# A BAFFLING MURDER AT THE MIDSUMMER BALL

## ALSO BY T E KINSEY

### Dizzy Heights Mysteries:

*The Deadly Mystery of the Missing Diamonds*

### Lady Hardcastle Mysteries:

*A Quiet Life in the Country*

*In the Market for Murder*

*Death Around the Bend*

*Christmas at the Grange*

*A Picture of Murder*

*The Burning Issue of the Day*

*Death Beside the Seaside*

*The Fatal Flying Affair*

# A BAFFLING MURDER AT THE MIDSUMMER BALL

T E KINSEY

This is a work of fiction. Names, characters, organizations, places, events, and incidents are either products of the author's imagination or are used fictitiously. Any resemblance to actual persons, living or dead, or actual events is purely coincidental.



Published by Thomas & Mercer, Seattle

www.apub.com



ISBN-13: 9781542021111
ISBN-10: 1542021111

Cover design by Tom Sanderson

Cover illustration by Jelly London

Printed in the United States of America

# A BAFFLING MURDER AT THE MIDSUMMER BALL

# Chapter One

***Friday, 26 June 1925***

'Tell me again why we couldn't have gone by train,' said Mickey Kent weakly as the motor coach clattered over another pothole.

Katy shook her head. 'We've been over this, darling. The charabanc is free – it was laid on by the family hosting the party. If we'd taken the train it would have come out of the fee. *Your* fee.'

Puddle looked up from her book. 'And it's door-to-door service – no need to traipse all the way to Paddington.'

'Lugging all our gear,' agreed Skins. 'It's all safely on the roof under a lovely big tarpaulin. Shut up and eat your sandwiches.'

Mickey turned slightly more green than is usual for a healthy person and looked out of the window. 'At least it's stopped bloody raining,' he muttered.

The Dizzy Heights were on their way to Oxfordshire where the band had been booked to play at a party at Bilverton House. Katy Cannon, their new manager, had been rather pleased with herself at having secured such a lucrative engagement before she'd even been officially appointed to the post. She had been doubly pleased when the family who made the booking had offered to provide transport in both directions in a 'luxury motor coach'. She wasn't sure that the twenty-seater vehicle that had turned up that morning quite counted as 'luxurious', but the paintwork was shiny and the wooden seats clean. She had tried her best to remain enthusiastic but Mickey's ceaseless complaints were making it increasingly difficult.

The coach was roomy for the eight-piece band and their two camp followers, and they had spread themselves out.

Singer Mickey Kent sat alone with his travel-sickness-induced bad temper. He was usually one of the more cheerful and easy-going members of the band, but coaches and lorries made him queasy. Being queasy made him irritable.

'Elk' Elkington, the banjo player, was sitting with Benny Charles (trombone) and Eustace Taylor (trumpet). They had been trying to play pontoon, but the same potholes that were causing Mickey such distress had bounced the cards off the bench once too often and they were now taking it in turns to make up filthy limericks.

The woodwind section – Isabella 'Puddle' Puddephatt and new girl Vera James – were sharing a two-seater bench in companionable silence as they read. Puddle had her book while Vera devoured a fashion magazine.

Ellie Maloney and manager Katy Cannon sat together at the front of the coach. Ellie had been involved with the band in one way or another since her husband, the drummer Ivor 'Skins' Maloney, and his bass-playing best friend Barty Dunn had formed it two years earlier. They had resisted the idea of employing a manager until only a week before, when Puddle had persuaded them to accept the services of her recently widowed sister, Katy. Ellie had spent the bulk of the journey so far explaining the band's complex financial arrangements and dietary requirements.

Skins and Dunn had been inseparable friends since childhood and had been making a comfortable living as 'the best rhythm section in London' since before the war. They had established themselves as musical pioneers, first with ragtime and then with jazz, and in the first few years after being demobbed they had sought out musicians who shared their passion. By 1923 they had found exactly the right mix of talent and enthusiasm, and the Dizzy Heights were born.

'I can't rhyme "twinkletoes" with "wrinkled hose",' said Dunn, wearily.

Skins pointed to a couplet further down the page. 'Yeah, but then you can have a line here about her shocking stockings.'

'It's supposed to be romantic.'

'Soppy, you mean.'

'You're a fine one to talk. I've put up with more than my fair share of soppiness between you and Ellie over the years.'

'Yeah, but it was my cheeky charm that won her over in the end, not the soppiness – everyone loves a bit of cheeky charm. Stick some jokes in it. The kids'll love it.'

Dunn shook his head.

'Are you boys behaving yourselves back here?' said Ellie.

She had stumbled the length of the jolting coach to join them. She sat down next to Skins.

'Barty's keeping me in order,' he said. 'He's come over all grown up this morning.'

'I'm just trying to write a decent lyric for this song,' said Dunn. 'It's not like I've taken holy orders or anything.'

'Keeps turning down my suggestions,' persisted Skins.

'Everyone turns down your suggestions, honey,' said Ellie. 'You're a goof.'

'He's an idiot,' said Dunn, without looking up.

Skins grinned. 'I prefer to think of myself as charmingly cheeky. Are we nearly there yet?'

'Not far now. I'm looking forward to this, I must say. We've not been away together for ages. Thank you for letting me tag along.'

'It's always a joy to spend time in your company, my perfect love.'

'See what I mean?' said Dunn.

'What does he mean?' asked Ellie.

'He thinks I'm soppy.'

'He's not wrong – you're as soppy as they come. But I'm still grateful to be coming out here with you. No one else brings their wives.'

'After all that business at the Aristippus Club they think of you as part of the band,' said Skins.

'We could do with a piano player,' said Dunn as he put away his notebook. 'You're always welcome to sit in.'

'That's a kind offer,' she said, 'but I'm mediocre at best. I'd be out of my depth with you guys.'

Dunn smiled. 'I disagree, but it's up to you. The offer stands. But what do we know about tonight's party? Who lives at Bilverton House?'

'The Bilvertons,' said Ellie.

'You say that like we should know them,' said Skins.

'Of Bilverton's Biscuits,' she said.

'Seriously?'

Ellie nodded.

'Oi, you lot,' said Skins. 'This shower we're playing for tonight own Bilverton's Biscuits.'

'We know,' chorused the rest of the band.

'Oh,' said Skins, deflatedly. 'How come you all knew?'

'I didn't know,' said Elk.

'How come everyone except Elk knew?'

'It wasn't hard to work it out, darling,' said Puddle. 'They live in a house in Oxfordshire called Bilverton House.'

'Yes, but—' began Skins.

'Oxfordshire,' said Benny. 'Where the biscuits come from.'

'And how would I know that?' asked Skins.

'It's written on the box,' said Eustace.

'Ah,' said Skins, with a triumphant wag of a skinny finger. 'That'll be it. The likes of me have servants to bring our biscuits on bone china platters. We don't deal with' – he sniffed – 'boxes.'

Ellie and Dunn ducked out of the way as Skins was pelted with sandwich wrappers and fruit peel.

Ellie returned to her seat next to Katy, picking up the litter and returning it to its owners as she went.

The journey proceeded uneventfully, with only three more stops for Mickey to be sick by the side of the road.

Shortly after midday, the coach passed through a stone gateway and on to a broad paved drive, then wound through woodland for a while before climbing towards an impressive Georgian country house. The drive was surprisingly steep, prompting jokes from the band that they might have to get out and push, but eventually they made it. The coach pulled up near the steps leading down to the servants' entrance at the side of the house.

'Everybody wait here,' said Katy. 'I'll go and find Mr Bilverton.'

She set off towards the steps, but stopped when she was hailed by a liveried butler. The band, still struggling to stir stiffly from their seats, looked on as Katy led the butler back to the coach. She gestured towards the open door and he stuck his head in.

'If you would be good enough to follow me, please, ladies and gentlemen, Mister Howard would be pleased to greet you in the Grand Hall.'

The Dizzy Heights, with only the smallest amount of complaining about their aches and pains, followed the butler towards the house, while the driver was left to make his own way to the servants' hall for a cup of tea and a sandwich.

◆ ◆ ◆

The freshly painted red front doors opened into a distinctly underwhelming vestibule: a tiled floor, a large coir mat, a modern mirror, a pair of doors set with cracked stained glass. No one in the band was expecting much by way of grandeur from the hall that lay beyond it. But there were gasps and at least one 'Bugger me!' from the assembled musicians as the butler flung open the doors with an impresario's flourish.

The Grand Hall was two storeys high with a broad stone staircase at the far end. The stairs split left and right at a landing and led up to a gallery that ran round all four sides of the hall, supported by elegant stone pillars. The floor was polished parquet, there were portraits on the stairs, and from the ceiling hung two elaborate chandeliers that had been adapted for electricity.

A man in his early twenties stood on the landing at the top of the first flight of stairs. He was dressed in a luridly striped blazer with a clashing bow tie, and his blond hair was slicked back with pomade. His smile was genuine and his arms wide in greeting.

'The Dizzy Heights, I presume,' he said warmly, descending the steps to the hall. 'Welcome to Bilverton House. I'm Howard Bilverton. Which of you is Mrs Cannon?'

Katy pressed her way through the little knot of gawping musicians.

'That'll be me,' she said. 'How do you do, Mr Bilverton?'

'How do you do?' he said. 'Please call me Howard – everyone around here's called Mr Bilverton. Frightfully confusing. I'm so glad you got here safely.'

'And we're glad you invited us. This is a magnificent house.'

'We're rather proud of it, I must say. Been in the family for . . . Actually, not that long, really. Since before I was born, though.'

'You should be very proud indeed,' said Katy.

'Thank you. I thought it would be fun to greet you all here as guests. To tell you the truth, I'm rather excited to have such a highly respected band playing for us tonight and I thought it would be a travesty to have you all skulking in through the servants' entrance, which was my father's plan.'

'That's very kind of you . . . Howard. Now, where would you like us to set ourselves up?'

'I have some good news on that front. With this awful rain we've been having all week we feared we might have to bring the festivities indoors – we usually hold the Midsummer Ball in the gardens, d'you see? Marquees and whatnot, I'm sure you know the drill. The invitations always say "Indoors if wet" and until this morning it looked very much as though you might be playing in here. But the gods have smiled on us with one sunny day. So the marquee has been decorated, a wooden floor put down and the stage set up.'

'That's lovely,' said Katy. 'We'll fetch our gear and get ourselves set up.'

Howard smiled. 'I'll take you out there myself. And don't worry about your . . . "gear". I'll get someone to take everything through for you. I promise the staff will treat it all with the greatest of care.'

Katy returned his smile. 'Oh. Well, thank you very much.'

Howard indicated a door in the corner of the hall. 'That door leads into the billiards room and I thought you might care to use it as your base for the evening. Your "green room", as they say – I was on the entertainments committee at my college, d'you see? We shut it off for parties and lock the doors – doesn't do to have drunken guests tearing up the old baize – so you'll be unmolested.'

'That all sounds splendid,' said Katy. This was her first engagement with the band and, in truth, she had absolutely no idea what they might think of as splendid. But she was a tiny bit intimidated by the exuberantly outgoing musicians and was determined to give at least the appearance of confidence.

'Well, then, that's marvellous,' said Howard. 'Simply marvellous. So, if you could all follow me, I'll show you where you'll be playing.'

He set off through a doorway at the end of the hall. They trooped through what looked like a library, then what seemed like a grand, airy sitting room, and out through double doors on to a flagstoned terrace.

On the other side of the low wall of the terrace was an area of level grass, now dominated by a huge white tent. Beyond a ha-ha, the parkland swept down a steep hill to a tree-lined lake.

Howard led them across some duckboards and through the canvas entrance to the marquee.

◆ ◆ ◆

The inside had been miraculously transformed into a ballroom. Swags of silk disguised the drab canvas roof, from which hung lightweight chandeliers set with electric lights, while the linoleum laid across the planks protecting the grass had been printed to mimic a polished wooden floor. Some servants were setting the circular tables for a summer banquet, and there were clinks and rattles of glass as others set up an impressive bar.

A stage had been built at the top end, upon which sat a Bösendorfer grand piano.

'Will that do you?' asked Howard, indicating the stage.

'Handsome,' said Mickey as he jumped up and surveyed the elegant outdoor room from the spot where he'd be standing that evening.

'Do you have any special requirements for the stage?' asked Howard. 'I can't do anything about the lighting, I'm afraid, although there will be lanterns dotted about the place and candles on the tables – perhaps we can put something on the stage. Would that help the old ambience, d'you think? I can't promise anything, but I'll look into it, and I'm sure we can arrange for anything else you need.'

'This will be perfect,' said Katy. 'We'll just need eight chairs, that's all.'

'I'll have some sent out. I couldn't remember if you needed a piano so I had them put one of ours on the stage for you.'

Ellie and Skins looked at each other.

'One?' whispered Skins. 'How many pianos do they have?'

'Thank you,' said Katy. She had no idea whether they needed or wanted a piano on the stage but, again, she was keen not to let on how little she knew about their requirements.

Howard beamed. 'Marvellous. Well done, me. I'll get our chaps to bring in your instruments and luggage, and then leave you to it, if I may. There's still rather a lot to do, I'm afraid. Just ask one of the servants if you need anything. I'll check on you later – you know, to make sure you have everything.'

With a cheery wave, he was gone.

'We've played worse places,' said Skins with a smile. 'You've done us proud, Katy. I knew we should have had a manager all along.'

'It's not half bad, is it?' she agreed.

'Just one thing,' said Eustace. 'Where are we sleeping?'

'They've a full house, what with family, guests and servants,' said Katy, 'but they've said we can kip down in the chapel. They've got some old army cots we can use.'

'The chapel?' said Eustace, as though she'd invited him to sleep in a water-filled ditch at the other end of the drive.

'Don't you listen to anything anyone ever says, Eust?' said Mickey, who was feeling less queasy now he was on solid ground, but no less testy. 'Not only is this place the seat of the Bilverton family, famed throughout the land as the owners of Bilverton's Biscuits—'

'Make your elevenses special with a Bilverton's Tea Break Assortment,' interrupted Elk.

'I love that advertisement,' said Vera. 'Such a pretty image of the young couple enjoying their . . .' She trailed off. 'Sorry, Mickey,' she said. 'But it is a lovely picture. Do carry on.'

'—it is also home to Bilver-Tone Records,' continued Mickey with a shake of his head. 'They've turned the deconsecrated sixteenth-century chapel next door to the house into a modern electronic recording studio. They've got all the latest gear from America.'

'I'm not sure how sleeping in a recording studio is a step up. It's still a draughty old chapel, no matter how many American toys they've put in it,' said Eustace.

'Give it a rest, Eustace,' said Dunn. 'Like Skins says, we've played worse places, and you've slept in worse places. But I'm sure you can find someone to drive you into Oxford if you'd prefer to spend your cut of the fee on a night in a posh hotel. It's up to you, old mate. Just say the word.'

'Yes. Well. I'm just used to better, that's all.'

'You and your missus live in a little flat in Kilburn,' said Mickey.

'Too right, we do. And not in a draughty, deconsecrated chapel full of American electronics and old army cots.'

'Excuse me, sir,' said a voice from behind them. 'We have a question about your luggage.'

It was the butler.

'Some of it's definitely very questionable,' said Skins. 'How can we help you?'

'Mister Howard suggested that your personal luggage might be better in the chapel since that's where you'll be staying, but we can leave it in the billiards room for the evening if you prefer. You'll be using it as your . . . I believe he said "green room".'

'Sounds good to me. We'll need the instruments and one or two of the bags on the stage, but the rest can go to the chapel like he says.'

'Indeed, sir. But we need some guidance as to which items you'll be needing on the stage, and which can safely be taken away.'

Ellie stepped forward. 'Lead the way, Mr . . . ?'

'Dunsworth, madam.'

'Lead the way, Mr Dunsworth. I'll give you all the guidance you need.'

'You're most kind, madam. Have you been offered refreshment?' he asked.

'We haven't,' said Ellie. 'I'm sure they'd welcome a "cuppa". If I've learned anything about you Britishers it's that everything is fuelled by tea.'

'I'll have some sent out. Please follow me.'

He retraced their steps back through the salon and library to the Grand Hall, where a footman was dropping off the last of the bags. Ellie scanned them quickly. The staff had had no trouble sorting the instruments into a pile of their own, and she pointed out which of the other bags would be needed on stage and which were just personal luggage.

'They really wouldn't mind coming back here and fetching this stuff themselves, you know,' she said.

'It's no trouble, madam. They'll be working hard enough this evening, I'm sure.'

'That's swell of you. Now, I don't want to embarrass you but what I could really do with is—'

'Up the left-hand stairs and turn left, madam. Second door on the right.'

'Thank you, Mr Dunsworth, you're a lifesaver.'

While Dunsworth and the footman started hefting the instrument cases on to a trolley, Ellie swished up the impressive staircase.

◆ ◆ ◆

When Ellie returned to the hall she found the bags and servants gone, and thought it best to have a quick look in the billiards room to check what had been set out for them there.

The room was, predictably, dominated by a twelve-foot billiards table, which, on closer inspection, she discovered had been set up for snooker. There were velvet armchairs between the windows along one of the long walls, and a scoreboard and a rack for cues and rests beside the fireplace on the other.

A card table by the window on the short wall was now home to an impressive selection of glasses, with a crate of beer and a half-dozen bottles of champagne on the floor beside it. Ellie surveyed the comfortably elegant room, feeling pleased. With the armchairs, a chaise longue and the few upright chairs beside the window to the front of the house, there was plenty of room for everyone to relax.

There was no sign of the luggage, which she presumed had been taken to their accommodation in the chapel, wherever that was.

The door at the far end was closed, and she checked to make sure it was locked as promised. It was, and the key was in the lock on this side. Curiosity got the better of her and she unlocked it and peeped through. She found a drawing room with all its furniture pushed back against the walls to allow guests to wander and mingle. Mildly worried that she might be discovered, she withdrew, relocked the billiards room door and went back out to see if she could retrace her steps to the marquee.

After finding her way to the library and back outside through the salon, she turned her face to the sun for a few moments, luxuriating in it. It seemed to have been wet and grey for days and she was glad of a touch of midsummer warmth.

In the marquee, all was abustle.

The Dizzies had a well-drilled routine for setting up. The trouble was that it didn't involve the whole band being present. As drummer, Skins had the most to do and would usually arrive at the venue first, accompanied by Dunn. While Skins assembled his drum set, Dunn would arrange the chairs and make sure they had everything they needed backstage.

As the appointed kick-off time approached, the other band members would drift in with their instruments and music stands and make themselves ready. Once everything was in order they would retire to whatever space had been set aside for them before making a dramatic and professional entrance and commencing their foot-tapping performance.

It didn't run nearly so smoothly when everyone was there.

Dunn couldn't set out the chairs on the stage because they didn't yet have any. Skins had tripped on Benny's trombone case, knocked over Puddle's music stand and walked into Vera. Twice.

'Steady on there, mate,' said Dunn after the second clash.

'Sorry, Vera,' said Skins. 'I'm not used to having people about when I do this.'

'Don't worry, sweetheart,' she said. 'We're all getting under each other's feet. I'll only complain if you actually manage to knock me over on me bum.'

A footman arrived with the first batch of smart-looking wooden folding chairs on a porter's truck.

'Blimey,' said Skins, 'you look all in, mate. Where are you having to go for those?'

'Down the chapel,' said the footman. 'They keep a big stack of them for the musicians. They've had symphony orchestras playing down there. Takes a lot of chairs to seat a symphony orchestra.'

'I can imagine. How many have you got there?'

'Just five, I'm afraid. Mr Dunsworth says you need eight.'

'To be honest,' said Dunn, 'we only desperately need five. Two of us stand up all night and he's got his own little stool, look.' He indicated Skins, who was, indeed, sitting on his own little stool and adjusting the tension of his snare drum head. 'The other three can wait till you're less busy.'

'That's very kind of you, sir, but Mr Dunsworth'll skin me if I don't do exactly as he said.' The young footman looked around to make sure he wasn't overheard. He leaned over the chairs and spoke more quietly. 'To tell you the truth, I'm pleased to be out of the way of the party preparations for a little while. I much prefer helping you. I love jazz.'

'Then it would be mean-spirited of us to deny you the chance for a skive,' said Dunn. 'Three more of your finest chairs, please, my good fellow.'

The footman grinned. 'Yes, sir. Right away, sir.'

Katy had been listening. 'I'm so sorry. I didn't know.'

'Didn't know what?' said Dunn.

'About the chairs. I thought you had one each.'

'Nothing to worry about. One each is a luxury, but if you're ever under pressure, five will do us.'

Katy took out a notebook and jotted this information down.

'Honestly,' said Skins. 'Don't worry about it. Look at the chaos here – half this shower don't have a clue what needs to be done. They just turn up with their little instrument cases and sit down like the fairies have magically done it all.'

'You're quite right, Skins darling,' said Puddle. 'We have servants to set everything up for us. We don't deal with' – she sniffed – 'chairs.'

'Help me out, Ells-Bells,' he said. 'She's being nasty to me.'

'She is, honey, I know,' said Ellie from the floor. 'You bring it on yourself, though. You shouldn't have been such a chump earlier.'

'I've only got myself to blame.'

Ellie called out to the rest of the band. 'Hey, I've checked the room Howard was talking about. Plenty of space, plenty of chairs, plenty of booze.' There was a ragged cheer. 'Before I tell them everything's OK, I just need to know: is everyone happy getting changed in the chapel or would you prefer the green room? They've already taken all the luggage down to the chapel, but I can easily get them to bring it back.'

'It'll save us lugging it all down there after the party if we just get changed in our billet,' said Mickey. 'I'm happy with that.'

The others agreed.

'What about you, ladies?' asked Ellie. 'We can change in the billiards room or upstairs in the bathroom. It's a lovely bathroom.'

'I don't mind changing with the boys, actually,' said Puddle. 'It's not like we usually have much privacy.'

'Vera?' said Ellie.

'I'm happy in the chapel if my case is already there,' she said. 'I've got clean drawers on.'

Katy was less keen.

'Just Katy and me for the bathroom, then. That simplifies things. Assuming they don't mind. They won't mind, will they?'

'You could ask,' said Skins. The young footman had returned surprisingly quickly with the second batch of chairs. 'The ladies can use the bathroom in the house to change, can't they?'

'That is the guest bathroom, sir, yes,' he said. 'The bedrooms each have their own.'

'Blimey,' said Skins. 'That's posh. There you are, then, Ells – you and Katy can titivate to your hearts' content away from the vulgar gaze of these ill-bred troubadours.'

Half an hour later the stage was neatly organized and everyone was happy with their seat. They shimmied through a couple of numbers while Ellie and Katy roamed the marquee to check how they sounded. It was, they declared, the perfect setting for a summer evening of jazz.

# Chapter Two

Guests for the Bilverton Summer Ball began arriving a few minutes before the appointed hour of seven o'clock. The dress code on the invitations had specified 'Swanky' and this had been liberally interpreted by the family's many friends, acquaintances and business associates.

Senior members of the Bilverton's board and their wives were in full evening dress, as were many of the local dignitaries and businessmen. Friends of the younger Bilvertons were mostly dressed in less-formal dinner suits and black tie, though Howard had elected to appear in a blazer with purple, cerise, pale blue and white stripes, set off with a cravat of drake's-neck green. The cream Oxford bags and two-tone wingtip Oxford brogues that adorned his lower half were positively conservative by comparison.

The host, John Bilverton, was greeting his guests at the bottom of the stairs with his wife Marianne by his side. He was tall and dapper, dressed in evening tails and white tie, while the much younger Marianne wore a floor-length evening gown of gunmetal silk.

The warm smile as John welcomed friends, business associates and even some rivals was genuine, but it vanished as he caught sight of his youngest son descending the stairs.

'What the devil do you think you're wearing?' he snarled.

'Supporting the local traditions, Pater,' said Howard. 'Oxford bags, Oxford brogues.'

'You look like a loafer. Go and change.'

'Right you are, Pa,' said Howard cheerily, though he made no obvious effort to do so. The young woman on his arm giggled. She was wearing an intricately embroidered white dress that John might have considered suitable for a ball had not the hem of the skirt reached only to her knees. They sauntered off together, John scowling at their retreating backs.

A short while later, a gang of similarly informal and thoroughly fashionable Bright Young Things arrived, and John Bilverton sullenly resigned himself to the realization that the country and its youth were going to the dogs.

Katy had discussed the dress code with the band during the week before the party.

'We've only got two options when it comes to dressing,' said Mickey. 'We've got dinner suits or flashy suits. Dinner suits'll do for most gigs, flashy ones for the cooler London clubs.'

'Well what does "swanky" mean, then?' asked Katy. 'How does one dress swankily?'

'I know it's a posh do,' said Skins, 'but who's likely to be going?'

'The Bilvertons are new money,' she said. 'John Bilverton is the head of the family. He's a Justice of the Peace, I think, and something big at the Oxford Chamber of Commerce. They'll have lots of crusty old friends. But his children range from stolid and staid to wild and wilful.'

'How on earth do you know so much about them?' asked Dunn, slightly impressed.

'Gossip pages. The papers and magazines were full of stories about them when John Bilverton married his secretary a few years after his wife died.'

'The secretary was young, I suppose?' said Ellie.

'She was twenty-six. He was fifty-five. She's less than a year older than his eldest son.'

'Blimey,' said Skins. 'No wonder the papers were talking about him. So it's a middle-aged "pillar of the community" type with a wife and kids in their twenties who wants a cool London jazz band for their Midsummer Ball. Flashy suits and dresses, I reckon. Let's give them what they paid for.'

'But what if the old boy only agreed reluctantly?' said Katy. 'What if he wanted a palm court orchestra playing selections from Gilbert and Sullivan? What if he doesn't really want us there at all? What if—'

'Katy, darling,' said her younger sister Puddle, 'do shut up, there's a good girl. Skins is right – they booked the cool London jazz band and we'll give them the coolest London jazz band they can imagine. Besides, I have a Paul Poiret that absolutely *needs* an outing.'

'You have a Paul Poiret?' said Vera.

'Well, sort of. I know a girl in Bethnal Green who makes the most marvellous copies. She—'

'I just don't want us to be underdressed,' interrupted Katy. 'You know, it's so easy to get these things wrong, I—'

'I shan't tell you again, sweetie,' said Puddle.

Katy had sighed, but relented.

As it turned out, their choice of attire was perfect. The older guests looked faintly disapproving and slightly intimidated, while one of Howard's friends was overheard in front of the stage declaring them to be the caterpillar's kimono. Lively debate ensued as the knot of excitable youngsters danced their way back towards the middle of the dance floor.

'I prefer oyster's earrings,' said one.

'Gnat's elbows,' said another.

'You're all a bunch of twerps,' said a third. 'They're self-evidently the kipper's knickers.'

Ellie sat with Katy to the side of the stage, sipping their chilled champagne and watching the dancing.

'Don't you find it a little frustrating?' asked Katy. 'Sitting here listening to these wonderful tunes and having no one to dance with?'

'I'm used to it. Even when Ivor's not playing I have no one to dance with – he won't dance.'

'Why ever not?'

'He claims he never learned how. When all the other boys were learning how to dance, he was playing in the band.'

Katy laughed. 'Well, I'm going to go and see if I can find a nice man to Charleston with. Coming?'

'No, I think I might take a wander into the house.'

Katy left the stage at the end of the next number and went off in search of a dance partner. Before Ellie could get up, Howard leaped energetically up on to the stage beside her, accompanied by the beautiful young girl in the white dress.

'Having fun?' she said.

'Rather. Just came to talk to the band. Do you think they'd mind?'

'I'm sure they'd love it.'

She stayed to earwig as the youngest Bilverton approached Eustace.

'I say, you chaps are bloody marvellous. Thank you so much.'

'Our pleasure,' said Eustace with a rare smile.

'Do you take requests? Do you know "Fidgety Feet"? Or perhaps "Tiger Rag"? By The Wolverines. New American band.'

'You know The Wolverines?' said Eustace. 'A man of taste. Both numbers are coming up later, as it happens. They have an astonishing cornet player, The Wolverines – Bix Beiderbecke.

Marvellous fellow. Such clarity. Such a beautiful tone. They record in Richmond, Indiana, you know. You'd have thought it would be New Orleans or Chicago, but—'

'He's gone, dear,' said Vera.

Like Katy, she had only officially been with the band for a week. The London jazz world was a small one, though, and she had known most of the individual members for quite a while longer. She'd always got on well with Eustace, but she was well aware of how he sometimes came across to others.

'Still,' he said. 'Nice to meet a genuine aficionado.'

Howard, by now, was talking enthusiastically to Mickey.

'This is Hetty Hollis. She's my best pal's fiancée. Kenneth Mary's his name, poor chap. He couldn't be here, though – family emergency – so I'm looking after her.'

'Nice to meet you,' said Mickey with a warm smile.

Hetty returned the smile. 'Charmed, I'm sure.'

Mickey's jaw dropped. Hetty looked almost entirely indistinguishable from hundreds of Bright Young Things he'd seen in nightclubs all over the country, but her voice . . . There was a warm silkiness to it that belied her age.

'Do you sing, Miss Hollis?' he asked.

Howard spoke up before she could reply for herself. 'That's rather why we came over, as a matter of fact. I . . . we were wondering if she might—'

'I'd love the chance to sing with you, Mr . . . ?'

'Kent, but call me Mickey.'

'I'd love to sing with you, Mickey. Do you think I might?'

Mickey glanced around at his colleagues but they were all engrossed in their own business. He made a decision.

'Next up is "All Alone". Irving Berlin. You know it?'

'I do.'

'What key?'

'F sharp, please,' she purred.

If Mickey were the swooning type, he would have swooned.

'You ready there, Mickey boy?' said Skins.

'Slight change of plans,' said Mickey. 'Let me do an intro.'

He stood at the front of the stage, briefly surveying the glamorous youngsters on the dance floor and the more mature guests reclining at the tables beyond. The meal had been sumptuously modern, and though everyone had eaten more than their fair share of roast haunch of venison, there was still room for the petits fours and yet more champagne being served by the uniformed footmen and housemaids who had been assigned to waiting duties for the evening.

'Ladies and gentlemen. We in the Dizzy Heights are always keen to show off new talent when we find it, so this next number is going to be sung by our new friend . . . Miss Hetty Hollis.'

There was a smattering of applause from the tables, and raucous whooping from Howard's young friends on the dance floor. The Dizzies exchanged cheerfully bewildered shrugs, but said nothing.

Mickey turned to the band. 'F sharp minor all right for you?'

There was a small amount of eye rolling, but no complaints as the band readied themselves to transpose the piece on the fly.

'Let's not leave the nice ladies and gentlemen waiting, then,' said Skins. 'I'll give you four for nothing . . .' He tapped his drum sticks together to set the tempo and they were off.

Howard retreated from the stage and rejoined his friends.

Hetty Hollis was a sensation. Her singing voice more than lived up to its promise, and even the more staid guests at the tables were clapping enthusiastically by the time she finished.

She beamed out at the partygoers and gave an awkward curtsey before turning back to the band.

'Do you think I might do another?'

'You can do the whole set,' said Dunn from behind his double bass. 'Mickey? Take the night off, mate.'

After a brief discussion they launched into a more upbeat number.

Ellie wanted to stay and listen, but she also wanted to explore. She had been married to Skins for six years and was well used to amusing herself while the band played. Not that she saw them every time they played – she often used his absence as an opportunity to catch up with her many friends.

In her elegant beaded dress, she made her way down the steps at the side of the stage and on to the crowded dance floor, where she quickstepped her way past the exuberant young dancers and weaved through the tables where the older guests were sitting in voluble clusters.

As she strolled along the canvas wall of the huge tent, she played a game she often played at social events when she was on her own. As a young girl before the war she had been taken to charity parties by her philanthropist mother, and had devised the game as a defence against the crushing boredom of having to spend time in the company of self-satisfied, rich old people. While feigning interest in the goings-on elsewhere in the room, she would listen discreetly to a conversation and try to divine the speakers' life stories from the clues she picked up.

Two people sat alone at one table with an unopened bottle of champagne in an ice bucket between them. They were clearly mid-argument, and Ellie wondered if the chilly atmosphere generated by the glowering couple rendered the ice redundant.

'. . . with my own father,' said the man. 'How could you, Charlotte? How bloody could you?'

'Keep your voice down, Gordon, for goodness' sake.'

'What, in case anyone finds out that you're a—'

'I'm a what, Gordon? Go on, say it.'

'You disgust me. He disgusts me.'

Ellie edged casually around the table to try to get a better view while pretending to watch the dancing. The man seemed to be in his late twenties and had a familiar look about him. She couldn't place him until it dawned on her that he must be a Bilverton. He somehow reminded her of enthusiastic young Howard without the enthusiasm, and there couldn't possibly be two unrelated people with a nose quite like that. The woman was young and blonde, but Ellie couldn't get a clear view and didn't want to be caught staring.

So . . . he was a Bilverton and she was his wife. And she'd done something with his father. But what? Something to do with the business, Ellie wondered. Embezzlement, perhaps? That was it. She and the managing director were stealing the biscuit company's money and were planning to invest it in . . . in a tea importer's.

She smiled and turned her attention back to the dance floor.

'If you weren't so pathetic, maybe I wouldn't have wanted to—'

The woman's words were cut short by the sharp sound of a slap. Ellie turned to see her clutching her cheek, stiff-backed. Calmly and coldly, she got up and left the man sitting alone.

Ellie's absorption in the intimacy of the moment had made the rest of the room fade away, and the bright conversation and laughter in the marquee seemed oddly loud now the spell was broken. Abandoning her game, she slipped away and hastened towards the fresh air.

Although the sun had gone down, the evening was still quite light, and the sky glowed a luminous blue. If she had looked to the west she would have seen thunderclouds on the horizon, but for now she savoured the warmth of a summer's evening.

She made her way across the duckboards and back to the salon. The room was large, roughly square, and decorated in a style that was just old enough to be 'classic' rather than old-fashioned. The chairs had clearly been chosen to match the rest of the furniture rather than for comfort, but they were plentiful and mostly occupied.

What set the salon apart from similar rooms in other houses was its domed glass roof. In the relative dark, it reflected the electric lamps that lit the room and the party guests below, but in the daytime it would fill the room with a glorious light of its own.

The lights in the house were brighter than in the marquee, but the atmosphere no less jolly. The guests were no less glamorous, either, and Ellie slipped among them after accepting a Sazerac from a silver tray proffered by a white-gloved servant – listening once more to their conversations.

'You should come down the club one night. Shouldn't they, darlin'?'

The speaker was a man in his forties wearing a fashionably cut dinner suit. His hair was slicked back and there were hefty gold rings on the fingers of both hands. His 'darlin'' was no more than twenty-five years old and was wearing an elaborately embroidered knee-length dress, the bottom six inches of which consisted entirely of tassels. Her headdress sparkled. Ellie wasn't sure if spending so much of the past month thinking about them was making her see them everywhere, but she would have sworn that the sparkle came from diamonds.

'That's very swell of you, old chap,' said a younger man in the group. 'I say, I don't suppose you've got any' – he sniffed loudly – 'on you, have you? I can pay.'

Ellie turned in time to see the older man's chummy smile replaced with a terrifying glare.

'Don't be a bloody idiot, son,' he said, coldly. 'Who the bleedin' 'ell do you think you're talkin' to?'

The younger man stammered an apology and scurried away.

'Bloody kids'll be the death of me,' said the slick-haired man. 'You try and run a respectable nightclub, and look what comes crawlin' out of the crevices.'

This one was too easy – the man was a gangster. She didn't even have to make that one up. She'd met many like him over the years, thanks to Skins's profession, and he conformed perfectly to the type, right down to the impressionable and bejewelled young lady on his arm.

The doorway to her left, Ellie remembered, led to the library. She turned quickly to the right, intending to find out what lay beyond the other door, and bumped into a middle-aged man. He was of medium height and stocky, though not yet running to fat. His greying hair was cut in a style that looked somehow military, and his extravagant moustache was waxed. He was holding a silver-topped walking cane in one hand and most of a glass of champagne in the other. With a smile, he transferred his glass to his cane hand and brushed spilt champagne from his jacket.

'Oh my goodness,' said Ellie. 'I really am most terribly sorry. Are you soaked?'

The man chuckled. 'Not at all, m'dear. Wouldn't be a party if there weren't spillages.' He inspected the front of his jacket. 'My man will get this out in a jiffy. Had worse things spilled on it, what?'

'I'm not usually this clumsy, I promise.'

'Think nothing of it.' He offered her his hand. 'Malcolm Bilverton – disreputable younger brother of our gracious host.'

Ellie shook the proffered hand. 'Ellie Maloney.'

'Are you one of the children's friends?'

'No, I tagged along with the band. The drummer is my husband.'

'Oh, I say, how very splendid. And what a marvellous band they are, too.'

'I'm rather proud of them, certainly. Do you like jazz? I know it's not to everyone's taste.'

'I love it. I love all music, though. I run Bilver-Tone Records. I'm glad I bumped into one of you, actually – I'd love to record the Dizzy Heights. Do you think they'd be interested?'

'I can't speak for all of them, but I know Ivor would love it. I'm sure the rest will be easy to persuade.'

'Good show, good show. Is their manager here?'

'She's in the marquee dancing, I think. Her name's Katy Cannon.'

'I shall seek her out. I think we might be able to strike a deal. D'you know I once—'

'Are you boring our guests again, Uncle Malcolm?' It was Howard Bilverton.

Malcolm chuckled indulgently. 'Cheeky young pup. You've met my nephew, Mrs Maloney? Howard Bilverton, layabout of this parish.'

'I welcomed them all to the house,' said Howard. 'And we met again a few moments ago on the stage.'

Ellie nodded a greeting. 'I'm surprised to see you here, actually. I thought you'd be listening to your friend Miss Hollis. She has quite a voice.'

'Oh, she'll be fine. I've heard her sing before – my pal Kenneth has dragged me to many a club to keep him company while he drools into his champagne and listens to her. I'm here in search of a little something more to eat. I heard there were cheese and biscuits.'

'New blood?' said Malcolm.

'Hetty Hollis, Uncle M. I introduced her to you yesterday.'

'So you did, so you did. I might go and have a listen. Always on the lookout for new talent for the record label. I shall leave you in each other's company while I sally forth into the thronging multitude. I'll see if I can track down Mrs . . . ?'

'Cannon,' said Ellie. 'Katy Cannon.'

'. . . Mrs Cannon while I'm there, too. Two birds with one stone, what?' Malcolm nodded his thanks and limped away.

Howard smiled fondly at his uncle's retreating back before returning his attention to Ellie. 'Your husband and his pals are the monkey's eyebrows, you know.'

'Absolutely the clam's garter, I'm told. They do seem to be going down rather well.'

'I'll say. I'm glad I managed to book them.'

'They're delighted to be here. Your family has a lovely home, Mr Bilverton.'

'I told you before – call me Howard. It's not bad, is it? The old manor house. Wouldn't fancy the upkeep, mind you. Though that's not likely to be something I'll ever have to worry about. Youngest son, d'you see? Big brother gets the spoils. And the bills. Ha ha.'

'Is your brother here?'

'We're all here. Three-line whip. Gordon's about somewhere. Tall chap. Miserable expression. Sour mood to go with it. Gorgeous wife, though – Charlotte.'

'Oh,' said Ellie. 'I think I might have seen them in the marquee.'

'Probably. Arguing?'

'I really don't know,' she lied.

'Oh, you'd most definitely know. It's all they seem to do these days. There are two sisters knocking about somewhere as well, but I'm dashed if I know where.'

'They're older than you, too?'

'They are indeed. Classic youngest child, me.'

Ellie laughed. 'I'm an only child. We have a reputation, too.'

'We should form some sort of society. But we oughtn't to be standing about here like a couple of lemons. Come with me, won't you? I'll give you the lowdown on all the fun people.'

Ellie happily allowed herself to be dragged off to the next room.

It turned out to be the dining room. There were more people here, milling around the huge dining table which had been pushed against the wall. The table was oak, and built to withstand the rigours of even the most rumbustious dinners, but it was so heavily laden with food that it was possible to imagine it bending under the weight. The Bilvertons had already fed their guests an elegant sit-down supper in the marquee, but someone in the family had clearly been worried it might not be enough and had provided this supplementary buffet indoors.

John Bilverton and his young wife brushed past them on their way out of the room, looking troubled.

'I'm not talking about this any more,' said John in a fierce undertone. 'Not one more bloody word.'

'And when *will* you talk about it, John?' said his wife. 'When are you going to stop being such a coward and address it?'

'How dare you talk to me like that, you little—'

Ellie never found out what she was a little example of, but she guessed it wasn't very nice.

Howard made a face. 'Families are always embarrassing, aren't they?'

'Always,' said Ellie. 'You can rely on me to pretend nothing happened, though. I've been living in England long enough to have learned how to do that, at least.'

'You're very kind.'

Howard led Ellie to a discreet vantage point in the corner of the room, next to a set of heavy velvet curtains. Or drapes, as Ellie still thought of them, much to Skins's amusement and their servants' bafflement. The slick-looking man Ellie had seen in the salon had followed them in, and Howard gave a subtle nod towards him.

'That fellow over there is our very own gangster.'

'I thought he might be,' she said. 'I overheard him talking to someone a little while ago.'

'Valentine Baisley. He runs a nightclub in Oxford for the moneyed and fashionable, from which he also supplies half the county with whatever chemical entertainment they desire. The muscular chap standing nearby . . .'

'The one who looks like he's imagining turning someone inside out?'

'Even he. That's Don Mowlam, Baisley's . . . Actually, I've no idea what his job title is.'

'Henchman? Minder?' suggested Ellie.

'Minder? Oh, how splendid – that's an ideal name for him. I say, you're not part of the underworld yourself, are you? I've not marked the poor lad for death at the hands of your own "minder", have I?'

'I move in an interesting twilight world – in the evening at least. The Dizzies play at a lot of clubs owned by men like him. One picks things up.' She looked around the room for another guest. 'Talking of my twilight world, is that Jo-Jo Furnace?'

'In the flesh. D'you know her?'

'Only to say hello to – she's been on the same bill as the Dizzies a few times. Such a voice. I remember one time she – holy Moses! Is that a leopard?'

Howard laughed. 'Surely you know about her pet? D'Arcy, I think his name is.'

'I've heard of it, sure. But I thought it was just a newspaper stunt. I didn't think she actually—'

'Takes it with her everywhere, apparently.'

'Not when I've seen her. Maybe the London clubs have a "no pets" rule.'

Howard laughed again. 'If they didn't before, they'd have instituted one pretty damn quick when she began turning up with D'Arcy by her side, leash or no leash.'

Ellie smiled. 'I think I recognize one of the women with her. Isn't that Felicia La Castra?'

'It is. You seem to know more people than I do.'

'Only because she's another *chanteuse*. She specializes in South American music. She has an impressive pair of maracas.'

Howard smirked. 'Doesn't she just?'

Ellie shook her head. It was like talking to Skins. 'Who's the third one? Dark hair and absurdly long cigarette holder.'

'That's Priscilla. I'm not sure she has a last name. Nor am I entirely certain what she does. I'm too afraid to ask, to be honest.'

'She does look rather forbidding,' agreed Ellie, enjoying the unexpected gossip with Howard, her eyes lingering on the remaining guests. 'How about those two striking older ladies over there?'

'The Bohemian-looking one on the left is "Dame Jelargy" – that's definitely not her real name, but that's what everyone calls her. There are rumours that she lives a second – much more mundane – secret life, but we just know her as our local sculptor and artist. And the other is Joanna Weston who owns a rather natty little boutique in Partlow's Ford. *Objets,* trinkets – you know the sort of thing.'

'They certainly look like fun. And those three ladies over there with the enormous drinks? They look rather fun, too.'

'Vivica Selway, Micki McNab and Lola Toft. Absolutely the best pals, and utterly charming ladies, but they're always plotting some sort of mischief. They call themselves "The Gang". You don't want to tangle with them. Unless mischief is your idea of a good time, of course, in which case I should definitely introduce you.'

'I get more than enough mischief hanging around with the band, thank you.'

'I'm sure you do . . . Now . . . let me see, who else would be worthy of the attention of the glamorous American sensation with the band . . . ? Ah, yes. The trio by the window? They might amuse you. Miss Crumlow, Miss Lundy and Miss van Beek. They run the ladies' archery club. There are rumours – unsubstantiated, of course – that one of them is the reason that chap over there' – he indicated a bearded man near the fireplace – 'walks with a slight limp. Bobby Scruggs, by name. They say he took an arrow in the calf for complaining about one of their dogs. Tittle-tattle, of course. Probably.'

Ellie chuckled. 'Most illuminating, thank you. I feel as though I know them all.'

'I wasn't joking, you know. All of this lot will have been stealing glances at you just as much as we've been surveying them. Who does your wardrobe, by the way?'

'You're too kind,' said Ellie, not minding the forward nature of the young Bilverton's chat – it was clear he was a dedicated socialite. 'I have a dressmaker in London. I like the clothes she puts me in very much, but she is always telling me off for not taking more of an interest.'

Howard laughed. 'If I ever need to impress a lady with a gift, I might need her card. Do you want anything more to eat?'

'I couldn't manage another mouthful, thank you.'

'Then let's see who's in the drawing room.'

Howard led them out through the other door and into a small hallway. Another door took them into the drawing room Ellie had seen earlier. There were more guests now, but Ellie's attention was on the piano.

'That's a beautiful instrument,' she said.

'Do you play?'

'A little.'

Howard gestured towards the Bechstein in the corner of the room. 'Be my guest.'

'Oh, I couldn't.'

'Of course you can.'

Ellie allowed herself to be steered towards the gleaming grand piano where, after a few experimental chords, she began to play a song she knew from a gramophone record that Skins often played at home.

'That's the ticket,' said Howard enthusiastically. 'Always loved "Singin' the Blues". Do you know it, Peter?'

He invited a man to join them as Ellie continued playing. He was only a few years older than Howard, but where the other younger guests had chosen more fashionable attire, he had opted instead for the full formal white tie and tails. The suit was exquisitely tailored and fitted him perfectly, but it still seemed to Ellie as though it were someone else's, as though he were playing a role and trying too hard to impress. Sucking up to the host, she wondered?

'Mrs Maloney, may I present my future brother-in-law, Peter Putnam. Peter, this is Ellie Maloney. Her husband is the drummer with the jazz band.'

'Hello,' oiled Peter, managing to make the simple informal greeting sound like a lewd remark. 'What a lucky man that drummer is.'

He put a hand on Ellie's shoulder. She tried to shrug him off as she continued to play, but he wouldn't take the hint. She caught Howard's eye and was thankful that he was a good deal better attuned to such things.

'I say, is that Betty over there? How's she enjoying herself this evening?'

At the mention of his fiancée's name, Peter hurriedly removed his hand from Ellie's shoulder and looked around. 'Where?'

'My mistake, dear boy. Sorry. Could have sworn it was dear Elizabeth come looking for you.'

'I'd better go and find her, though, eh?' said Peter. He oozed away.

'Thank you,' said Ellie over the recently mauled shoulder.

'I'd like to say he means well . . . But he really doesn't. I don't know what she sees in him.'

'Families, eh?' said Ellie as she expertly played on.

◆ ◆ ◆

The invitations had said 'Carriages at One'. The evening had been dry and warm, but by the time the chauffeurs and taxi drivers began to line up their vehicles on the drive, it was raining heavily.

By two in the morning, most of the partygoers had returned home and the rest had retired to the guest rooms on the second floor. The Dizzies, meanwhile, packed up their instruments and cleared the stage, still buzzing with the thrill of performing. The servants were already busy clearing up, so the band trooped out of the marquee with their gear into the pouring rain. A flagstone path ran along the rear of the house, past the walled garden and along a bowered passage to the old chapel. Skins always had the most to carry, but the others helped and they managed to get everything to their billet in one trip.

Just that short walk had left them all soaked through, and there was a scramble once they were inside to find places to hang clothes where they might dry.

The army cots had been set up for them in two rows of five on either side of what had once been the aisle. Ellie and Katy moved one of them so that the six men and four women could sleep on opposite sides.

'Do you want a screen down the middle?' asked Katy.

'Can *you* be bothered to do it?' asked Puddle.

'Well . . . I just thought . . .'

'Then no, we'll be fine. They've resisted our charms so far, after all.'

'It's not that we don't love you,' said Dunn. 'It's just that we're knackered.'

'See?' said Puddle. 'Shut up and get some kip, sis.'

# Chapter Three

***Saturday, 27 June 1925***

The Dizzies slept well, and the first of them began stirring at about ten the next morning.

The men had all served in the war, and Ellie had been a nurse in the First Aid Nursing Yeomanry, so most of them were used to roughing it. Vera and Puddle had grown accustomed to dossing down with their bands when they played engagements far from home. Only new girl Katy had struggled.

'You never told me I'd be living like a tramp,' she said to her sister. 'I thought being a jazz band's manager would be a sight more glamorous than this.'

'This is luxury,' said Puddle. 'You should see some of the places we've kipped in over the past couple of years.'

'I think I might give touring a miss in future. I'll be one of those managers with an office in Denmark Street. I'll smoke cigars and hire a dishy secretary so I can flirt with him. And I'll not sleep on army surplus cots in shabby old chapels.'

There was movement on the other side of the room.

'Anyone mind if I go first?' said Elk.

There were mumbles of consent and Elk got up and lumbered towards the chapel vestry, which had been converted into a bathroom. While he saw to his ablutions, a rota quickly evolved to get the Dizzies washed and dressed.

'What are the arrangements for breakfast?' asked Eustace.

'They promised me they'd have something ready for us in the kitchens,' said Katy. 'If a couple of you would be absolute poppets and nip up there to get it, we can eat down here.'

'If I can have the bathroom next,' said Mickey, 'me and Elk can go as soon as I'm dressed.'

The two men set off in the rain shortly after that.

There was an urn on a table at the back of the chapel to keep the studio's clients supplied with tea during a long working day. While Mickey and Elk were gone, Dunn fired it up and was already handing out cups and mugs of tea by the time they returned, utterly sodden. Fortunately the much-awaited breakfast was covered.

'It's bedlam up at the house,' said Mickey as he set down the tray of food. 'Guests everywhere. The hall's full of baggage. Looks like an evacuation.'

'That will be the overnighters going home,' said Katy. 'Quite early, isn't it? I suppose they have places to be. Young Howard Bilverton was charmingly apologetic about having to put us up down here, by the way. "Plenty of spare beds," he said, "but they're all taken – family friends and whatnot." I said we wouldn't mind. Perhaps I shouldn't have.'

'It was only one night,' said Vera. 'It was an adventure. Like camping.'

The others politely agreed.

They sat on their cots to eat their breakfast, with a few of the boys chattering eagerly about the exotic electronic recording equipment they'd found in a side room.

'It's good, then, is it?' said Katy.

Mickey nodded sagely. 'I should say so.'

'Why? What's so special about it?'

'Well . . . it's . . . it's electric, ain't it?'

Katy laughed. 'I see. Well, I'll have to take your word for it. Does that mean you'd be pleased if your new manager had arranged for you to make a recording in here today?'

Eating and conversation stopped abruptly.

'Pleased?' said Mickey. 'I should bloody well say so. You little darlin'.'

'Nice one, Katy,' said Elk.

The rest of the band began talking all at once, excitedly speculating on what it would be like to make a proper modern recording.

Breakfast was down to the last few rounds of toast when they heard the clatter of the latch on the old chapel door.

'Are you decent?' a voice called.

Mickey gave a falsetto giggle. 'No, but you can come in anyway.' He grinned at his friends and bit off another mouthful.

Malcolm Bilverton came in. He was dressed in tweeds, and his elegant walking cane of the evening before had been replaced by a more robust, bucolic stick. He limped into the body of the chapel among the munching band members on their old army cots.

'Morning all,' he said, giving the semblance of a bow. 'Malcolm Bilverton of Bilver-Tone Records at your service. How wonderful to meet the Dizzy Heights in person at last.'

'For our sins,' said Skins, who was the only one of them without a mouthful of food. 'Nice place you've got here.'

'I'm glad you like it – I have a proposal for you. Do you have any plans for the rest of the morning? Young Howie tells me you're stuck here till the charabanc arrives at lunchtime to take you all back to London.'

'Well, I don't. What about you lot? Did anyone have anything they particularly wanted to do?'

'I would have quite liked a walk in the grounds,' sighed Puddle, 'but not in this weather.'

'Well, quite,' said Malcolm. 'You see, the thing is I spoke to Mrs Cannon yesterday and asked if you'd like to cut a couple of discs while you're here.'

'Did you?' said Mickey. 'Katy, why didn't you tell us?'

'Ignore them, Malcolm,' said Katy. 'I told them just now. They were positively giddy.'

Malcolm chuckled amiably. 'You're keen, then? It's just that I was thinking I have one of London's hottest jazz bands trapped here in my lair for the morning. It would give me an opportunity to hear you all again, and you'd end up with some recordings you could use for promotion.'

'No need to try to convince us,' said Skins. 'You should have heard the reaction when she told us about it.'

'Well, that's a relief. I had a speech prepared, but it wasn't a terribly good one. So we shall make a recording or two for your own use. Although Mrs Cannon and I might even strike a commercial deal. One never knows.'

'Well . . . I . . .' said Katy.

Malcolm smiled. 'Splendid, splendid. Why don't you and I have a little chat while your chaps set up? The cots live in the storeroom over there.'

He took Katy into the corner and left the overexcited band to convert their dormitory back into a recording studio.

It took the Dizzies quite a while to tidy everything away and then set themselves up to play. It took Malcolm even longer to find exactly the right spot for his microphone. He began by having the band play as normal and then walking around until he heard roughly the sound he was hoping for. Then he had them shift their chairs backwards or forwards as a way of balancing the different instruments. Skins and his drum set ended up at the back.

Next, he spent almost half an hour arranging a number of what looked like oversized hospital screens hung with thick blankets around the room to 'control the reverberation', as he put it. Then he would make his way surprisingly nimbly back to his chosen spot, listen intently, nod sagely, and set off to make more adjustments.

Finally, he seemed satisfied.

'How's that for everyone?' he said as he set the heavy iron microphone stand in place.

'We'll get used to it,' said Skins. 'I can't hear Barty so well. To tell the truth, I can't hear anyone too well. You'll all just have to follow me.'

'It's a revelation for me,' said Barty Dunn. 'Without that wiry little idiot banging and crashing next to me, I can hear things I've never heard before.'

They rehearsed a couple of numbers while Malcolm checked the sound on the loudspeaker in the side room. He came out and excitedly told them everything was set up perfectly.

'Are you ready to make a record?' he asked. 'It's going to be marvellous. Absolutely marvellous. I'm so glad you all agreed to do this. So very glad. Glad indeed.'

Skins gave Ellie a bemused frown. 'All right then, Malcolm, m'boy, let's go.'

But as Malcolm set off at an unexpectedly energetic trot towards the control room, Eustace piped up. 'We don't want to record the count-in, do we?'

They didn't.

'And Skins can't use his stick like a conductor's baton because he's at the back and we can't see him.'

They couldn't.

'So how will we know when to come in?'

Ellie was at the other end of the room. 'I can conduct,' she said, making her way down towards the band. 'It's not like I haven't heard your entire repertoire a million times before. Ivor can give me the tempo, then I can give you one bar for nothing once the recording doodad is doing whatever it is recording doodads do.' She was one of only a very few people anywhere in the world who ever called her husband Ivor.

'That'll work,' said Eustace. 'Thank you.'

And that's how it went. Skins tapped his sticks. Ellie did a little jig on the spot to keep the tempo fixed in her head. In the side room that housed all the equipment, Malcolm lowered the stylus on to the shellac recording disc and switched on the red light to signal that everything was working. Ellie conducted one bar and they were off.

Then, as stealthily as she could, Ellie slunk to her seat in the lounge area by the tea urn, where she sat with Katy in perfect silence until the number was over and Malcolm had emerged from his lair to give the thumbs-up. They whooped and whistled.

'That's one for posterity,' said Malcolm. 'Care to try another before the muse leaves you?'

The band enthusiastically agreed and Malcolm disappeared once more to change the disc.

The same procedure followed, though this time Ellie stayed near the microphone to try to get an idea of how it might sound on the disc.

Malcolm had originally intended just to record two numbers so that they could have a few copies of a single disc duplicated for their own use. They had proven so suited to the recording process, though, that he decided to record a few more songs just in case anything came of the ongoing negotiations with Katy.

They were part way through the sixth number when the chapel door clattered and creaked open. Malcolm lifted the recording stylus and hurried out to stop the band.

'Come in if you're coming,' he called.

The entire rain-drenched Bilverton family trooped in, led by John Bilverton and his young wife.

'Not come at a bad time, I hope,' said John.

'Of course you have, dear boy,' said Malcolm. 'But it's my fault – I did suggest you all came down here, after all. I need to install a red light on the outside of the door to match the one in here.'

'It would make the place look like a Parisian brothel,' said Howard from the back of the group.

'Must you always be so vulgar, you obnoxious little twerp?' said the man Ellie had heard arguing with his wife at the party.

'That'll do, boys,' said John. 'Not in front of guests.'

He completely ignored Katy and Ellie and walked down towards the band, his family trailing behind him.

'I hope you don't mind, but we find ourselves confined to barracks by the rain and I thought it might be a treat – since we have what my children tell me is one of the "hottest jazz bands in London" staying with us – if we all came down to Malcolm's little studio and spent some time listening to music. After all, we'll lose you to the bright lights of London as soon as the charabanc arrives.'

His position at the back of the band put Skins closest to John, so he decided to speak for them all.

'Don't mind at all,' he said. 'Always happy to have a captive audience. We're the Dizzy Heights, but you knew that. We've got Barty Dunn on bass and Elk Elkington on banjo.' He indicated the two men, who each gave a small wave of greeting. 'Then we've got Eustace Taylor on trumpet and Benny Charles on trombone.' Eustace waved, while Benny gave a warm smile and a nod. 'The woodwind section is Isabella "Puddle" Puddephatt on sax, clarinet and occasional flute, and Vera James on clarinet and sax.' The two women just smiled. 'Mickey Kent is our singer and I'm Ivor Maloney, but everyone calls me Skins.'

'Do they, indeed? And what do you do?'

'I just came in to read the gas meter.'

The man laughed. 'Jolly good. Well, if we're doing introductions, I suppose I ought to introduce my lot. This beautiful lady is my wife, Marianne. Then we have my eldest son Gordon and his wife Charlotte.' He indicated the arguing man and the slapped woman, who were both still looking hostile. 'My daughter Elizabeth and her fiancé Peter Putnam.' A short woman and the oily man Ellie had met while she was playing the piano at the party. 'That's my daughter Veronica.' Taller and more athletic, but somehow less graceful than her sister. 'Youngest son Howard and his . . . pal, Henrietta Hollis. But I believe you've already met.' The two youngsters from the previous evening were familiar to the whole band. 'I'm John Bilverton and you already know my little brother, Malcolm. Welcome to my home.'

'Pleasure to meet you all,' said Skins, still in the role of spokesman. 'Oh, and lest we forget: the two ladies in the comfy chairs by the tea urn are our manager Katy Cannon and my own wonderful wife, Ellie.'

'Splendid, splendid,' said John. 'Well, if you've no objections, we'd like to listen in.' He finally acknowledged the existence of Ellie and Katy in the battered armchairs. 'Do you mind if we join you, ladies?'

'Be our guests,' said Ellie. 'The more the merrier, as you say.'

The family arranged themselves on the mishmash of chairs and old sofas that had been brought down from the main house to provide visiting musicians with somewhere to relax between recordings.

'Shall we try another take?' said Malcolm.

The band agreed and Ellie excused herself to go and count them in.

'We need absolute silence in the cheap seats,' called Malcolm. 'This is the last number we're recording today so you can gabble away all you like once we're done, but for now, not a peep.'

The final recording went without a hitch.

◆ ◆ ◆

Ellie had been fascinated by the way the family had arranged themselves on the many chairs. It came as no surprise that Gordon and Charlotte weren't sitting together, given what Ellie had heard the night before; but given what she'd heard, she was slightly puzzled that Charlotte chose to sit next to John.

Marianne, seemingly oblivious to whatever was going on between her husband and his son's wife, was sitting with Elizabeth and Peter. Howard's pal, the singer Hetty Hollis, was sitting with Howard's sister Veronica, leaving Howard himself free to chat to Katy.

Everyone was talking animatedly in their little groups, and Ellie was free to listen in.

'Is it you?' said Elizabeth.

'Is what me, love?' said Marianne with a puzzled frown.

'Father has put what he's called a "budget cap" on the wedding. Was that your doing?'

'Why on earth would I do that?'

'Because you're a gold-digging little tart,' snarled Elizabeth.

'And you're a spoilt brat,' said Marianne breezily, 'but I can't see any benefit in sabotaging your wedding. The sooner you're out of my house the better, as far as I'm concerned.'

'It's *my* house.'

'Everything all right over there?' said John.

'Yes, thank you, darling,' said Marianne. 'Just discussing the wedding.'

'Jolly good.'

'He's also planning to make changes to your allowance, by the way,' Marianne continued, calmly and quietly. 'With Peter to look after you after the wedding, there'll be no need for your father to pay for quite so many dresses and hats. But it's still nothing to do with me.'

'You've had your claws into him from the very beginning,' said Elizabeth. 'Even before Mama died. And now you're making sure he doesn't spend any of his money on the people who actually love him – all the more for you.'

'Steady on, darling,' said Peter. His manner when talking to his fiancée was a good deal more deferential than when he had greased his way to Ellie's side the night before. 'No need for all that. You know it's me he doesn't like. But we'll soon be rid of him.'

Meanwhile, Veronica was talking to Hetty.

'You're walking out with one of Howie's friends, I gather?'

Hetty nodded. 'Kenneth Mary, yes. Lovely chap. Devastated that he couldn't manage to get here this weekend.'

'Ah, yes. Howie did say. Glad you could make it, though. You were quite a hit last night. Well done, you.'

Hetty affected a completely unconvincing look of modesty. 'Well, I don't know about that.'

'Oh, come now. You should think about doing it professionally. Perhaps Uncle Malcolm could introduce you to some people.'

'Oh, gosh, do you think he would?'

'I'm sure of it. He knows everyone who's anyone. I'll mention it to him.'

'That would be super, thank you. Howie tells me you're a schoolteacher. It must be a trial being a teacher sometimes. I was beastly at school – I certainly shouldn't have liked to try to deal with me.' She looked around to check she couldn't be overheard. 'Honestly, though, if I didn't already know and I'd been forced to guess, I would have assumed it was fussy old Elizabeth who was the teacher.'

Veronica laughed. 'No, it is I. Perfect little Betty went to her finishing school, came home, attached herself to the first witless wonder with an income she met, and lives the approved life of a good little bourgeois daughter. Charity committees and secretary of the parish council. I'm the black sheep with a job and an opinion.'

'Heaven forbid we should have those.'

Ellie looked around the chapel. The Dizzies were chatting, too – apparently trying to decide what to play next. Malcolm was busy in the side room with his mysterious equipment. Ellie could hear the sound of one of the earlier performances being played back from the disc until he closed the soundproof door.

She caught Skins's eye. He beckoned her to come down and join him.

'You looked a bit lost,' he said when she arrived.

'I was quite enjoying myself, actually,' she said. 'This is some family.'

'Really? How's that?'

'I'll tell you later. You wanted me?'

'Always. I just wondered if you'd like to sit in on piano for a bit. You missed your chance last night.'

'I played in the drawing room.'

'Did you, indeed?' he said. 'How about reprising your triumphant drawing room recital with the rest of the band?'

'They won't mind?'

'They'll love it. It's what we do. Just play something – I guarantee they'll join in.'

'Can I invite someone else, too?'

'Always.'

Ellie turned to Hetty Hollis. 'I'm going to play with the band. Do you want to join us?'

Hetty was delighted. 'Oh, may I?'

'Of course,' said Skins. 'Come down and meet the workers.'

Hetty almost knocked her chair over in her haste.

Skins was right. Ellie had no idea what she should play, so she just tried a little Chopin. One by one the Dizzies joined in, and within a few minutes they had turned the gentle nocturne into a syncopated dance number with Hetty improvising a lyric about a couple walking in the rain.

All conversation at the other end of the chapel stopped as the family turned to listen. They greeted the end of the tune with enthusiastic applause and cries for more.

'That really is splendidly clever,' said John. 'Bravo. Well done all.'

'Hear, hear,' said Elizabeth.

John stood. 'I should love to hear more, but I have to get some important papers sorted out before Monday. I'll be in my study for a while.'

'Oh, Papa,' said Veronica. 'Don't be so rude. Can't it wait until tomorrow? The band will be gone soon.'

'I might need tomorrow as well. I told you all I was going to have to work this afternoon. But the sooner I start, the sooner I'll be back. I'll join you all for tea at four, but not a second before.'

He took his coat from the rack and rummaged in the huge earthenware vase by the door. It was mostly filled with Malcolm's spare walking sticks, but he eventually found the only umbrella and set off into what had now developed into a rather impressive storm. The rain, which had varied indecisively for most of the week between moderate drizzle and steady showers, had finally settled on the idea of a torrential downpour. Occasional crashes of thunder added to the theatre. John slammed the chapel door shut behind him and hurried off towards the house.

The band, as bands do, played on.

◆ ◆ ◆

The household had been told that the Dizzies were expected to leave around lunchtime, so no one had thought to offer them any lunch. By half past three, though, the motor coach had still not arrived and they were getting more than a little peckish. Fortunately, the excitement of hearing the band again had meant that most of the Bilvertons had skipped lunch too, and so they were similarly afflicted.

Elizabeth took charge.

'Since we're all having such fun down here, why don't we have an indoor picnic?' she said. 'I hate to impose upon guests, but if you wouldn't mind lending a hand, Mrs Cannon, we can scurry up to the house and get Mrs Radway to put something together for us, then we can help bring it all back.'

'I'm more than happy to help,' said Katy. 'I could do with stretching my legs.'

Ellie looked up from the piano. 'Me too,' she said. 'As much as I love playing with the Dizzies, I do feel the need for a little exercise. We've been cooped up in here for ever. I'll even brave the rain.'

'Thank you,' said Elizabeth. 'Come along, Ronnie, you can help, too.'

'Of course I can,' said Veronica. 'Heaven forfend the boys should have to dirty their manly hands with something so domestic.'

'Oh, do shut up, there's a love,' said Elizabeth.

Ellie looked at Katy and raised her eyebrows, but neither said anything. Sharing a grin, they followed the Bilverton daughters to the door.

'Are you sure you want to come?' said Elizabeth. 'You've no raincoats. I thought there was an umbrella here but Papa must have taken it.'

'A little rain won't hurt us,' said Ellie. 'We'll only be outdoors for a few moments.'

Elizabeth opened the door and the rain lashed in.

'Are you sure?' she said. 'It's a good deal more than "a little rain". There's really no shame in backing out.'

'No, I really could do with a break,' said Ellie. 'Katy?'

Katy didn't look at all keen. 'Well . . . I mean . . .'

'Why don't you stay here and organize the boys?' suggested Elizabeth. 'There are trestle tables in the storeroom – they can set those up for us.'

Katy nodded gratefully and retreated into the shelter of the chapel.

'Onward to glory and all that,' said Elizabeth, and led Ellie and Veronica into the storm.

They took the short journey along the bowered path at a run. Even under the shelter of the arching trees they were getting wet, but as soon as they broke cover and began to run past the walled garden, 'wet' was an entirely inadequate description – they were drenched.

They passed the garden gate and hurried on towards the house. Veronica had overtaken her sister, and was already a couple of yards past the rear door and on her way to the servants' entrance at the other side of the huge building when Elizabeth called her back.

'Quicker to go in through the house,' she shouted.

Veronica doubled back and the three of them bundled into the salon, trailing mud and rainwater on to the tiled floor.

'Mrs Freeman will have a fit,' said Veronica.

'Our housekeeper,' Elizabeth explained to Ellie. 'But I think she'd rather organize the cleaning up of a bit of mud than have to deal with three drowned corpses on the servants' steps.'

'Light summer dresses aren't at all suited to rain,' said Ellie, glad to be indoors. 'One might have thought, given your climate, that you Brits would have thought to invent a waterproof summer dress by now.'

They walked through to the library, still dripping.

'I believe the rainproof summer dress was invented in 1781 by George Yandle, a haberdasher from Taunton,' said Veronica. 'But it was deemed that wearing it would indicate a lack of backbone in the face of perfectly ordinary summer rain, and it was declared un-British. Yandle died a pauper a few years later, having been ostracized by his community for being openly unpatriotic in a time of war.'

'You do talk rot sometimes, Ronnie,' said Elizabeth.

'It sounds convincing to me,' said Ellie. 'The Revolutionary War might have gone the other way had your side not been held back by lily-livered cowards like George Yandle.'

'Was your family there?' asked Veronica.

'Fighting in the Revolutionary War? They were indeed. The Wilsons had been in the Province of Maryland for more than a hundred years before anyone even thought of revolting.'

'How exciting. You're proper American aristocracy, then. Not like us. We're "new money", you see.'

'Is that bad?'

'I should say so. Earning money is frightfully vulgar. One has to inherit it down through the generations.'

'Someone had to earn it in the first place, though, right?'

'Good Lord, no. Real wealth was granted by the king. Or stolen from another lord. Earning is for the middle classes.'

'I see.'

'Worse still, we made our money from biscuits.'

'Everyone loves cookies.'

'That's what pastry cooks are for. Buying them from a shop? Well, I mean, really.'

'You'll have to excuse my sister,' said Elizabeth. 'She somehow manages to be simultaneously embarrassed by her wealth and irritated that she's not more highly respected for being so wealthy.'

'Except I'm not wealthy, am I?' said Veronica. 'It all goes to Gordon.'

'Can we argue about this later? Poor Mrs Maloney is starting to shiver. Go up to the linen store and get some towels. We'll go down to the kitchens and start packing everything up while you do that. The ovens will still be on down there, too – that'll help.'

Veronica set off towards the hall and the main stairs while Elizabeth led Ellie down a flight of much less ostentatious stone steps to the servants' lair in the basement.

Ellie found herself in a long, stone-floored corridor that seemed to stretch the entire width of the house. On the opposite wall, slightly to her left, was a large open doorway from which came kitcheny sounds and smells. This was clearly their goal.

'Come on in here,' said Elizabeth. 'The ovens in this place are never allowed to go out. We'll get you warmed up.'

There was a flurry of activity in the spacious kitchen as Mrs Radway, the Bilverton House cook, bustled about, issuing orders to her kitchen maids as she went. It was a warm, cosy place and Ellie felt immediately better for being there.

'Afternoon, Mrs Radway,' said Elizabeth.

'Hello, Miss Elizabeth, my love. How are you? Did you enjoy yourself last night?'

'Do you know, I really rather did. Thank you so very much for all your hard work. I do hope you had a few moments to enjoy the results of your labours.'

Mrs Radway chuckled. 'I might have had a port and lemon once all the serving was done.'

'There was so much delicious food,' said Ellie. 'I hope you sampled some of that, too.'

The cook looked quizzically at Elizabeth.

'This is Mrs Ellie Maloney. She's married to the drummer in the jazz band.'

'I didn't know they was American,' said the cook.

Ellie smiled. 'They're not. Just me.'

Mrs Radway seemed unconvinced, but declined to pursue the matter further. Instead she turned the conversation to safer ground. 'No one sent down for lunch. Will you be wanting afternoon tea?'

'You read our minds,' said Elizabeth. 'We're all in the chapel listening to the band while they wait for their charabanc to arrive, and lunch completely slipped our minds. Do you think we might have an indoor picnic?'

With a wave of her arm, Mrs Radway indicated three hampers piled beside the huge preparation table.

'I packed you all up some leftovers and salads from last night, along with some fresh sandwiches. There's beer and wine, as well.'

Elizabeth was delighted. 'I say. Well done, you.'

'We'll give you a hand getting it all down the chapel.'

'No need for that, Mrs Radway. If we can borrow the footmen's porter's truck we should be able to manage. There are three of us. Ronnie's upstairs fetching some towels to dry us all off.'

'If Mr Malcolm would put a bell in the chapel you wouldn't have needed to get so wet. You'd have thought with all his gadgets and whatnot he could wire up a bell push down there.'

'He has other priorities, Mrs Radway, so for now we have to brave the rain. We ought to see if we can find umbrellas for the journey back.'

While two kitchen maids went off hunting for the porter's truck, Veronica arrived with the towels and handed them to Ellie.

'Sorry it took me so long,' she said. 'The blessed linen store is all the way up on the second floor.'

'Thank you so much,' said Ellie. 'Elizabeth was suggesting we find umbrellas for the return trip.'

'Or raincoats at the very least.'

'Should we tell your father we're about to eat?'

'What time is it?' Veronica looked at the large clock on the kitchen wall. 'Nearly four. Yes, that should be all right. As long as we wait until the grandfather clock in the hall chimes four, we'll be fine. He has few eccentricities, our dear papa, but he has a real bee in his bonnet about having tea at four. Did you hear him earlier? "Not a second before." And he meant it. He's been known to get fearfully cross with people offering him food before the clock strikes four.'

Mrs Radway's chuckles rippled across her aproned body. 'She's right. None of the staff will go near him till that clock in the hall strikes four.'

'He wouldn't shout at me, surely?' said Ellie. 'I'm a guest. But I don't want to upset him so I'll be sure to wait for the clock. Why don't I take the booze up with me and then go and get him while you sort out the food? I'll see if I can find some umbrellas in the entrance hall while I'm there, then we can all go down together.'

'All right, but on your own head be it. He'll be in his study – it's the door opposite the billiards room, next to the clock.'

Ellie smiled and staggered upstairs with the heavy hamper of wine and beer.

She left the basket just inside the library and walked back out into the cavernous Grand Hall. The longcase clock ticked solemnly, and a glance at its face showed Ellie that it was still two minutes to four.

She walked stealthily past the study door towards the entrance hall and the promise of umbrellas, but nearly jumped out of her skin as the sound of a clarinet blared out from inside the study. She stopped to listen. It was a recording of Gershwin's 'Rhapsody in Blue', but louder and clearer than any gramophone she had ever heard. She listened for a few moments and shocked herself by being able to name the clarinettist in the Paul Whiteman Orchestra – Ross Gorman.

'You've been hanging about with those jazz boys far too long,' she said to herself.

There was another oversized vase by the front door – the twin of the one in the chapel – containing half a dozen umbrellas of various sizes. She grabbed four and returned to the hall, where she tiptoed once more to the study door and listened to the music while she waited for four o'clock.

With a whirr and a mechanical clonk, the clock began to chime the hour.

As the fourth chime died away, she was about to knock but was startled into inaction when she heard another completely unexpected sound from inside the room.

A gunshot.

# Chapter Four

Ellie hammered on the study door. 'Mr Bilverton!'

The music inside played on.

She tried the handle but, as she'd expected, the old oak door was locked. She beat it with the flat of her hand and shouted louder. 'Mr Bilverton! Are you all right? Mr Bilverton!'

She hammered again.

'Mr Bilverton! John! John Bilverton!'

She turned to see Elizabeth and Veronica, who had dropped the two heavy picnic baskets in the library and were hurrying towards her.

'What's the matter?' asked Elizabeth, breathlessly.

'Is it Papa?' said Veronica. She was slightly less out of breath than her sister, but there wasn't much in it.

'I heard a gunshot,' said Ellie. 'Now there's no reply.'

Veronica put her ear to the door. 'How can you be sure it was a shot over that music?'

'Have you tried the handle?' asked Elizabeth.

Ellie stood aside and let them try the door for themselves.

'Where's the spare key?' said Veronica.

'Dunsworth must have one,' said Elizabeth. 'If he's not about, I'd bet it's on that board thing just inside his door.'

Veronica dashed off towards the stairs in search of the butler and his spare key.

'How high are the windows on the outside?' said Ellie. 'Can you see in?'

Elizabeth frowned as she tried to remember. 'Pretty high. We used to make a game of trying to peek in when we were children.'

'But it can be done?'

'If you're nimble.'

'I'm nimble enough. You wait here for Veronica, I'll see what I can see through the window. I might even be able to get inside.'

'Thank you,' said Elizabeth anxiously. 'Do be careful.'

Ellie trotted back to the entrance hall and grabbed an oiled rain cape before wrenching open one of the huge front doors and heading out into the storm.

She hurried through the rapidly forming puddles towards the study window. The windowsill was above her head and she couldn't immediately work out how the young Bilvertons had been able to see in. She decided the agile children must have been able to grip the sill and clamber up on the stone skirting. Or was it called a plinth course? Either way, she wasn't convinced it was something she'd be able to do in her increasingly heavy summer dress, despite her claims to nimbleness.

She looked around for something to stand on, but the outside of the front of the house was as neat and tidy as the inside. She put her head down and ran towards the corner – maybe there would be something there, out of sight.

The gardeners had helpfully left a wheelbarrow and a couple of old tea chests by the garden wall. She loaded them up and trundled everything back to the study window, where she managed to make a wooden tower tall enough to be useful and dangerous enough to add an element of peril to future retellings of her exploits.

Gripping the wet stone of the windowsill, she peered into the study. There was an electric lamp on the desk, faintly illuminating the room. The chair was facing towards the locked door but she could see there was someone in it. It looked like John Bilverton, and he appeared to be slumped to one side with his arm dangling over the armrest.

Ellie banged on the window and called his name, but he didn't respond. She wondered for a moment if the loud music might make it difficult to hear her, but realized, pressed up to the pane, that the record had long since ended.

The window didn't yield to her efforts to open it, so she gingerly clambered down from her precarious perch and went back to see how the Bilverton sisters were getting on in their attempts to gain entry by the more conventional route.

She found Veronica holding a key nervously in both hands.

'Dunsworth was nowhere to be seen,' she said. 'So I nabbed the key from his room. But it doesn't work.'

Elizabeth, meanwhile, was on her knees, trying to squint through the keyhole.

'There's something in there,' she said. 'That's why it won't open. It's probably Papa's key.'

'So it's locked from the inside?' said Ellie.

'It seems that way,' said Veronica. 'Did you manage to see anything?'

'Yes. He's in his chair, but he's not moving. We've got to get in there. Right now.'

Elizabeth stood. 'Do you think we could break it down?'

'If we threw all our weight against it we might,' said Ellie as she shrugged off the dripping oilskin.

'We'd not all fit in the doorway,' said Veronica. 'Let me try.'

She took a few steps back and charged. She turned her shoulder towards the door as she approached and made violent, clattering contact. There was plenty of noise, but the door didn't budge.

'Buggering hell, that hurt,' she said. 'Worth another go, though.'

She tried a few more times with a similar lack of success, though on the last effort they did hear a slight cracking sound.

'Nice one, Ron,' said Elizabeth. 'Sounds like we're nearly in. Let me have a go before you break your shoulder.'

More cracking followed Elizabeth's attempts but she, too, had to retire. Both women were now nursing aching shoulders.

'Who would ever have thought doors would be so difficult to smash open?' said Ellie. 'Do you mind if I have a go?'

'You go ahead,' said Elizabeth. 'We must be close to breaking in by now. It should only take a few more goes. Alternate your shoulders, though. I wish I had.'

Ellie smashed into the door with all her might. Pain exploded in her arm and her nurse's training helped her imagine all the damage she might be doing to herself. She definitely felt a little give from the door, though.

She braced herself for another try, this time leading with the other shoulder. 'I figure one more ought to do it.'

She charged and, finally, the door burst open. The sudden lack of resistance made her lose her balance and she stumbled into the room, where she slipped on a small puddle of rainwater and landed in an awkward heap on the polished wooden floor. Elizabeth and Veronica were close behind.

They rushed to their father, leaving Ellie to pick herself up and follow.

She stood to find the sisters standing with their hands to their mouths.

John Bilverton was very obviously dead. A gun lay on the floor beneath his outstretched left arm.

The record on the new electric gramophone was still spinning. Ellie went over to it and switched it off.

'We need to telephone the doctor,' said Veronica.

Elizabeth looked at her angrily. 'And what will he do?'

'What?'

'The doctor – what will he do? Will he bring him back to life?'

'No, but—'

'We do need to notify the authorities,' said Ellie, kindly. 'I'll telephone the doctor for you if you like.'

Elizabeth didn't move.

Veronica shook her head. 'Thank you, but I'll do it.'

She picked up the telephone receiver and Ellie put her arm around Elizabeth's shoulders and led her gently out of the room. There were a few chairs around the walls of the hall and Ellie directed Elizabeth to one of them.

'I'm so sorry,' said Ellie. 'I don't know what else to say, but I really am sorry. If there's anything I can do . . .'

Elizabeth spoke softly. 'Can you tell the others, please? They ought to know. Gordon, Howard, Uncle Malcolm. They'll need to know.'

Ellie noticed that she hadn't mentioned John's wife, Marianne, but now wasn't the time to point that out. Instead she said, 'I'll go as soon as Veronica has finished on the phone.'

She didn't have long to wait before Veronica appeared in the study doorway.

'The telephone's not working.'

'It must be the storm,' said Ellie. 'You two wait here while I go and tell the others, then we'll work out what to do next.'

She picked up the oilskin from its puddle and set off for the chapel.

◆ ◆ ◆

Ellie burst through the chapel door and slammed it behind her. The noise of her explosive entry made the band stop playing mid-bar. The Bilverton family, strewn across the cluster of mismatched dilapidated furniture, turned towards her as one.

'I say, old girl,' said Malcolm. 'Steady on. Get yourself out of that wet coat and come and sit down – you're drenched. Are the girls on their way with the scoff?'

'Something terrible has happened,' said Ellie. 'Elizabeth and Veronica are very shaken and asked me to bring you the news. I'm afraid . . . I'm afraid John Bilverton is dead.'

There was a moment's shocked silence before every member of the family started asking Ellie urgent questions. Ellie prided herself on her calmness under fire, but after the horror of finding their host shot to death, she found herself overwhelmed by their clamorous interrogation. Holding back tears, she shrugged apologetically and turned away, leaving the Bilvertons to turn their questions on each other.

Skins left his seat with the band and marched briskly to his wife.

'Are you all right, Ells?' he said. 'What happened?'

'It looks like he shot himself,' she whispered. 'It was awful.'

Skins pulled his wife into an embrace, and only then did she realize that she was trembling. Whether with cold or shock she wasn't sure. Perhaps both.

'Where are the daughters?' he said.

'I left them in the hall. Veronica tried to call the doctor but the telephone isn't working.'

Gordon came over to them – he seemed to have appointed himself family spokesman.

'The phone's not working?' he said.

'No,' said Ellie. 'Veronica tried to call the doctor but the line's dead. It must be the storm.'

'We'll have to get help,' said Gordon. 'Howard? Take the car into Partlow's Ford and fetch the doctor. Uncle Malcolm? Come with me – we need to look after the girls. Everyone else, stay here until . . . until we've got everything . . . everything cleared up.'

'I ought to be with Elizabeth,' said her fiancé, Peter.

'Quite right, quite right. You come with us.'

'I'm coming with you,' said Marianne.

Gordon frowned. 'I don't think that would be wise.'

'Oh do shut up, Gordon,' said Charlotte. 'We're both coming.'

Marianne looked disdainfully at Charlotte. 'I don't think I need you, of all people, to speak up for me.'

'Do you want to go to the house with the men?'

'Yes, but—'

'Then you can shut up as well. We're coming, Gordon. Don't be such an ass.'

Gordon threw up his hands in despair, but relented.

Ellie was abruptly aware that she and the band had no part to play in this family tragedy. She had been at the heart of it for a brief moment, but now she was cut adrift. Still, she felt compelled to try to help.

'If there's anything we can do . . .' she said.

'Thank you, Mrs Maloney.' For the first time, Gordon seemed unsure of himself. 'Yes. Thank you. I'll . . . er . . . we'll . . .'

'Come on, lad,' said Malcolm.

The family set off into the rain. Hetty Hollis paused for a moment, uncertain whether she was invited, but she made up her mind and followed them, leaving Ellie and Skins to return to the band.

'What happened?' said Dunn.

Quickly and concisely, Ellie told them about hearing the music and gunshot, about the locked door and looking in through the window, about breaking in and, finally, finding John Bilverton dead in his chair.

'Blimey,' said Mickey. 'Messy way to go. You all right?'

'Messy?' said Ellie.

'We had a lieutenant in the war shoot himself. Nasty business.'

'This wasn't like that,' said Ellie. 'Just a single bullet hole in his left temple.'

Mickey frowned. 'You sure?'

'I saw bullet holes in the war, too, Mickey. I know what I was looking at.'

'Did you see the gun?'

'It was on the floor. A small-calibre pistol. A Smith & Wesson .22.'

'It'd still leave a mess if he held it up to his head. A little .22 round could go straight through.'

'What was the wound like?' asked Dunn.

'A small round hole,' said Ellie.

'What colour?'

'Wound-coloured.'

'Any little black dots round it?'

She thought for a moment. 'No. No, there weren't. The edge of the hole was darker, I guess. A lot darker now I think about it, like it was bruised, but there were no little dots.'

'He didn't shoot himself,' said Mickey and Dunn together.

Skins nodded. 'I saw a few wounds in my day, too. If you fire a gun up close, powder and bits of other crud embed themselves in the skin. If it's more than . . . what do you reckon? Two feet?'

'I'd say two feet,' said Mickey. 'Maybe a little more.'

'More than two feet away,' continued Skins, 'the powder and other rubbish doesn't hit the skin.'

'What about if the muzzle is touching the skin?' said Ellie.

'Makes a horrible mess,' said Mickey. 'That's what happened to the lieutenant. Rips its way in, then rips its way out again.'

'Whereas,' said Dunn, 'if you shoot someone with a little pop gun like that from a few feet away and the bullet makes a neat little hole with a black ring around it, it's probably not going to come out the other side.'

'But the room was locked from the inside,' said Ellie. 'He must have done it himself.'

'I suppose you could hold a gun at arm's length,' said Mickey, miming the action. 'But there's a fair chance you'd miss unless you were looking straight at it.'

'No, he was shot in the temple.'

'You'd have to pull the trigger with your thumb, too,' said Skins. 'I reckon it would spin out of your hand when you fired if you didn't have a proper grip on it.'

'And the pistol was lying on the floor underneath his outstretched arm,' said Ellie.

'Which arm was it?' said Skins.

'Left. The wound was to his left temple and the gun was on the floor to the left of his chair.'

'You saw him earlier. Was he left-handed?'

'I've no idea,' she said. 'But if he shot himself in the left temple with his left hand, I'm willing to bet he was.'

'Still doesn't explain the wound,' said Skins. 'What do you reckon we should do about it?'

Ellie touched his arm. 'When Howard gets back with the doctor, you three can explain your thoughts about the wound. Then we'll all retire discreetly back here to leave the family to grieve in peace while we wait for the motor coach to take us home to London. Where is it, do you think? It was supposed to be here by lunch.'

'Delayed, I suppose. By the weather,' said Skins, looking unusually thoughtful. 'What a rotten business. I can't even imagine what they're feeling.'

'Which is why we need to gently say our piece and then get out of the way,' Ellie reiterated. 'They need each other, not a jazz band.'

'They could probably do with a cup of tea as well,' said Dunn. 'Any of you lot want one? I'll make a pot.'

Everyone did.

It took Dunn quite a while to make and pour ten cups of tea in the eclectic assortment of crockery. It seemed that all the odds and ends from the house ended up in Malcolm's studio, from lone bone china cups to army surplus tin mugs, and Dunn was amused, as always, by the frugality of the moneyed classes. His landlady could ill afford to throw out old cups and saucers, but she would be mortified to serve her guests tea in mismatched crockery. These people, though, could buy an entirely new set every time someone so much as chipped a cup handle, but they clung to the oddments and unembarrassedly displayed them to strangers.

A few minutes later, Howard clattered into the chapel, a burst of rain blowing in with him, and the Dizzies fell silent as he slammed the door.

'What did the doctor say?' asked Ellie.

'Couldn't get off the estate,' said Howard. 'Main road's a good three feet deep. Tried going down the track and out the back on to the lane, but that's flooded, too. The river must have burst its banks. We're the only thing above water for miles around.'

This provoked a groan from the band.

'We're stranded,' said Benny, softly. 'That'll be why the motor coach hasn't come to pick us up.'

‘I’m supposed to be takin’ the missus to see her mother tomorrow,’ said Elk. ‘Sunday lunch with all the trimmings. She does a lovely roast, my mother-in-law.’

Howard shrugged apologetically. ‘Obviously you can stay for as long as needs be.’

The band’s complaints melted to sympathetic murmurs.

‘None of us has much of an appetite, as you can imagine, but Mrs Radway has set out some afternoon tea if you’re hungry. You should feel free to come up to the house.’

‘Thank you,’ said Katy. ‘We’ll try not to intrude.’

‘It can’t be helped. We’re going to move my father to the ice house for the time being, and then try to get by as best we can until the flood recedes.’

With a forlorn shrug, he turned and left.

While the rest of the band cleaned and packed away their instruments, Skins, Ellie and Dunn went down to the lounge area at the other end of the chapel.

‘What are we going to do?’ said Ellie.

‘I thought we could nip up to the house and get some pork pie and beer,’ said Skins. ‘Then wait to see what the arrangements are going to be for dinner.’

‘You know what I meant. What are we going to do about John Bilverton?’

‘There’s not much we can do, is there?’ said Dunn.

‘We said that about the missing diamonds and the Aristippus Club,’ she said. ‘But we stuck our noses in there and solved it. And I have to do something to distract me from worrying about the children. We told them we’d be back this evening.’

‘I doubt they’ll remember the exact time and date,’ said Skins. ‘And Nanny Nora will keep them happy and busy.’

‘But she’ll worry, too, if we can’t contact the house.’

'I understand that,' said Dunn, 'but how will poking our noses in here actually help anyone? There's plenty of other things we can do to distract ourselves.'

Ellie frowned. 'Don't you think these people would prefer to know the truth?'

'At least one of them wouldn't,' said Skins. 'If he didn't kill himself, then one of *them* did it. And they definitely wouldn't want people to know that.'

'None of the family can have done anything,' said Dunn. 'Everyone was here in the chapel when he copped it.'

'Everyone except Elizabeth and Veronica,' said Ellie.

'But you were with them.'

'Not the whole time. I was on my own when I heard the shot.'

'And where were they?'

'Down in the kitchens with the servants.'

'QED,' said Dunn. 'You said they came up together, and they couldn't have got out of the study and down the stairs after shooting him because you were outside the door when you heard the shot and you didn't move until they reached you.'

'So it must have been one of the others,' said Ellie. 'Or one of the servants.'

'But the room was locked from the inside,' said Dunn. 'And they were all in the chapel with us, anyway.'

'The killer could have jumped out of the window and run back. I bet you weren't keeping tabs on all of them.'

'I'd swear they were all there, but you can check with Katy. She was sitting with them. I'd have noticed that one of them was wet, though, even if I had lost track of them for a few minutes. I mean, look at the state of you. It's impossible to get to the house and back in this weather without getting so much as a drip on you.'

'Unless . . .' said Skins.

'Unless what, mate? Unless there's a magic cabinet that made them disappear from the study and reappear in the chapel? Or they were hiding under the desk, and Ellie and the sisters didn't notice them? Then when they all left, the killer sneaked out and raced back to the chapel by a covered pathway we don't know about, and arrived just before they got here?'

'No, I was going to say, "secret passageway". You know what these old places are like.'

'That's entertainingly imaginative of you, but I tell you, they were all accounted for,' said Dunn.

'You were the one who said he didn't shoot himself,' said Ellie. 'Now you're doing all you can to argue that no one else could have done it, either.'

'I'm not saying that. I'm saying it couldn't be one of the family.'

'Then who?'

'A servant with a grudge? A party guest?' suggested Dunn. 'They hid themselves away when everyone was leaving. Then they came out when the old bloke went into his study, shot him—'

'And then what? A servant would just melt back to their job, but where would this mystery party guest go?'

'They went back to their hiding place, waited for you three to come back here and then scarpered out the front door.'

'And how far will they get?' said Ellie. 'You heard Howard – the whole place is flooded.'

'It's a right old puzzle and no mistake,' said Skins with a grin.

Ellie shook her head. 'We need to get some pork pie and beer into you.'

'Hunger impairs the cognitive whatnots. It's been proven.'

'Then let's go up to the house,' she said. 'We can see about searching that study while we're up there.'

They collected the others from their comfy chairs and set off.

◆ ◆ ◆

Back at the house, the members of the Bilverton family were scattered among the ground floor rooms, sitting quietly alone or in small groups. None of them had eaten, but someone had put the picnic tea out on the dining table.

Veronica was on her own in the salon when the Dizzies arrived.

'Hello,' she said. 'You remember where the dining room is?' She indicated the door to her left. 'Please help yourselves.'

'Thank you,' said Ellie. 'If there's anything any of us can do to help. Anything at all. You only have to say the word.'

'You're very kind. I think we just have to try to get through as best we can until civilization is restored and we can go through all the . . . all the formalities.'

'Of course,' said Ellie. 'We'll try to keep out of the way. Is there anywhere we can sit to eat where we won't be disturbing anyone?'

'For some reason no one likes the garden parlour, so that'll probably be empty.'

'Where's that?'

'The door in the hall next to Papa's study.' She stopped, and swallowed a small sob.

Ellie held the young woman's clasped hands for a moment but said nothing further. The others took this as their cue to slip quietly into the dining room.

There were, as promised, pork pies and beer, as well as everything else they could imagine being served at a posh picnic. Not that many of the band had ever been on a posh picnic, but they'd read about them in books.

Skins filled two plates and went out into the Grand Hall, then through the door to the garden parlour. If the sun had been shining it would have been a light, airy room. Double glass-paned doors sat between enormous windows, all of which looked out on to a walled formal garden. In better weather it must have been magnificent, and Skins was struggling to imagine why the family might dislike it.

He sat on one of the comfortable chairs that lined the walls and tried to balance his plate on his lap. He was soon joined by Ellie and the remaining Dizzies.

'It's rather nice in here,' said Katy. 'I wonder why the family don't like it.'

'South-facing,' said Elk. 'It'll be a suntrap in the summer. It'll get really hot.'

The rest of them goggled at him.

'What?' he said. 'I might not be as well read as some of you lot, but I can tell north from south.'

'How?' said Vera.

'I know it was cloudy when we arrived but you could still see where the sun was. This room faces south.'

'You're a source of constant amazement,' said Dunn.

'Well, I think it's a charming room,' said Katy. 'I'm not sure about these dreary paintings, but the room itself is a delight.'

'Hear, hear,' said Puddle. 'Now then, you lot . . .'

'Which lot?' said Skins.

'You lot. You, and Ellie and Barty. What were you talking about back in the chapel? Were you planning one of your investigations?'

'Investigations?' said Vera. 'Oh, like at the Aristippus Club. Was that an "investigation"? I thought you just stumbled into all that. Was it . . . you know . . . a proper thing?'

'They were working for the rozzers,' said Puddle.

A piece of Scotch egg paused on its way to Vera's mouth. 'You never were. Well, I'll be blowed.'

'It's true,' said Skins. 'We know a detective from Scotland Yard. Well, sort of. And Ellie's got a couple of pals down in Gloucestershire who do a bit of detecting on the side.'

'On the side of what?'

'Well, they're ladies of leisure these days,' said Ellie. 'But they used to work for the Secret Service. And you're right, Puddle, we were wondering what we should do.'

'I think we should sit tight and wait for the doctor,' said Katy. 'I'm happy to book engagements, negotiate fees and try to get some champagne in the dressing room, but I didn't sign up to be a detective.'

'Oh, Katy, you stick-in-the-mud,' said Puddle. 'You've always been like this. Live a little.'

Katy harrumphed.

'Actually,' said Ellie, 'I think we ought to find out what's been going on before the doctor gets here. If they get the family doctor in, they'll make sure he tells the coroner it was suicide and no one will ever know the truth – the murderer will get away with it. We have to have incontrovertible evidence of foul play before he arrives.'

'I say,' said Puddle. 'How exciting. What do you want us to do?'

'Just keep your eyes and ears open when the Bilvertons are around, really – that would be tremendously helpful.'

'Is that all?'

'Well, there is one thing you can do right now. Would you be an absolute darling and pretend you have no idea where we are while we sneak next door and have a look round John Bilverton's study?'

'Of course,' said Puddle. 'I am the very soul of dissemblement. Is that a word? It is now.'

'You're going into the room where he shot himself?' said Katy.

'He didn't shoot himself, sweetie,' said Puddle. 'You heard the boys.'

Katy harrumphed again. 'He still died in there. You're all mad.'

'We'll keep you covered if anyone comes in here looking for you,' said Elk.

'But there's not much we can do to make you invisible out in the hall,' said Vera.

'Or if one of them decides to take a look in the study themselves,' said Puddle.

Ellie frowned. 'You've got a point. But I don't think that's very likely. They're all in a bit of a state – they're not going to want to go in there if they don't have to.'

'When are you planning to go?' asked Puddle.

Ellie looked at Skins and Dunn. 'Now?'

Skins nodded, his plates empty. 'No time like the present.'

'I'll take a look and see if the coast is clear,' said Dunn. 'No point in us all barging out of here and barrelling straight into a Bilverton or one of the servants.'

He went to the door and looked about as casually as he could manage.

'There's no one about,' he said. 'Let's go.'

# Chapter Five

Dunn led the way with Ellie close behind and Skins at the rear of the column, keeping an eye open to make certain they were unobserved.

'We're not on patrol in no-man's-land, mate,' said Dunn, when he saw the way Skins was prowling behind them. 'No one wants to shoot you.'

'I'd not be so sure about that,' said Skins. 'If we're right, there's definitely someone here who likes to shoot people. But that's not the point. I don't want to upset them, that's all. We're going to be nosing about in the room where their old man died. If we get caught we're not going to be the most popular people in the place, are we?'

'Fair dos. But you do look a bit of a nit, tiptoeing about like that.'

Skins tried to relax. 'Have you ever noticed how difficult it is to walk normally once you start thinking about it?' he said. 'I mean, you do it all day but as soon as someone says you look like a nit, controlling your legs is suddenly the hardest thing in the world. Imagine being a spider and having to deal with eight of them when your mate says you look like a nit.'

Dunn shook his head and turned his attention to the study. The door and its burst lock had been pulled to, but he only had to push it open to gain entry. He did so gingerly, afraid it might creak, but the hinges were well oiled and it swung silently inwards.

John Bilverton's body had been taken away and there was little to show that anything horrible had happened. The books on the shelves were arranged alphabetically by author but some had been replaced unevenly, giving the impression they were regularly used. The fireplace was clean and stacked neatly with new logs. There were papers on the desk, as though he were still working on them, and his pen lay uncapped on the topmost document. There was a decanter and a glass of Scotch beside the blotter.

The only things that looked in any way out of the ordinary were the splintered segment of door frame with the lock keeper still screwed securely to it lying on the floor, and a tasselled brocade cushion propped up on the windowsill.

'That cushion isn't from this room,' said Ellie.

'How can you tell?' asked Skins.

'Look at it. That pattern matches the chairs in the library. Everything in here is leather and mahogany. It's a man's room with a capital M. He wouldn't have something so . . . so . . . oh, what's the word?' She looked at the boys, but they offered no help. 'You're useless. Well, whatever the word is, this cushion belongs somewhere else.'

'He might have had piles.'

'It would be on his chair, then,' she said.

'It might have fallen off when they moved the body,' said Dunn.

'Maybe. But make a note of it. It's wrong.'

Skins was looking at the gramophone.

'This is a tasty bit of gear,' he said admiringly. 'You seen this, Barty? It's all electric, like the studio. I didn't even know they were out yet. I read about how they were starting to make them in America. Must have cost a fortune.'

'It did,' said a voice from behind them.

The three friends looked round to see Veronica standing in the doorway.

She came in. 'Uncle Malcolm bought it when he equipped his studio. Actually, he bought two – the other one is in the drawing room. What are you doing in here?'

Ellie thought for a moment. If they were serious about trying to solve this mystery, they'd need an ally in the household. Sneaking about undetected was clearly going to be tricky, and having a family member to vouch for them would help. She looked at the boys, but once again they offered her nothing. So she made a quick decision.

'We're investigating . . . recent events.'

'Papa shooting himself?' Veronica didn't seem quite as upset as Ellie expected.

'Yes,' she said. 'Or, rather, no. We don't believe he did shoot himself – we think he was murdered.'

'What on earth makes you say that?' exclaimed Veronica, looking suddenly alarmed. 'He was alone in a locked room.'

'The boys in the band can explain it better than I can, but it has to do with the nature of the wound.'

Skins nodded. 'The wound Ellie saw could only have been made by a bullet fired from more than a couple of feet away. It had to be someone else. Was your dad left-handed?'

'He was, yes.'

'Oh. Still, it just means the killer knew him well enough to remember.'

'The whole household knew – he never stopped going on about how inconvenient everything was. "Whole bloody world's designed for right-handers." How could anyone have done it, though? The room was locked and no one was in the house except Ellie, Elizabeth and me.'

'We don't know that ourselves, yet,' said Ellie gently, 'but that's what we want to find out for you. If we can establish how it happened, we might discover who did it.'

'Well, if it was murder, you won't be short of suspects,' said Veronica. 'He wasn't . . . how best to put it? He wasn't a "nice" man. Honourable, law-abiding, a pillar of the community – he was all of that and more. But at the core of it all was a cold, manipulative, dislikeable human being. And he raised a family of cold, manipulative, dislikeable children. Any of us could have killed him. Lord knows I wanted to many times.'

'But you didn't,' said Dunn. 'Did you?'

'No. But if he didn't kill himself, I'd like to know who did.'

'Even though it might be one of your brothers?' said Skins. 'Or your sister?'

'I didn't like him, and I may have daydreamed about killing the old bastard, but he was my father and I loved him. Grudgingly, most of the time, through tears and gritted teeth, but one loves one's parents no matter what. And he didn't deserve to die. Justice needs to be done and all that.' Veronica stood to her full height in her black evening dress, having changed out of her sodden things. Ellie admired her strength and composure.

'We'll do our best to see that it is,' she said. 'We'd rather keep our suspicions to ourselves for the time being, though, so it would help enormously if you could . . . "cover for us" isn't quite the right phrase – it makes it sound like we're up to no good – but if you could help keep what we're up to away from the others, that would be swell.'

'Whatever you need,' said Veronica.

Skins, meanwhile, had been examining the papers on the desk.

'Is this as you found it earlier?' he said. 'Nothing's been moved?'

Veronica looked for a moment. 'I can't be sure, but it seems to be about the same. Why?'

'When people commit suicide they usually leave a note. Explanation. Apology. Even accusation, sometimes. There's nothing here.'

'I confess that's what I originally came in looking for,' she said. 'I never thought him the type to take his own life, so I very much wanted to read his explanation.'

'Well, if he left one, I can't see it.'

'Another minor argument in the case against suicide,' said Ellie.

There were footsteps in the hall.

Elizabeth called from outside. 'Ronnie? Where are you?'

'I'm in the study.'

'Good Lord, what are you doing in there?'

'I just wanted to be alone for a moment. I'll be with you presently.'

'Have you checked on the musicians?'

'Yes. They're fine.'

'I'll be in the library with Peter.'

'Right you are.'

Veronica waited until she heard the library door close, then looked out into the hall.

'All clear,' she said. 'You'd better get back to your pals before anyone else comes wandering about. Would you like to be my guests at dinner, whenever and whatever that is? It might give you a chance to get to know the family a bit.'

'That would be grand,' said Skins. 'Do you think the others would mind? If you can swing it, it would be really useful.'

'I'll see what I can do.'

She slipped quietly out through the door with the three friends close behind.

The rain had eased by early evening, so the majority of the Dizzy Heights had returned to their base in the chapel with their food, leaving Skins, Ellie and Dunn to dine with the family.

The twelve around the table had split into several smaller groups.

Newly widowed Marianne was deep in conversation with Uncle Malcolm and Hetty Hollis. Eldest son Gordon was with his sister Elizabeth and her fiancé, Peter. His wife, Charlotte, meanwhile, had chosen to talk to youngest son Howard. Veronica was trying to bring Skins, Ellie and Dunn up to date with all the family relationships as quietly and discreetly as she could.

'We're just your average, run-of-the mill capitalist exploiters of the proletariat, really,' she said. 'But we make biscuits and popular gramophone records so nobody complains too loudly about it. We are the modern purveyors of bread and circuses.'

'Are you a Bolshie, then?' said Skins.

'Good Lord, no,' she said. 'Well, maybe a little. As Ellie heard earlier, I'm a complicated bundle of contradictions, me. I love our money, but I feel the appropriate level of guilt about us having it while others are struggling. I'm proud we made the money by making things rather than from just owning land, but I'm resentful of the way Old Money looks down on us.'

'Do the others feel the same?' asked Ellie.

Veronica laughed. 'I don't think many of them are capable of any sort of self-examination. As long as they've got the oof for trinkets and treats, they're not given to pondering their place in the world.'

'Give us the lowdown, then,' said Skins. 'Who are the runners and riders?'

She cast her eye around the table. 'Let's see . . . where shall we begin? How about my darling stepmother, Marianne? Mama was taken ill early in 1920 and died in April that year. Papa was devastated, but it didn't last long and three years later he and Marianne were married. She was his secretary, and the gossips have it that she wasn't the first – nor the last – of his younger . . . "conquests".'

Dunn remembered the conversation before the party. 'She's about your brother's age, isn't she?'

'A few months older than Gordon, yes. She's not a bad old stick, really. She's friendly and kind. Only averagely bright, but chaps prefer that, don't they?'

'Not me,' said Skins.

Veronica eyed him appraisingly. 'Anyway, it can't have been easy joining a family like ours, but she did her best. At least we were all grown up so she didn't have to be a mother. Well, little Howie was nineteen but he was already up at Oxford. Betty – Elizabeth – hates her, but only because she thinks Marianne is plotting to cheat her out of her inheritance. There's little else to dislike.'

'You said she wasn't his last conquest,' said Ellie. 'I . . . well, I think I overheard something at the party. Gordon and Charlotte were arguing, and it sounded like . . .'

Veronica laughed. 'A proper family scandal. They managed to keep it secret for a while but it came out last week that our dear father was, indeed, diddling his son's wife.'

'Blimey,' said Skins.

'Blimey, indeed. There was screaming and shouting at first. Recriminations, threats . . . and then we quickly retreated to the traditional English response to a family squabble: seething, unexpressed anger and resentment.'

Even after living in the country for six years, learning its customs, adapting to the strange way the locals used her own otherwise familiar language, Ellie still hadn't mastered the English art of understatement. Given a thousand years and a million guesses, she would never have hit upon 'squabble' as an appropriate word to describe the consequences of a betrayal like that. She decided not to pursue it, and instead said, 'Are they staying together?'

'It seems so. Gordon is absolutely besotted so I rather think he'll forgive her eventually. He's angry with her, of course, but that will pass. And it's nothing compared with the way he felt about Papa – he was furious with him. That was the greater betrayal in his eyes.'

Ellie suddenly wished she had a notebook, but she was sure she could remember these few details until she was able to write them down. It wasn't as though they weren't thoroughly memorable.

'Malcolm seems like a decent sort,' said Dunn.

'He's a sweetheart. Papa got the business acumen and the steely ambition while his brother got the heart and compassion. He's the only one of them speaking to poor Marianne, did you notice? He was a soldier for over twenty years, which I never quite understood, to be honest. I always wondered how a man as kind and gentle as Uncle Malcolm could have served in the army, but he loved it. Well, he loved it eventually. He saw some terrible things fighting the Boers in South Africa and they say he almost resigned his commission over it, but he came home and stuck at it. He worked as a military adviser but eventually transferred to Sandhurst to try to train the next generation of officers to be a little less brutish. That was interrupted by the Great War. He lost his leg, and then retired as a full colonel in '19. He tried working at the biscuit factory but his heart wasn't in it, so he sort of drifted into the music recording business. He likes to tell everyone about how he built the studio up from nothing by the sweat of his brow. If he wants extra sympathy, he'll tap his false leg with his cane.'

'He didn't do that,' said Dunn.

'He would have if he'd seen an opportunity,' she said with an affectionate laugh. 'He usually does it when he's trying to talk someone into something. It's part of his tried and trusted technique for getting his own way.'

'He certainly knows his onions,' said Skins. 'Even listening to them from outside you could tell that those recordings he made of us are fantastic.'

'It's his passion,' said Veronica. 'That's one thing we Bilvertons are known for – we do get a little obsessed.'

'Take us round the rest of the table,' said Ellie. 'What's Gordon's obsession?'

'Biscuits, I think. Or the business of making them, at least. Gordon worked out early on that he was going to inherit the family firm and set about learning everything he could. He lives and breathes the biscuit business. It's no wonder Charlotte's eye wandered. I'd be bored to tears in no time if my other half were obsessed by bloody biscuits.'

'But it wandered to another man obsessed by biscuits,' said Ellie.

'Ah, no. Papa, you see, was obsessed by money and younger women. The making of biscuits was a means to an end – doubloons and dalliances. That's more than enough to catch many a pretty maid's eye.'

'What sort of man is Gordon, though?'

'He's not the easiest fellow to get along with, but that's what older brothers are supposed to be like, isn't it? It's part of the duties?'

'I wouldn't know, I'm afraid,' said Ellie. 'Only child.'

Dunn looked up from his consommé. 'And what about you? Are you easy to get along with?'

Veronica laughed. 'Well, now, that rather depends upon one's point of view. I like to think of myself as refreshingly direct and honest, but that's not always how others see it.'

'And how do others see it?' asked Ellie.

'I think the most common reaction is, "For goodness' sake, Veronica, do you always have to be so rude?" But if someone's a pill, then pretending they're not just to be polite doesn't really help anyone, does it? It's just a lie. It certainly wouldn't help you, and I do want to help you. I mean, I don't know you all from Adam, but you seem like decent folk. You say Papa was murdered and for some reason I believe you. Does that sound feeble?'

'Not at all,' said Dunn. 'It's a bit of a relief, to tell you the truth. We're well aware that we're just the hired help—'

'Stylish and fashionable hired help,' interrupted Skins.

'Talented and hardworking, too,' agreed Dunn, 'but hired help nonetheless. We've got no business interfering and well, I don't know about these other two, but I fully expected you all to close ranks and tell us to bugger off.'

'Oh, that's certainly my instinct, if I'm honest. Lord knows the idea of exposing the family to scandal fills one with absolute horror. But the thought that someone *murdered* Papa fills me with something worse. Rage. They have to be brought to justice.'

'Even though it could very well be one of the family?' said Ellie.

Veronica looked uneasy. 'Well, I know you mentioned that before, but . . .'

Skins leaned in and spoke quietly. 'I understand. But all the guests were gone, and all the band were accounted for. That leaves your family and your servants.'

'Oh, it can't be the servants – why would they want to kill him?'

'Which leaves . . .'

'I see what you mean,' said Veronica, looking pale but stoic. 'Well, in that case I'd better carry on dishing the dirt, as Ellie's countrymen say. Where were we?'

Ellie smiled. 'Elizabeth?'

'The second-born. The perfect daughter. Charitable works, bridge evenings, and organizing sophisticated soirées to further the career of her ambitious husband-to-be.'

'Doesn't sound like you're impressed,' said Skins.

'She's all right, I suppose, but she's as boring as Gordon. Mama and Papa never tired of saying, "Why can't you be more like your sister? She knows how a lady should behave."'

'And how should ladies behave?'

'I could never quite fathom that out, but I know they're not supposed to get a job as a schoolteacher and try to make their own way in the world without a husband.'

'That's what you do, is it?'

'It is. And they all hate it. Apparently I should be engaged to a nice boring solicitor like boring Peter and live a boring life like my boring sister.'

'So Peter's a solicitor, then?' said Ellie, keen to derail this particular train of thought.

'Set up his own boring practice in Oxford last year.'

'How well did he get on with your father?'

'Swimmingly until a couple of weeks ago. Papa was a JP – a Justice of the Peace.'

Ellie looked to Skins for help.

'Magistrate,' he said.

'Just so,' continued Veronica. 'Papa said . . . something or other and put the kibosh on something Peter was doing. I honestly didn't care enough to pay any attention. But they fell out over it, whatever it was.'

Ellie was desperately longing for her notebook now. Peter was the one who had tried it on at the party and she would have put a few nastier personal traits above 'boring' if she were trying to describe him. 'What about the next group?'

'Charlotte. We've already discussed her. Another boring, perfect woman. Charities, supporting boring Gordon. The only spark of interest she ever had in her was indulging her natural urges with dear Papa. Next to her is baby brother, Howard. Just come down from university with a degree in . . . I want to say he read history, but it was probably PPE or something equally ghastly. He's managed to fall into a job in the City. Something dreary to do with finance. Which is a shame – he's the only one of us who's ever been any fun, aside from yours truly of course. I like him a lot. He's a sweetheart.'

'How well did he get on with your father?'

'As I say, no one really got on with our father, but Papa was always especially infuriated by Howard. "Feckless and facetious" was Papa's verdict. It drove him mad that Howie never took anything seriously and wasn't interested in doing something to further the family business. He threatened to cut him out of his will if he didn't buckle down at university. He scraped through with a third, which bought a stay of execution, but then he took his City job thanks to a pal's father and was on the chopping block again. There was always talk of a new will, mind you.'

Ellie frowned. 'I'd have thought he'd be proud his son was making his own way.'

'Any normal father would, but it was seen as disloyal. "Damn layabout ought to be putting his meagre talents to work for the Bilverton name."'

'Oh,' said Ellie. 'And what about his pal? Do you know anything about her?'

'His "pal", yes. Don't know very much about Hetty Hollis at all, I'm afraid. She's Howie's best pal's sweetheart, but that's as much as I've been able to glean.'

Skins looked over at the young woman. 'She can sing up a storm, though.'

'I'm as surprised as you are. She was quite a hit last night.'

'She was indeed,' said Ellie. 'And what of you? Where do you teach?'

'In the little school in Partlow's Ford – the nearest town.'

'Is that where you live?'

'Sadly, no. I still live here. I've my salary and an allowance, and together they'd be able to pay the rent on a nice little cottage, but the allowance is contingent on my living here until I'm twenty-five or married. On its own, the salary from the school would barely pay for a room in a lodging house. If there were any rooms available. So I'm stuck here.'

'There are worse places to be stuck,' said Dunn.

'Oh, absolutely. It's a lovely house. Not decorated entirely to my taste, but it's a beautiful place to live.'

'I love these old houses,' said Skins.

'They have a certain charm, definitely.'

'And they're fascinating. Any secret passages?'

Ellie rolled her eyes. 'Take no notice of him – it's his latest obsession.'

But Veronica's own eyes had lit up. 'Oh, I do so wish I could find it.'

'You mean there is one?' said Skins.

'Probably not, actually. But there are stories. I've spent my whole life looking. What's your interest in secret passages?'

'It's just something that happened to us a few weeks ago. Secret passages, hidden treasure . . . It made quite an impression on dear Ivor.'

'Oh, I'm not sure there's any treasure here. It would be wizard if there were, but the stories never mention any.'

'Ah, well,' said Skins.

A bread roll clattered into Veronica's cutlery. 'Oi, Ronnie!' said Howard. 'What are you four muttering about over there? Stop monopolizing the fashionable folk. We need an injection of style into this dreary gathering.'

Further details of the lives and loves of the Bilverton clan would have to wait. It was time to be sociable.

◆ ◆ ◆

It was almost midnight by the time the three friends made their way back to the chapel. Skins and Dunn, with an umbrella each, flanked Ellie and provided her with cover from the slackening rain. Ellie put a hand against the small of each man's back and pressed them onwards.

'Come on, boys, let's not dawdle out here in the wet.'

'That was a much less unpleasant experience than I'd been expecting,' said Skins.

'Being shoved about by your missus?' said Dunn. 'I thought it was a bit rude, to be honest.'

Ellie thumped him.

'Now that was definitely rude,' said Skins. 'But I meant the dinner.'

'I thought it would be a sight more miserable than that, yes,' said Dunn.

'Once the shock of it wore off, I think they realized how little they liked the old boy,' said Ellie. 'Actually, Veronica doesn't have a particularly high opinion of any of them.'

Skins nodded, then realized they couldn't see him in the dark. 'She was a bit dismissive, wasn't she?'

'I need to make some notes before I forget everything. They all had a reason for wanting to get rid of him, and we only scratched the surface. Everyone's a suspect.'

Skins forgot once more that it was dark, and frowned. Then he remembered and said out loud, 'Everyone?'

'Sure,' she said. 'Gordon because the old boy was sleeping with his wife. Marianne because he was sleeping with Gordon's wife. Peter because he did something that set his business back. Howard because he was going to be disinherited.'

'That's not everyone,' said Dunn. 'What about Uncle Malcolm? Or Elizabeth? Scarlet Charlotte? Even our new pal Veronica?'

'It's still more than half of them. And I bet the more we dig, the more we'll find.'

'We still have to work out how it was done,' said Skins.

'We're easily up to the task,' said Ellie. 'Now let's get in out of the rain and tell the others.'

She opened the chapel door and ushered them in. The lights were on, which was an encouraging sign, and she was hoping for a chance to share their discoveries with Puddle and the others. There was no chatter, though; only the sound of slow, steady breathing and an occasional snore. That was less encouraging.

'They can't all be asleep,' she said as they walked into the main body of the chapel.

But they were. Still fully dressed. Vera, Puddle and Katy were in a tangled heap on Puddle's bed. Mickey, Benny and Eustace were slumped in chairs around a table where they had obviously been playing cards with Elk, who had fallen from his chair to the ground.

'What the bleedin' 'ell . . . ?' said Skins.

Ellie rushed to check them. 'They're all breathing OK, but they're out cold. Completely unresponsive. Drugged, I'd say.'

'Seriously?' said Dunn. 'How?'

'Can't be the food,' said Skins. 'We all ate the same.'

'Drink, then,' said Ellie. 'Look – they all have Scotch.'

Skins scanned the room. 'It's the decanter from the study,' he said, pointing. 'Mickey must have half-inched it on his way back with the nosh.'

'Well, that confirms it,' said Ellie. 'John Bilverton had a glass on his desk. He'd have been out cold if he'd drunk it, so he definitely can't have shot himself.'

'You're sure the drug didn't kill him? You're sure it won't kill them?' said Dunn, looking more than a little anxious.

'I can't be sure he didn't die before he was shot, but I'm pretty sure it won't kill this lot. Everyone's breathing just fine. Elk's snoring louder than usual but other than that, I don't see any problems. They'll be a bit woolly in the morning, but they'll get a good night's sleep.'

'Maybe we should have a snifter ourselves, then,' said Skins. 'Might help you forget how uncomfortable these cots are.'

'I think the three of us need to stay clean in case any of these guys get into difficulties, honey. Give me a hand getting them all into safe positions so they don't choke to death in the night. I'll show you how.'

They arranged the slumbering band members as best they could and retired for a much less sound sleep of their own.

# Chapter Six

***Sunday, 28 June 1925***

The Dizzies were very much living up to their name as they began to struggle towards consciousness on Sunday morning. There was some moaning, a little staggering, and more than the normal amount of head-clutching.

'We must have had quite a night,' said Mickey on his way back from the bathroom. 'I can't remember a thing.'

'Not a thing?' said Ellie.

'We ate dinner. We drank a little Scotch. And then I woke up on my bed fully dressed. No idea how I got there.'

'We know how you got to bed, mate,' said Skins. 'We bloody put you there. You aren't half heavy when you're out cold.'

'You? What you talking about?'

'We got in about midnight and you were all spark out. I was all for leaving you there but Ellie said you might choke to death so we put you all to bed.'

'Lucky we've got an ex-nurse on the strength, then,' said Mickey. 'Thanks, Ells.'

'Entirely my pleasure,' said Ellie.

Elk was just coming to. He sat up groggily and scratched his face. ''Ere, how come I've got the three of clubs stuck to my cheek?'

‘We found you on the floor,’ said Dunn. ‘We didn’t think to check your face for cards. You wouldn’t, would you?’

‘We were all out?’ said Puddle. ‘How odd. I was sitting on Katy’s bed with Vera. I only had a couple of sips of Scotch.’

‘Were you all drinking the Scotch Mickey and the boys brought back from the house?’ asked Ellie.

‘It’s all there was after the boys had drunk all the beer from the hampers,’ said Katy. ‘I don’t really like whisky, to be honest, but needs must when the Devil’s locked the drinks cabinet. I certainly didn’t drink enough to render me pie-eyed, though. I only had a couple of sips, too.’

‘Same here,’ said Vera. ‘Look – there’s my glass on the floor. None of this makes any sense. I’ve always been able to hold my drink.’

Ellie took a good look round the huge space. Sure enough, there were three mismatched glasses on the floor beside Katy’s bed, all of them containing a decent measure of whisky. There were four more on the card table, also largely undrunk.

‘None of you had very much, actually,’ said Ellie. She raised her voice a little so everyone could hear. ‘Don’t panic, Dizzies, but I think you were all drugged—’

There were murmurs of consternation, but no actual panic.

‘My best guess is that it was something like Veronal, and I’d put serious money on it being in the Scotch.’

Katy’s hand went to her mouth. ‘Oh my goodness. Who would want to drug us? Are we in danger?’

‘Mickey,’ said Ellie, ‘did you by any chance find that rather attractive decanter standing unattended in John Bilverton’s study?’

‘Well, now,’ said Mickey. ‘The thing is, you see . . . I nipped in there to have a look. Curiosity and all that. It’s not often you see the scene of a possible murder. And it was a bit of a disappointment, if I’m honest. We’ve played in loads of posh gaffs and I’ve seen a dozen studies just like it. Only this one had a full decanter of Scotch in it. And it wasn't like the old boy was going to be drinking it. So it came back here with us. I'm sure he wouldn't have wanted it to go to waste.'

'Then the good news is that no one wanted to drug us – they wanted to drug John Bilverton. The bad news is, that means the murderer planned everything very carefully. They wanted him out cold before they shot him.'

There were more concerned murmurs.

'Is everyone accounted for?' asked Mickey, looking around.

Elk pointed to the bed next to his. 'Actually, Eustace hasn't stirred yet.'

'He's dead,' wailed Katy, without actually looking. 'He's overdosed on the Veronal and died. We've got to get out of here.'

Ellie crossed the chapel and put her fingers to Eustace's neck, checking for a pulse.

'He's not dead,' she said, patiently.

At that moment, Eustace snorted and startled himself awake.

'What's going on?' he slurred. 'What are you doing over here?'

Ellie quickly explained what had happened and reassured him that he was going to be all right.

'All right for now,' said Katy. 'I swear our next date will be in a nunnery.'

Benny had been listening quietly and decided that a change of subject was in order. 'Are you three playing flatfoots again?'

'We just can't help ourselves, mate,' said Dunn.

Benny chuckled. 'No, no, I don't think you can. But maybe we can help you. Is there anything we can do?'

Skins and Dunn looked at each other and shrugged.

'Don't ask me, mate,' said Dunn.

'Nor me,' said Skins. 'What do you reckon, Ells-Bells?'

'There could be something to be said for having us all milling about the house – it might make searching the place a bit less conspicuous. But actually I think we might make better progress if you all hang about down here. Do you mind awfully?'

'Not sure what we'd do up in the house, to be honest,' said Mickey. 'And we don't have to mind our Ps and Qs if we're down here.'

'A woman's place is in the recording studio,' agreed Puddle. 'Just get me fed and watered and I'll be fine. What's the plan for breakfast, does anyone know?'

'No one mentioned breakfast,' said Katy.

'Maybe we should all just go up to the house,' said Vera. 'We could eat in the servants' hall if they don't want us in the dining room making the place look untidy.'

After a brief discussion, it was agreed, and everyone set off together.

The rain had eased to a gusty drizzle, so the rest of the band made their way round the house to the servants' entrance while Skins, Ellie and Dunn let themselves into the salon through the French doors.

The three friends went from the salon to the dining room, but of the family there was no sign.

'Looks like the Bilvertons are having a nice little lie-in,' said Skins, as they wandered out into the hall. 'I can't even hear anyone moving about upstairs.'

'There's not a lot to get up for,' said Dunn. 'They're obviously not churchgoers or they'd not have deconsecrated the chapel and turned it into a recording studio. And even if they were, they couldn't get to church because of the floods. What else would they be doing at this time on a Sunday morning? I'll be honest, I don't even know why we're up.'

'Because I spent three years trying to learn how to sleep comfortably on army cots,' said Ellie, 'and I never mastered it. I honestly began to wonder if the stone floor would be any better. I'd rather be up and about than lying on that thing.'

'She makes a good point, mate. Nice of them to give us somewhere to kip, but it's not somewhere you want to linger.'

'Fair dos,' said Dunn. 'What do you reckon, then? Another squizz at the study? See if we can find the secret doodah?'

Ellie frowned quizzically. 'What secret doodah?'

'It's like Skins said – there's always a secret doodah. It'll be where the killer hid.'

'You're as bad as each other,' said Ellie. 'I'm going to go ahead and hope it's just because you're both hungry. Let's go downstairs with the others before you say anything else dumb.'

She led the boys to the staircase outside the library that she'd used the day before.

'Weird place to have a staircase,' said Dunn. 'It's nowhere near the dining room. You'd think they'd want direct access.'

'There's another set of stairs,' she said. 'But I wasn't sure where they came out so I thought we'd use the ones I know.'

'They come out in the dining room, I'd imagine.'

'She's right, you know, mate,' said Skins. 'You're a grumpy git when you're hungry.'

'I never said he was grumpy,' said Ellie. 'I said you're both stupid.'

Dunn scowled. 'Not half as stupid as an architect who puts the servants' stairs a mile from the dining room.'

They traipsed down together and walked into the kitchen.

The Dizzies had been welcomed by the staff, and the atmosphere in the kitchen was unexpectedly jolly. Mickey, Benny and Eustace were lapping up the attention, most of which came from

Lily, the young kitchen maid, who was in danger of being reprimanded by Mrs Radway for paying more attention to the musicians than to her work. Katy, Vera and Puddle were standing in the doorway that led to the larder, chuckling quietly. And Elk was chasing a chicken.

'How's it going, ladies and gents?' said Skins.

Puddle gave a cheery wave. 'Not so bad,' she said. 'Mrs Radway has offered to let us eat in the servants' hall.'

'Very kind of you, Mrs R,' said Skins. 'So . . . ah . . . what's Elk up to?'

'He's chasing a chicken,' said Eustace in a tone that very much suggested it was a stupid question.

'That's what I thought. Elk, mate? Why . . . ?'

Elk looked up briefly from the chase. 'Why what?'

Skins sighed. 'Why are you chasing a chicken round the kitchen?'

'Because it keeps getting away.'

'I'm getting nowhere here,' said Skins. 'Want to have a try, Barty?'

'Elk,' said Dunn, 'why is there a chicken in the kitchen?'

Elk stopped and stood upright. 'For the eggs.'

'But that's a—'

That set Puddle off again. 'No, darling, don't tell him. We're waiting to see if he works it out for himself.'

Elk resumed his pursuit.

'I still don't understand why—' began Skins.

Puddle tried to calm herself. 'We offered to help. There was nothing much to do, but young Lily here had been sent out to get some eggs and Elk volunteered to do it for her. He trotted out and returned a few minutes later with that chicken.'

'It's where eggs come from,' said Elk, defensively.

'Wait,' said Skins. 'So you thought it was like milking a cow? You bring the chicken in, give her a helpful squeeze and say, "Come on, then, Clucky. We need half a dozen eggs. Off you go"?'

'We get our eggs from the grocer's,' said Elk. 'I don't know how chickens work.'

'Didn't you look for eggs in the coop?'

'In the what?'

'The little house where the chickens live.'

'Why would I look in there? This one was walking about outside so I just grabbed her and came back in here.'

The chicken crowed aggressively.

The three women in the pantry doorway were laughing properly now. Mrs Radway shook her head, but there was a smile on her face, too.

'Hang on a minute . . .' said Elk.

'Keep going, son,' said Dunn. 'You'll get it in a sec.'

'That's a—'

'Yes, mate,' said Skins. 'Yes, it is. Even if chickens worked the way you thought they did – which, for future reference, they don't – this one couldn't help you. This is what those in the poultry business call a cockerel. It's a boy chicken.'

'Buggerin' 'ell,' said Elk. 'Well, that was a waste of ten minutes. Give us a hand, would you? If we can round it up, I'll take you outside and you can show me where the eggs are, given you're such an expert.'

Skins approached the cockerel and grabbed him gently but firmly mid-crow.

'Did you not notice the comb on his head?' he said to Elk. 'Or these little dangly bits round his chops?'

'Well, yes,' said Elk. 'But what am I supposed to know about chickens? I just thought it was part of its, you know, its chickeny decoration and that. I grew up in New Cross. No one had chickens. Now shut up taking the rise and just help me get rid of him.'

Skins smiled. 'Lead the way, Elkie boy. We'll get this lad back to his lady friends and see if they've paid the rent. Bring a basket.'

Elk walked out of the kitchen with Skins and the cockerel close behind.

'So we're having eggs, then?' said Ellie, when they were gone.

'I wouldn't count on it,' said Mrs Radway. 'Not after all that palaver. But there's sausages, bacon, tomatoes, mushrooms. I've got a kedgeree on the go an' all. Is there any sign of the family?'

'Not yet, no. We had a look before we came down here. And don't give up on the eggs – Ivor's a very resourceful little fella. Is there anything useful we can do?'

'No, ma'am, thank you. You just make yourselves comfy at the table and let us take care of you.'

They were about to set off for the servants' hall when Howard appeared in the doorway.

'What ho, you chaps,' he said brightly. 'Morning, Mrs R. And Lily – how the devil are you?'

The kitchen maid blushed and curtseyed but said nothing.

'I'm all alone upstairs – would any of you Dizzy Heights like to come up and keep a chap company?'

There was a chorus of mumbles and a fair amount of looking at shoes before Ellie said, 'I'd love to. Barty? You'll keep us company, won't you? And Ivor will join us, I'm sure.'

'Wizard. Are you sure I can't tempt the rest of you?'

There was more apologetic mumbling and Howard smilingly took the hint and left them to it.

Ellie and Dunn followed Howard out the door and on towards the other flight of stairs.

The stairs ended at a small landing where they found a table and a cabinet. Howard turned the knob on the door in front of them. It opened into the dining room.

They found Veronica sitting at the table with her feet up on the chair next to her.

'What ho, Ronnie,' said Howard with a grin.

Veronica waved in reply. 'Morning all. Is breakfast on its way?'

'Its delivery is imminent, old thing.'

They were joined almost at once by Skins, slightly out of breath from his poultry-related adventures.

As the four new arrivals sat down, Skins looked back at the door they'd just come through. It was perfectly ordinary from the staircase, but from the dining room it just looked like a section of wall and had been papered to match. Only a small, discreet brass doorknob gave it away.

'I love the way they do that in these old places,' said Skins. 'Loads of hidden doors and secret passages.'

'I don't know about "loads",' said Howard. 'That's one of the only ones I know about.'

'That's a shame. I thought a house like this would be full of them.'

'They all conceal servants' staircases, as far as I know. There's that one there. There's one just outside that leads up to the first floor, with another pair to match on the opposite side of the house next to the library. Those both have concealed doors on the first-floor landing, and they both carry on up to the servants' quarters and storerooms on the third floor. There are no doors at the very top.'

'I confess to being a bit disappointed. I was hoping for priest holes and secret passageways.'

'Imagine how disappointed you'd have been if you'd lived here all your life and found nothing,' said Veronica.

Howard nodded. 'Well, quite. I think the place is too modern for priest holes, though. It's Georgian, I think.'

'It certainly looks like it,' said Ellie.

'When were priest holes, then?' asked Skins.

'Elizabethan.'

'You're going to have to give me more than that.'

'Late 1500s,' said Ellie with a smile.

'Actually, the chapel's Elizabethan, come to think about it,' said Howard.

Skins was still trying to sort out the dates. 'And Georgian was . . . ?'

'Early 1700s to early 1800s, give or take,' said Ellie. 'I can't remember the exact dates.'

Skins looked at Howard and Veronica apologetically. 'Sorry. We did the Romans, 1066, and why the British Empire is the greatest thing in the history of the world, but we skipped over a lot of bits in between. Well, I did, anyway. And I never quite understood the Empire thing. I could never work out why it's supposed to be so great to invade someone's country, treat them like dirt and nick all their stuff. Seems like piracy to me. But what do I know? I'm just a drummer.'

Howard laughed. 'Don't let Gordon hear you talking like that. He'll denounce you as a Bolshie or a traitor – or both – and then chase you out with a horse whip. You might have an ally in Ronnie here – or "Veronica" as she prefers to be known now' – Veronica stuck out her tongue, but he carried on undaunted – 'but dear old Gordy's got the Union Jack stamped through him like a stick of Blackpool rock. Won't hear a word about how, as you put it, "invading countries and nicking their stuff" might not have been such a terribly virtuous thing to do. He thinks they're all savages who need the firm guiding hand of the white man.'

'He must have had a fit when he saw Benny.'

'Your gorgeous trombonist?' said Veronica. 'I don't imagine he was best pleased.'

Skins shrugged. 'Benny's been dealing with idiots like your brother – no offence – ever since he came over to France from

Antigua in the war. He was in the British West Indies Regiment. Volunteered to fight for king and country. I don't reckon he should have to put up with it, but it never changes. Best trombone player on the circuit, but most of them look down their noses at him. I thought we were supposed to be better than that.'

'Well, Gordon isn't better than that, I'm afraid,' said Howard, with a shrug of his own.

The concealed door opened and the two kitchen maids entered bearing heavily laden platters, bowls and tureens, which they arranged on the sideboard. It took them several trips to carry everything in, with the last consignment being of silver pots of tea and coffee.

Dunn thanked them and started pouring steaming hot drinks while Howard invited his musical guests to help themselves to food.

'Maybe we should open a restaurant, you know,' said Dunn as he sat down. 'Did you know Mickey was a cook in the army? Quite a good one, as it happens. He could run the kitchen and we could play in our own place without having to scrape around for club dates.'

'Oh, but you'd not be available for any more of our parties,' said Howard.

'That's the beauty of it, though. If we had our own place, always ticking over, always taking money, we could book other bands to play the restaurant and we could play wherever we liked.'

'What would we call this dream palace?' asked Ellie.

'Eleanora's.'

'That's very flattering.'

Dunn shrugged. 'It's only fair. You'd be putting up most of the money as soon as your inheritance comes through.'

She laughed.

'Oh,' said Howard. 'Inheritance. I'd completely forgotten about that. I wonder what the old codger left me.'

'I've been wondering the same,' said Veronica as she speared a sausage with her fork.

'Did your father ever talk about his will?' asked Ellie.

'Not in any helpful detail,' said Howard. 'It was used more as a weapon than anything else.' He slipped into a passable impersonation of his father. '"If you don't sort your life out, you worthless idler, I'll cut you out of my will. Don't think I won't."'

Veronica nodded. 'Mine was always, "If you don't give up these stupid dreams of independence, I'll cut you out of my will. Why can't you be more like your sister?"'

'But he never revealed any details about the will,' said Howard. 'I expect Gordon knows. Elizabeth, perhaps?'

'Was her fiancé his solicitor?'

Howard laughed. 'Good Lord, no. He never thought much of Peter, did he, Ronnie? Especially not his abilities as a lawyer. He used some old crony of his. Big firm with offices at Oxford and London. Bristol, too, I think. Again, Gordon will know. Gordon will contact them. Gordon will be executor. Gordon will get the lion's share of the estate.'

'Surely John wouldn't let you both starve,' said Ellie.

'I think he'd have loved nothing more. He genuinely once said, "Eversion's too good for you."'

Skins looked blank.

'Turning inside out,' explained Dunn. 'Nice bloke, your dad.'

'Well, quite,' said Howard. 'You can see why my expectations are low.'

'He didn't approve of your new job, I gather,' said Dunn.

'He didn't, as a matter of fact. How did you—'

'I told them last night,' said Veronica. 'I told them all about us.'

Howard chuckled. 'Did you, by crikey? Was there any family secret you didn't blurt out to our guests?'

'Well, the poor souls are being forced to endure our company for a good deal longer than they bargained for – I thought it only fair to warn them of the full potential horror of it. Forewarned is a four-poster bed or whatever the phrase is.'

'It's something like that, certainly.'

Hetty arrived, yawning, at the door.

'And here's the divine Miss Hollis,' said Howard. 'Did you sleep well?'

'Not at all badly, thank you, sweetheart. Is everyone well?'

'As well as can be expected under the circumstances,' said Veronica.

Hetty was ambitiously filling a breakfast plate. 'Yes. Quite. Once again, I'm so sorry about your father. Is there anything useful I can do today?'

'Not a thing, old thing,' said Howard. 'We're just stuck here waiting for the floodwaters to subside before life can resume and matters progress. What are you chaps doing?'

'Us?' said Ellie. 'Well, I . . . I don't really know. The band will probably play cards in the chapel and keep out of the way, I expect.'

'That's the plan,' agreed Skins. 'As far as I know.'

Hetty's sleepiness suddenly disappeared. 'Will you be playing again? Would you mind awfully if I came down to join you?'

'I say, old girl, steady on,' said Howard. 'It's bad enough that the poor blighters are stuck here without you latching on to them.'

Hetty seemed crestfallen. 'Oh.'

'We'd like nothing more,' Dunn reassured her. 'If anyone wants to come down they'll be more than welcome. It'll be either cards or jazz, and both of those are better with more people.'

'Thank you.' She beamed.

She sat down next to Dunn and tucked into a heroic breakfast while chattering eagerly about the latest recordings from America.

◆ ◆ ◆

As predicted, the weather was still too miserable for anyone to want to be outside, and the family spread themselves around the house while the Dizzies retired to the chapel.

Ellie, Skins and Dunn took up residence in the comfy chairs by the tea urn while the rest of the band attempted to organize a seven-handed poker game.

Ellie had her notebook and Dunn, once more, was in charge of making the tea.

'I need to run through the suspects again,' said Ellie as she flicked to another page in the book. 'I'll make a list.'

'All right,' said Skins. 'Gordon. He was angry with his old man for having it away with his missus. He's got to be the odds-on favourite.'

'Inheriting the business and the house wouldn't hurt, either,' said Dunn, handing them their cups of tea. 'Keep going, I'll just take these down to the others.'

Ellie started making notes. 'So a simple crime of passion, then. Revenge for the cuckolded eldest son.'

'It's a strong motive,' said Skins. 'And Veronica said he was a bully, so he's clearly not a nice bloke.'

'Did you meet him? I saw him at the party. I'm pretty sure he slapped his wife.'

'Slapped her?'

'They were arguing – presumably about her affair with John – and while I was discreetly looking away there was a slapping sound. When I turned back she was holding her cheek.'

'Blimey. It takes a nasty bloke to do that. A nasty, arrogant bloke to do it in public.'

'He's top of my list, then. What about the widow, Marianne?'

'She's pretty much in the same position as Gordon. The avenging betrayed wife. And she's bound to benefit from the will, too.'

'OK, so quite high up then. What about Charlotte?'

'Gordon's adulterous wife? I can't see it. Why would she kill him? From what you say she's more likely to want to kill Gordon.'

'I don't know. Some sort of twisted guilt? Or maybe it wasn't a two-way thing?'

'John coerced her, you mean?'

'It happens all the time.'

'All right,' said Skins. 'We can include her, but I'll not be convinced without more evidence.'

'Sounds fair. What about Uncle Malcolm?'

'Long-standing family feud? Resented his big brother for getting all the money?'

Ellie chewed the end of her pencil for a moment. 'That's a thought. Family resentments run deep, after all.'

Dunn had returned. 'Where have we got to?'

'Elizabeth,' said Skins.

Dunn shook his head. 'Boring Elizabeth? She has it all.'

'She hates Marianne, though,' said Ellie. 'Could you hear them talking in here yesterday? John was threatening to cut the spending on the wedding and reduce her allowance, and Elizabeth blames Marianne.'

'That would make her want to kill Marianne, though,' said Dunn. 'Not her dad.'

'There's that business with her bloke, though – Peter,' said Skins. 'John did something to put the kibosh on something he was working on. Might have lost a lot of money.'

'That's certainly a motive for Peter,' said Ellie. 'But unless Elizabeth has a good deal more about her than people make out,

I can't see her shooting her father over the price of a few bouquets and a couple of new hats.'

'But it would be helpful to know exactly what it was that John did to Peter,' persisted Skins. 'I think he's a definite possibility. There's something about him.'

'I'll write it down,' said Ellie. 'What about Veronica?'

'Would she be helping us investigate if she were the murderer?' asked Dunn.

'It could be a double bluff. Or she could be getting close to us to find out how much we know, and then steer us in the wrong direction if we get too close. She's not especially loyal to the family, either, is she? She couldn't wait to dish the dirt.'

'She doesn't have much of a motive, though,' said Skins. 'Other than whatever objections she might have to the family because of her Bolshie tendencies, she doesn't seem all that bothered by them or anything they do. She's just getting on with her own life. Why would she want to kill him?'

'Fair dos,' agreed Ellie. 'Howard?'

'Too obvious,' said Dunn. 'The old man bullied him.'

'I'm not sure the courts see "too obvious" as a line of defence.'

'All right then, it's too improbable. The happy-go-lucky life and soul of the party patiently devises a means of shooting his dad in a locked room and making it look like suicide. If he were going to kill him it would be part of a screaming row over John's endless needling. Everyone would see it.'

'If you're going to use "improbable" to rule them out, mate,' said Skins, 'then none of them did it. The locked door makes everyone unlikely.'

'But we agree someone did do it,' said Ellie. 'Don't we?'

'Wrong kind of bullet wound. Drugged Scotch,' said Dunn. 'So, yes, we agree.'

'Then what about Hetty Hollis?'

'She doesn't even know the family, from what I can make out,' said Skins. 'She's a friend of a friend. What possible motive could she have?'

'John had an eye for the young ladies. Maybe he made a pass at her.'

'No,' said Dunn. 'Even if he did, the murder took planning, didn't it? We're agreed on that. If he tried it on and she lost her temper and shot him . . . I mean, where did she get the gun? How did she lock the door from the inside? How did she get out while Ellie and the Bilverton sisters were outside?'

'What if he had the gun out to clean it? She picked it up . . . Bang! Then she hides in the secret room.'

'What secret room?'

'The secret room Veronica's looking for.'

'And then what?'

'Actually, yes,' said Ellie. 'Then what?'

Even Skins was beginning to get a little puzzled. 'Then what what?'

'How did she get out of the room?'

'She waited till . . . Oh, I don't know.'

'I mean, clearly something weird happened,' said Dunn, 'but she wouldn't have been able to improvise it all on the spot.'

'She's a bright girl, mind you. Thinks on her feet. You saw her yesterday singing with Mickey – she was keeping up with him on songs they'd never sung together. Takes brains, that.'

Dunn shook his head. 'Maybe so. But even if she could come up with a brilliant plan like that on the hoof, how did she get there in the first place? Before the girls got to the study, I mean.'

'She ran.'

'All right, how did she run to the study while she was singing with us in the chapel?'

'And what about the drugged Scotch?' added Ellie. 'Where does that fit in?'

Skins looked crestfallen. 'You've got me there. But it doesn't really matter anyway. Barty's right – how did any of them get into the study while they were all sitting with us? Everyone was here when you and the sisters left to get the picnic, Ells.'

'And no one was wet when we got back,' agreed Ellie. 'We were soaked, but everyone else was dry. If one of them managed to sneak out before John left without us noticing, they also managed to stay completely dry while they made the return journey in the pouring rain.'

'And sneak back in without any of us noticing,' said Dunn.

'And yet we still agree he didn't shoot himself,' said Ellie. She frowned. 'So there's someone else in the house, or there's something we're missing.'

'We need to—'

Dunn's musings on whatever it was they might need to do were interrupted by the arrival of Malcolm Bilverton.

# Chapter Seven

Malcolm seemed to be limping a little more than Ellie remembered as he walked into the chapel and sat down with them on one of the upright chairs near the urn. Dunn offered him a cup of tea, which he gratefully accepted.

'How is everybody?' he asked.

'We're fine,' said Ellie. 'But more importantly, how are you?'

'Shocked. Saddened. Angry.'

'Angry?'

'Perhaps that's the wrong word. Frustrated, perhaps? Guilty?' He thought for a moment. 'No, definitely angry. With myself, that is. He was my brother. I should have been able to see that he was getting desperate enough to . . . Well, you know.'

'Ah, yes,' said Ellie. 'Of course.'

'But enough about me. I came down here for a little diversion. I wondered if your chaps might be playing.'

'No sign of it so far,' said Dunn. 'As you can see, there's us having a chinwag up here, and there's a dodgy-looking card school down the other end.'

'If my time among musicians has taught me anything,' said Malcolm, 'it's that they're generous and friendly, that they'll always help one out if one finds oneself in dire need, but that one should never, ever, under any circumstances, play cards with them.'

Skins laughed. 'Especially not this lot. They'll rob you blind.'

'I'm tempted to say that some of them cheat,' began Dunn, 'but that wouldn't be true.'

'No?' said Malcolm.

'No,' said Skins. 'It's not just some of them who cheat – they all do. It's like it's part of the game.'

'So if you're not cheating along with them,' said Dunn, 'they'll have your last farthing.'

'It seems as though the original advice was sound,' said Malcolm. 'It's still disappointing to find the studio free of music, though.'

Skins nodded. 'It has charms to soothe the savage beast, music. That's your actual Shakespeare, that is.'

'It's William Congreve,' said Dunn. 'And it's breast. "Music has charms to soothe a savage breast." Although some Roman bloke said it moved savage beasts, so you might be on to something.'

Skins made a face.

'What?' said Dunn. 'I live alone. I—'

'—read a lot. Yes, we know.'

'If you want to play something yourself, someone might join in,' said Ellie. 'Look what happened to me yesterday. It's your studio – there's nothing to stop you.'

'Only my lack of talent. I'd be terribly self-conscious playing in the presence of real musicians.'

'We're less judgemental than you think,' said Skins. 'But no one's going to force you.'

'Tell you what,' said Dunn. 'I wouldn't mind learning a bit more about this studio of yours, if you want something to take your mind off things.'

Malcolm smiled. 'I could bore for Britain on the subject of my studio. Are you sure you want to know?'

'Not half,' said Skins. 'You coming, Ells-Bells?'

Ellie held up her cup of tea. 'Thank you, but I think I'll sit this one out and finish this.'

'Can't say I blame you,' said Malcolm with a chuckle.

'I might play the piano myself, in a bit,' she said.

The three men got up and left her to finish her tea.

'You've seen what we do out here,' said Malcolm as he led them down towards where the altar had once stood. 'The microphone I spent so long setting up yesterday converts the sound into an electrical signal. It runs through this wire . . .' – he picked up a cotton-wrapped length of flex – '. . . and into the gubbins in here.'

They followed the wire into a side room full of arcane electronic boxes, a recording gramophone, two regular gramophones and a large loudspeaker.

'This is very impressive,' said Skins, as Malcolm described the function of the various pieces of equipment. 'Can you play us back something we recorded yesterday?'

'Of course. Give me a moment.'

It took Malcolm a couple of minutes to retrieve one of the shellac discs from a rack against the wall and put it on to one of the playback gramophones. The boys smiled as they listened to the sound of their own band coming back at them from the loudspeaker.

'We're not half bad, you know,' said Skins, when the number was over. 'We should probably take up music professionally.'

'It's worth considering, certainly,' said Dunn. 'The others would like to hear this. Can this loudspeaker be moved outside?'

'Sadly not,' said Malcolm. 'I've got the stand screwed down to try to minimize the vibration. I've got another pair on order so I can put them out in the main room for playback, but it'll be a while before we get them.'

'It wouldn't be a problem putting them outside? Don't they have to be near the other equipment, you know, like the horn on a gramophone has to be connected to the box?'

'No, that's the beauty of it. It's an electrical signal, so there's a theoretical limit to how far away you can put loudspeakers before it degrades, but in practical terms, as long as you've got a long enough piece of wire, they can go anywhere.'

'That would be handy,' said Skins. 'What other changes would you make?'

'I'd like to be able to use more than one microphone, but I can't fathom out how to blend the signals together. I'm sure the chaps in America are working on something. Other than that, I'd just welcome any developments to improve the fidelity of the recording and playback. Can you imagine a recording so clear it's impossible to tell whether you're listening to real musicians or a gramophone record?'

'That would be something,' said Dunn. He reached out and put his hand near one of the amplifiers. 'I reckon a way of keeping the room cool would be handy.'

'Why's that?'

'Surely it gets hot in here. You keep the door shut while you're recording and all this kit will generate quite a bit of heat. It must get uncomfortable during a long session.'

'You'd think so, wouldn't you? But no, this room's always blissfully cool. It sometimes gets a little chilly, actually. But that's old churches and chapels for you, eh? A bit draughty.'

'Maybe you could open a studio in a purpose-built place,' suggested Skins. 'Design it exactly how you want it.'

'Perhaps. But this old chapel has an . . . "ambience", wouldn't you say? As well as the splendid acoustic qualities of the place, there's a certain atmosphere here. Perhaps it's the old stone, perhaps it's a memory of what it used to be – I have no idea. But it seems to bring out the best in performers. I think we'll stay here for a while. And, to be honest, it was hard enough to raise the capital to convert this place – I can't even imagine where we'd get the money for a new building.'

'I'd have thought people would be falling over themselves to invest in gramophone recordings,' said Dunn. 'People love records. And look at all the juke joints in America – bar owners are actually playing records instead of hiring musicians. We've got to start making records if we're going to survive, I reckon.'

'I thought the same. But investors want mines and factories. Even at the artistic end of things, they want grand paintings and theatre shows. It was a struggle to get someone interested.'

'But you managed it,' said Skins.

'Eventually, yes.'

'Good for you.'

While they'd been talking, Ellie had been messing around with a few tunes on the piano. They stopped to listen just as she was joined by two saxophones and the warm, velvet voice of Hetty Hollis.

'Is everything set up?' asked Skins. 'Could you record this?'

'Of course. It'll take a few moments to put a disc on. Hold on.'

Ellie, Puddle and Vera played in the chapel, accompanying Hetty's singing, while Malcolm, Skins and Dunn listened in the control room. They managed to capture snippets of two of these semi-improvised songs before Ellie began playing an introduction to a gentle love song that perfectly suited Hetty's warm, sensuous voice. Malcolm had set up a new disc just in time, and was able to record the whole thing. This, thought Dunn, was the future of music.

When they'd finished, Skins called Ellie, Vera, Puddle and Hetty into the control room.

'Come and listen to this, ladies,' he said.

The room was crowded with seven people in it, but they were so thrilled at the idea of hearing themselves play that the minor discomfort this brought was forgotten.

'That's astonishing,' said Puddle. 'I'd never heard myself play before this weekend.'

'It's a pity my piano-playing isn't up to the same standard,' said Ellie. 'But it is rather wonderful to hear it all back.'

Hetty just stood with her mouth open, staring at the equipment.

'Are these discs expensive?' she asked.

'Not prohibitively so,' said Malcolm. 'Why?'

'I'd like to buy this one from you. I've never heard myself, either. I might be able to use it to get work.'

'Oh, my dear girl, don't be so silly. Discs are all part of the expense of the business. You can have it with my blessing. Better yet, why don't we cut another complete song with the band. That would really get you noticed.'

'Oh, I say. Really? That's absolutely the most marvellous thing. Thank you so very much.'

'Think nothing of it, dear girl.'

'Oh, but it's everything. I can't tell you how much this means to me. It's my dream come true. One can scratch a living in the small clubs, but something like this would open doors for me. I'd be able to get on the bill with bands like the Dizzy Heights.'

'You'd be welcome at any of the clubs we play,' said Skins.

'Even more so with a record in my hand.'

Malcolm smiled indulgently. 'Let's see what we can do for you, then.'

It might not have been hot in the little control room, but it was certainly getting a little claustrophobic.

'It's a touch cramped in here,' said Ellie. 'Would you mind awfully if I ducked back out into the main room?'

Malcolm waved airily. 'Be my guest, dear lady. The room certainly wasn't designed for seven.'

'And we ought to get out and get the band ready for your recording,' said Dunn.

After some amount of shuffling and shunting, accompanied by huffing, puffing and profuse apologies, they eventually managed to work out a way of getting back out through the door and into the cavernous chapel, but Hetty stayed with Malcolm.

Skins and Dunn rounded up the Dizzy Heights from their raucous card game and herded them back to their instruments. There was a brief discussion about what song might best suit Hetty's range, and after a few minutes they were ready to play.

Hetty reappeared, flushed with excitement, and joined them. They told her what they had in mind and she agreed enthusiastically. Malcolm gave the signal that everything was running, Mickey counted them in, and they were off.

When they were finished, the young songstress all but bounced into the control room to listen to the playback.

Most of the Dizzies resumed their seats at the card table, while Ellie, Skins and Dunn returned to what they were coming to think of as the lounge area.

After what seemed like an age but was probably closer to fifteen minutes, Hetty emerged and joined the card school, followed by Malcolm who limped down to join Ellie and the boys.

He sat and accepted a tin mug of tea from Dunn.

'You seem to have made an impression there,' said Ellie, nodding towards Hetty.

Malcolm sipped his tea. 'She's a remarkably talented young woman. Ambitious, too. And very keen to learn – she had so many questions.'

Skins chuckled. 'I remember being young and enthusiastic. What was she asking about?'

'Absolutely everything, dear boy. The business – how to get bookings, how to spot the reputable agents, how to sell gramophone records. The technicalities – how all the equipment works, what that button does, what's on that shelf there, what's in that cupboard, where to stand, how to sing into a microphone. I don't think there was anything in my little control room she didn't prod or poke, and I'd be surprised if there were anything she couldn't operate on her own by now.'

'If the singing career doesn't take off, maybe you should offer her a job,' said Dunn.

'I could do worse, certainly, but I feel she has a bright future ahead of her. No need to lurk in the shadows if she can be standing in the limelight, what?'

'Is that how you see yourself?' asked Ellie. 'In the shadows while everyone else gets the glory for your work?'

'Heavens, no, dear lady. We all have our part to play. You chaps make music, I record it. The men and women on the factory floor make biscuits, John sat in the boardroom and made what he always called "the tough decisions". I always imagined it in white on a black background, like one of those cards at the cinema. "The Managing Director Makes the Tough Decisions".'

Ellie laughed. 'And then they cut to a well-dressed man with a pensive expression, surrounded by board members, eager for his wisdom.'

'That's the ticket. Actually, that's exactly how I remember John from the few board meetings I could bear to attend.'

'Do you mind talking about John?' asked Skins. 'Do say if you'd rather not.'

'There's not much to tell, I'm afraid. Not really.'

'It's just that Howard booked us to come down here for the party, not John, so we didn't really have many dealings with our host. We saw him for a couple of minutes here and there, and now he's gone. It would be nice to know a little bit more about him – I'm sure you and the rest of the family would prefer we remembered the man he was rather than what happened to him.'

Malcolm touched Skins's arm. 'That's rather thoughtful of you. Thank you. Though I confess he might not come out too well from a full and frank account of his life.'

'Surely he can't have been as bad as all that,' said Ellie. 'Everyone has at least one redeeming quality.'

Malcolm chuckled. 'I suppose he must. Dashed if I can think of one offhand, though.'

The three friends laughed.

'What was he like as a boy?' asked Skins. 'Were you mates?'

'I don't know – he's seven years older than I. By the time I wanted a playmate he was away at school most of the time. I saw him during the holidays, of course, but I'd not say we were pals. He always thought of me as an annoying little twerp and wasn't shy in telling me so. Mother used to say it was just our ages, but we had such different personalities that I doubt we'd have been friends even if we were twins. He had no imagination, for one thing. He was angered by my flights of fancy. I remember playing with our toy soldiers one day. It wasn't something we did often, so there must have been exigent circumstances – I imagine we were stuck indoors because it was raining.'

'It seems to do that a lot round here,' said Dunn.

'Well, quite. Anyway, we set up a mighty battle between our forces. I was outnumbered and outflanked, but I summoned up the massed ranks of my wooden farm animals and routed his cavalry to claim a historic victory. Or I would have, had he not refused to accept that my general was also a powerful wizard, trained in the mystic arts by Merlin himself and able to control the beasts of the field.'

Ellie smiled. 'It does sound a little like cheating.'

'He certainly hated cheating, but what bothered him most of all was that my attack came from my "stupid made-up world" and not the real world as he knew and understood it.'

'What happened?' asked Skins. 'Did he win?'

'No, I sneaked a sniper on to the high ground – the back of an armchair – while he was engrossed in putting his infantry in neat lines. Shot his general. He conceded that one because marksmen are real. That the man couldn't possibly have scaled the armchair, nor made the deadly shot from that distance, didn't seem to bother him nearly as much as the idea of being overrun by sheep and pigs.'

'He could have ridden up on the back of a goat,' said Skins.

'That was surely going to be my defence if challenged.'

'Were there just the two of you?' asked Ellie.

'No, I'm the youngest of four. I have two sisters: Violet and Sylvia. I was closer to Sylvia – she's just two years older than I. She and her husband live in Scotland. There are so many people who need to be told.'

'What did he do next?' asked Dunn. 'University?'

'Indeed. University, then straight into the biscuit company. The gaffer had founded the company a couple of years before John was born. Started out making crackers for cheese, and by the time John joined the firm they were experimenting with all manner of sweet biscuits, too. The old man retired in 1900 but John was more or less running the place by then. As soon as the gaffer was out of the way, John put all his plans and schemes into action. He launched the Tea Break Assortment a short while later and we haven't looked back since.'

'It's very popular even now,' said Ellie. 'The band was talking about it just the other day.'

'It changed the family's fortunes, that's for sure. Things had been ticking along well enough, but the Tea Break Assortment took the business to an entirely new level – it was a runaway success. It bought him this place a couple of years later.'

'I imagined you'd all lived here for ages,' said Skins.

'Good Lord, no. The family was hardly poverty-stricken before – had a nice place at Oxford – but this is a relatively recent acquisition in the grand scheme of things. They moved here in 1903 – it's the only home the children remember. Gordon would have been . . . five, I think, which would make Betty four and little Ronnie two. Howie was just a bump under Christina's dress.'

'That was John's first wife?' asked Ellie. 'What was she like?'

'I adored her. Everybody did. Even John, in his own way. Although that didn't stop him breaking the seventh. Or the tenth, come to that – he coveted every man's wife if they were young enough.'

'Why did Christina put up with it?'

'It's what people do, isn't it? What were her options, after all? Scandal? Divorce? She'd have lost her home. She might even have lost her children. She thought it was far better to endure.'

'You talked to her about it?'

'She wrote to me often. She couldn't talk to her friends about him, and certainly not her own family. But I knew what he was like so she felt safe telling me.'

'When did it all start?'

'Well, they married in '97 and his eye was roving before the ink was dry in the parish register. They were always younger than he, always pretty. You met him – he was a handsome chap, and he could be as charming as anything when he wanted to be. They just seemed to fall at his feet. I'd have given him what for if I'd been here, but I was never around. Not sure he'd have paid any attention if I had, mind you. Christina was just part of his organized, regimented plan, d'you see? Successful business. Beautiful young wife. Children. Country house. It wasn't that he didn't love her, he just thought of her as another accomplishment to be noted in life's ledger. And being faithful to her wasn't really part of the plan. He saw no reason not to bed every young popsy who caught his fancy.'

'I know one shouldn't speak ill of the dead, but I'm afraid I like him less and less the more I hear of him,' said Ellie.

'You're not thinking anything that many, many others haven't thought.'

'How did you come to get involved in all this?' asked Skins, indicating the chapel and its electronic equipment. 'Why a recording studio?'

'Once I resigned my commission, I used to spend my time travelling the world listening to music. Concerts, opera festivals, nightclubs in the capitals of Europe. Even just a few locals playing traditional folk songs in a backstreet taverna – you name it, if there was someone making music, I wanted to be there listening. Expensive business, though, with just an army pension and dividends from my shares in the family firm. Army had been my life, you see? Took me to most of the places I wanted to go. Joined in '96. Fought in South Africa. Posted all over the Continent after that – military adviser stuff, you know? Then the big one.' He tapped his right leg with his cane. It clonked hollowly. 'Lost this in '17. Retired not long after it was all over – couldn't face the thought of a desk job at the War Office. So I thought, why not make the music come to me? Started out with some mechanical kit and recorded a few sides for local chaps. Reputation grew. Soon found my ambition had outstripped the facilities, so I started looking round. Raised some finance and imported the latest kit from America.'

'It's like nothing I've ever seen or heard before,' said Dunn.

Malcolm inclined his head in acknowledgement. 'It's the future of music.'

'I was thinking the same thing a few moments ago.'

The iron door handle clattered and Veronica came in.

'Ah, there you are, Uncle Malcolm,' she said. 'Everyone's been wondering where you'd got to.'

'It's seldom a mystery,' he said. 'There aren't many places I'm likely to be.'

'Hence my venturing here to your not-so-secret lair. It seemed the likeliest of all.'

'Is my presence required elsewhere?'

'Gordon wants to talk to you about something, but I'm not part of the inner circle, I'm afraid, so I'm not allowed to know what.'

Malcolm grinned. 'I shall go and see him and then report straight back. I can't have my favourite niece left out of the inner circle.'

'Thank you,' she said. 'You know, you really should get a telephone out here.'

'It's on my list. I just need to sort out running a cable from the house.'

He hauled himself out of the chair and stood for a brief moment to gain his balance before setting off for the door.

'What's the weather like?' he called over his shoulder.

'It's clearing up nicely. I saw the sun briefly on the way here. Peter says he thinks it'll clear up completely by teatime, but I've no idea what he's basing that on.'

Malcolm opened the door. 'A feeling in his knees, I expect. That's why I struggle to forecast the weather.' He tapped his false leg. 'Only one knee, d'you see?'

Veronica winked at the three friends. 'Gosh, Uncle Malcolm, do you only have one leg? You should have mentioned it.'

He chuckled. 'Cheeky wench.'

And was gone.

The card school was breaking up, and one or two of the band members were getting up to stretch their own legs.

'I was thinking of going up to the kitchens and seeing if they had anything for lunch,' said Mickey. 'Any requests?'

'Nothing too heavy,' said Puddle. 'I'm still full from breakfast.'

'I think Mrs Radway is putting something together from the remnants of yesterday's picnic tea,' said Veronica. 'None of the family ate anything so there's plenty left to make a decent luncheon for everyone, and she's not one to let anything go to waste. To be honest, there's enough for at least fifty people. She does tend to overdo things, our Mrs R.'

'Handsome,' said Mickey. 'Come on, then, you lot, let's go and chat her up, see if we can get the good stuff before it's gone. Be nice to get some fresh air an' all.'

'If the weather's warming up, perhaps we can eat al fresco,' said Puddle.

Chairs scraped, cards were put away, and Mickey led the way out of the door.

Ellie, Skins and Dunn made to follow, but Veronica held them back.

'Do you chaps want a squizz round the house while everyone is occupied?' she said. 'I thought it might help with your . . . investigations.'

'Sounds like a grand idea,' said Skins. 'We'll give that lot a couple of minutes to get down to the kitchens, then we can make our own way to the house with no one thinking anything of it.'

They entered, as usual, through the double doors to the salon. The sun was temporarily obscured by a cloud, but the skies had lightened, and for the first time it occurred to Skins to look up at the ceiling.

'Bloody hell,' he said. 'Has that glass roof been there all along?'

'Since before we moved in, certainly,' said Veronica. 'Have you really only just noticed it?'

Skins smiled apologetically. 'Well, what with the gaudy furniture and the ugly paintings – no offence – there was plenty to look at down here. And it's been dark most of the time.'

'It is all a bit tacky in here, isn't it? I like to hope Gordon will redecorate in a more modern style, but then I remember I'm talking about Gordon and my hopes fade. This place will remain a monument to Georgian bad taste until we can no longer afford to run it and we give it to the National Trust. Although they might not want it, of course – they might not be able to afford to keep it, either.'

'I think it's charming,' said Ellie.

'Oh, it has charm. It's just that it's like living in someone else's house. Or a museum. Very much like a museum, in fact. I'm hoping for enough of a bequest in the will that I can get a place of my own somewhere, but I fear that's as forlorn a hope as the one that Gordon will turn out not to be boringly bourgeois. But, anyway. The house was built in 1742 by Elias Dunweasel, who made his fortune from a weaving device, the Dunweasel Jiggler. He wanted a home for his three wives and their fourteen children, where they could live a life of—'

'Really?' interrupted Ellie.

'No, not really. Sorry. The truth doesn't interest most visitors so I invented Dunweasel when I was little. He's much more fun, don't you think? Anyway, this is the salon. When the sun's out in the morning it's as beastly hot in here as in the garden parlour, but in the afternoon it becomes quite pleasant. The paintings are . . . probably a job lot from a local dealer, knowing Papa. Or perhaps they came with the house. They want putting on a bonfire – that much I do know. The delicious piano over there is the Bösendorfer we put on the stage for you, by the way.'

'So there's a Bösendorfer in the salon,' said Dunn, 'a Bechstein in the drawing room and a Steinway in the chapel. You could just sell the pianos and be able to afford a place of your own.'

'Quite possibly, although I'd have to be a little careful what I said about this one when I put it up for sale. I usually tell anyone who stands still long enough that we shouldn't keep it in here, but my warnings about the frame warping in the heat fall on deaf ears. Although, actually, I don't think it's faring too badly, and I don't have to pay to have it retuned, so I suppose I shouldn't care quite so much.'

She walked through the door to the right. 'This is the dining room, but you've seen it already, so shall we skip it? We'll have to get out of the way before they start congregating in here for the picnic, anyway.'

'Unless Puddle persuades them to eat outside,' said Dunn.

'That's a point. But the staff will be back and forth either way, so we'd better not linger. The décor is in the same style, which I believe is known as Regency Ghastly. Note the particularly unappetizing painting of a bowl of fruit. The oak dining table is William IV, and is inscribed underneath with the initials of all four Bilverton children, carved when Gordon was given a new penknife for his birthday.'

'You make Gordon out to be so dull,' said Ellie. 'But he joined in with that.'

'In fact, no. I "borrowed" the new knife and carved my own initials, but then realized it would be a bit of a giveaway if the vandalism were discovered so I carved everyone else's as well by way of covering my tracks. I made rather a neat job of it, even if I say so myself.'

'Cunning,' said Ellie.

'Thank you. To be honest, I don't think anyone would be in any doubt as to who had done it, but so far my handiwork remains a secret and I am, as yet, unaccused. Now, if we go through this door here we'll find ourselves in a little vestibule where I used to lurk when Mama and Papa were entertaining – I was a great one for earwigging at keyholes. Here's another secret staircase leading upstairs . . .' She indicated what looked like an ordinary panelled wall, but headed straight past and instead opened a more conventional door. 'And this is the drawing room. This room, I actually like. The furniture is far from modern, but it's a good deal more comfortable. There's room in here for us all to gather and enjoy a post-prandial cup of coffee and still not feel as though we're on top of each other. This is where the Bechstein lives – it's a much better place for a piano.'

'It's beautiful,' said Ellie. 'I played it on Friday.'

'And another gramophone,' said Skins. 'Any secret doors?'

Veronica laughed. 'Not as far as any of us knows, no. I've checked most thoroughly. There might be something at the back of the fireplace, but I'm not sure how it might be opened, nor where it would lead if we managed it.'

Skins nodded sagely. Ellie rolled her eyes.

Veronica moved on. 'This,' she said as she led them through the door at the other end of the drawing room, 'you also know. It's the billiards room. For billiards. Although we mostly play snooker.'

'Who's the best?' asked Dunn.

'At snooker? Me, probably. I used to come in here a lot when we were all small. Boring Bossy Betty would never let my dolls join in with her tea parties so I used to come down here where they could play each other at snooker instead. We children used to have our own little cues and a stool to stand on, so I was able to keep myself amused in here for hours.'

Skins made as though to speak.

'No,' said Veronica, 'there are no secret doors in here, either. Though if you set the top score to sixty-six and pull down on the sixth cue from the left you'll open a portal to hell, and one of Beelzebub's demonic minions will emerge to offer you gifts beyond the dreams of mortal man in return for your eternal soul. Or so they say. I've never tried it myself, though it might account for Gordon's successes. The boy was always such a dullard, and yet here he is on the verge of controlling a biscuit empire to rival Peek Freans and McVitie's.'

She peered out through the door the band had been using on Friday night.

'Come on,' she said, 'the coast's clear.'

They hurried across the Grand Hall to John Bilverton's study.

'Papa's study you know, too,' said Veronica as Skins pushed the door shut behind them. 'We were never allowed in here, so of course I was always fascinated by this room as a child. Papa forbade us to come in when he was working, and the door remained locked when he wasn't.' She paused. 'Before you ask . . . Skins . . . May I call you Skins?'

'Everyone does,' he said.

'Not everyone, honey,' said Ellie.

'No, fair dos. Ellie doesn't, but she has special dispensation to use my given name on account of how I love her so much. And because I'm too terrified of her to tell her not to.'

'As you should be,' said Ellie. 'It's the basis of a happy marriage.'

Veronica smiled. 'Thank you. As I was saying, Skins, I don't know of a secret door in here, though with none of us ever having been allowed in, that's more difficult to confirm.'

'We need time and privacy to have a good poke about,' said Dunn. 'So far it's the only idea we've got for how someone might have shot your dad from inside a locked room.'

'I understand. We've no time now, though – someone will come looking for us if we don't show up for lunch soon. But I'll work out a way of getting you all back in here again later on. Leave it to me.'

Dunn nodded. 'Thanks.'

'You spent some time in the garden parlour yesterday. Do you want to see it again?'

'No,' said Ellie. 'If time is tight, I'd rather have a good look at the . . . library?'

'Yes, the library is the only other room on the ground floor. Walk this way.'

'If I could walk *that* way—' began Skins, but a swat on the arm from Ellie dissuaded him from saying anything more.

They left the study and walked the length of the hall, past the massive staircase and through to the short corridor that led to the library.

'Two secret doors for you here, Skins,' said Veronica. 'The one on the left leads down to the servants' area—'

'We used those stairs this morning,' he said. 'But the door was open – I didn't realize it was a secret one.'

'And now you do. And to the right is the servants' staircase that'll take you up to the first floor without having to use the main stairs.'

She indicated what looked at first glance like another panelled wall. On closer inspection, though, one of the panel frames was cut in at about waist height to provide a recessed handle.

'Give it a firm pull,' said Veronica, indicating the handle.

Skins put his fingers in the slot behind the frame and tugged. With the click of a simple catch, a previously invisible door opened and swung towards him.

'Nice,' said Skins with an appreciative nod. 'Whoever built this gaff didn't mess about, did they? That's very neatly done.'

'I've always liked that door,' said Veronica. 'And I've always liked this next room, too.'

She led them into the library.

Floor-to-ceiling bookcases lined the walls, precluding the hanging of the paintings of which Veronica so stoutly disapproved – in here the impressive book collection was the main event. There were four wing-backed leather armchairs, each with its own side table and electric lamp. There were other, less impressive chairs and small tables dotted about, as well as a sofa. Last, but by no means least, was a set of steps in the corner, like a miniature four-tread spiral staircase, which could be moved around the room to reach the high shelves.

'When my dolls weren't playing each other at snooker, I used to spend most of the rest of my time in here. I've read almost everything apart from some of the more tedious political books on that wall over there.'

'I would have done the same,' said Ellie. 'We had a decent enough library in the house in Annapolis, but it didn't have the . . . the warmth of this one. It has an atmosphere, don't you think?'

'I know exactly what you mean. I lobbied to put my bed in here, but it was never allowed.'

Howard suddenly appeared in the other doorway.

'There you are,' he said. 'What are you up to, lurking in here? Come on, you lot – luncheon is served on the terrace.'

The tour was temporarily halted for lunch.

# Chapter Eight

The servants had put two large tables together on the terrace. The air was heavy as the sun shone from the cloudless sky and warmed the waterlogged ground. Summer, at least, was back to normal.

Dunsworth, the butler, had stationed himself near the foot of the steps leading down from the French doors, alert to the goings-on at the table and ready to anticipate the needs of the family and their unexpected guests. He smiled a greeting as Veronica led her tour party down the steps and accompanied them to their seats.

Mrs Radway had provided a sumptuous spread of cold meats and salads, with leftovers from Friday's feast baked into pies or repurposed as rissoles. There were jugs of iced cordial as well as the ever-present champagne. Most of the family were drinking the cordial. Most of the band were drinking the champagne.

The Bilvertons and Dizzies were already seated, leaving five vacant places. Ellie carefully totted up who was present and found that Hetty Hollis was the fifth absentee. The other empty chairs were arranged in two pairs. Veronica and Dunn took one, putting Dunn next to Elizabeth's fiancé, Peter. Ellie and Skins sat together in the other pair, with Skins next to Elizabeth and Ellie beside Gordon. With a wave of his hand, Dunsworth summoned a footman to hold Veronica's chair while he took care of Ellie.

'Good afternoon, Mrs . . . Maloney,' said Gordon. 'I've remembered that right?'

'You have,' she said. 'But please call me Ellie.'

'Thank you, Ellie. I don't think I said so yesterday but the party was a great success, thanks in no small part to the splendid efforts of the band – your husband and his colleagues did us proud. I can only apologize for the dreadful circumstances of your enforced stay. I took a stroll down the drive this morning and it's still not possible even to get off the estate, much less into town.'

'It's scarcely your fault. And you have our deepest sympathies, of course.'

'Thank you. It was a shock, I have to admit. Deeply saddening for all of us. He was a remarkable man. A great man. I'm sure you've worked out by now that . . . Well, let's just say that my father was a difficult man, too, but great men often are, aren't they?'

'I'm sure he'll be missed,' said Ellie.

'He will. Terribly.' He paused for a moment, looking off into space before abruptly pulling himself together. 'I say, is everything all right with your accommodation? We hadn't anticipated that you'd have to stay more than one night.'

'We'll be fine. The boys are used to roughing it occasionally when they're on the road.'

Gordon frowned. 'I'm sure they are, but it's not how we prefer to treat our guests – for guests you are, Ellie. It hasn't gone down too well with certain people' – he glanced across the table at Peter – 'but I decided under the circumstances that we couldn't just treat you as staff. It didn't feel right, somehow.' He called across the long table. 'Marianne!'

Marianne looked up. 'Yes?' she said coldly.

'Why haven't we offered the musicians the guest bedrooms?'

'I've spoken to Mrs Freeman and it's all in hand. I'm not entirely certain why you think it any of your concern.'

'Insufferable woman,' he muttered. 'Thinks she owns the place.'

Charlotte was sitting a couple of seats away and couldn't resist the opportunity to needle her husband. 'Technically, darling, she very well might. Until the will is read and we learn differently, the house is hers and everything that's in it.'

'When I wish to hear the opinions of street girls I shall go to Jericho. They've a damn sight more honour and integrity, so it might be a journey worth making.'

'I was given to understand you have a discount as a regular customer, darling.'

Gordon seethed for a moment. Then, as though nothing had happened, he turned back to an embarrassed Ellie.

'I'll ensure the servants make up the guest rooms for you all,' he said, as though oblivious to the fact that Marianne had already seen to it.

Ellie tried to smile. 'Umm . . . Thank you. I'll let Katy know.'

'I do feel for you all being stuck here with us. Is the band losing work?'

'They have a residency at a London club – the Augmented Ninth, do you know it? They play there on Monday nights, and I heard something about them playing at a new club on Wednesday, but those are the only engagements in the diary for the rest of the week, as far as I know. The clubs will wonder where they are if we don't get back and no one manages to call them in time, but Katy will explain as soon as she can. They have a great relationship with the Augmented Ninth so I know they'll understand. They might not get invited back to the new one if they let them down, but there are new clubs opening all the time so it's no great loss to the Dizzies.'

'There won't be consequences for breaking the contracts?'

'It's not really their fault, is it? Katy will claim exigent circumstances. Or Act of God. I'm sure it'll work out OK.'

'That's something, at least. Mrs Cannon knows we're still paying for the motor coach, I hope. Perhaps I ought to tell her. I foresee a good few days of having to tell people things.' He paused for a moment in thought, then continued, almost as though talking to himself. 'Oh, dear Lord, the board of directors is going to be a nightmare. I need to talk to our solicitor. I need to see that will . . . I'm so sorry, Mrs Malo— Ellie. Here I am wittering on about work again. I'm a dreadful host.'

'Nonsense,' said Ellie kindly. 'You've a lot to deal with.'

He glanced over at Charlotte, who was talking to Vera. 'Don't I just?'

Ellie chose not to say anything.

Howard caught her eye and winked. 'Are you boring our guest, Gordy?' he said. 'I got them all the way down from London to entertain us, and you repay them by being a tedious old pill.'

Gordon flushed red. 'Do shut up, Howard, there's a good boy.'

'Would that I could, old horse, would that I could. But if I don't tell you you're a crashing bore, no one will. It's for your own good, and the good of society at large.'

Gordon stabbed angrily at a slice of ham with his fork.

◆ ◆ ◆

Skins, meanwhile, was talking to Elizabeth.

'It's so frightfully exciting to have an actual jazz band staying at the house,' she said. 'Under other circumstances I rather fear we'd be taking unfair advantage of having such talented guests.'

'It's never an imposition,' said Skins. 'We love to play.'

'How long have you been together?'

'The Dizzy Heights? A couple of years now. But Barty and I have been mates since we were kids. Do you play?'

'I played the violin as a girl, but I haven't touched it for years. I can peck out a tune on the piano.'

'Were you any good? At the violin, I mean.'

'Not bad, I suppose.'

'You're welcome to play with us if you fancy something to divert you from . . . Well, you know. Things.'

'That's very kind, but I'm not up to your standard. Wretched Ronnie's the one with the talent.'

Skins glanced across the table, but Veronica was busy talking to Dunn and hadn't heard them. 'You don't get on, then?'

Elizabeth thought for a moment. 'Honestly? No, not really. She's such a . . . Oh, I don't know. She calls me Boring Bossy Betty and I tell her she ought to be more ladylike. She really ought, you know. She ought to make something more of herself.'

'I thought she was a schoolteacher – that's something to be proud of, surely?'

'It would be if only she were a little more . . . I struggle to describe it. She has all these ideas about independence. She sneers at me for getting engaged to a solicitor and preparing to be a "dutiful wife". She thinks that's boring. But looking after a family is important, don't you think? I'd be keeping up my charity work, too.'

'I can't say you're wrong – it's what Ellie chose to do, after all. But . . . Well, it's not my place to get involved in a family's business, but the point is that Ellie chose to do it. Isn't it up to Veronica what she does?'

'Of course. In a way. I just wish she wanted to live a more conventional life.'

'What does the rest of the family think? Did your father approve?'

'Heavens, no. But he disapproved of almost everyone.'

'Even you? What did you do?'

'I got engaged to Peter. He massively disapproved of Peter. He called him a second-rate failing lawyer and accused him of being a gold-digger. "That fool's barely competent to write wills for maiden ladies leaving their meagre fortunes to their lapdogs. He's only interested in you because of my money." I was, apparently, a fool for falling for him.'

'But you could have weathered that one, surely. He'd have come round in the end. Peter seems all right to me.'

'He's an absolute darling and I love him more than I can adequately express. But that was when Papa started talking about changing his will. He was planning to give Marianne a controlling stake in the company – it had always been promised to Gordon – and cut Howard out completely. Which was fine by me – I don't care who runs the stupid biscuit factory – but it meant the money-grabbing little witch started getting proprietorial about "her" money. That was when the budget for my wedding got cut. And my allowance.'

'What did Gordon think of all this?'

'He was furious. He's always been the blue-eyed boy, the heir apparent, the chosen bloody one. Suddenly his precious biscuits are going to his stepmother.'

'So the will has been changed?'

'I've no idea. I don't think so. I'm sure there would have been a grand announcement if it had. He loved letting everyone know how little he thought of us all. Kept us on our toes, apparently. Or in our places. Or something.' She paused for a moment. 'It was so completely out of character. You know . . . taking his own life. That wasn't Papa's style at all. If he were going to do anything to upset us, he'd want to witness the consequences. He'd want to see the looks on our faces, hear the outrage in our voices. Just bowing out without being able to gloat over our distress wasn't him.'

'So you think someone killed him?'

'How could they? The study was locked from the inside – it took Ronnie, Ellie and I about five minutes to break in. There was no one lurking in there and no way for them to get out. Ellie checked the windows from the outside.'

Skins shook his head. That was very much the problem they were trying to solve.

Suddenly, there was a commotion at the other end of the table. Charlotte threw her napkin towards her plate and it caught Vera's champagne glass on the way. As the glass smashed on the table, she stood so forcefully that she knocked her chair over. Without a word, she stormed away, her heels clicking as she hurried in through the French doors.

Everyone pretended not to notice and carried on eating.

Ellie looked around, still bewildered by the English and their reactions to awkward social moments, while Dunsworth and the footman discreetly cleared away the broken glass and checked that no one had been splashed, before setting Vera up with more champagne. Ellie nudged Skins and gave him a questioning look, but he just grinned, shrugged and returned to his pie.

◆ ◆ ◆

On the other side of the table, Veronica had become entangled in a conversation with Howard about some family matter Dunn didn't really understand, so he turned to his left and introduced himself to Peter Putnam.

'We've not met properly,' he said. 'Barty Dunn. Bass player with the Dizzy Heights.'

'Peter Putnam. I'm engaged to Elizabeth.'

They awkwardly shook hands without standing.

'Veronica has been trying to explain everyone to us, but it's not easy keeping it all straight. You're the solicitor, aren't you?'

'That's right. I have a practice at Oxford. Just a small one, you know? Wills, a bit of conveyancing – nothing fancy, but it pays the bills.'

'As long as you enjoy it, that's all you need.'

Peter laughed. 'I say, steady on. I'd not say I enjoy it. I don't hate it, but "enjoy" is a bit steep.'

'Really? Then why . . . ?'

'A chap has to earn a living. I come from a long line of solicitors, so it was just sort of what I expected to do. If my father had been a miner, I'd have worked down the mine. If he were a cobbler, I'd mend shoes. But he's a solicitor, so I solicit. And it's much less important now that I'm marrying one of the richest gels in the county, what?' He winked.

Dunn winced inwardly but decided not to respond. Instead he said, 'Did you handle John's will?' He already knew the answer, but he was keen to hear what Peter had to say on the matter.

'Gracious, no. It's a very personal thing, a will. You don't want family members getting involved in that – even prospective family members. It opens up the possibility of the will being challenged, as well.'

'It does?'

'Of course. Let's say I drafted the will and he left an enormous legacy to Elizabeth but disinherited one of the others. They could say that I'd written it in my bride-to-be's favour, and the courts might agree with them. Far better to get it done by a disinterested party.'

'That makes sense. But surely he put some work your way now and again.'

'From time to time. I act for Malcolm more often. He trusts me to handle quite a bit of Bilver-Tone business.' He looked towards the other end of the table to check that Malcolm couldn't overhear.

'He recommended me for some other work. Might have been a bit of a leg-up, but it all came to nothing in the end.'

'What sort of work?'

'Just some conveyancing for a local businessman. You've heard of Valentine Baisley?'

'I confess I haven't. Local musician?'

Peter chuckled. 'Hardly. He describes himself a businessman, but he fancies himself as an American-style gangster. Among his many enterprises, he runs a swanky nightclub in Oxford.'

'There's a lot of that about. London has more than its fair share of clubs run by shady blokes.'

'Well, Baisley has Oxford to himself. As well as his club where he likes to show off to the local well-to-dos, he owns a couple of pubs and a row of houses in Jericho. He's an entrepreneur. Or ontro-pron-ewer, as he so eloquently and elegantly says it.'

'How does that make him a gangster?'

'Well, we've not banned booze like the Yanks, but they say he has complete control of the local drugs market. Gambling, too. There are rumours that he even runs the local protection racket, but I'm not sure I completely believe any of it. I strongly suspect it's an image he likes to cultivate because he thinks it makes him seem more glamorous and exciting.'

'There's a lot of that about, too – there's a particular kind of bloke who gets caught up in the romantic image of villainy. They forget it's mostly about frightening little old shopkeepers out of their hard-earned money.'

'Well, quite.'

'So why would you want to be involved with a bloke like that?'

'Business is business and money's money, old chap. It would still pay my bills, no matter where it came from. That's rather been Malcolm's attitude, too, I think.'

'So how is Malcolm linked to Baisley?'

'Baisley put up most of the money to get Bilver-Tone Records started.'

'Blimey. That can't have gone down well with his brother. I shouldn't imagine John would have wanted the family linked to a dodgy geezer – even if the dodginess was put on.'

'There was a fair amount of frostiness, I believe. For his next birthday John bought Malcolm a long spoon.'

'For supping with the Devil.'

'Precisely. But Malcolm didn't care. He insisted that many of the characters John dealt with were no less unpleasant in their own ways. One of John's landlord friends putting a family out on the street for not paying their rent, he argued, was no different to Baisley having a man's fingers broken for not paying his gambling debts.'

'So Malcolm bought into the gangster thing?'

'Everyone does. It's reached the point where it doesn't matter whether it's actually true – people accept that he's a violent thug. John huffed and puffed about the legality of it, of course, but he was an honourable man himself and he could see there were ethical – or rather unethical – similarities between Baisley and some of his own business acquaintances.'

'John was straight, then?'

'As a die. He was a JP with a reputation for being strict, fair and thoroughly incorruptible.'

'Sounds like a nice bloke.'

Peter laughed again. 'Ye gods, no. He was a thoroughly dislikeable man, but a decent and honest one.'

Dunn nodded.

◆ ◆ ◆

When lunch was over, servants materialized as if from nowhere to clear everything away, and the house's inmates split into their customary groups. The family disappeared indoors while the band tried to agree how to spend the afternoon. Although the weather had cheered up, the ground was still sodden, so the proposed games of rounders, French cricket and five-a-side football were all vetoed. Eventually they decided to retire to the chapel with its never-ending supply of tea, where they could have another game of cards.

Skins, Ellie and Dunn stayed behind on the terrace, promising to join them all in a short while.

'So what did you learn?' asked Ellie as she drew her notebook from her pocket.

'Why do you assume we were trying to learn things?' said Dunn. 'I might just have been passing the time of day with our gracious but reluctant hosts.'

'If you weren't trying to learn things, Bartholomew Dunn, you're in serious trouble.'

'Yes, ma'am.'

'That's better. And what did you make of that business with Charlotte? Did you hear her and Gordon going at it? He called her a "street girl" right there in front of everyone. I take it Jericho is where the hookers hang out and I haven't misunderstood.'

'It's in Oxford,' said Dunn. 'North of the city, by the canal. And yes, it is.'

'I shan't ask how you know.'

'We played some dates in Oxford before the war. You pick things up.'

Ellie raised her eyebrows. 'Hmm. And what about her storming off like that?'

'Malcolm said something to Marianne,' said Dunn, 'but I couldn't hear what. Marianne looked very upset. Charlotte remonstrated and he told her to shut up and mind her own business.'

'Good Lord,' said Ellie. 'What's going on there?'

Skins shook his head. 'I doubt they'll ever tell us.'

'I don't suppose they ever will,' said Ellie. 'So what did you pick up?'

'Well, Elizabeth is pretty much just as Veronica makes her out to be. An ordinary woman. Didn't much like her dad and it really cheesed her off that John didn't like her bloke . . .'

'Peter,' said Dunn.

'That's him. She's not keen on her sister and she doesn't like her stepmother, either. Says she's trying to manoeuvre things so she gets all the money. She said something about a new will.'

'He made a new will?' said Ellie, raising an eyebrow as she made notes. 'Did she know anything about it?'

'I think it was just a planned new will – she didn't know if he'd actually written one. All she knew for certain was that the idea was to give Marianne a bigger share of the biscuit business and that Gordon was furious.'

Ellie made another note. 'That makes him even more of a suspect. Kill the old man for sleeping with his wife and do it before he changes the will.'

'It makes Marianne less of a suspect, too,' said Dunn. 'She'd want to make sure the new will was in place before she bumped him off for knocking off his daughter-in-law.'

'Good point. Gordon's a nasty piece of work. Did you hear the way he talked to Marianne and Charlotte?'

'He made sure we all did,' said Skins. 'Quite the bully.'

'Very unpleasant,' agreed Ellie.

Dunn nodded. 'Did he say anything about his father?'

'Nothing bad. He acknowledged that John was . . . What did he say? A "difficult" man. But he didn't seem to despise him.'

'I don't think any of them liked him much. But if Gordon had done him in, he *would* play it down, wouldn't he? He'd not be sitting there ranting about how much he hated the old bloke in case anyone worked out it was murder rather than suicide. He'd want to keep up the impression that he found him "difficult" but loved him all the same.'

'Elizabeth is wondering whether it really is suicide,' said Skins.

Ellie looked up from her notebook. 'What?'

'She says it was completely out of character. She said if he was going to upset people, he'd want to be there to see it. She doesn't reckon suicide was his style.'

'If that's true, she's not likely to be the only one who thinks it,' said Ellie. 'What about Peter?'

'He didn't mention suicide,' said Dunn.

'No, you chimp, what did you make of him?'

'As ordinary as his affianced. Seems like a bit of a plodder. I got the impression his ambitions outstrip his abilities. He spent most of the time talking about the local gangster, though.'

Ellie had returned to her note-taking. 'I want to say Beasley, but I know that's not right.'

'Baisley. Valentine Baisley. How do you know about him?'

'Howard pointed him out to me at the party while you were corrupting the assembled throng with the Devil's syncopation and all his demonic harmonies.'

'We are a degenerate influence, it's true,' said Skins. 'So who is this bloke?'

'He's a local businessman,' said Dunn. 'Among other things he runs a nightclub and likes to play the gangster. Peter thinks it's put on, but he still seems to find him quite glamorous. Wanted to work for him, but it fell through.'

'Howard believes it,' said Ellie. 'And so do others. I heard a young guy asking him not so subtly for some cocaine.'

'Well,' said Dunn, 'maybe there's something in it, maybe not. But he put up the money for Malcolm's record business, so he can't be all bad.'

'Rules Malcy-boy out, then,' said Skins. 'He wouldn't have cause to kill his brother if his funding was coming from somewhere else. He might profit from the will, but he doesn't need it.'

'Did Peter say anything about what John had done to make them fall out? Veronica just knew it was something to do with Peter's practice.'

'Didn't mention it at all,' said Dunn.

Ellie finished off her notes. 'There might be something in that – we'll have to do some more digging. I'm going to go through the list again – can I have a yes or no, please. Malcolm?'

Skins frowned. 'Leave him as a possible. I can't see a motive. It would be difficult for him to get to the house and back in a hurry on his false leg, too.'

'Marianne?'

'Yes,' said Dunn. 'Revenge for the infidelity and securing her inheritance.'

'Assuming the will was changed in her favour,' said Skins.

'OK,' said Ellie. 'Gordon?'

Skins nodded. 'Yes. Inheritance if the will hasn't already been changed. And revenge, of course.'

'Charlotte?'

'Don't know anything about her yet, but I can't see what she'd have to gain from it.'

'I'll put her as a no in this round, then. Elizabeth?'

'No,' said Skins. 'Too . . . wet.'

'I don't think "being a little insipid" is a valid defence in court, but all right. Peter Putnam?'

'No,' said Dunn. 'Same defence. And neither of them seems to have a decent motive.'

'Hmm,' said Ellie. 'He's a bit slimy.'

'If being wet isn't enough to get someone off, being slimy isn't enough to convict.'

'You wouldn't say that if you'd seen him in the drawing room at the party, but all right.'

'Wait a moment,' said Skins. 'You didn't tell me about that. What happened?'

'It was when I was playing the piano. He oiled up to me and put his clammy hand on my shoulder. Howard had to peel him off.'

'You should have said something – I'd have given him what for.'

'That's precisely why I didn't mention it, honey. No point in starting a fight over it. He's not tried anything since.'

'I'll slosh him one if he does.'

'Thank you,' she said. 'What about Veronica?'

'I'll slosh her, too, if you really want me to, but I quite like her.'

Ellie rolled her eyes. 'As a suspect.'

'Put her down as a yes,' said Skins. 'She's as brainy as they come, so helping us could be a clever double bluff. She's none too keen on the rest of her family and she doesn't mind who knows it. Especially her old man – she really wasn't a fan of his. I'd always put a tanner each way on the outsider.'

'I thought you said you liked her?'

'What can I say? I'm attracted to dangerous women.'

'Hmm,' said Ellie with a frown. 'I'm not so sure, but OK. Howard?'

'Yes,' said Dunn. 'Again, contingent on the will. If he's not already been disinherited he'd want to kill his old man and get his share of the loot.'

'Hetty Hollis?'

Dunn shrugged. 'Haven't spoken to her yet.'

'That's a point,' said Skins. 'Where is she?'

'I've not seen her since before lunch,' said Ellie. 'We can talk to her later. Staff?'

Dunn shrugged again. 'Could be any of them – who knows who he might have upset? Who even knows how many of them there are? It doesn't seem like something they'd do, though. If your employer upsets you, you just leave, don't you? I mean, you might put a couple of kippers in an air vent, but you'd just pack your bags and do a moonlight. You'd not stage an elaborate murder and then hang about.'

'Fair enough. Valentine Baisley?'

'No,' said Dunn. 'He's not here, unless he's hiding upstairs. He'd get one of his thugs to do it, anyway – and they'd definitely be too dim to stay out of sight this long.'

'That's everyone, I think,' she said, closing her notebook.

'Unless it was one of us,' said Skins.

'No motives,' said Ellie. 'And no opportunity – we know where we were the whole time.'

Veronica had appeared at the doors behind them. Ellie couldn't help wondering what, if anything, she'd overheard.

'Ah, there you are. Do you want to continue our tour?'

Veronica led them back through the salon and the library to the Grand Hall. From there, they went up the broad stone steps to the first landing, where she paused.

'Left, I think,' she said, after a moment's thought.

They trailed up after her.

'We can start at my room. All the others are broadly the same save for decoration and whatnot, so it'll give you an idea.'

They turned right at the top of the second flight of stairs.

'On the left is another of our secret staircase doors – that one leads upstairs to the second floor as well as back down to the secret door outside the dining room. The main staircase for guests is over on the other side.'

'What's up on the . . . second floor?' asked Ellie. She still sometimes struggled with the English custom of naming their floors from zero. Surely, she thought, the first floor you walked into was the first floor. Not here. The first floor was the ground floor. Which made the second floor the first floor. Still, she should think herself lucky they didn't go all nautical and call it the orlop floor, or the quarter floor.

'Guest bedrooms. The layout is much the same as down here.'

'Or the poop floor,' said Ellie out loud.

'I beg your pardon?'

'End of a conversation in my head. Ignore me. Actually, I did know what was upstairs – Howard told us earlier. I'm sorry.'

Veronica frowned quizzically. 'Righto. Then there are servants' quarters and storage on the attic floor,' she said. 'We'll see it in a minute.'

She reached for the handle of a conventional door in the corner next to the secret door.

'Welcome to my humble abode. It's not much, but it's home.'

The three friends were reluctant to invade the young woman's bedroom, so they peered in through the door. There was a bed, a chest of drawers, a dressing table and a large wardrobe. The furniture was elegant without being extravagantly "antique". A large window looked out on to the parkland at the rear of the house. Veronica, it seemed, was a tidy person and there was little clutter.

'The one concession Papa made to modern living was to provide each bedroom with its own bathroom,' she said. 'The alterations meant we lost a few guest rooms, but we're not part of the "country house weekend" set, so we never have many guests anyway. And it's such a joy not to have to share. It's over there on the left.'

Leaning in through the doorway, they could just about see another door in the corner of the room and took her word for it that it led to a bathroom.

'Swanky,' said Skins.

'It's not a bad place to live, certainly,' said Veronica. 'Most of the bedrooms are the same – there's just a little variation in size.'

She closed the door and led them clockwise around the gallery. There were doors to their left, and to the right a view of the Grand Hall over an ornate balustrade.

'Next to mine is Howard's – his room's a little smaller, which pleases me more than it ought.' She walked on. 'Then there's a view of the glass roof of the salon and the park beyond. And then a guest room where Peter stays when he's here. Which seems to be most of the time. It's a mirror of Howie's room, and Boring Betty has the room in the other corner, which is a mirror of mine. And that bothers her more than it ought – she thinks she should have a larger room.'

She turned the corner.

'That's the concealed door for the secret stairs back down to the door outside the library, and the main staircase up to the guest rooms above us.'

She led them on past the other arm of the main staircase and along the gallery.

'Gordon and Charlotte are in here,' she said, indicating a door about halfway along. 'With Papa and Marianne next door. Theirs is more like a suite – they have room for a sofa and chairs.'

Huge windows formed the far wall of the gallery, looking out across the entrance hall on to the drive. They crossed to the other side of the house and Veronica resumed her guided tour.

'Uncle Malcolm has the suite on this side. He often sits up here if he wants to be alone. Then there's a bathroom—'

'Where Katy and I got changed for the party,' said Ellie.

'Ah, of course. And finally another guest room. Hetty Hollis has been staying here. Hello, she's left her door open.'

She knocked on the door. 'Hetty? Are you in there?'

There was no reply. Veronica opened the door a little wider and peered in.

'Hetty?'

She turned back to the friends.

'I think she's on the floor by the other side of the bed. I can just see her shoes.'

Ellie pushed past and entered the room.

'Miss Hollis?' she said. 'Hetty?'

As the others followed her in, she knelt down beside the bed.

'Don't touch anything,' she said. 'She's dead.'

# Chapter Nine

Veronica hurried to the other side of the bed. 'Are you sure?'

'I'm afraid so,' said Ellie calmly.

'Any signs of foul play?' asked Dunn.

'Nothing obvious, but don't touch that glass of Scotch on the bedside table – it could be poisoned.'

Veronica put her hand to her mouth. 'Poisoned? So we have two killers?'

'How do you mean?' asked Dunn.

'Well, killers stick to one method – everyone knows that. It's in all the stories. And Papa was shot.'

'He was drugged first,' said Ellie. 'There was something in his Scotch – I guessed Veronal but the police will be able to test it – to knock John out and make it easier to stage the fake suicide. But an overdose can be fatal, and if the killer had access to a supply of Veronal to drug John, they might have had enough to kill poor Hetty.'

'But if it is poison, she might have taken it herself,' said Veronica, as though she were trying to wish away the possibility of two murders.

'Easy enough to check,' said Dunn.

He scanned the bedside table and found only a book and a travel clock. Hetty's clothes hung in the wardrobe, with several items, including an impressive selection of shoes, on the shelves. He looked through them and then took down the suitcase from the top. He found nothing he wasn't expecting to see. Hetty's make-up case and spongebag were in the bathroom and they, too, yielded nothing out of the ordinary.

'No sign of any other pills,' he said. 'I can't see anything she might have kept them in, either. Unless she was carrying drugs loose in her pockets, anything in the Scotch glass that isn't whisky was brought in by someone else.'

Ellie stood. 'Obviously it could be natural causes, but she's a fit and healthy young woman in the prime of life. There are no obvious signs of a heart attack, but that doesn't prove anything. And there are any number of other things that might have killed her – a brain aneurism, perhaps.'

'It's certainly suspicious, though,' said Skins. 'One death in a house is rare. Two in the same house in the same weekend . . . there's got to be something going on.'

'Whatever happened, it was recent and quick,' said Dunn. 'She was with us in the chapel, but she didn't show up for lunch.'

'Was anyone other than us late for lunch, I wonder?' said Ellie. 'Can you ask around, Veronica?'

'I'll try to think of a way to make it sound like an innocent enquiry.'

'Thank you.'

'But we really need the police here now,' said Veronica, looking pale. 'There's a murderer in the family. *My* family. They killed Papa, now possibly poor Henrietta—'

'Who?' said Skins.

Dunn rolled his eyes. 'What did you think Hetty was short for, mate?'

'Oh, right. But without the phone, and without a way to get on or off the estate, there's no one coming, I'm afraid.'

'There's not,' said Ellie. 'Gordon says the roads are still impassable. That's why it's up to us. Will Gordon start investigating, do you think? Start trying to figure it out?'

'No,' said Veronica. 'He won't believe it's murder. And even if he does, he'll fuss and bluster and tell us all to wait for the police.'

'What about the others? Anyone else fancy themselves as an amateur detective?'

'Oddly enough, it's not the sort of thing that comes up in family discussions.'

'No, of course not. Sorry. We've got to tell everyone, though.'

Ellie put an arm around Veronica as they filed out of the room. It was obvious that she was shaken and, like them, wondering who in the poisonous Bilverton family was capable of murder.

They found Gordon sitting alone in the drawing room.

'Oh, dear Lord,' he said when Ellie explained what they had found. 'Not another thing to deal with.'

'I do think you could be a little more sensitive about it, Gordon,' said Veronica, visibly upset. 'Someone has died. Another murder. In our house.'

'What do you mean, "another murder"?'

'First Papa, now Hetty.'

'Don't talk such rot, Ronnie, you utter fathead. Father killed himself and Hetty collapsed.'

'Have it your way, brother dear. But there's a woman's body in the guest bedroom on the first floor, and since you're so keen on taking charge I shall leave you to sort it out.'

She stomped out of the room, leaving the three friends to offer Gordon embarrassed shrugs and trail after her.

They stood in the Grand Hall for a few moments, trying to decide what to do next.

'We ought to get back down to the chapel and tell the others,' said Dunn.

'And I could do with joining in the card game,' said Skins. 'I need something to clear my head.'

They set off towards the library and their footsteps echoed loudly around the hall. Suddenly, Ellie motioned for them to stop. She listened intently for a few seconds.

'You boys go on to your card game. I want to check on something.'

'What is it?' asked Skins.

'Can't you hear?'

'After a lifetime of drumming, I'm lucky I can hear you, never mind anything else.'

'Can't you hear it, Barty?'

Dunn shook his head. 'After a lifetime of standing next to this wiry idiot while he plays the drums, I'm even luckier that I can hear anything at all.'

'Well, why don't you two old fellas toddle off back to the chapel for a nice sit-down, and I'll find out what the noise is.'

Skins and Dunn obediently set off for the studio while Ellie turned towards the source of the noise that had caught her attention. She paused at the door to the garden parlour and listened again. It was a woman crying.

Without knocking, she gently opened the door and stepped in. Marianne started, and hurriedly wiped her eyes with her handkerchief.

'I'm so sorry,' said Ellie, 'I had no idea there was anyone in here. Am I disturbing you?'

'No,' said Marianne, 'it's quite all right. Please come in. It's lovely in here in the afternoon, don't you think?'

Ellie approached the sofa and looked out through the large windows into the walled garden.

'It is,' she said. 'I don't quite understand why the family doesn't like it.'

'Nor do I. It's my favourite room.'

Ellie turned and looked down at Marianne. 'If you don't mind me asking, are you OK? You look as though you've been crying.'

Marianne sniffed. 'I'm fine, thank you. Things have just suddenly got on top of me, that's all.'

'I can understand that. Can I get you anything?'

'What? Oh, no, thank you. You're very kind.'

Ellie smiled. 'I should leave you in peace – I don't like to intrude.'

'No, please stay. It would be nice to talk to someone who isn't a Bilverton.'

Ellie sat at the other end of the sofa. 'I noticed the way they treat you.'

'I can sort of understand it, I suppose. I'm only nine months older than Gordon, after all. I was his father's secretary, and then suddenly one day I was his stepmother.'

'Being a stepmother of any age must be hard, I'd have thought.'

'I've always imagined so. It might be easier if the children are young, but this lot were all adults. Well, nearly – Howard was nineteen by the time John and I married, but that's not far off. The upshot is that they've never really thought very highly of me. I'm a gold-digger, obviously. And a scarlet woman – it wasn't hard to work out that I must have been having an affair with John while their mother was still alive. But I loved him, you see? Even when I found out he was sleeping with Charlotte.'

'Really?'

'I'm not naive. He had an affair with me while he was married to Christina, after all. But I'd always hoped . . . It sounds as stupid now as it was then, but I'd always hoped that maybe . . . maybe I would be enough.' She swallowed a sob. 'Eventually I just stopped noticing . . . the lipstick marks, the late nights. The perfume on his shirts. I turned a blind eye. I wasn't happy about it, not at all, but I never stopped loving him. And that made it worse, of course.'

'Worse? How so?'

'Instead of storming out like a betrayed wife, I stuck with him. That confirmed the gold-digger theory, didn't it? I must be in it for the money if I stayed after that.'

'Did they really think that?'

'They've always thought that. I was John's secretary so I'm not "one of them". Which meant, of course, I was only with him because I wanted the big house and the fancy frocks. They couldn't imagine it any other way.'

'That's awful.'

'I'm used to it. Look, you don't mind me talking like this, do you? I just needed to get it all out.'

'You go right ahead. We're not so afraid of personal stuff as you English.'

'Ah, of course. Are you American? Or Canadian?'

'American. From Maryland.'

'I'm afraid I don't know where that is. Is it nice?'

'It is, actually, yes. Beautiful.'

'Don't you get homesick?'

'Not any more. I served as a nurse in France during the war and I felt it terribly there, but London is my home now.'

'Good heavens. That was brave.'

'Going to France? Perhaps. Or foolhardy. I was chasing a man.'

Marianne laughed for the first time. 'Did you catch him?'

'I married him.'

'Ah, yes, you're married to one of the musicians, aren't you? The tall one or the short one?'

It was Ellie's turn to laugh. 'The short one.'

'I can see the appeal.'

'He was worth chasing halfway round the world for.'

'He seems like a nice fellow. They all do, though. We often have musicians down in the chapel with Malcolm and they're not always as pleasant as your lot.'

'Are they not?'

'Not always, no. Some of them are a bit . . . dodgy. But Malcolm doesn't seem to mind. How are you all getting on with him?'

'He seems like a nice fellow, too.'

Marianne smiled and then nodded towards Ellie's elegant dress. 'Do musicians earn a lot?'

'They get by.'

'That's a lovely frock, though. Am I right in guessing that you come from money, too? You'd fit in round here, at least.'

'My family is wealthy, yes. I don't inherit for a while yet – there was a weird clause in my father's will. It's complicated.'

'Oh my goodness, don't talk to me about wills. That's what got me so upset in the first place.'

'I'm sorry, I wasn't thinking.'

'Oh, don't be silly. I was the one who asked. John had made a new will. He thought it was time the children all stood on their own two feet and he wasn't shy about telling them so. Everyone suspects he changed the will to give them less of an inheritance. They all think it's my fault but I had nothing to do with it. All I ever wanted was John. Even if I couldn't have him all to myself, I'd rather have had whatever part of him he was prepared to share than have another penny of his money. But he wanted to give me the house and shares in the company.'

'And that was a change to the will? Weren't you getting all that anyway?'

'Most of it was going to Gordon before whatever changes he made. The other children got a little, and I was to be assured of a roof over my head and a handsome income. But then John took it into his head to "shake the idle beggars up a bit", as he put it, and suddenly I'm supposed to get the house, a big interest in the company, and Lord knows what else besides. I actually tried to talk him out of it, you know? I don't need any of that and the children would be apoplectic. Gordon particularly. But he wouldn't hear it.'

'Have you not seen this new will, then?'

'No, he said he wanted to finalize everything first.'

'That makes sense. And how do you feel about it? Is it a good thing, or bad?'

'I was wondering about it all while I sat here, as a matter of fact. I worked at Bilverton's for nearly nine years before John married me so I'm sure I understand the business as well as Gordon, but I don't know if I have any real interest in running it. I didn't hate it, but I never had a passion for it. That boy lives and breathes biscuits. So I actually think I'd like to come to some sort of arrangement with Gordon where he gets the business and the house, and I get enough to buy myself a nice little flat in London and to provide a comfortable income. Start a new life, far away from them. I'll pack my bags, and this sorry lot can bicker themselves to death for all I care.'

'Why London?'

'I've no family here – I lost both my parents to the flu in '19. And London's exciting. I want to live a little.'

'It's certainly a fun town. I like it there.'

'I think I would, too. But listen to me blithering on. You ought to be getting back to your friends.'

Ellie looked at the clock on the mantel. 'Actually, I probably should. The boys were about to join a card game.'

'Oh, I love cards. Do you play?'

'No, I was just going to make sure Ivor hasn't gambled away our house. Or the children. But you're welcome to come along if you want.'

'That's very kind, but I think I'd prefer a few more moments with my thoughts. Some other time, perhaps?'

'You're always welcome in the chapel. They're a friendly bunch.'

'I'm sure they are. Thank you for listening to me. It all feels a little less oppressive now I've said it out loud.'

Ellie stood. When she'd seen how upset Marianne had been she had been hesitant to mention the recent tragedy, but she decided now it would be worse to say nothing. 'Look, I don't want to worry you unduly – you're already upset – but something else awful has happened.'

'Oh, no. What?'

'I didn't know whether to say anything, but . . . you see . . . I'm afraid we just found poor Hetty – Howard's friend – dead in her room.'

Marianne put her hand to her mouth. 'Oh my word. How awful. Why didn't you say something sooner? I've been wittering on about my own petty problems and there's a girl dead upstairs.' She blanched. 'How did she die?'

'We're not sure. Veronica was showing us round the house. We saw her door open, went inside, and there she was.'

'Gracious. Have you told—'

'We've just told Gordon. Veronica left him to get on with things.'

Marianne stood. 'But no one else? I should tell Howard – she was his friend.'

'I think that's a good idea. And I'd better get back to the band. Can I get to the chapel if I go out these doors?'

'Of course. There's a gate in the wall over there to the left – it'll bring you out on the main path.'

'Thank you. We'll see you at dinner, I hope.'

Ellie left through the double doors into the walled garden.

◆ ◆ ◆

Ellie opened the chapel door and was greeted by a discordant cacophony from the band, who were playing an out-of-tune, out-of-time rendition of 'Twinkle Twinkle'. It was a genuinely unpleasant sound. The saxophones were honking, the trumpet squeaking. Skins's drums sounded as though they were being played by a particularly uncoordinated gibbon.

She hurried in, worried they might all have been drugged again, and wondering what on earth she might be able to do about it. As she skidded to a halt on the tiled floor, she saw at once the reason for the musical chaos – they were playing each other's instruments. Even Katy had joined in, on her sister's clarinet. The song ended to cheers and guffaws.

'What the heck . . . ?' she began, as the laughter died down.

'Hello, love,' said Skins, taking a saxophone from his lips. 'They got bored of cards.'

'So I see. But . . . I mean, did you even tell them about Hetty?'

'He did, sweetie,' said Puddle from behind Skins's drum set. 'But there's nothing to be gained from us moping about, so we decided to lighten the mood. Can you play the flute?'

Ellie shook her head. 'Not even a little bit.'

'Perfect. Grab mine and join us. It's the small case under Skins's chair.'

'I don't even know how to put it together.'

'Even better. We're trying "Frère Jacques" next.'

Elk waved Eustace's trumpet. 'What key?'

'If you can play it in any key I'll give you a fiver,' said Dunn.

'It comes in three pieces,' said Ellie.

Skins looked over. 'What does?'

'This flute. Look.' She held up the sections of the disassembled flute. 'How the heck . . . ?'

'Take the bit with the lump with the hole in it, and put it in the long bit . . . No, other end . . . That's it. Now take the short bit with the keys on and put it in the other end of the long bit . . . No, other way round.'

'How should it all line up?'

'Don't ask me – I'm just the drummer. It probably doesn't matter. Can you get a note out of it?'

Ellie had seen flutes being played and knew it was something like blowing across the top of a bottle. She knew how to do that. She tried it. The instrument emitted a mournful hoot.

Puddle tapped the drumsticks together. 'That's it,' she said, delightedly. 'Everybody ready? After four. One, two, three, four.'

Once again, the tuneless din began. It had vaguely the rhythm of the familiar French nursery rhyme, but none of the assembled – otherwise highly skilled – musicians was able to get anywhere close to the tune. Ellie tapped at the flute's keys and managed to change the pitch of the hooting. She was beginning to imagine that she was approaching something vaguely like the melody, but hysterical giggling from the rest of the band brought it all to a premature end before she could claim fully to have mastered it.

Katy was smiling, but was less amused than the musicians. 'Can we do something else now? Something I'm good at. How about charades?'

There were murmurs of agreement before Dunn played a perfect 'Shave and a Haircut' on the trombone. The others attempted the 'five bob' response, but it was as chaotic as before.

'Cheat!' said Puddle. 'You never said you could play the trombone.'

He stood and placed Benny's instrument carefully on the chair. 'You never asked.'

'It was implicit, sweetie. The idea was that we pick an instrument we can't play.'

'I can get a tune out of all of them,' he said with a smile. 'It's funny how many things you pick up if you live long enough.'

'Ten bob says you can't,' said Mickey.

'If you want to lose your money . . .'

'Talk is cheap, mate. Let's see the cash.'

Dunn fished in his pocket and produced ten shillings. He placed it on the lid of the piano. Mickey put his own pile of coins next to it.

'Mrs Maloney,' said Dunn, 'you're an independent. Do you know the "Colonel Bogey March"?'

'I do,' said Ellie. 'In D?'

Dunn thought for a moment. 'I think B flat would be easier on most of these idiot things. Any objections?'

'Sorry, mate,' said Mickey with a wicked grin. 'You said you could get a tune out of all of them. As written, if you'd be so kind.'

Dunn shrugged. 'D major, then, please, dearest Eleanora.'

'Your wish is my command,' she said, and sat down.

Dunn grabbed a saxophone. 'Ready when you are.'

Ellie played the two-bar introduction to the famous march, and then Dunn came in with the first phrase. He managed to swap to the clarinet for the second. Ellie slowed occasionally to allow him to rush from chair to chair, and by the end of the second verse he was sitting beside Ellie playing the tune as a duet on the piano. Ellie carried on playing while he hurried to the drum set and motioned politely for Puddle to vacate the stool. He sat down and rattled out a military-style accompaniment on the snare drum until Ellie reached a suitable stopping point.

He took a bow as his colleagues applauded.

Puddle was especially delighted. 'Why have you never let on that you can do that?'

'It's never come up.'

'I had no idea,' she said. 'Did you know he could do that, Skins?'

'Of course,' said Skins. 'I thought everybody knew. I was surprised Mickey made the bet, to be honest. Although, of course, now I know nobody had any idea, I'm disappointed in you, Barty boy. You should have raised the stakes a bit. All that talent for ten bob . . . Doesn't seem worth it.'

'I couldn't take all the poor lad's money – it wouldn't be fair,' said Dunn. 'I made a sacred vow only to use my powers for good.'

'Big of you,' said Mickey, handing over Dunn's winnings.

'Ta very much. Now, then – what are the teams for charades?'

Before anyone could answer, the chapel door opened and two footmen appeared.

'Hello, lads,' said Skins. 'Fancy a game of charades?'

'That's very kind of you, sir,' said the elder of the two, 'but we've been sent to speak to Mrs Cannon.'

'Katy,' called Skins. 'Two gentlemen here to see you.'

While Katy dealt with the footmen, Ellie took Skins and Dunn to one side. Quickly and concisely she recounted her conversation with Marianne.

'I'm still in two minds about her,' said Skins, when she had finished. 'On the one hand she loved him too much to bump him off. Even the . . . "dalliance" with Charlotte didn't put her off. But then again, if she really did love him, she'd have been broken by a betrayal like that. That sort of feeling can lead to murder.'

'And she could be lying, anyway,' said Dunn. 'If the new will is signed, she'd have every reason to get rid of him, take the money and do a bunk to the bright lights of London Town.'

'I didn't get the impression she was lying,' said Ellie. 'She seemed very sincere. The tears were real.'

'We really need to see this will everyone's going on about,' said Skins.

Dunn nodded. 'We need to get away later and search the study. Properly, this time.'

'But we can't all go,' said Skins. 'It'd be easier to keep it on the old QT if just one of us was in there.'

'I agree,' said Ellie. 'Who?'

'You'd probably have a better idea of what we're looking for,' said Dunn.

'I don't know about that. What do you think, Ivor?'

'You'd certainly know a will from a wedding invitation.'

'So would you, you idiot. Actually, why don't one of you do it. I'd quite like to hang around the family some more – see what else they might reveal.'

'You go, mate,' said Dunn. 'You like all that sneaking-about stuff.'

'Can't deny it. I'll slip out after dinner.'

'That's that settled, then,' said Ellie. 'But I think our presence is required in a game of charades for now. Come on.'

Teams had been organized and the game had begun, but there was a brief interruption when Katy told the band that if they packed their bags, the footmen would take everything up to the house. They would be sleeping in the guest rooms that night.

'Gamble?'

'Sounds like "gamble"? It's only one syllable, mate. How can it be "gamble"?'

'Oh, right. How about . . . Oh, oh, "bet". Sounds like "bet"?'

'Looks like it.'

'First syllable "ham", second syllable sounds like "bet"? What sounds like "bet", though? Wet? Set? Get? Met? Net? Fret?'

'Oh, for heaven's sake, Elk,' said Dunn. 'It's *Hamlet*.'

'Ohh,' said Elk. 'Of course. Wait, he said it was a play.'

'It's a play. Shakespeare.'

'Oh, right. Point to us, though, eh?'

'Point to us. Well done.'

Puddle got up to mime for her team, but before she could begin, the door opened yet again.

'Ah, good,' said Howard. 'Glad you're all here. Saves me traipsing about the place trying to round everyone up.'

'We're all here,' said Ellie. 'Are you OK, honey?'

'Why shouldn't I be?'

'Has no one told you?'

'About . . . ?'

'Oh,' said Ellie, going over to him. 'There's not an easy way to say it, I'm afraid. It might be best if you sit down. It's your friend Hetty, Howard. She's . . . Well, I'm sorry to have to tell you – we found her in her room a little while ago. Dead.'

Howard gaped for a moment, looking round at the sympathetic faces of the Dizzy Heights. 'Dead? How?'

'I'm afraid we don't know.'

'Oh my word. I need to tell her family. And poor Kenneth. He's an absolute ass, but he loved her.'

'Is there any news on when we'll be back in touch with the rest of the world?'

‘That was what I came to say. I’ve been out, and we’re still stuck – all the roads are completely impassable in every direction. The water levels have gone down since yesterday, but not by much. I fear we shan’t be able to get the car through to Partlow’s Ford until Tuesday—’

There were groans all round.

‘It can’t be helped,’ said Ellie. ‘We’ll just have to make the best of it. Is the phone working yet?’

‘Afraid not, no. Sorry to say we’re completely cut off for at least another day, but more likely two.’ Howard sat for a moment, staring blankly towards the vaulted ceiling of the chapel. At length, he lifted himself wearily from the arm of the sofa and quietly said, ‘I ought to be getting back to the house,’ before walking slowly back towards the door.

Once he had gone, Ellie pulled Skins and Dunn to one side.

‘Two murders,’ she said. ‘And unless we can work out what’s going on, the killer might have two more days to kill again.’

‘Steady on, Ells-Bells,’ said Skins. ‘There’s nothing to say they’ll kill again.’

‘No, but there’s nothing to say they won’t.’

‘I’ve been thinking about it, though,’ said Skins. ‘I mean, we reckon someone killed John over the will. Or some family thing at the very least. But Hetty was just a weekend guest. A friend of a friend. Why would anyone kill her?’

‘Remember what Lady H told us when we were trying to work out what was going on at Tipsy Harry’s?’ said Dunn. ‘She reckons there are only three motives for murder – passion, money and covering up another crime. So . . . Howard could have been in love with her and killed her out of jealousy because she was in love with his mate. Money . . . money . . . No, I’ve got nothing on money. But what if she saw something? What if she suspected one of them of killing John? Subtly covering up the first murder with the mysterious death of a dangerous witness would fit.'

'It would,' agreed Ellie. 'And that means they might kill again. If anyone else saw something, they'd be next.'

Dunn smiled. 'If you're looking at it like that, we could be next. If the killer gets wind of our suspicions, *we* might wake up dead.'

'Then we need to be swift and circumspect. We need to figure out what the heck is going on and not let anyone know what we're up to.'

'Anyone else,' Skins corrected her. 'Veronica already knows.'

'We're all in trouble if it's her,' said Dunn.

Ellie shook her head. 'It's not her. The double bluff just doesn't fit. She's being too helpful. She'd be steering us in the wrong direction if it were her. She's just agreed with every request we've made.'

'Until we make a request that'll lead us to the truth. Then it's good night, Dizzy Heights.'

'You're a Gloomy Gus, Barty Dunn. Didn't you see how shaken she was when we found Hetty?'

'That may be, but better a Gloomy Gus than a Murdered Marvin. We've got to get cracking. You've got to find that will this evening, mate.'

Skins made a face. 'What if I find it and it doesn't tell us anything?'

'That very fact will tell us something, surely?' said Ellie. 'It'll help us rule some people out.'

'I'll find it,' said Skins. 'You just make sure no one comes looking for me.'

'Don't worry, honey, we'll keep you safe. We'll run interference back in the dining room.'

Dunn looked blankly at her.

'American "football" term, mate,' said Skins. 'You'll be responsible for blocking the running whatsanames and . . . doing something to the quarterbloke. Or something. Just keep the Bilvertons out of the study.'

'That sounds easy enough,' said Dunn. 'What shall we do till dinner?'

'I'm going to read my book,' said Ellie.

'I was going to have a quick kip,' said Skins.

'I'll have to find someone else to play with, then,' said Dunn.

Ellie patted his arm. 'Attaboy. Play nice, now. We'll call you in at dinnertime.'

# Chapter Ten

The Bilvertons dressed for dinner, and the Dizzies wore their dinner suits. In spite of everything, the atmosphere in the dining room that evening was reasonably jovial, no doubt helped by the generous amount of drink that had found its way to the table. John Bilverton had kept an impressive cellar and Gordon was an unstinting host, so the wine flowed and the conversation with it.

They had broken up into their usual groups, with Ellie, Skins and Dunn chatting once more with Veronica. She was a keen observer of other people's characteristics and foibles, with a gift for describing them in a way that was funny without being cruel. She had a wealth of stories about the family, their friends, the staff, the people in Partlow's Ford, the children at her school, their parents, the other teachers . . .

Skins, though, was only half paying attention. He'd been watching the comings and goings as people excused themselves from the table, and was on the lookout for the right moment to get up and go snooping. He reasoned that at some point everyone would be sufficiently engrossed in their own conversations that they wouldn't notice if someone got up and didn't come back for a while. Then he would slink out.

Veronica noticed his inattention. 'Are you still with us, Mr Skins?'

'What? Oh, yes, sorry. Just a bit distracted. Nothing personal.'

'As long as you're well.'

'Right as rain,' said Skins with a smile. He looked around. 'Would you excuse me for a moment, though?'

Veronica returned his smile and nodded her assent.

Smoothly and without further fuss or fanfare, he stood up and left the dining room. He didn't look back.

They had been sitting near the door to the salon, so he had to take the long way round to get to the hall. The advantage, he decided, was that he'd only have to walk along one side of the echoing hall to get to the study in the corner. It shouldn't make too much difference, and no one would be listening for footsteps anyway, but he felt safer as he walked beneath the gallery on the balls of his feet. He would have preferred to describe his progress as 'stealthy' rather than 'tiptoeing', but he couldn't help feeling that he must look as comical as his children did as they tried to sneak undetected past the dining room at home when they were supposed to be upstairs in bed.

He reached the study and pushed the door open, looking again at the battered, black-painted lock with its scratched screws and the splintered door jamb as he closed it behind him. The key was still in the lock, and he was reminded once more that they were chasing a murderer who couldn't possibly have committed the crime. He stared at the lock, wondering how anyone could shoot John in a locked room, then leave without the three women outside seeing anything, and all while the door remained so firmly locked that the women had to break in.

He realized with a shock that he'd been standing there gawping at the door for a few minutes. He was there to find a will. A will, he remembered, that might not even exist.

'Now then,' Skins said quietly to himself, 'if I were an imaginary will, where would I be?'

He scanned the bookshelves on either side of the fireplace and, as expected, found them to be almost entirely filled with books. There was one shelf of box files all neatly labelled 'Household', and a quick inspection revealed that the first two held invoices and receipts for maintenance work carried out on the house. Opening the others, Skins saw that they all contained assorted domestic papers. It was possible John might have stashed a will in there, but it didn't seem likely. A will was personal – this was all just household stuff.

He put the last one back and looked at them again. As well as saying 'Household', the labels all had a date range and they were not in the right order. It could be that John had been slapdash, but the books on the shelves above were neatly ordered by subject and author. It seemed more likely to Skins that someone else had been through the files and had been careless about putting them back.

He turned his attention to the desk. When he'd explored the room with Ellie and Dunn the previous evening he'd quickly scanned the desk, and noted that John's pen was lying on top of a pile of papers. It was still there, exactly as he'd last seen it, so he judged it less likely that anyone else had moved it. Carefully noting the position of the pen and its cap, he lifted them clear and scanned the topmost document. It was something legal, but not a will. He riffled through the rest; they were all incomprehensible court papers. There were several manila folders, each containing what appeared to be John's handwritten notes on cases he'd recently been involved in at the magistrates' court. Skins noted the names on the files, but none of them seemed significant.

The two desk drawers were unlocked. They contained new notebooks, some ink and a few other odds and ends of stationery, but no papers. There were two screwdrivers in the right-hand drawer, as well as an old rag and a cleaning rod. Skins recognized the familiar smell of gun oil – this was obviously where John had kept the pistol that now sat on the corner of the desk.

He looked around. There was nothing else on the shelves except some framed photographs. On the chimneypiece there was a cricket ball on a wooden stand and what appeared to be a trophy in the form of a gilded biscuit. He got up and inspected them. The ball was to commemorate taking the winning wicket in a staff cricket match, while the trophy had been awarded by a local magazine in 1920 for 'Best Biscuit Product'.

Skins sat back in John's chair. The room was lived in, but it wasn't chaotic. Nothing was especially neat, but there was order. There were no random piles of tat. He could see no hiding place he might have overlooked. He leaned back.

'Where the bleedin' 'ell did you pu' it, you old codger?'

Skins had worked hard since he met Ellie in 1910 to lose his accent. Or at least to soften it a bit.

'She's wealthy, ain't she?' he'd said to Dunn after his first meeting with her at Weston-super-Mare. 'Refined and that. She won't want no gorblimey little bloke from norf London. She hangs about with toffs and la-di-das.'

In moments of stress, though, or private contemplation, his north London accent came shining through.

He leaned back a little further, still pondering the location of the alleged will.

There was a heart-jolting moment as the chair overbalanced and began to topple backwards. Skins reached out and grabbed the desk and just about managed to stop himself from falling.

Heart still pounding, he sat upright for a moment, contemplating the potential embarrassment of having fallen off the chair and knocked himself unconscious while snooping about in the dead man's study. Lucky he had those catlike reflexes and was able to grab the desk in time, he thought. He relived the almost-fall in his head. The thrill of the moment when gravity got the better of him, the sudden grab, the feel of the underside of the desk . . .

The underside of the desk didn't feel at all how he'd expected it to.

He reached out and ran his fingers along the wood. What was odd about it? What had he—?

He pushed the button and a secret drawer sprang open.

Inside there were yet more files and loose papers, including one document headed 'Last Will & Testament'.

He opened it up and began reading.

◆ ◆ ◆

Skins returned to the dining table and sat down with as little ceremony as possible.

'Hi, honey,' said Ellie. 'How lovely to have you back.'

'Of course it is – I'm a lovely bloke. Was I missed?'

'Not for a second.'

'Oh. I'm not sure how I feel about that. I expected at least one person to look up from their mutton cutlet and say, "Where's old Skins gone? It's just not the same without him."'

'I missed you terribly, of course.'

'Well, that goes without saying.'

Dunn sighed and shook his head. 'You two are quite sickening sometimes, you know.'

'You tell us often,' said Skins. 'Where's Veronica?'

'Call of nature. Did you find anything?'

'Many things,' said Skins. 'Things of wonder. Things to amaze and delight kings and princes. Things—'

'Skins, mate?'

'Yes?'

'Did you find the will?'

'I found books, household bills, pens, paper, stationery, a cricket trophy, another trophy in the shape of a gilded biscuit, a—'

'I *will* kill you. Did. You. Find. The. Will?'

'I found a secret drawer in the desk' – he held up his hand to forestall Dunn's protest – 'inside which was a brand-new will.'

'Good work,' said Ellie. 'What did it say? What was he leaving them?'

'I haven't the foggiest,' said Skins.

Ellie made a face. 'How can you not know? Didn't you read it?'

'I know exactly what he *planned* to leave them – it was a few grand and an interest in the biscuit company for our Veronica, for instance – but the will was unsigned. Whatever they're all actually getting will be in the older version, and that wasn't there.'

Ellie harrumphed.

'It was all pretty much as everyone's been saying, though,' said Skins. 'Marianne was going to get the house and a big share in the business, so if Gordon was expecting to get the lot he would have been badly disappointed. Elizabeth was getting cash and jewellery, but not much of either. Howard was getting nothing. John specifically mentions that he was excluding Howard in a lengthy paragraph about the boy's many failings – it would have been an uncomfortable moment at the reading. Meanwhile, Malcolm would have got some cash and some keepsakes, as well as a guarantee that he'd be able to operate Bilver-Tone Records from the chapel no matter who owned the house. Marianne had to agree to that as a condition of getting the place. There was a lot of other guff about what would happen if she refused, and who'd get it then and . . . To be honest I didn't pay a lot of attention to the details. There was a lot of "thereinafter" and "heretofore" and "notwithstanding" – I glazed over a bit. But then it got back on track. There were a few other bequests to people I didn't know, but that was about the stretch of it.'

'No real surprises, though,' said Dunn. 'It's pretty much what everyone has been saying. So where does all this leave our list of suspects?'

Ellie thought for a moment. 'I'd say it rules Gordon out, and Marianne back in. If Gordon wasn't getting as much under the new will, he'd want time to work on his pa, try to change his mind. Killing him would do him no good. Whereas Marianne stood to get a fortune as soon as John copped it.'

'But what if they knew it hadn't been signed yet?' said Dunn. 'Everyone assumes Gordon got the lion's share under the old will. If he knew the new one hadn't been signed, he'd want to bump the old boy off before he could scribble away his inheritance. Same for Marianne, but the other way round. She'd want to keep him alive until the fortune was hers and *then* do him in.'

'It rules Howard in, either way,' said Skins. 'If he knew it was unsigned, he'd protect whatever he got in the original. But if he thought it was signed, he knew John was prepared to publicly disown him. Money or revenge – both good motives.'

'On the whole, then, it looks like the new will tells us nothing,' said Ellie. 'But well done for finding it, Ivor.'

'Thank you kindly, ma'am,' said Skins. 'Just doin' my job.'

'You've known me for fifteen years and that's the best American accent you can do?'

'I thought it sounded just like you.'

Ellie huffed. 'Did you? Did you really? And who says, "Thank you kindly, ma'am," anyhow?'

'I read it in a Western,' said Skins.

'It was pretty dreadful, mate,' said Dunn.

'You do better, then, go on.'

Veronica sat back down and took a sip of her champagne. 'Better at what?'

'An American accent,' said Skins.

'Oh, I'm hopeless at accents. I can just about do Oxford, but you'd expect that.'

'From all your wild nights out at the local nightclubs?' asked Dunn.

'Heavens, no. I seldom go out. Not for want of wanting, mind you – I should love to get out more. There's something about this stifling place that saps the life out of one and I never seem to get round to it. Even when we're not flooded in, I feel so trapped. Oh, but perhaps I've inherited enough to get me out. Actually, do you know what? Why don't I get out anyway? I sometimes think I'd rather sleep in my classroom than spend any more time here.'

'Don't take one of the cots from the chapel, though,' said Ellie.

'Are they not the comfiest?'

'You can only begin to imagine. I was telling these two earlier that I seriously wondered if the floor would be more comfortable.'

'We're such terrible hosts. I'm so sorry. I'll see if we can do something about it.'

'You're very sweet, but two burly footmen arrived in the chapel this afternoon to take our bags up to the . . . second floor?'

Veronica laughed. 'The second floor, yes.'

'Where I grew up that would be the third floor.'

'Which would be logical, but also terribly, terribly wrong.'

'Ivor has tried to explain it many times and it still makes no sense. But Marianne arranged for us to be moved into the guest rooms, so we're going to be fine.'

'I'm so pleased. Have you had any more thoughts about' – she looked around to see who might overhear – 'the case?'

'No,' said Skins. 'We keep coming back to the same list of suspects in the same order.'

'What about me?' asked Veronica. 'Where do I fit into your list of suspects?'

'Way down at the bottom,' said Dunn.

'That's hardly fair. Why not me?'

'Did you kill him?'

'No.'

'There you go, then.'

'I could be lying.'

'You could, but you've got no real motive. And you were with Ellie when he was shot.'

'Actually, I was with Betty in the kitchens.'

'Did she do it?'

'No, but—'

'That rules you both out, then. She's got no motive, either. If she didn't want him dead you'd be an idiot to rely on her as an alibi. She'd shop you in a heartbeat.'

'She might have wanted him dead, too.'

'Did she?'

'I don't know. Maybe over that business with Peter?'

Dunn laughed. 'The mysterious business with Peter. All right, then, you're in it together and you're both back on the list.'

'I just want to be treated fairly, that's all. You can't claim to be proper detectives if you're going to exclude people from your investigations just because you like them.'

'Who said we like you?'

'Everybody likes me once they get used to me. I turn out to be delightful.'

Dunn laughed again.

Ellie was distracted by something at the other end of the table. Charlotte and Marianne were deep in earnest conversation. It didn't seem heated or antagonistic, but it was definitely very intense. She was about to nudge Skins to point them out to him, but at that moment Marianne rose from the table, put down her napkin and swept out of the room. She was the only one of the family who had opted to dress in mourning and her long black evening gown gave her sudden departure an air of intriguing elegance.

Before Ellie could say anything, they were interrupted by the arrival on their side of the table of Howard, bearing a fresh bottle of champagne.

'I'm so frightfully bored of that lot over there,' he said. 'I've come to spend some time with our more glamorous guests. Budge up, Ronnie. Make some room.'

Howard settled himself between Ellie and Veronica and refilled everyone's glasses. Ellie wondered if he had any idea what his father had written about him in his will.

'How are you feeling, honey?' asked Ellie.

Howard shrugged. 'Honestly? Rather more upset than I would have expected, but the champagne helps. I'm dreading having to tell Kenny, but I'm spared that terrible duty for another day or two. Can't work out if that's worse, mind you. Might be better to get it done.'

'The waiting's often worse,' agreed Skins. 'That was the bit that always got to me in the trenches.'

Howard smiled. 'Another chap with a wealth of war stories, eh? You and Uncle Malcolm would get along swimmingly.'

'They don't talk about it much,' said Ellie. 'If at all.'

'That's because no one could possibly ever want to listen to our boring war stories,' said Dunn.

Howard raised his glass. 'To boring war stories.'

Ellie, Skins and Dunn joined the toast.

'I was brought up on boring war stories,' continued Howard. 'Uncle Malcolm never tired of regaling anyone who would sit still long enough with tales of his daredevil exploits.'

'Tired?' said Ellie. 'Past tense? He doesn't do it any more?'

'No. By the time he retired he'd lost his passion for it. Talks endlessly about bally music now.'

'We can do that, too, if you like,' said Dunn.

'That's awfully kind of you, but I think I'll pass, thank you. But how are you all coping under these unfortunate circs? What have you been up to?'

'Oh, you know,' said Skins. 'Just mooching about the place. Veronica gave us the tour.'

'I thought I saw you trooping about. I hope she didn't bore you too much.'

'Not in the least,' said Ellie. 'You have a lovely home.'

'Did you find the priest hole?'

'Don't tease me, Howie,' said Veronica. 'There's one here, I know there is.'

'I think it's exciting,' said Skins. 'We got involved in some business with secret treasure in Mayfair a few weeks ago. I might have found a new hobby. I could become a finder of secret rooms.'

'I did all the work there, honey,' said Ellie. 'Maybe it should be *my* new hobby.'

'Fair enough. It can be a family thing. We can do it together. Oh, and we can send the kids into the nooks and crannies we can't get to.'

'Mayfair?' said Howard. 'Not that business at Tipsy Harry's? That was you?'

'It was us,' said Skins, proudly. 'We got 'em bang to rights. Joint effort. Us, the rest of the band and the rozzers.'

'I say. Well done, you.'

'So you know a thing or two about finding hidden rooms, then,' said Veronica.

'Ells-Bells does, certainly,' said Skins.

'Only I'm stumped. I mean, completely stymied. I swear I've looked absolutely everywhere, really I have.'

Ellie smiled. 'What makes you so sure there's a priest hole here?'

Howard grimaced. 'Honestly, Ellie darling, don't get her started. We'll be here hours.'

'No, I'm as interested as Ivor,' she said. 'You keep mentioning this secret room, but we've never given you a chance to talk about it properly.'

'Up till now you've made entirely the right decision,' said Howard. 'She absolutely must not be allowed to bore new friends with wild tales of priests and their secret holes.'

'She absolutely must,' said Ellie with a laugh. 'Go ahead, honey – bore away.'

'Well,' began Veronica. 'Our story begins in 1572 when John Mattingly, the eighth Baron Elsfield, lived in this very house.'

'I thought it was Georgian,' said Ellie.

Veronica nodded. 'The present house was built in 1793, but there's been a manor house here since the 1300s. Now, Lord Elsfield was a Catholic, and under Good Queen Bess, that was a frightfully dangerous thing to be.'

She was warming to her role of storyteller. Howard was rolling his eyes and pouring more champagne.

'The chapel where you've been staying was used for Catholic mass, and Lord Elsfield had a priest hole built within the house to hide his father confessor should the authorities come calling. Which they did. More than once. But the family refused to recant their faith and soon fell from favour. Their land was forfeited to the Crown and the house was bought and sold several times over the next two hundred years, with many additions and changes made to the building. Then it was bought by Charles Hopson, a local brewer with links to the East India Company, who decided to completely rebuild the old house. He left the chapel where it stood, but he wanted to impress his friends with his modern tastes, so he had the original house completely demolished and rebuilt it as you see it now. But he loved the idea of the priest hole, so he had a new one incorporated—'

'So the rumour goes,' interrupted Howard.

But Veronica was not to be deterred. 'So he had a new one incorporated into his design.'

'But no one has ever found it?' said Ellie.

'It would be somewhat tricky for anyone to find it,' said Howard, 'what with it not actually existing.'

'It would be fantastic, though, wouldn't it?' said Skins. 'I mean, it would solve the conundrum of your father's death, for one. And it would be . . . well, priest holes and secret passages are so "old house", aren't they? I wonder if we've got any at our gaff.'

'You're not to go looking,' said Ellie. 'And you're not to encourage the children, either.'

Skins grinned. 'I'll just have to see what we can find here, then, won't I? I've got to say, though, Howard might have a point – I mean, it's a long shot, isn't it? You've lived here . . . how long?'

'I was almost two when we moved in,' said Veronica. 'I don't remember living anywhere else.'

'So you've been here all your life, near as dammit, and you've never found it. It's not really likely there is one, is it?'

'You see, Ronnie?' said Howard. 'I love you dearly, but even when you meet new friends who have every reason to indulge you out of sheer politeness, they apologetically explain that you're a loony.'

'I certainly wouldn't say that,' said Skins. 'But you must have been over every inch of the place by now.'

Veronica harrumphed. 'Well, I don't care what any of you say. There's a priest hole here and one day I'm going to find it.'

'Let me know when you do,' said Skins. 'I want to see it.'

There was movement on the other side of the table.

'We're all off to the salon for a sing-song,' said Mickey. 'You coming?'

'Just try and stop us,' said Howard.

◆ ◆ ◆

Ellie was puzzled by the party mood. The head of the household, as far as they knew, had taken his own life. A house guest had died in mysterious circumstances. And here they all were about to enjoy an evening of songs and music as though nothing had happened. All of them apart from Marianne, that is, who had not returned to the table. Her behaviour, at least, was easy to understand. Or most of her behaviour. Ellie still couldn't quite work out why Marianne seemed to have such a cordial relationship with Charlotte, but everything else about her made sense. As for the rest of them, though, they seemed decidedly odd to her. Suspicious, even. But then again, perhaps it was yet another English thing she would never understand.

Puddle was judged the most capable pianist – much to Eustace's annoyance – and had ensconced herself at the piano. She played a few exploratory chords and pronounced the instrument more than satisfactory.

'I could never be truly comfortable in a house where they don't look after their piano properly,' she said. 'I was worried what it might be like, what with it living in here in this sunny room—'

Veronica smiled, and winked at Ellie.

'—but this is splendid.' She played a little more. 'So, come on, then – let's be having you. Who's first?'

The Bilvertons nudged each other shyly, but no one volunteered.

'I'll give you one,' said Benny.

He had a brief, whispered conversation with Puddle.

'You want something they can join in with,' she said. 'But something familiar to all of them. They're not the hippest crowd, so . . .'

'Gilbert and Sullivan?' suggested Benny.

'Perfect. Do you know "I Am a Pirate King"?'

'It's a role I was born to play. We're all pirates at heart in the West Indies.'

Puddle played the introduction and Benny's mellifluous baritone brought the role of the Pirate King to life in a country house in Oxfordshire. They had chosen well, and the entire Bilverton clan joined in with 'Hurrah for the Pirate King' at the appropriate moments.

With the ice well and truly broken, Puddle had to turn from chivvying them along to trying to persuade them to keep quiet and take their turn. Over the course of the next hour or so, everyone joined in with the singing while Eustace, Veronica, Charlotte and Elizabeth all took a turn at the piano.

Skins leaned over and whispered into Ellie's ear. 'Elizabeth told me she could "just about peck out a tune". She's a damn sight better than she makes out.'

'It's that English understatement thing you all do,' she whispered back. 'I swear I'll never understand it if I live to be a million years old.'

'It doesn't do to be too full of yourself – no one likes a show-off.'

Ellie tutted but said nothing further. Instead she cast her eye about the room to see how the family were grouped. There was little to surprise her.

Howard, as usual, was with Veronica, and they were giggling together like naughty children. Uncle Malcolm and his niece Elizabeth were deep in some earnest conversation Ellie couldn't quite hear. She thought she heard the words 'factory' and 'house' but it probably wasn't anything suspicious – the consequences of

John's death were on everyone's mind, so of course they'd be talking about the future of both the family business and the family home. Gordon Bilverton was telling Peter a joke, and from the few words Ellie had heard so far, it was a filthy one. If it was the one she was thinking of, she vaguely remembered the punchline and hadn't found it nearly as amusing as Skins had. Nor, it seemed, as amusing as Peter did – he roared with laughter and almost threw his brandy over himself in his delight.

Ellie nudged Skins.

He frowned and mouthed, 'What?'

'Did you see Marianne and Charlotte at the dinner table?'

Skins was puzzled by the change of direction. 'Can't say I did. Why?'

'They were sitting next to each other.'

'It's a big table, love, but sooner or later you're going to end up sitting next to everyone.'

'But Charlotte was furgling Marianne's husband. You wouldn't expect them to sit together.'

'Well, when you put it as delicately as that . . .' He grinned.

'If I'd had an affair with Elk, would you sit next to him at dinner?'

Skins laughed. 'Is that likely?'

'Hardly. But do you see what I mean? It doesn't make sense. They've been almost pally.'

'I think you're seeing stuff that isn't there. We don't know whether they were friends before. Maybe they got past the whole furgling thing.'

'I still think it's suspicious.'

The mood was fully relaxed now, and there was a lot of movement as people nipped discreetly out and returned a few minutes later looking a great deal more comfortable.

Mickey was clearly enjoying himself and seemed worried that the party might break up.

'Anyone else for a turn on the old Joanna?' he called. 'What about you, Mrs M? You play lovely – we've heard you.'

Ellie put down her gin and stood up. 'Well, if you insist.' She walked slightly unsteadily to the piano and sat down, swaying a little. 'I think someone put something in my drink.'

This got the laugh she'd been hoping for.

'Now, what can I play for you lovely ladies and gentlemen?' she said. 'Something from the Old Country? I can do you "Yankee Doodle"? "Home on the Range"? Oh, who knows "Camptown Races"?' She played a few bars. 'No, wait, I've got it. "He'd Have to Get Under". Help me out, boys and girls.'

She launched into the intro and Puddle dutifully joined in with the opening verse in her beautiful contralto voice. By the time they reached the chorus, the whole room was singing about how poor Johnny O'Connor had to get out and get under to fix up his little machine.

The mood was extremely jolly by now, and Ellie no longer had to feign drunkenness to keep them on her side. She had decided to accept the oddly cheerful mood as some sort of defence against the horrors of the weekend and had thrown herself enthusiastically into a selection of popular tunes which made the mood jollier still.

After a particularly spirited rendition of 'McNamara's Band', she spotted Malcolm returning to the room, having been the latest one to be absent for a couple of minutes.

Howard noticed him. 'You've been terribly quiet so far, Uncle M,' he said. 'Come on. Do your party piece. You know you want to.'

Malcolm grinned. 'My party piece, you say?' he said loudly.

'Yes,' chorused the family.

'I should give you a little song, d'you think?'

'Yes, Uncle Malcs,' said Veronica. 'Do the song.'

The other Bilvertons joined in. 'Sing the song.'

With a theatrical flourish, Malcolm approached Ellie at the piano.

'Do you know "Modern Major General"?' he asked quietly.

'I think Puddle's your girl for Gilbert and Sullivan,' she said. 'Puddle, honey, can we prevail upon you for your D'Oyly Carte expertise?'

Puddle resumed her seat at the piano, and after a brief consultation with the singer, began to play.

The Bilvertons were giggling and nudging each other, and Ellie was wondering what the gag might be. But as soon as Malcolm opened his mouth, she knew.

He was awful. Truly, ear-shatteringly, teeth-grindingly dreadful. He had the words down pat, and the performance was gleefully exuberant, but he was entirely unable to get anywhere even close to the melody.

The Bilvertons were in fits. Malcolm, meanwhile, pretended not to understand what all the fuss was about and continued to bellow tunelessly.

He finished to rapturous applause from the family and the band, but instead of sitting back down, went straight into an equally terrible rendition of 'Tit Willow'.

By the time he'd finished, Howard and Veronica were wiping their eyes.

Gordon stood up and raised his hands for silence. 'On that note—'

'Which note?' called Howard. 'He didn't hit a single one.'

'On those many delightful notes,' continued Gordon, 'I think it's about time I turned in. Goodnight, everyone.'

He left.

'I'd quite like to call it a night,' said Ellie. 'Do you mind?'

'Not at all,' said Skins. 'I'll join you. Any of you lot coming?'

'Oh, don't go,' said Malcolm. 'The party's just getting started.'

'I'll stay up for a bit,' said Elk.

'Me too,' said Vera.

'I'll keep you all company,' said Dunn.

'Well, if they're staying,' said Puddle, 'it would be rude to leave them without a decent pianist.'

'That's the spirit,' said Malcolm eagerly. 'Let the old fuddy-duddies take to their beds. We'll party till dawn.'

Ellie and Skins, though, set off towards the second floor and a more comfortable night's sleep.

They only had to climb up two floors, but the journey seemed much longer at the end of the day. Skins was used to late nights, but the increasingly alarming circumstances surrounding their stay at Bilverton House were making him wearier than usual.

As they plodded along the first-floor gallery, it belatedly occurred to him that they had no idea where they were going.

'How will we know which is our room?' he said. 'We've not even been up there.'

'If the worst comes to the worst, we can just try every door until we find our bags. It's not like we're going to be disturbing anyone – they're all downstairs singing.'

They arrived at the top of the stairs and looked out on to the second-floor landing. The carpet running along the centre of the corridor was the same as on the floor below, and the walls were painted the same shade of pale green. There was no view down into the hall, though, just a wall hung with more paintings.

There was something else pinned to the wall opposite the staircase. In what they presumed was Veronica's neat hand, it said, 'Dizzy Heights Luxury Accommodation – This Way'. Underneath was a list of the band members' names with arrows indicating the quickest route to their rooms.

They turned to the left and found the door labelled 'Mr and Mrs Maloney' at the end of the corridor.

'Isn't John and Marianne's room below us?' asked Skins.

Ellie turned the handle. 'Yes. Looks like we got the luxury suite.'

They went inside.

As with the rest of the house, the furniture was old but not shabby. Skins surprised himself by recognizing its style.

'Nice Georgian furniture,' he said. 'Must be worth a few bob.'

Ellie was no less surprised. 'How on earth do you know that?'

'My Uncle Billy had a junk shop. See all that dark wood? Walnut, that is. And look at the elegant curves. The marquetry inlays on that chest of drawers. Typical Georgian. And see that sofa down the end – all spindly legs and high arms? Definitely made for looking at, not for sitting on.'

Ellie smiled. 'You have hidden depths, Ivor Maloney.'

'This bed is a bit of all right, though.'

He flopped down on to the huge bed. Its sturdy wooden frame was of the same dark wood as the chest of drawers, with the same skilful inlays.

'I'm disappointed by Veronica's flimsy story about the priest hole,' said Ellie as they settled into bed in the darkness. 'I honestly thought that would explain John's murder.'

'She said she's never searched the study, though. There might be one there. I'm still going to look for it.'

'Of course you are, honey. You wouldn't be you if you didn't.'

He smiled in the darkness and the faint clicking sound of his lips moving against his teeth made Ellie smile, too.

'You know I can't see you smiling, right?' she said.

'But you know me well enough to know I am.'

'I do. Malcolm is a hoot, isn't he?'

'Not half. I would have put money on a bloke so obsessed with music being able to at least sing in tune. I don't know where he gets his confidence from.'

'It's a class thing, I bet. Don't they teach that sort of thing at your public schools?'

'Confidence? No idea. Probably. The officers I met were never short of it. Some you wouldn't trust to lace up their own boots, but they'd arse it up with such confidence they'd make you think you were the stupid one.'

'And what were Charlotte and Marianne doing?'

'Chatting.'

'Yes, but—'

'Ells-Bells?'

'Yes, honey.'

'Go to sleep.'

# Chapter Eleven

***Monday, 29 June 1925***

Skins woke to the rattling of a teacup on its saucer.

'Rise and shine, little drummer boy,' said Ellie.

'Blimey, Ells. You made me tea? That's lovely of you.'

'I'd like to take the credit, but I wandered down to the kitchens and once they'd got over the shock of having a guest in their midst, they made me some tea. The butler guy – Dunsworth – offered to send someone up with it but I stood my ground. Actually I sat my ground. I had what you would have described as "a good old chinwag" at the kitchen table. Mrs Radway, the cook, is lovely. And young Lily the kitchen maid is perfectly charming once she gets past her shyness. And she makes great tea, apparently. She loves jazz. You guys should go say hello.'

'We should. Was there any gossip?'

'Nothing we haven't already heard from Veronica.'

'Did they notice anything odd on Saturday when John died?'

'I was going to ask but I didn't want to be too obvious about it. I want to gain their trust a bit before I go in like Ellie of the Yard with my notebook and my questions.'

'Fair dos. It's Monday, isn't it?'

'It is. We have twenty-four hours. Maybe a little more.'

'Until we can go home?'

'Yes.' She put her hand to her mouth. 'Oh.'

'Oh?'

'The lawyers are coming on Wednesday. What if we're not back in time?'

'Surely they'll make allowances – the flood will be in the papers.'

'Oh, sure, but my father's will was quite specific. Once a year we have to satisfy them we're happily married, that we're not behaving irresponsibly and that you're not squandering my allowance. Being stranded away from home at a party and leaving the children with Nanny is hardly responsible.'

'We'll be fine,' said Skins. 'We can sweet-talk them if it comes to it.'

'I guess. So now we just have to find out who the murderer is without getting ourselves killed.'

Skins sat up and picked up the cup of tea from the bedside table. 'Well, there's that little obstacle, yes.'

'I hope the children are OK.'

'Nanny Nora will keep them entertained. They probably won't even notice we're not there.'

'That's even worse. I hate not being able to let people know where we are and that we're safe.'

'Just imagine how people got on before telephones.'

'Before telephones they wouldn't be sixty miles from home and stuck in a country house with a murderer. They'd have trotted to the local market in their horse and cart and would be back in time for supper. They'd not need to telephone anyone because they'd almost always be at home.'

Skins sipped his tea. 'You make a good point, my love – and Lily does make a cracking cup of char, by the way – but fretting about it isn't going to mend the phone lines.'

'Fretting about Lily's tea-making skills?' she said with a wink. 'No, that won't get the phones reconnected.'

'That really is annoying, isn't it? You must hate it when I do that.'

'It really is. But you're right about the phone lines. They'll be fixed when they're fixed, and no amount of worrying will make it happen quicker. You're becoming very wise.'

'It's old age,' he said. 'Give it a couple more years and I'll be sitting on a mountain top with a long grey beard and adoring acolytes at my feet.'

'Adoring acolytes, eh?'

'Besotted with me, they'll be.'

'I'm sure they will.'

'Such will be my fame that they'll come from far and wide to hear my words of wisdom.'

'Proud of you, honey. Now put on some pants and we can have breakfast.'

'Will I ever persuade you to say "trousers"?'

'Nope. I love the way everyone's eyes goggle when I talk about their pants.'

'I'll be as quick as I can.'

◆ ◆ ◆

Most of the rest of the band were already in the dining room. After helping themselves to heaping plates of food from the sideboard, Skins and Ellie settled themselves at the table.

'Morning, all,' said Skins. 'Just us lot for breakfast, then? Where's the family?'

Mickey attempted an impersonation of Dunsworth the butler. 'Some members of the family are taking breakfast in their rooms, sir.'

'Are they, by gawd? How the other half lives, eh? Why don't we have breakfast in bed, Ells?'

'I brought you a cup of tea,' she said. 'What more do you want?'

'Fair dos. Any coffee in the pot?'

'Only if you want it black, I'm afraid,' said Eustace.

'I quite like black coffee,' said Skins.

'Me, too,' said Ellie. 'Have we run out of milk? We had some in our tea earlier.'

Mickey looked up from his scrambled eggs. 'I think you might have got in just before rationing started. Mrs Whatsherface, the cook, said the milkman hasn't been able to get here since Friday. They're going to have to eke it out, apparently – there's not much left and she needs most of it for cooking. Black coffee, and lemon in your tea from now on.'

'We'd send Elk out to see if there were any cows on the estate,' said Puddle. 'But . . . well . . . you know how the chicken thing turned out.'

'I told you before,' said Elk. 'I grew up in New Cross. We didn't have chickens. Or bleedin' cows.'

Dunn walked in. 'It doesn't matter, mate. If there were cows that needed milking, someone would have done it by now. Can't leave cows unmilked for a whole weekend.'

'Hello, Barty boy,' said Skins. 'Sleep well?'

'Like a baby. Actually, no, not like a baby at all. I've been at your gaff when your two were babies. They wake up every couple of hours and scream the place down.'

Benny was tucking into some sausages. 'How's the investigation coming along?'

Ellie quickly ran through everything they'd learned so far.

'Blimey,' said Benny. 'You've not been letting the grass grow, have you?'

'It doesn't sound like you're any closer to working it out, though,' said Eustace.

'It just seems to be getting more and more confusing,' agreed Ellie. 'What about you guys? Have you noticed anything odd?'

'Like what?' said Benny.

'Oh, you know – conversations that don't make sense, people acting strange?'

'Nothing I can think of,' said Benny.

'That Peter's a bit oily,' said Puddle, with a shudder. 'And I overheard Gordon and Charlotte having the fiercest row before dinner last night, but that's all. I didn't catch any details, and nothing came of it – she just went off and sat next to Marianne.'

Katy took two slices of toast from a rack on the table and buttered one of them. 'I've got to be honest, I'm still wondering why you don't just leave it to the authorities. I mean, even if you really believe they were both murdered, why not just let the professionals deal with it?'

'Once the doctor has signed the death certificates,' said Dunn, 'the police won't question it, the coroner won't question it, and they'll get written up as a tragic suicide and an equally tragic accident.'

'And why would that be so bad? It's not your job. It's not your family. It's not your problem.'

'Seriously?' said Puddle. 'You think someone should just get away with murder because it's too much trouble to catch them?'

'Well, no. But, I mean, what actual difference does it make to any of us if some jumped-up biscuit merchant knocks off their old man? They're not going to kill again, are they? You're not protecting society from some evil maniac, are you?'

'We think they have killed again, though,' said Ellie. 'I don't think Hetty's death was an accident. Someone drugged her.'

'Like they drugged us,' said Puddle, in a sudden panic.

'No, I think you drugged yourselves – it was light-fingered Mickey Kent filching the Scotch from the study that led to you all conking out in the chapel.'

'Still,' persisted Katy, 'it's all just a private family squabble.'

'So if I strangle you right now, we could just write that off as a private family squabble?' said Puddle. '"Musician kills sister in fit of pique." You'd not want me brought to justice?'

'I'd be dead, darling – what would I do with justice? It wouldn't bring me back to life, would it?'

'I love a philosophical discussion as much as the next girl,' said Ellie, 'but you're not going to change my mind. I want to see this through. If what they say about the floods is true, we've got until tomorrow morning before the doctor gets here and someone gets away with murder. And I, for one, am going to do everything in my power to make sure they don't.'

Katy shook her head. 'As you wish. What about you two?'

'I'm with Ellie,' said Skins. 'Always.'

'Whither go the Maloneys, there go I,' said Dunn. 'And if either of them ever kills me, I *definitely* want them brought to justice.'

'We'd never kill you, honey,' said Ellie.

'I might,' said Skins. 'Don't get complacent, mate.'

Katy shook her head. 'I still think you're on a hiding to nothing, but it looks like I'm in the minority.'

Ellie smiled and looked around the table. 'Anyone got anything else that might help us?'

'I was sitting near Charlotte and Marianne last night,' said Vera. 'Thick as thieves, they were. I reckon you need to find out more about them.'

Ellie poked Skins in the chest. 'What do I keep saying to you?'

'You keep saying there's something odd about the way those two are thick as thieves,' he said.

'Damn right.' She looked back at Vera. 'What were they saying?'

'They were talking very quiet – I couldn't hear. But the tone wasn't angry – they weren't having a row. It was . . . you know . . . chummy.'

'Chummy, Ivor. They were chummy. One woman was sleeping with the other woman's husband, and they were chummy.'

'Chummy,' said Skins. 'Very odd.'

Ellie poked him again.

'Why don't I try getting one of them alone?' asked Dunn. 'Give them a bit of the old Barty magic – see if I can't charm something out of them.'

Puddle winked. 'I'd tell him anything, wouldn't you, girls?'

'Oh, in a second,' said Vera, fluttering her eyelashes and holding her hands coquettishly beneath her chin.

'You can take the mickey all you like,' said Dunn. 'I've still got the magic.'

Ellie touched his arm. 'Of course you have, honey. So you're in charge of finding out what's going on with those two.'

'I've got magic,' said Skins.

The four women laughed.

Ellie kissed him on the cheek. 'In spades, honey. But best keep it under wraps for now – who knows what the Bilverton girls might do if they come under your influence? We don't want to cause a riot.'

'I'm immune to it, meself,' said Mickey. 'But to be on the safe side, I'm off back down to the chapel. Anyone coming?'

Elk and Benny joined him, leaving the rest to finish their breakfast.

A little later, the Bilvertons began drifting in.

Dunn was halfway through his second cup of coffee and trying to decide whether to have another boiled egg when he spotted the first of his potential interviewees.

Marianne came into the dining room and headed straight for the sideboard. She helped herself to a surprisingly large amount of food, then looked around to see who else was at the table. Before Dunn could catch her eye, she spotted Malcolm at the other end and joined him.

'Never mind, mate,' said Skins. 'You'll be able to work the magic later, I'm sure.'

Dunn held up his hand. 'Shh.'

'What?'

'I'm trying to listen,' said Dunn under his breath.

'What are they saying?'

'I don't know – some skinny idiot keeps talking to me and I can't hear them.'

'Sorry, mate.' Skins turned to Ellie and whispered, 'We've got to keep quiet, he's trying to earwig.'

'We'd better shut up then,' she whispered back.

'Better had.'

'Oh, for crying out loud,' said Dunn. 'You two are as bad as each other. Are you going to eat that toast?'

'Help yourself,' said Skins, pushing the plate across.

Skins and Ellie talked about their children and made plans for a trip to the seaside now the weather had properly cheered up, while Dunn ate the toast and waited for an opportunity to get Marianne on her own. He thought he saw an opening when Malcolm rose from the table, but he was just refilling his plate.

His hopes rose again when Charlotte appeared at the door, but she looked quickly around the room and left without coming in. Dunn put down his coffee cup.

'You going to follow her?' said Skins. 'You might be able to catch her before she disappears back upstairs.'

'Thanks for the help, mate. Always good to get advice from a professional investigator.'

'I'm just saying . . .'

Before Dunn could stand up, Marianne wiped her mouth, put her napkin on the table and made her excuses to Malcolm. She left the room.

'Better get your skates on, Barty boy – they're both on the loose now.'

Dunn followed.

He hurried out of the dining room, through the tiny vestibule with its secret door to the servants' stairs and out into the Grand Hall. He came to a skidding halt behind one of the stone pillars supporting the gallery when he heard women's voices ahead. He stood still, hoping they hadn't heard his rushing footsteps. Realizing how peculiar it would look if someone saw him, he took his notebook from his breast pocket and leaned on the pillar. If anyone chanced upon him and wondered what he was up to, he'd say he'd just had an idea for a song and had to stop to write it down before he forgot.

He listened carefully, trying to make out the voices in the echoing hall.

'We've got to come clean,' said Charlotte.

'It will destroy them,' said Marianne. 'They can't ever know.'

'It's the only way. It's secrets that tear families apart. They can deal with the truth, whatever it is, but secrets will eat away at all of us.'

'We can't. Just think of the trouble—'

Marianne stopped abruptly at the sound of fresh footsteps on the stairs.

'What ho, ladies,' said Howard from the landing. 'Lovely day again.'

'Yes,' said Marianne. 'It looks as though the weather's finally turned.'

'Might be worth a quick run down the drive in the old MG after breakfast and see how the floodwater's doing.'

Howard was getting closer, and Dunn found his confidence in the 'just writing a song' ruse ebbing away. He pushed himself upright and stepped out, trying to make it look as though he'd just come from the dining room.

'Morning, Dunn,' said Howard.

'Morning, Howard.'

'Any breakfast left?'

'Plenty. Not much milk, though.'

'Ah, of course, should have thought of that. Milkman can't get through. We shall have to make do. I was just telling the ladies I'll pop out later and check on the flood. I doubt we'll have to wait more than another day before everything's back to normal.' He looked guiltily at Marianne. 'Well, I mean, not normal . . . but . . .'

'It's all right, Howard,' she said. 'I know what you mean. You go and have your breakfast.'

'Right you are.'

Howard strode towards the dining room, giving Dunn a little shamefaced grimace as he passed.

'Good morning, Mr Dunn,' said Marianne. 'I didn't see you there.'

'Just this second come out of the dining room,' he said, tucking his notebook back in his pocket.

'This must be awful for you,' said Charlotte. 'Being stuck here, I mean. Are you losing work?'

'We'll miss our regular slot at the Augmented Ninth tonight, but they'll get by without us.'

'The Augmented Ninth, eh? A nightclub?'

'Yes. Not too big. Knowledgeable crowd. Love their jazz.'

'How delightfully glamorous. I say, Marianne, should we see about paying them for their time? We've had plenty of entertainment, after all, and if they're losing work because they're stuck here . . .'

Marianne looked at him appraisingly. 'We'll have to see what we can do.'

'There's no need, really,' said Dunn. 'It's not like it's anyone's fault, is it?'

'I suppose not,' said Charlotte.

Dunn smiled. 'Well, I'm just on my way upstairs. Shall I see you later?'

'I'm sure you shall,' said Marianne.

Still smiling, he swept confidently past and set off up the stairs. As he turned left on the landing he could just about hear Charlotte whispering.

'Do you think he heard us?'

'I think he was there longer than he claims. We'll have to be more careful.'

'You're the one who needs to be careful. I really don't think you should go—'

Having already reached the gallery, Dunn had no excuse to linger, so he headed for the second floor and never heard where Marianne shouldn't go, nor why it might be cause for concern.

Dunn returned to his room and sat on the bed. He had no reason to be there and nothing to do, but he needed to make it appear as though he really had been on his way upstairs and that he hadn't been lurking in the Grand Hall, earwigging.

After what he considered a suitable length of time, he stood and made his way back down.

He returned to the dining room where he found Skins and Ellie deep in conversation, as they so often seemed to be, with Howard and Veronica.

'And here's the very man,' said Howard.

Dunn frowned. 'The very man for what?'

'It seems you are part of a democracy, old chap. A workers' collective. Your pals here refused to commit to our proposal until you returned to cast your vote.'

'Ah, I see. Well, you know – all for one and up the proletariat and all that. What proposal?'

'The younger Bilvertons here have something to take our minds off our prolonged incarceration,' said Skins. 'They're going to have one last hunt for the priest hole. You coming?'

'Are you going, Ellie?' asked Dunn.

'I think they're quite mad,' she said. 'But I can't deny my interest is piqued. I said I'd tag along.'

'Go on, then,' said Dunn with a sigh. 'It's not like I've got anything else to do.'

'That's the spirit,' said Howard. 'Spoken with the weary resignation of a true Englishman. If it helps, you can console yourself with the fact that you're doing yours truly the most enormous favour. When we've scoured the place top to bottom one last time and found nothing, Ronnie will be forced to shut her trap about it forever more.'

'Just you wait and see,' said Veronica.

'My breath is bated. I am positively agog with electric anticipation. The mysteries of our nation's persecutory past await, I'm sure. But they'll have to wait a tiny bit longer – I've promised everyone I'll check the roads. Load your packs. Don your sturdiest boots.

Alert the bearers to our imminent departure. I shall be with you before you can say, "Complete waste of a morning."'

He grabbed another slice of toast and munched it as he swept out of the dining room.

◆ ◆ ◆

Howard didn't hang about and was back in the Grand Hall with his report in less than a quarter of an hour.

'The roads remain impassable,' he said. 'But the levels are still falling. I stand by my estimate of tomorrow morning.'

'Boo and hurrah,' said Ellie. 'In that order.'

Howard laughed. 'I just need to tell Gordy, then I'll be with you. Oh, and there seemed to be some chaps off in the distance shinning up the telegraph poles. At least, I assume they were telephone engineers. Could have been anything, what?'

'They could have been circus performers practising a tightrope act,' suggested Skins.

'Well, quite. Still, there's a reasonable chance the telephone might be back on soon.'

It took him another few minutes to find Gordon and return.

'Are you ready now?' said Veronica.

Howard struck a heroic pose. 'As I'll ever be. Lay on, McRonnie, and damned be him that first cries, "Is it time for elevenses yet?"'

Shaking her head, Veronica led them towards the study.

'Why are we starting here?' asked Howard. 'What about the billiards room? At least I could practise my game while you're fossicking in the fireplace for your secret room.'

'You don't have to come, you know. I have new friends now.' She swept her hand to indicate Skins, Ellie and Dunn.

'I wouldn't miss it for the world, dear heart.'

They arrived at the study door and Veronica pushed it open.

Skins quickly scanned the room for signs of anyone else having been in there since his own visit. As far as he could tell, it looked exactly as he'd left it.

'We were never allowed in here as children unless Papa was here,' Veronica said, 'so I've honestly never had a chance for a good old nosy round. That's why I wanted to come here first. I had hours to go over all the other rooms, but the study was always locked and out of bounds unless Papa was working.'

She went straight to the fireplace and began to inspect the mantelpiece. She ran her hands along the top, then down the carvings of the stone surround. She put her hands on either side and pushed hard. She pulled out the fire basket, inspecting and then pushing at the stonework at the back of the firebox. Finally she reached up into the chimney itself. Her hands returned soot-blackened but empty.

'No luck, old horse?' said Howard.

Veronica dusted her hands together to get rid of the worst of the soot. 'Not yet, no. But I've only just started. You could help instead of sneering, you know.'

'I was always told one should play to one's strengths. Sneering is what I do best.'

'Why don't we try to approach this logically?' suggested Ellie. She stepped over to the wall on the hall side and hit it with the side of her fist. 'This wall is good and sturdy, but you can see from the doorway that it's only a foot or so thick. You'd not conceal any sort of secret room in there, and it's probably a supporting wall anyway so you'd not want to weaken it.'

'I say,' said Howard. 'Are there architects in your family? "Supporting wall", eh?'

'I've never met an architect, but it stands to reason, don't you think? How else would the upper floors stay up?'

'No idea, Mrs M. By magic?'

'Supporting walls or magic, yes. And of the two options, it's far better to rely on a solid structure. So the same applies to the wall with the window. It's good and thick, but we can see roughly *how* thick so we know there's nothing inside it. That leaves the wall behind the gramophone, the outside wall with the bookcases and fireplace, and the floor.'

'Trapdoor, you mean?' said Veronica.

'Possibly. It would be harder to conceal, but we can't rule it out as easily as these other two walls.'

'This is the woman you should have consulted years ago,' said Howard. 'She's made more sense in the last two minutes than you have in the last twenty years.'

Ellie ignored him. 'So why don't Howard and Veronica take the right-hand bookshelves, Ivor and I will take the left, and Barty can see what lurks behind the gramophone equipment?'

'Ivor?' said Veronica.

'Me,' said Skins.

'What a nice name. Do you mind if I . . . ?'

'I'd honestly rather you didn't. I've been Skins to everyone except Ellie since I was a nipper. And my mum, of course.'

'But why "Skins"?'

'Drum skins,' said Dunn.

'Oh, of course. I feel such a fool. Skins it is, then,' said Veronica. 'Sorry. Shall we?' She indicated the wall of bookshelves.

They split into their assigned groups and began the search.

Ellie started on the bottom shelf, pulling each book in turn.

'What are you doing?' said Skins, looking down.

'One of these might be a secret lever. I'm sure I read it somewhere once. Some Gothic horror thing where the dungeon was concealed behind a fireplace. The latch was operated by a book on the shelves.'

'Secret latch? I was expecting something a little more . . . I don't know . . . ordinary, I suppose. Like we give it a shove and it turns out to be a door.'

'I know you must all be getting frightfully weary of the way I keep pouring cold water on all this,' said Howard, 'but I really do think they're going to turn out to be a good deal more like ordinary bookcases.'

Skins, though, had clearly thought of something. Ignoring the higher shelves, he ran his fingers along the underside of the two at about waist height. Each shelf had a rounded, downward lip. Slowly and carefully, he traced along the back of each lip on first the upper, then the lower shelf. He found nothing on the upper, but after a few moments his fingertips caught on to slight imperfections on the lower. They might otherwise pass as the outline of a knot in the wood, but Skins was looking for a button like the one on the desk. He pressed it. Nothing happened. He pressed again, more firmly this time.

The was a loud clonk, and the left-hand side of the bookshelf moved ever so slightly away from him.

The others stopped and turned.

Skins pushed against the bookcase and the left-hand side swung into the wall on smooth hinges to leave an opening about eighteen inches wide. There was a light switch just inside. Skins flicked it on to reveal steep steps leading downwards.

◆ ◆ ◆

'This is entirely unfair,' said Howard. 'We've lived here all our lives and Ronnie here has searched every inch of the place. You've been here five minutes and you walk straight in and open the secret door. How on earth . . . ?'

'Nimble fingers, mate,' said Skins with a grin. 'I could have been a concert pianist.'

'What stopped you?'

'Can't play the piano.'

'I can see how that would be a disadvantage. Do you want to lead the way?'

'I think Veronica should go first – she's the one who's been looking for this all these years.'

'Actually, that's a splendid idea,' said Howard. 'I couldn't agree more.' He touched Veronica's arm. 'I take back everything I've ever said. You were right all along and I apologize for doubting you. Lead the way, old girl.'

Veronica smiled and edged past them all so that she could squeeze through the narrow entrance and down the stone steps. The others were close behind.

Skins was at the rear, and paused for a moment to make sure he knew how to open the door from the inside, just in case it should close behind them. He found the latch and satisfied himself that they wouldn't be locked in, then made his way down to join the others.

At the bottom of the steps, he found them crammed into a small stone-flagged room, about ten feet by six. There was a desk with a reading lamp at the far end, and the walls were lined with shelves. Once he joined them, they could barely move, and certainly couldn't examine the contents of the room.

'Didn't think this through,' said Howard. 'It's a bit cramped in here with all five of us, don't you think? What say we take turns? Ronnie can have first dibs, then we can come down one by one to have a look for ourselves without feeling like we're in an impromptu game of sardines.'

'Sounds like a good idea,' said Ellie. 'Lead the way, Ivor.'

They dutifully trooped back up the steps and into the study, leaving Veronica to explore on her own.

'Not much use as a priest hole,' said Dunn as they clustered around the bookcase waiting for her to return.

'How's that?' said Skins.

'Priest holes always had two exits. No good hiding in a little room with only one way out if the queen's agents find the secret door – you'd be trapped.'

'It's not a real priest hole, though, is it? Not if Veronica's story about the brewer bloke . . . ?'

'Hopson,' said Ellie.

'It would be, wouldn't it?' said Dunn. 'And his partners, Barleyford and Yeasten.'

'Anyway,' continued Skins. 'If he just had it built because he liked the idea of it, it didn't need to be a proper escape route, did it?'

'Then what's down there?' asked Howard.

From downstairs, they heard a muffled but hearty laugh.

'I think we're about to find out,' said Ellie.

Moments later, there were rapid footsteps on the stone steps and Veronica emerged holding one of the small boxes.

'You're never going to believe this,' she said as she put the box down on the desk and lifted the lid. 'Take a look at what Papa was hiding down there.'

The box was crammed tightly with what looked like postcards. Ellie pulled a few out and spread them out on the table.

The others looked and then they, too, began to laugh.

'The dirty old bugger,' said Skins.

John Bilverton, it seemed, had been the owner of one of the largest collections of 'naughty' French postcards in all England.

'Well,' said Dunn, 'that's a turn-up.'

# Chapter Twelve

Skins hunted for the bell push and within moments had ordered a pot of coffee from the ever-friendly butler. It took only a few minutes for a tray to arrive, borne by one of the young footmen, and Skins was driven to assume that they must have pots of coffee pre-prepared at that time of day, ready for just such a request.

He poured three cups, still without milk, and then joined Ellie and Dunn, who were looking out through the French doors on to the formal walled garden.

'I sometimes wish we could have a garden like this,' said Ellie as Skins handed her a cup.

'We've got our garden,' he said. 'And there's all the parks in London for the kids to play in.'

'Oh, I'm not complaining, but look at this. It's magnificent. Ordered and precise like something from a story book.'

'I'll take our little patch of grass and our swing on the apple tree any day.'

'True. I've got everything I need.'

'But you don't have an enormous stash of filthy French post-cards,' said Dunn with a grin.

'I'm sure I could do without those,' she said. 'I mean, I'm no prude, but a whole roomful?'

'They're probably worth a few bob,' said Skins. 'I mean, they're not that easy to come by. And there are some connoisseurs about who'd pay handsomely for decent ones.'

'Do I want to know how you know this?'

'We knew a bloke in the war, didn't we, Barty? He made a mint.'

'Dirty Dudley,' confirmed Dunn. 'Always had a few in his pack for the lads, but he made his real money selling them to the officers.'

'Each to his own, I guess,' said Ellie. 'But finding the room opens the case up, wouldn't you say?'

'I'd not be so certain,' said Skins.

'Sure it does. We've been wondering how the killer got out of a locked room with the key still in the lock on the inside, but now we know they didn't have to get out at all – they could have been hiding among the dirty postcards the whole time. When the girls and I left, they could have sneaked out and joined the others to make it look as though they just got there.'

'It's an attractive idea, but no one's been down there for weeks.'

'How can you possibly know that?'

'When I first flicked the light on there was at least a month's worth of dust on those steps. If anyone had been down them there'd be footprints, but the dust was thick. Undisturbed. And did you see the state of them cobwebs? They'd have been brushed out of the way, too.'

Ellie sighed. 'Oh. You're sure?'

'Absolutely, sorry. Veronica was the first person down those steps for ages. I'd bet my pension on it.'

'Blimey, have you got a pension?' asked Dunn.

'Well, no. But if I did have, I'd bet it all on us being the first ones to open that door for a good few weeks. Longer, maybe.'

Ellie sighed again. 'And where does that leave our opinion of Howard and Veronica?'

'I'm tempted to rule them both out completely,' said Dunn. 'It doesn't make sense for it to be either of them.'

'Fair dos,' said Skins. 'So that's two off the list and good news all round.'

'How's that?' asked Dunn.

'Well, I doubt those postcards are in the will,' said Skins. 'What with them being illegal and all that. So if they play it right, they've got everything they need whatever the will says. Just sell the postcards to some other connoisseur and Bob's your uncle. Sounds like a happy ending to me.'

Ellie smiled. 'To me, too. Oh, Barty, you haven't told us what happened when you followed Charlotte and Marianne outside.'

'Oh, of course. Sorry. I didn't want the Bilvertons to hear. It was pretty odd. Charlotte wants to tell everyone, and Marianne won't let her. Says it would destroy the family.'

'Tell everyone what?'

'That's all I heard before Howard came along.'

'Tell them about how they murdered dearest Johnny B, I reckon,' said Skins.

'But why?' asked Dunn.

'What if he'd given Charlotte the old heave-ho? Then it would be the jilted lover and the betrayed wife banding together for revenge on the man who done them wrong.'

'It's possible, I guess,' said Ellie.

'If we can work out how they did it, I'd say it puts them squarely in the frame,' said Skins.

Ellie was still doubtful. 'Maybe. We'll have to think about it. Hey, is it lunchtime yet?'

Dunn looked at his watch. 'It's only just gone eleven.'

'So it's time for cake? Can we order cake? Why didn't they bring any with the coffee?'

Skins laughed. 'She needs her cake, mate, what can I say?'

He once more rang the bell and they placed an order for cake, which they ate while pondering their next steps.

◆ ◆ ◆

Coffee drunk and slices of Battenberg eaten, Ellie took the lead as they left the garden parlour and headed for the salon and the main doors to the rear of the house.

Skins was telling a joke. ' . . . so the barman says—'

Ellie stopped dead, holding up her hand. 'Shush.'

'You have no respect for the comedic arts, Ells-Bells. I was just getting to the punchline.'

'Just shut up for a second – you can tell him later. He's probably heard it before anyway. I know I have.'

Dunn shrugged. 'I didn't want to say anything, mate.'

'Will you shut up, as well? I can hear something.'

'Again?' said Skins. 'Another crying woman?'

'As a matter of fact, yes. You two really do need to get your hearing checked, you know. It's coming from the library. You carry on through and I'll stop and find out what's going on.'

With a shared grin, Skins and Dunn breezed through the library without looking round. Ellie waited a moment and then followed.

She was half expecting to meet Marianne again, but to her surprise she saw Charlotte in a chair by the unlit fireplace. She hadn't really paid much attention to her before, simply filing her away as 'Gordon's wife' or 'the woman having an affair with John Bilverton'. But now she looked properly, she saw that she was actually rather attractive. Her blonde hair was cut in a fashionably boyish bob, and her face had a soft beauty that Ellie thought wouldn't be out of place on a movie star.

Ellie scuffed her feet on the rug as she approached, to alert Charlotte to her presence.

Charlotte wiped her eyes with a handkerchief which she hurriedly stuffed into the sleeve of her pale blue cardigan.

'Hello, there,' she said. 'It's Ellie, isn't it?'

'It is. We've been here all this time, and you and I haven't spoken properly yet.' She sat down in a chair on the opposite side of the fireplace. 'Are you OK, honey?'

'I'm fine, thank you,' said Charlotte wearily.

'If you don't mind my saying so, you don't look at all fine.'

Charlotte offered a tiny smile. 'Americans are always so direct.'

'Sorry. I forget where I am sometimes.'

'No, no, it's rather refreshing in a way. No, I'm not really fine. But it's nothing to worry about. Just a . . . a personal matter.'

'John's death has hit everyone hard.'

To Ellie's surprise, Charlotte laughed. 'John? That miserable old ratbag? I'll not be missing him.'

'You're going to have to excuse some more American directness, then, but I thought you and he were having an affair.'

Charlotte laughed again. 'You're not alone there.'

'So you weren't?'

'Good Lord, no. Can you imagine? One shudders even to think of it.'

'Then why does everyone think you were?'

'Because we let them.'

'We?'

Charlotte looked at her for a moment. 'I've so wanted to explain it to someone – do you mind it being you? It would help to say it out loud to someone who isn't part of the family, but I must insist on your absolute discretion.'

Ellie was struck by the similarities with the conversation she'd had with Marianne the day before. Both outsiders, both keen to confide in another outsider. She was also suddenly afraid that she was about to be made an accessory after the fact. But her curiosity got the better of her. 'Sure. Mum's the word, as you say over here.'

'I *was* having an affair, but not with John.'

'Then who?'

Charlotte looked at her quizzically. 'With Marianne,' she said, as though it were the most obvious thing in the world.

Ellie was so surprised it was all she could do not to laugh. Gathering herself together, she said, 'But the whole family thinks it was John.'

'Yes.'

'Even Marianne told me you were sleeping with him.'

'She loved John, so she went along with the lie for his sake.'

'I don't quite understand.'

'He caught us a couple of months ago. There was a fearful row. There was a lot of bluster, of course. Anger. Confusion. Hurt. But then resignation. He said he wouldn't stop us, but he begged us never to let on. If any hint of an affair got out, we were to say it was with him, not Marianne. He'd been the villain before and could take all the disapprobation that went with it, but he couldn't bear the thought of people knowing his wife had been with another woman. Obviously word did get out – last week, in fact – and we dutifully went along with the story.'

'And now he's gone?'

'Now he's gone we don't need to keep it a secret, but Marianne insists. She says that with Gordon having forgiven me—'

'He's forgiven you?'

'He couldn't bear any sort of scandal, either, so divorcing me was always out of the question. With him forgiving me and the man he believes I was having an affair with dead, Marianne thinks we can pretend it's all over. We've avoided any possible trouble and we can all carry on as normal.'

'But you don't?'

'I . . . Well, I love her. Marrying Gordon was the most frightful mistake. I can never be happy as the dutiful wife of a biscuit-maker. I want to tell them all the truth and go to London with Marianne.'

'And she doesn't want that?'

'I thought she did. But I'm not certain any longer. I don't know what to do.'

'Well, I'm sure—' Ellie stopped as she heard footsteps outside.

Gordon appeared in the doorway. 'Ah, there you are, darling. I've been looking for you. How are you fixed for a game of croquet? The lawn's dried out nicely. Betty and Peter are playing.'

Charlotte pasted on a big smile. 'That would be delightful. Will you join us, Ellie?'

'That's very kind,' said Ellie, 'but I promised I'd join Ivor and Barty in the chapel.'

'You're all welcome,' said Gordon. 'The more the merrier.'

'Thank you. I'll let them know.'

With a smile to Charlotte, she left the library and headed for the stairs.

◆ ◆ ◆

Ellie found Skins and Dunn lounging on chairs at the end of the chapel, chatting with Mickey and Benny.

' . . . so the barman says—'

'Hello, boys,' said Ellie. 'Can I have a quiet word?'

'Really?' said Skins, exasperatedly. 'Can I not be allowed to get this punchline out just once?'

Dunn laughed.

'And you can shut up as well,' said Skins.

'I've got to be honest with you, mate, this is funnier than that old joke ever could be. What's the news, Ellie? Anything good?'

'Walk this way and I'll tell you,' she said, and stood up.

As she walked off, Skins heaved himself to his feet. 'If I could walk *that* way, I wouldn't need—'

'Shut up, Ivor,' she called over her shoulder.

She led Skins and Dunn to a quiet corner.

'Who was in the library, and what have you found out?' asked Dunn as Ellie turned to face them.

'It was Charlotte, and I found out what she and Marianne were talking about when you overheard them in the Grand Hall.'

'They murdered John,' said Skins.

'They're sisters,' said Dunn.

'They're part of a secret society controlling the world by exerting their sinister influence on England's rich and powerful families,' said Skins.

Ellie laughed. 'Where do you get this rubbish?'

'It was a pamphlet some bloke in a raincoat was handing out up the West End one night.'

'No, it's altogether much more straightforward than that. Charlotte *was* having an affair, but not with John Bilverton—'

'Uncle Malcolm,' interrupted Skins.

'Peter Putnam,' said Dunn.

'Dunsworth the butler,' said Skins.

'No, you goofs. Marianne Bilverton.'

'Now hang on a minute,' said Skins. 'Everyone – including Marianne – told us she was having it away with the old feller.'

'Everyone – excluding Marianne – was mistaken. And Marianne was lying. It was something to do with protecting John's pride. I think both the women had one eye on their inheritance – or Gordon's inheritance in Charlotte's case – so they went along with a fiction John concocted for them. It seems John would rather have been known as a degenerate roué than a cuckold even if it destroyed his family, so he made them promise to tell the lie that *he* was the lucky recipient of Charlotte's favours, and not Marianne.'

'She's a good-looking girl,' said Dunn. 'Once we'd heard what John was like, I had no trouble believing he'd have wanted her.'

'Well, whether he did or not,' said Ellie, '*she* wanted his wife, not him.'

'So where does that leave them as suspects?' asked Skins. 'Did they want John out of the way? Or did his existence make no difference to them?'

'As far as I can make out, Marianne really did love him so she wouldn't have wanted him dead. But Charlotte claims to love Marianne, so she might have wanted him out of the way.'

'Is she bright enough to pull it off?' asked Dunn.

'How would we know? Whoever did it is a good deal brighter than us – we've still no idea how they did it. But I couldn't tell from my brief conversation. She didn't come across as an idiot. But then again, none of them does.'

'We'll figure it out,' said Skins.

'Sooner rather than later,' said Ellie. 'There are two dead already and anyone could be next.'

'Even us,' said Dunn.

Skins looked thoughtful for a moment. 'There's got to be a simple answer to John's murder. Another way out of the room, maybe. We didn't look for a trapdoor, after all. Or a secret mechanism on the window so you can open it without opening it.'

'What?' said Dunn.

'Like a latch or something so you can open it sideways instead of lifting the sash.'

'How would that help?'

'I don't know – I'm just trying to come up with ideas. What about the ceiling? Did either of you look up there? A hatch with a ladder?'

'Just your bog-standard moulded ceiling rose with an electric light fitting.'

'One of them big ones? That could be the hatch. There could be another secret passageway between the floors.'

'It's all getting a little wild now, honey,' said Ellie. 'Why don't we let it percolate for a bit and join the others?'

'Good idea,' said Dunn. 'If we don't stop him soon he'll have Father Christmas coming down the chimney and shooting John before being pulled back up by his elves.'

'Don't be daft, mate,' said Skins. 'It's June. Everyone knows Father Christmas is still at the North Pole in June.'

'Can't be him, then. Easter Bunny?'

'Too late – she's back in her burrow painting eggs for next year.'

'A witch on her broomstick.'

'Halloween's not for ages.'

'Leprechaun?'

'Oh, do stop it,' said Ellie. 'And everyone knows leprechauns only come out on St Patrick's Day, anyway.'

'He could be guarding his gold at the end of a rainbow,' said Dunn. 'We haven't looked outside for ages. There could have been a rainbow.'

'I'm going back to the comfy chairs.'

As she left she could still hear them.

'Cupid?'

'He takes a few months off in the South of France after Valentine's Day.'

'How about . . .'

Lunch was served once more on the terrace, where the sky was blue and the sun deliciously warm. Skins and Ellie were sitting with Gordon and Peter, who were talking excitedly about the future.

Gordon was gesturing with a slice of ham on the end of his fork. 'Look, the thing is, I'll most likely be inheriting the business, and I'll need a decent solicitor to look after the firm's affairs. Do you think you can handle that?'

Peter looked as though he was going to burst with pleasure. 'I say. Well. Yes. Heavens, yes. I'm already dealing with most of the Bilver-Tone work so I might have to engage another junior. Maybe two. But the Bilverton's Biscuits account would make it worth it. Oh.'

'Oh?'

'Well, what about John's lawyers? Won't they be dealing with everything?'

'I've been studying that business since I was a lad. One of the things I learned was that my father surrounded himself with people he knew and trusted. The current firm – Dog Cart, Wimple and Fetlock or whatever they're called – are *his* pals, not mine. I want to build up my own circle of advisers.'

'Well, gosh. Thank you.'

'You'll be part of the family soon – it would be good to have you helping with the family business. We'll sit down after the reading of the will and thrash out the details.'

'How very splendid. Thank you, old chap.'

'Think nothing of it. But we seem to be talking shop and ignoring our guests. Are you fellows enduring your incarceration without too many problems?'

'We're finding ways to amuse ourselves,' said Ellie.

'That's the spirit. Howie says the roads should be clear tomorrow, so if we can get word out we might even have you home soon.'

'That would be wonderful. I'm missing my children very much.'

'Good heavens. I hadn't even thought about that.'

'They probably haven't actually noticed we're not there, but we've not been able to telephone, obviously, so Nanny will be worrying.'

Gordon looked puzzled for a moment. It had clearly not occurred to him that a musician and his wife might employ a nanny. 'Howie suspected the telephone might be back on soon, too, so you'll have to call your nanny and let her know where you are.'

'Thank you.'

Skins had lost interest and was looking around the table. As always, he was struck by the bright mood, and intrigued by the tangle of unlikely alliances and the muttered conversations. Only Marianne had ever seemed properly upset, and even she was joking with Veronica.

He turned his attention to his surroundings. The terrace was obviously well looked after. The flagstones were free of weeds and the ornamental stone flowerpots appeared to be conscientiously tended. There was a wood and canvas contraption leaning against the wall, and it took him a few moments to work out that it was probably some sort of sun shade that could be fitted to the table. It was as well maintained as everything else, with the canvas canopy clean and bright and the woodwork neatly varnished. One of the screws had clearly been removed for some reason. The heads of all the screws had been varnished over, but the brass of this one was shining through where the varnish had been scratched off by the gardener's screwdriver.

He stood up and bent to whisper in Ellie's ear. 'I've just thought of something. Back in a sec.'

He walked quickly through the salon, the library and the Grand Hall on his way to John Bilverton's study.

Once inside the study, Skins checked that no one had followed him, then squatted down to inspect the lock. There was nothing exotic about it. It was a factory-made lock of the sort he'd seen on hundreds of doors. He'd had to replace a similar surface-mounted lock once before and had learned that it was referred to in the locksmith trade as a 'rim latch'. It was a rectangular box of pressed metal, painted black, with a brass doorknob and a keyhole, still containing its key.

It showed signs of wear. The edges of the keyhole were bent where the key had scraped it and there were a couple of dents in the casing, but like everything else in the house, it was well maintained. It had been given a fresh coat of black paint at some point which, just like the varnish on the sun shade, had covered the screws that affixed it to the door. And, as with the sunshade, the paint on the screw heads had been scratched, exposing bright, shiny brass. Someone had removed and replaced the lock recently enough that the brass hadn't had time to tarnish.

Skins turned the key.

Nothing happened. It just rotated inside the lock, and the bolt stayed resolutely in place.

He stood and looked around the room. He wanted to get a proper look at the lock and that would mean taking it off the door and opening it up. He needed a screwdriver, but where would he find one? Hadn't he seen one in the desk?

He rummaged through the drawers once more and, sure enough, there was the gun-cleaning kit and the two screwdrivers.

'Got to admire a practical bloke,' he said, and picked the larger of the two.

As he suspected, the screws moved easily, and within moments he had the lock in his hand. He removed the key and turned the case over. There were more screws, also scratched, on the other side. He cleared a space on John's desk and laid the lock down so he could try to open it.

Again, the four screws moved easily and within moments he was prising off the cover. He was going slowly now, though. He had dismantled too many contraptions over the years, and had experienced too many disastrous explosions of springs, widgets and whatnots not to be cautious when opening something new.

He lifted the cover clear and narrowly missed being struck in the face by an escaping spring.

'Bugger,' he said as he scoured the rug to find it.

He retrieved the mutinous spring and placed it on the desk with the screws.

Skins was no locksmith, but he could see there was something not quite right with the lock. He picked up the key and placed it into the mechanism. Holding it in place with one hand, he turned it. Whatever it was supposed to turn or move was absent. He poked at the bolt, which moved freely.

He thought for a moment, then picked up the stiff spring. It looked newer than the rest of the mechanism – it was obviously not an original part.

There were scratches on the plate that held the bolt, and corresponding scratches on the case at about the same level. He managed to fit the spring into the gap and saw that it was definitely the cause of the scratches.

With one hand on the spring to stop it bursting out again, he tried the bolt, and this time it was held firmly in place by the spring.

He sat back. Someone had altered the lock. They'd removed part of the mechanism and replaced it with a simple spring. But why? What good would that do? The bolt was held in place by the spring, but that would stop the door closing, surely. How did that help? He had no idea, but he was certain the killer must have had something to do with it. Nothing else made sense.

He was about to leave everything and go to tell Ellie and Dunn what he'd learned, but it occurred to him that if the killer saw the dismantled lock on the desk, they'd know someone was on to them. He screwed the cover in place and reattached the whole thing to the door.

He returned the screwdriver to the desk drawer and set off to return to the terrace.

◆ ◆ ◆

The crowd at the lunch table had thinned, and Ellie and Dunn were on their own. Skins stood beside them.

'What was that all about?' asked Dunn.

'Just me being a genius.'

'And we missed it. Damn.'

'You can still bask in the glory of it, though,' he said enthusiastically. 'Just walk this way and I'll tell all.' He turned, ready to lead them back towards the chapel.

'If I could walk *that* way—' began Ellie.

Skins grinned. 'That's quite enough of that, Eleanora Maloney.'

They strolled along the path until Skins was certain they couldn't be overheard. He briefly described his recent discoveries.

'So someone tampered with the lock,' said Ellie when he was finished.

'But in a way that meant that you couldn't shut the door after it was done,' said Dunn.

Skins nodded. 'Exactly. So what's going on there? Someone rigged the whole thing so the door would stay locked and the key wouldn't do anything. But how did they get it closed in the first place? Like you say, once the thing's set up, the bolt's out and the door won't shut.'

'Unless you fit the lock when the door's closed. Maybe John did it. Maybe he really did shoot himself.'

'But why go to all that trouble?' asked Ellie. 'He could get everything he wanted just by locking the door. All this must be for something else.'

'To make it look like murder? To frame one of the others?' suggested Dunn.

'It's not very . . . effective,' said Skins. 'I mean, it's taken us two days to get this far and we're the only ones who even began to wonder if it might be murder. If he wanted to set someone up he'd have made it a sight more obvious than that.'

'Yeah, you're right,' conceded Dunn.

'What if there were a way to hold the bolt back and make it pop out only when the door was shut?' said Ellie.

'Like a pin or something?' said Skins. 'That might do it. But I didn't see a fresh hole in the cover. Any holes at all, in fact. How would you get the pin out?'

'And you'd still have to be inside the room to pull it out anyway,' said Dunn.

Skins frowned. 'Right. So we're assuming the whole thing was supposed to be a way of making it look like the door was locked from the inside with the key still in it, but whoever did it wanted to be on the outside.'

'It's the only thing that makes sense,' said Ellie.

'Thinking about it, the pin's a rubbish idea. If it wouldn't come out, or if the thread broke, they might be fiddle-faddling about for ages trying to get it fixed – they'd not want to get that far and then get caught because their trick lock didn't work first time. And if it did work exactly as planned but they somehow couldn't pull the pin back out under the door, they'd leave evidence behind . . .' He looked thoughtful. 'They'd leave evidence behind on the floor,' he said slowly. 'Ells – tell us again what happened when you broke in on Saturday.'

'We went at it like human battering rams for what seemed like hours, but was probably just a few minutes. The Bilverton girls went first, then me. After about the three hundredth go, the door gave way and I pretty much fell into the room.'

'You fell?'

'No . . . no, actually, I didn't. I mean, I fell flat on my face, but I slipped. There was the tiniest puddle of rainwater on the floor. Not much, but enough to make me lose my footing.'

'Where had it come from, though?' said Skins. 'That door's well inside the house on the ground floor – it couldn't be a leak.'

'Oh,' said Ellie.

'Exactly,' said Skins.

'Not with you,' said Dunn.

'Ice,' said Ellie and Skins together.

Dunn smiled and nodded. 'Clever.'

'Push the bolt back against the spring,' said Skins, 'and hold it in position with a little chunk of ice. Not too much or it won't melt in time. Not too little or it'll get crushed and lock too soon. Put the lock back together, screw it in place, shut the door and go. When the bolt clicks into place, you're miles away and it looks like the door was locked from the inside the whole time. The only evidence is a little puddle of water.'

Ellie frowned. 'How do you know how much ice is just right?'

'I'd bet that's not the only one of those locks in the house. I'd bet that one's not the lock that was usually on that door, too. So how about the killer modified another lock and experimented with the ice until it was working just the way they wanted? They could set it up to give themselves enough time to get everything done, with the door locking itself within minutes of them leaving.'

'Well, that's one part of the puzzle solved,' she said.

'Probably,' corrected Skins.

'One part of the puzzle probably solved,' she agreed. 'Now, we just need to work out how they got out of the room while the girls and I were standing outside, and how the heck they got to the room and back without getting wet.'

'Before tomorrow,' said Dunn. 'And we need to work out what happened to Hetty.'

'Someone slipped her a Mickey Finn – not much of a mystery there.'

'Yes, but who? When? Why?'

'She saw something she shouldn't have,' said Skins. 'It's the only reason.'

'What, though? She was with us in the chapel when John was killed.'

'Maybe she saw who left,' suggested Ellie. 'Maybe she asked them about it and got herself poisoned for her trouble.'

'Maybe,' said Dunn. 'Maybe.'

# Chapter Thirteen

While Ellie, Skins and Dunn had been chatting, the rest of the band were setting up.

Skins walked over. 'Lovely. A quick session?'

Puddle looked up from assembling her saxophone. 'If there's a chance we could be going home tomorrow, we might still be able to play our date at the Preening Parrot on Wednesday. We thought we ought to run through a few new numbers.'

'I'm in,' said Eustace.

'This is such a great place to play,' said Dunn, taking his bass from its case. 'You know, we should all chip in and buy a deconsecrated church somewhere.'

'I thought we were starting a club,' said Vera.

'With Mickey as chef,' agreed Elk.

'Why not a club in an abandoned church?' said Dunn. 'Tables in the main bit, stage where the altar used to be, bar along the back wall. Kitchens in a side room. Lavs in the vestry.'

'I'd love to run a nightclub,' said Katy. 'It'd be no good if it were as out of the way as this place, though – no passing trade.'

'No, but we'd make it a "destination",' said Dunn. 'People will travel miles to get to the hottest clubs.'

'We've already got a decent reputation,' agreed Mickey. 'I reckon it would work.'

'There you go, then, Katy,' said Puddle. 'Your next job as manager is to get us a deal on an abandoned church, get planning permission to convert it to a nightclub, raise the money for the conversion, get all the licences, book the bands, source the food, sort out the publicity and plan a whizzo opening night.'

'Well, that's Wednesday sorted out,' said Katy. 'What do you want me to do for the rest of the week?'

'Yeah, yeah,' said Dunn. 'I know. It's a pipe dream, but at least I have a dream.'

'It's a lovely dream, honey,' said Ellie. 'Don't let them crush it.'

'I still think it's a pretty good idea,' said Mickey.

'Me too,' said Skins. 'But for now, how about "Ostrich Walk"? I'll give you one bar for nothing. Watch the tempo in the stops. Everybody ready?'

They launched into the song they'd learned from a gramophone record by the Original Dixieland Jass Band, and Ellie joined Katy on the comfy chairs at the end of the chapel by the giant – now dormant – tea urn.

'How goes the Sherlocking?' asked Katy as Ellie sat down. 'Oh, or are you more like Tommy and Tuppence?'

'You read Agatha Christie?' asked Ellie.

'All four. There's supposed to be a new one out but I've not seen it yet. I'm terribly excited.'

Ellie laughed. 'And you're the one who's been pooh-poohing our efforts as amateur sleuths. I should have thought you'd be all for it.'

'Oh, I love to read about it, but I'm well aware it's all just fantasy. I don't actually believe normal people stumble on crimes and solve them. Well, mostly. I was a bit surprised to hear about you lot and the diamonds, I must say. Izzie's told me all the gory details.'

'Izzie? Oh, of course. Sorry. You know I've never called her anything but Puddle.'

'Isabella managed to make a feature of our ghastly family name. You know, one of the many, many delights of my short marriage to Roger was being able to change my name to Cannon. I'm not sure I could have gone on much longer as a Puddephatt.'

'Puddle suits her.'

'I've grown accustomed to it. Mother and Father aren't so enthusiastic. But I was saying . . . I didn't mean any offence. I just never really believed it was something the likes of us could or should be getting ourselves involved in. As much as I love mystery books, I do often think, "Oh, just leave it to the police, for heaven's sake." You know?'

'I do. And we shall. But in this case we still think the police will just write the two deaths off as a suicide and an accident if we don't find out what really went on.'

'You're still certain John Bilverton didn't commit suicide, then.'

'Even more so now. Ivor figured out how the killer got away and left the door locked from the inside.'

'I say, well done, Skins. What was it? Trapdoor? Trick lock?'

'It was a trick lock. You do read a lot of mysteries, don't you?'

'Not so many as all that. It just seems like the easiest way to do it.'

'It wasn't you, was it?'

'I was in the chapel the whole time, guv.'

'That's the problem,' said Ellie. 'So was everyone else.'

'Except someone wasn't, were they? Unless it was one of the servants.'

'We've discounted the servants – they have nothing to gain. But we did wonder if it could have been one of the party guests – you know, the ones who stayed overnight. They could have remained hidden upstairs for quite a while, but when we moved into the guest rooms on the second floor they had nowhere to hide. We'd have seen evidence of them by now.'

'True, true. You need to get your Ivor to apply his mighty brain to the matter of how to get to and from the house without anyone noticing.'

'Don't let him hear you describing his brain like that – we'd never hear the end of it. He was convinced it was a secret passage, but we found the hidden door and it just led to a room full of French postcards.'

'Mucky ones?'

'The muckiest. Worth a few bucks, the boys think, but no actual help to us.'

'I'll have to give it some thought. Do you want to listen to this?'

'The rehearsal? I always enjoy listening to them, but I'm happy to miss it. Why?'

'I could murder a cup of tea and this thing will take an age. Shall we go back to the house?'

They left the Dizzies to their rehearsal and went off in search of tea.

With cups of tea in hand, Ellie and Katy found their way to the garden parlour where they sat enjoying the sunshine and the view of the garden.

'You don't mind my coming in and taking over running the band?' asked Katy.

'Mind? Why on earth would I?'

'Well, Izzie said you were managing them before I came along. I felt like I was ousting you.'

'Lord, no. That was just a ruse to get me into the gentlemen's club where they were working. I've never had anything to do with running the band. The most I've ever done is to make sure Ivor has remembered to put on a clean shirt before he goes out to play.'

'I'm sorry, I got completely the wrong end of the stick.'

'Easily done. They've never had a manager. They talked about it – endlessly – but they never did anything about it. Instead they just muddled along as best they could. Their idea of managing their own affairs was to complain about having to manage their own affairs. They'd moan about how tiresome it was to make their own bookings. Then they'd grouse about the dressing room. Then they'd grumble about getting the wrong beer in the dressing room. Essentially, there was a lot of bellyaching but very little actual managing. You're a godsend.'

'Well, that's a relief. I blame Izzie, of course. She said I'd be saving you from a job you hated, and that it would all be fine, but I still couldn't get it out of my head that you might not be so pleased to have someone coming in and shoving you aside. If she'd explained it properly I'd have known the score. Sisters, eh?'

'I'm an only child, I'm afraid. I have a cousin I could cheerfully kill, mind you, so I sort of understand what you mean.'

Katy laughed.

Ellie was about to ask what it had been like growing up with Puddle, but she was interrupted by a familiar, yet unexpected, sound.

A telephone was ringing.

Ellie and Katy stood up to investigate. Once out in the Grand Hall, they could hear that the ringing was coming from more than one place, but the nearest was John Bilverton's study. They waited for a moment, expecting the butler to arrive to answer it, but when it became obvious that he wasn't coming, they hurried into the study where Ellie picked up the receiver.

'Hello,' she said. 'Bilverton House.'

There was a pause. The line crackled. 'Hello?'

'Yes, hello. This is Bilverton House.'

'To whom am I speaking?' said a distorted woman's voice.

'This is Ellie Maloney. I'm a guest here.'

'But you're American.'

'I am, but it's not entirely my fault. Is there someone you wish to speak to?'

'This is the operator from the exchange at South Barlington. I'm calling to inform you that the telephone line to your property has been restored.'

'That's very kind of you. Would you like to speak to a member of the family?'

'There'll be no need. Thank you.'

The line went dead.

'Well, the phone's working,' said Ellie. 'That was the GPO. We should tell the family. I'll call Dunsworth – he must be getting sick of me by now.'

Before she could even find the bell push, though, Dunsworth appeared at the study door.

'Did I hear the telephone ringing, madam?'

'You most certainly did, Dunsworth. That was the GPO calling to tell us that the line "has been restored".'

'My apologies, madam. I would have answered it but I was decanting some claret for this evening's dinner and I couldn't get to an instrument in time.'

'Please don't worry. I enjoy answering the phone occasionally.'

'You're very kind to say so, madam. I shall inform Mr Bilverton at once.'

'Right you are. We'll tell the band.'

Dunsworth disappeared as silently as he had arrived.

'Some good news, at last,' said Katy as they returned to the garden parlour.

'Good and bad,' said Ellie. 'I'm hoping to be able to call home and check on the children, to let Nanny and the housekeeper know what's happened, so that's a relief. But it also means the Bilvertons will be calling the doctor about John's "suicide" and Hetty's "sudden illness". And that means we're running out of time to prove they were both murdered.'

'I hadn't thought of it like that. You see why I'd be no use as a sleuth? But if there's anything I can do, just let me know.'

'Thank you. As soon as we work out what we're doing next, we'll know how much help we need.'

◆ ◆ ◆

News of the repaired telephone line spread rapidly. Ellie and Katy went down to the chapel to tell the band, and by the time they all returned to the house, the Bilverton clan were also aware that their watery incarceration might soon be at an end. An impromptu afternoon tea party had broken out in the dining room and there was a buzz of excitement. It was like the end of the school term.

'Ah, there you are,' said Veronica. 'Have you heard? The telephone is back on.'

Ellie smiled. 'I took the first call – an operator telling us the line was restored.'

'Oh, that was you, was it? Stupid Gordon was a bit vague. More interested in when he'd be able to get back to his precious biscuit factory, I bet.'

'I don't suppose there's any news on the roads?'

'Gordon telephoned the doctor in Partlow's Ford and he agrees with Howie – he thinks the road should be passable by tomorrow morning. So then Howie put in a call to the motor coach company and they're going to try to get your charabanc here after lunch. If all's well, we should be able to get you fellows on your way tomorrow afternoon.'

'Oh, that's wonderful. Do you think anyone would mind if I telephoned our nanny? She must be frantic by now. And I'm sure the married boys in the band would appreciate being able to try to get messages home.'

'It's already in hand – Betty has taken charge as usual. She'll make a list of all the trunk calls so she can try to book them all at once.'

'I'll spread the word.'

While Ellie was telling the band about the plans for calling home, Skins helped himself to a ham sandwich.

'Have you solved it yet?' asked Veronica.

He hurriedly swallowed a mouthful. 'Not quite, but we're getting there. How do you feel about finally finding the priest hole?'

'I'm thrilled to have found it at last, but a bit disappointed by what we found inside.'

'Why?'

'Well, it's all a bit sordid, isn't it? One doesn't like to imagine one's own dear papa collecting mucky postcards in secret.'

'I've been thinking about that, though. I mean, as treasure goes, it doesn't have the glamour of a ruby-encrusted golden platter or a religious statue set with emeralds and diamonds, but if you're just talking about its value . . . Well, a collection like that would be worth a mint. I mean, you'd have to be canny about how you flog them – you can't just go down the local auction house with a stash of illegal postcards – but one of the boys in the band knows a few dodgy geezers who could get a good price. And if you're happy to go to a bit more trouble, you'd get even more if you broke the collection up and sold it off in smaller lots.'

She laughed. 'You really have been thinking about it, haven't you?'

'It's what you said about wanting to get out that made me wonder. There's no guarantee you or Howard will get anything from the will, but a stash like that could see you both right. I mean it about getting help from one of the lads. Mickey knows some right shady characters – I'm sure he'd make the introductions.'

'We have our very own shady character, don't forget. Mr Valentine Baisley, gangster of this parish.'

'Oh, yes, I'd forgotten him – the money behind Bilver-Tone Records.'

'You know about that?'

'Peter told Barty the other day. He might know some likely people if he moves in the right circles, but he might cheat your boys. He sounds like the sort.'

'And Mickey's dodgy friends wouldn't?'

'It's a risk, I grant you, but the ones I'm thinking of have been his mates for years. They met in the army. There's loyalty, there, you know? Like there's a sort of honesty to their dishonesty – they'd certainly not rook one of their mates. I'd trust them to get the best deal and pass it on. I mean, don't get me wrong, they'd want a cut, but it would be a fair one. You'd pay any middleman a percentage, after all.'

'I'll mention it to Howie. I'm rather hoping we can share the proceeds between us. The others are going to be getting businesses and houses and goodness knows what. It would be nice if we youngsters got a few bob out of it, too.'

'You do that. Honestly, though, I'd be wary of this Baisley bloke – he sounds like a nasty piece of work from what Barty said. You can trust Mickey, though.'

Dunn had joined them. 'Trust Mickey? Course you can. Just make sure you count your rings if he ever kisses your hand.'

Veronica smiled. 'Duly noted. Have you put in a request for a phone call?'

'No one to call,' said Dunn. 'Mrs C doesn't have a phone and all my mates are here.'

'Who's Mrs C?'

'My landlady. Mrs Phyllis Cordell. She's a lovely old girl but she won't be panicking just because I haven't come home for a few nights.'

'She is lovely,' agreed Skins. 'Can't argue with that. And he's a dirty stop-out, so she's well used to his shenanigans.'

'I assumed you'd have a gorgeous wife waiting for you,' said Veronica.

Skins looked at his friend and laughed. 'You're on your own, mate. I'm not even going to try to explain your love life.'

'I'm very single,' said Dunn with a sigh. 'Very, very single.'

With another chuckle, Skins walked away to find Ellie, leaving them to it.

◆ ◆ ◆

Once the excitement had died down and the telephone schedule was organized, the crowd dispersed once more, leaving Ellie, Skins and Dunn in the dining room with Veronica.

'You know this house like the back of your hand, I bet,' said Skins.

'Almost,' said Veronica. 'Until earlier today I'd have said, "Yes, definitely," but then you lot went and found a secret room no one knew even existed, and now I'm beginning to doubt everything I thought I knew about the place.'

'But apart from the secret room,' said Ellie, 'there's nowhere here, inside or out, you don't know?'

'Almost certainly. I was the absolute queen of hide and seek. Why?'

'It's like this,' said Dunn. 'We're pretty sure now that your father really was murdered. We know how the killer got out and made it look like John had locked himself in the room alone. Well, more or less. Getting out while you were outside is still a stumper. Ellie heard the shot, then you all tried to break in . . . But leaving that for a bit, what we also can't figure out is how the killer got from the chapel to the house and back without anyone knowing.'

'Is there a covered walkway?' asked Ellie. 'Or just a sheltered route. Is there another way into the chapel other than through the main door?'

'There are only a couple of ways to get to the chapel. I've never wondered how sheltered they are, though.'

'Do you mind showing us?'

'Not at all. Walk this way.'

Skins glanced at Ellie. The look on her face persuaded him to say nothing.

They followed Veronica to the front door.

'From here we can see the delightfully symmetrical front elevation of Bilverton House. Typical of the Georgian period, the house was . . . It's no good, I can't keep it up. I'd be no use as a bear-leader.'

'A what?' said Skins.

'Bear-leader. You know, the chaps who used to take young toffs on the Grand Tour.'

'I live and learn.'

'Anyway, I'm afraid that for all I know about the history of the house, I'm a duffer when it comes to the technical stuff – the architecture and whatnot. But I do know my way around, at least.'

'That's all that matters.'

'Well, quite. So if we turn to our left, we pass Papa's old study, then a little way on, we'll go left again at the corner of the building. Hello, what's that wheelbarrow doing under the window?'

'Oh,' said Ellie, 'that was me. I needed something to stand on so I could look into the study on Saturday.'

'I say. How enterprising. Where did you find it?'

They rounded the corner, where Ellie pointed to the garden wall about five yards ahead. 'Just over there.'

'Of course. You've seen the garden from the garden parlour, I assume. That gate there will let you in, and there's another on the opposite side that will let you out again on to the path that runs along the back of the house.'

'The route we usually take to get to the chapel,' said Skins. 'Leads on to the bit with all the trees growing over it and that.'

'Our "bowered path", yes. But if you follow the wall all the way to the end we find . . .'

'Apple trees,' said Ellie. 'They'd provide pretty good cover.'

'Ah, yes,' said Veronica. 'But there's a problem with that. Follow me.'

She led them to the end of the wall, where they found themselves in a small orchard. In contrast to the formality of the walled garden, the orchard was a higgledy-piggledy collection of trees of various sizes and ages that had been left to grow entirely as they pleased.

'It must have been fantastic growing up with your own supply of fresh apples,' said Skins. 'I love an apple.'

Veronica led them towards the first trees. 'You'd think so, wouldn't you? Trouble is, these are cider apples. Perfectly edible, of course, but hardly the treat you might imagine.'

'On the other hand,' said Dunn, 'it must have been fantastic as a youngster having your own supply of cider.'

‘That was definitely fun, yes. We used to sneak into the brewing sheds over there and help ourselves.’

‘Any trapdoors in there?’ asked Skins.

‘Sadly not. Just solid wooden sheds with flagstone floors.’

Ellie, meanwhile, understood why Veronica had said there was a problem. Although the low canopy formed by the jumble of trees might provide limited shelter from the rain, the ground – even after more than a day of sunshine – was a morass.

‘I see what you mean,’ she said. ‘No one could get through all that mud without getting covered to the ankles in it. It would be even more noticeable than damp clothes.’

‘And they’d leave tracks,’ said Dunn. ‘No one’s been over there for days.’

‘Certainly doesn’t look like it,’ agreed Skins. ‘What happens if you go round it?’

Veronica pointed ahead. ‘Then you end up along the side wall of the chapel. Do you see?’

‘And is there another way in?’

‘There’s a side door that used to open into the vestry, but that’s the bathroom now so it’s been blocked off from the inside. The door’s still there, but if you can get it open – and I honestly don’t know if you still can – you’d just find yourself facing a blank wall.’

They carried on past the orchard to the chapel, where they saw that there was, indeed, a side door. The gap between the door and its frame had been filled with plaster and varnished over. The keyhole was similarly filled and painted black to match the other fittings, while the handle, when Skins tried to twist it, turned out to be welded in place.

‘Purely ornamental,’ said Veronica.

There was a path of sorts along the chapel wall where the ground had been cleared of weeds, and the four explorers followed it to the main door.

'You'd get a little shelter from the weather if you hugged the wall,' said Dunn, 'but you'd already be soaked by the time you got here.'

'Or muddy,' said Skins.

'Or both,' said Ellie.

They stood together by the main door and looked along the bowered path.

Skins sighed. 'So that's it, then. If you leave here by the main chapel door, you get wet whether you go to the back door of the house or the front.'

Ellie nodded. 'And you get wetter still on the way back.'

'And no one was wet,' said Dunn. 'Or were they?'

'I didn't notice anyone dripping,' said Veronica.

'And we're sure there was no one missing?' asked Ellie.

Veronica shook her head. 'No one. Uncle Malcolm was in his control room – we could hear him in there playing back his recordings. You lot were all in your seats with your instruments. Let me see . . . Down at our end, Papa was with Charlotte. Marianne was with Betty and Peter. I was with Kenny. Howard was with your manager, Katy. And you were sitting on your own until you got up to play the piano.'

'Where was Gordon?' asked Skins.

'Do you know, I have no idea,' said Veronica.

'He was sitting on his own,' said Ellie. 'I remember that much. So that's everyone.'

'It is. That's how we stayed from when Papa got up to go to the house until you and I went with Betty to fetch the hampers. Apart from visits to the loo, obviously. Everyone was back and forth to the little bathroom the whole time.'

'Who was sitting nearest to the door?' asked Ellie.

'Gordon, I think.'

'And you're certain he didn't leave?'

'Not *certain*, but we'd have heard the door, surely?'

'Not if everyone was concentrating on the band,' said Dunn. 'We're pretty loud.'

Veronica thought for a moment. 'All right, I'll concede that. But we've just established that he couldn't have got to the house and back without getting soaked, haven't we? There's no sheltered route between here and the house. But no one said, "Gosh, Gordon, you're frightfully wet." And he didn't reply, "I was just thinking that. Must be a leak in the roof." No one said anything at all.'

'People don't notice things,' said Dunn. 'No one was talking to him, after all. And by the time we all realized how hungry we were, all eyes were on you and Elizabeth while you organized the catering party. He could have sat there quietly dripping without anyone paying him the slightest bit of attention.'

Ellie nodded. 'He'd have been even drier by the time I came back over here with the news.'

'And everyone just wanted to find out what was going on,' said Dunn. 'So there still wasn't any reason for anyone to notice that Gordon was a bit damper than usual. Even if they did, he'd only have been a little wetter than everyone else. You all got soaked getting over here. I think he's our main suspect.'

Skins made a face. 'I'm still not convinced.'

'It all fits, though,' said Dunn. 'He had more than one motive. As far as he knew, his dad was sleeping with his wife—'

'As far as he knew?' interrupted Veronica. 'We all knew.'

'Yes, of course, sorry. So he knew that. One way or another he was going to inherit the business. Men have been driven to kill for much less.'

'Yeah, but . . .' said Skins. 'I mean . . . Well, look. Whoever did it went to a lot of trouble over that lock. It was all well planned. I can't believe they'd have done all that and then just taken a chance on no one noticing them coming and going. They'd have it better organized than that.'

'Maybe he just saw his chance and took it. Everyone was here, distracted by us lot . . . It was a perfect opportunity.'

'We all knew Papa was going to be working on Saturday afternoon. He'd made a big thing of it,' said Veronica.

Dunn nodded enthusiastically. 'Exactly. So having everyone still in the chapel listening to us probably changed the murderer's plans a bit. He'd have been expecting everyone to be in the house so he could come and go as he pleased. When he found himself sitting in the chapel, he had to improvise.'

'I'm afraid I've another objection,' said Ellie. 'I'd not thought of this before, but I heard the gunshot at four o'clock. That means the killer must have been in the room then. We started out thinking the killer must have been hiding in the room somehow, so I never questioned it, but thanks to Ivor, we now know he was able to get out and leave the door locked behind him. We've just been talking as though we assume the killer struck before I went back to the house with the sisters. But if John was already dead, how did I hear the shot at four?'

Skins spun round and looked at them. 'The gramophone record.'

'The what?'

'Oh,' said Dunn. 'Very clever.'

Skins turned back towards the house. 'Come on, then, let's have a look.'

He raced down the bowered path with the others close behind.

Skins and Dunn almost pushed each other over in their hurry to be the one to switch on the gramophone in John Bilverton's study.

Skins won, and while the valves in the amplifier were warming up, he lifted the record and examined it closely.

'Gershwin's "Rhapsody in Blue" by the Paul Whiteman Orchestra,' he said. 'Looks exactly like our copy. The label's properly stuck down. Can't see anything odd about it at all.'

He put it on the turntable and set down the needle. He, Ellie and Dunn knew the piece well and it played through exactly as they'd been expecting. They listened in silence until it reached the end, then Skins lifted the needle and switched everything off.

'So much for that,' said Dunn.

'It was a good idea, though,' said Ellie.

'What were you hoping to find?' asked Veronica.

Skins pointed to the electric gramophone. 'I thought the sound of the gunshot might have come from this thing. There's equipment in the chapel for making recordings on discs and everyone has access to it.'

'So if the killer wanted it to sound like the shot happened at some other time,' said Dunn, 'he could record it on the disc, maybe set up some sort of timer, and be long gone by the time someone heard the bang. John said he wanted tea at four, so there was a good chance someone would be outside to hear it if the timer were set for then.'

Skins flopped dejectedly into the chair. 'But the record is just the record, and there's no sign of any sort of timer.' He sighed. 'That's that then, isn't it? The old proverbial wild goose whatnot. John really did shoot himself and the trick lock was just some sort of joke – a last laugh at everyone else's expense.'

'What about the wound, though, mate?' said Dunn. 'He can't have shot himself and left that sort of wound. It was the first thing we agreed on.'

'We must have been mistaken, then.'

'So we're just giving up, are we?'

'To be honest, we might as well. The family doctor will be here tomorrow and it'll all be explained away. There'll be a funeral, and the reading of the will, and everyone will get on as normal. If things work out, Howard will do something splendid with his share of the spoils from the postcards. You'll get a place of your own somewhere, Veronica. Everyone else will do whatever it is they want to do and we'll play at the Preening Parrot as if nothing ever happened.'

'Yes, but—'

'He might be right, Barty,' said Ellie. 'We might have been barking up the wrong kettle of fish the whole time. Maybe we should just enjoy dinner with everyone one last time and say our goodbyes as though we never thought one of them was a murderer.'

'But one of them is a murderer,' said Veronica forcefully. 'You've convinced me. There's too much that's not right. Papa wasn't the sort of man to kill himself. You said the wound couldn't be self-inflicted. The lock was modified. Nothing adds up.' She looked around the room. 'And what's that bloody cushion doing in here? That's from the library.'

'Maybe the killer brought it in here to muffle the sound of the shot,' said Dunn. 'But he decided he didn't need it because the thunderstorm was so loud.'

'You see? Another thing that doesn't add up. Please don't give up. Someone in my family is a murderer and I won't be able to sleep soundly until I know who. They might come after me next.'

Ellie put a hand on Skins's shoulder. 'We'll just let it all percolate again. If we forget about it for a few hours and clear our heads, one of us might still have a brainwave before it's too late. Let's get back to the others and see about some early evening cocktails.'

Cocktails, though, were to be delayed.

Ellie, Skins and Dunn walked out into the Grand Hall.

Skins had begun a joke. 'So this Great Dane walks into a post office, and he picks up a telegram form—'

The three friends stopped in their tracks. Lying in an impossibly contorted position at the foot of the stairs was the body of Marianne Bilverton.

Once again it was Ellie who collected her wits quickly enough to rush forward and check for signs of life.

'She's breathing,' she said. 'Pulse is weak, but it's there. Ivor – hold her head very still while I check her for injuries.'

Skins knelt at Marianne's head and gripped her tightly while Ellie ran her hands along her limbs and around her body.

'No sign of anything broken,' she muttered. Then, more loudly, she said, 'Marianne. Marianne. Can you hear me? Don't move, but if you can hear me, squeeze my finger.'

There was no response.

'Is everything all right down there?' called Gordon from the gallery.

Another door opened and Malcolm leaned over the balustrade.

'I say, is she all right?'

Gordon was already on his way down the stairs, closely followed by Peter. Charlotte had emerged, too, and she and Malcolm arrived at the bottom of the stairs together.

'Oh, my goodness,' said Charlotte, her hand flying to her mouth. 'Is she . . . ?'

'She's alive, and I can't find any obvious broken bones,' said Ellie. 'But she has a terrific bump on the back of her head and she's unconscious. I can't rouse her at all.'

'Should we move her?' asked Gordon.

Ellie felt Marianne's neck again before indicating that Skins could safely let go. 'There's no damage to her neck, so it would probably be good to get her into bed and comfortable. Can somebody stay with her? She needs someone to keep an eye on her. Head injuries can be very dangerous.'

'I'll do it,' said Charlotte quickly. 'I'll sit with her.'

Gordon had already rung the servants' bell, and a few moments later Dunsworth appeared.

'We need to move my stepmother,' said Gordon. 'Do we own a stretcher?'

'No, sir. Not so far as I know.'

'We can improvise one,' said Ellie. 'We need two long poles and a blanket. I'll show you how to fold it.'

Dunsworth nodded. 'Right you are, madam. I think I know what you intend. I've seen it done in the trenches.'

'Good man,' said Gordon.

A few minutes later, Ellie showed Gordon and Dunsworth how to fold the blanket over the two poles to form a makeshift stretcher, and Marianne was carried upstairs, followed by a visibly distressed Charlotte.

'Nothing to be done now till the quack can get here in the morning,' said Malcolm. 'Important to keep up morale, what? I declare cocktail hour.'

Ellie, Skins and Dunn, though, made their excuses and set off to their rooms, promising to return later for dinner.

# Chapter Fourteen

***Tuesday, 30 June 1925***

Skins drank too much at what they'd all assumed would be their final dinner together at the house, and had slept badly. It had been a sombre evening, and although the food was as delicious as ever he had felt gloomy and uncomfortable, and had tucked away quite a bit more wine than he'd intended.

As always when he'd been drinking, he woke early, feeling more weary from the lack of decent sleep than groggy from the booze. Ellie was still fast asleep, so he pulled on his clothes as quietly as he could and set off downstairs.

Despite having servants at home, it still made him uncomfortable to summon someone just to make him a cup of tea. It was different if it was for the whole family, or for guests, but if it was just him, he'd honestly rather make it himself.

He ventured cautiously down into the kitchens. Although the household had been patient with the band's carefree wanderings, he was well aware that it was most definitely frowned upon for house guests to go roaming about in the servants' domain.

Lily was alone at the stove.

'Morning, Lily,' he said with a grin. 'Any tea in the pot?'

The young kitchen maid blushed.

'Good mornin', sir. You should have rung. We'd have brought you one up.'

'I know, but it seems a shame to put you out when all I want is a cuppa. All right if I help myself?'

'Of course, sir.'

Skins found himself a cup and saucer and poured out the strong dark brew from the heavy teapot.

'Is there news of Mrs Bilverton?' he asked. 'Marianne?'

'No, sir. Last I heard she was still abed with Mrs Bilverton by her side keepin' watch. Guilt, I reckon.'

'Guilt?'

'Over what she done. You know . . . Mr John.'

'Ah, yes. Right.'

Lily fell silent, but was fidgeting about, looking for all the world as though she was wrestling with a weighty dilemma.

'You all right there, love?' said Skins.

She blushed again. 'I am, sir. It's just . . . Can I have your autograph? I've been wantin' to ask but Mr Dunsworth told us we wasn't to bother you. I've got a book, see? My auntie give it me. I collect autographs from famous people. I've got a load from the music hall, and from a pantomime we all went to see last Christmas. But I love jazz. I stood outside the marquee while you were playin' the other night. You're wonderful. Would you?'

Skins smiled. 'Of course.'

He expected her to scurry off and fetch the book, but she just reached into the pocket of her neatly pressed uniform.

'I've been carryin' it about in case I met any of you.'

She handed him the book and he drew a pen from his jacket pocket. He signed it, 'To Lily, the jazz lover,' and drew a cartoon drum set beside his name before handing it back.

'We've been playing in the chapel,' he said. 'You should have come over.'

'I wanted to come over on Saturday, but we weren't allowed. The whole family went over and I thought we were going to get our chance, but Mr Dunsworth said no. I thought I was going to get a chance to meet someone when one of you came down here in the afternoon but I couldn't get away from my peelin'.'

'One of us came over?'

'On Saturday before Miss Elizabeth and Miss Veronica came down for the picnic. I didn't see who it was. They just went in the larder and then disappeared before I could nab them. Then we heard the terrible news about Mr Bilverton and I never got another chance. When you all came down and mucked about with the chicken, I didn't have my book. And anyway, Mrs Radway would have skinned me if I'd been cheeky and asked for autographs.'

'But it was definitely one of us? Not the staff?'

'They went in the larder, so it had to be a guest or family. They goes where they likes, see, even when they're not supposed to, but none of the other staff is allowed in there. Only kitchen maids allowed in the larder. Mrs Radway—'

'—would skin them, yes. Well, I don't know which of us it was, but I wish you'd said hello.'

Lily blushed. 'I wish I had, too. Do you think I'll be able to get the rest of the band to sign?'

'I'll send them over myself. I'd take the book, but it's more fun to be there when they sign, isn't it?'

'It is, sir. Thank you, sir.'

'Well, I'll not hold you up any longer – I'll go and find somewhere to sit.'

'I recommend the library.'

'Library it is, then. Hang on to that autograph book – I'll be sending the Dizzies down as soon as they're up.'

He set off back upstairs.

◆ ◆ ◆

He'd never been much of a reader, but something about books – especially large collections of books – fascinated him, so he was more than happy to follow Lily's suggestion.

Selecting a book at random from a shelf beside the fireplace, he settled into one of the armchairs, took a sip of his tea and began to read.

His choice was not a good one. The author, it seemed, had spent some time on a walking tour of the Alps, and was keen to share a detailed account of absolutely everything he saw along the way. No wayside flower was too insignificant to be intricately described, no passer-by too unremarkable to be remarked upon at length. After reading eight pages in which the author catalogued the contents of his own knapsack, Skins decided that he might be better off with something altogether less thorough.

He put the book back where he had found it and scanned the shelf for a more appealing title. Nothing caught his eye, but it did occur to him that the bookshelves had obviously been built by the same carpenter who had built the ones in the study. They were made of the same wood. They had the same proportions, the same polished finish and even, he noticed, the same downward lip on the leading edge of each shelf. He frowned.

On a whim, he ran his fingers along the lip of one of the waist-high shelves to the left of the fireplace. He found nothing.

He tried the lower one, as he had in the study. Still nothing.

Feeling slightly foolish, he repeated the process on the shelves to the right of the fireplace. On the lower shelf, he found a familiar imperfection. He pressed hard, and with a resonant clonk, the bookcase swung inwards an inch.

'Well, I'll be buggered,' he said.

He pushed the bookcase to reveal a familiar set of stone steps, though this time going to the right instead of left. He was about to flick on the light switch and set off to see where the stairs led when he heard footsteps and voices in the Grand Hall – it sounded like Gordon and Charlotte. Now, he decided, was not the time to get caught snooping about, most especially not if this turned out to have anything to do with John's death.

He pulled the bookcase closed as quietly as he could and resumed his seat. The voices disappeared, presumably to the dining room.

A few minutes later, Gordon poked his head round the door.

'Morning, Skins,' he said. 'Just seeing if there's anyone about.'

'Just me at the moment. Is there any news about Marianne?'

Gordon shook his head sadly. 'Still out cold, I'm afraid. Charlotte has been taking care of her but there's been no improvement.'

'I'm sure she'll be all right. I've seen blokes recover from worse.'

'I do hope so. I say, is it worth getting the staff to bring up some breakfast yet, do you think? I know you musicians are late risers.'

'Usually, yes, but the band will be down soon, I reckon. Give it half an hour and people should start turning up.'

'Marvellous. I'll have a word with the kitchens. Be nice to give you a good start to your last day here.'

'Last day, eh? You still reckon the roads will be clear?'

'They seem sure of it in the village. I've told the doctor what's happened and he's going to try to get here at nine. We'll know what the going's like then.'

'Then I look forward to a hearty breakfast with my comrades before we pack our gear and move out. It'll be like being back in the army.'

'But without anyone shooting at you, what?'

'Yeah,' said Skins with a slight frown, 'that's always a bonus.'

'Marvellous. I'll tell Mrs R to get cracking. Say an hour?'

'I'll let people know once they start coming down.'

'Good man. Toodle-oo.'

Gordon disappeared once more.

As soon as he was sure Gordon had gone down to the kitchen, Skins double-checked that the bookcase was closed and then ran up to the second floor as fast as he was able. He pelted to his bedroom where he found Ellie awake, but still lying in bed.

She smiled up at him. 'You need to take more exercise, honey. You're puffed.'

'I . . . ran . . . from . . . the . . . library,' he panted.

'Chased by the ghost of Bilverton House, huh?'

'No . . . I—'

'Hey, do you think they have a ghost? I've always wanted to stay in a haunted house. England's supposed to be full of them, but I've never been to one. Do you think—'

'Ellie . . . love?'

'Yes, honey?'

Skins was getting his breath back. 'Shut up a sec, there's a poppet.'

'Shutting up now, dear.'

'I've found another secret door.'

Ellie sat up abruptly. 'In the library?'

'Yup. It's in the bookcase, just like in the study. Same sort of mechanism, same sort of doorway, same sort of stairs.'

'Same room full of French pornography at the bottom?'

'I didn't get that far. I was about to have a nosy when I heard Gordon and Charlotte outside, so I closed it up quick. If we're going down there, I reckon we need a lookout up top. It was all right in the study – most of the family don't seem to want to go in there – but they're in and out of the library all day.'

'It's a thoroughfare, that's why. You have to go through either the library or the dining room to get from the hall to the back door.'

'Exactly. So we can't go poking around with the bookcase open, or someone's going to see.'

'We can just shut the door behind us.'

'And what happens when we open it to get out and Killer Gordon is standing there looking for a book on shooting?'

'When who's doing what?'

'Oh, nothing. I'm coming round to the idea of it being him. Something he said to me just now. We were talking about breakfast and I said eating with all my mates before shipping out would be just like being back in the army and he said, "But without anyone shooting at you." I mean, no one mentioned shooting. He's got it on the brain.'

'You did mention the army, though, honey. That's kind of its *raison d'être*, wouldn't you say? Shooting at people? It's not an entirely peculiar thing to say.'

'Yeah, well. I wasn't sure it was him yesterday, but now I've seen there's another secret door, and found out he's obsessed with shooting at people, I agree with you and Barty now. You thought it was him when we were at the chapel.'

'Hold on there, cowboy, we don't even know where the stairs go yet. Yesterday you were lukewarm on the idea of Gordon as the killer, but today you've got him tried and hanged just because you've found some hidden stairs in the library. Let's at least have a rummage about down there first.'

There was a knock on the door.

'Are you decent?' It was Dunn.

'As long as you'll not be embarrassed that I'm still in my night-dress,' called Ellie.

'Only, the last I heard was you suggesting he have a rummage about down there.'

Ellie laughed. 'Come on in, you dope.'

'Oh,' said Dunn as he opened the door and found a fully dressed Skins leaning against a chaise longue while Ellie sat in bed. 'That's not nearly so exciting as I imagined.'

'We're married, mate,' said Skins. 'It never is.'

'Hey,' said Ellie, throwing one of her pillows at him.

'You can see why I've always been so reluctant to get hitched,' said Dunn.

'Hey,' said Ellie again, but thought better of throwing her remaining pillow.

'So what's going on?' asked Dunn. 'I heard someone running.'

'That was me,' said Skins. 'There's been a whatsaname. A development.'

Skins recounted the events of the morning so far while Dunn made himself comfortable in an armchair.

'So how did none of them know the door was there?' asked Dunn, when Skins had finished.

'Same way none of them knew about the one in the study,' said Skins. 'The buttons are well hidden. But John knew, and I'm betting at least one of the others knows.'

Ellie nodded. 'And I was saying that before we get too carried away, we need to explore it to find out what's down there.'

'Ah,' said Dunn. 'That explains what I heard from outside. I thought—'

'We know what you thought, mate,' said Skins. 'Oh, and I nearly forgot. I spoke to Lily while I was getting myself a cuppa.'

'Lily?' said Dunn.

‘That pretty kitchen maid. Oh, I said I’d get everyone to sign her autograph book, by the way. Anyway, she said she saw someone go into the larder on Saturday afternoon.’

‘Who?’ asked Ellie.

‘She didn’t see. But adds fuel to the idea that someone was over here from the chapel.’

Dunn nodded. ‘It does. No doubt getting the ice. So what are we doing sitting here?’

Ellie sat up a little straighter in bed. ‘Well, I’m still in my nightdress, for one, and Ivor is counselling caution.’

‘You? Caution?’

‘I can be circumspect when the situation calls for it,’ said Skins. ‘We just need a lookout so no one catches us poking about. I was thinking Veronica would be just the girl.’

‘Then let’s go and get her.’

‘After breakfast, I think,’ said Ellie. ‘Ivor’s right – we need to make sure no one’s about. There’ll be a ton of coming and going until everyone’s had their breakfast.’

‘Then let’s go to breakfast.’

‘Can I at least get dressed first?’

‘Course you can.’

‘With you not in the room?’

‘Oh. Yes. Right. Sorry.’

‘Come on, idiot,’ said Skins. ‘Let’s leave the poor woman in peace. See you down there, Ells-Bells.’

Skins and Dunn left Ellie to get dressed and set off for the dining room.

Breakfast was cheerfully chaotic, with the end-of-term feeling even stronger than the day before. Many of the Dizzies had already started packing and all were talking excitedly about leaving at last. Even Mickey, who was actually dreading the nauseating journey in the motor coach, couldn't suppress his pleasure at the prospect of returning to his normal life.

'Don't get me wrong,' he said between mouthfuls of kedgeree, 'I've enjoyed our time here, but I can't wait to get home.'

'Well, we've appreciated your company,' said Howard, raising his teacup. 'You've all made a difficult time a good deal more bearable.'

'Yes, thank you,' said Gordon.

Skins, Ellie and Dunn, meanwhile, had managed to get Veronica on her own and were describing their plan.

'Oh, how exciting,' she said. 'Another hidden passage, and in my favourite room. I'll keep cave for you as long as I get to have a nosy afterwards.'

'It's your gaff,' said Skins. 'It would be rude to keep you out. All you have to do is make sure no one knows we're down there. As soon as we've worked out what's what, we'll cover for you and you can have a look for yourself.'

'But we think it's best that no one else knows the door even exists for now,' said Ellie.

'You can rely on Ronnie B. When are we off?'

'After this lot has dispersed a bit,' said Dunn. 'Give us a chance to get in and out without anyone wondering where we've got to.'

'I can hardly wait,' said Veronica. 'It's just like—'

All conversation stopped suddenly at the clangingly unfamiliar sound of the doorbell.

Gordon stood up. 'That will be Dr Hurlston. Malcolm? Howard? We ought to see him together, I think.'

Malcolm nodded and stood, but Howard looked round at his sisters.

'What about the girls?' he said. 'Shouldn't they come, too?'

'Don't be an ass, Howard. We'll be taking him out to the ice house.'

'Yes, but—'

'It's no place for the ladies. Now, are you coming or not?'

With an apologetic shrug, Howard joined his brother and uncle as they went to greet the family physician.

The mood was broken and breakfast was completed in near silence. As soon as the remaining family members finished their food, they left, and the band began to go their separate ways, too.

'Mickey, mate, do us a favour?' said Skins as Mickey rose to leave. 'Can you nip down the chapel and pack up my drum set? You know where everything goes.'

'What did your last servant die of?' said Mickey.

'I drugged him and threw him in the Thames for his insolence. Look, we've got one or two things to do . . . You know . . . about the you-know-what. Just pack up for me – I might not have time.'

Mickey nodded sagely. 'Say no more, mate. Consider it done.'

'Thanks. If anyone asks, you've not seen us.'

'Mum's the word.'

Mickey left the three friends and their lookout to wait for their chance to go exploring.

They sent Veronica on a scouting mission and she came back to report that most of the family seemed to have returned to their rooms, while Peter and Elizabeth were bickering in the drawing room.

'Oh dear,' said Ellie. 'What about?'

'Oh, the usual. She was berating him for not being ambitious enough, and for letting Father push him around. There was the usual thing about Papa thinking Peter was a gold-digger. He pointed out that her father wouldn't be able to do that now he was dead, and that he was about to start working with her brother as the company's lawyer. He didn't add, "So yah-boo to you," but it was implied.'

'It's all working out for Pete, then,' said Skins. 'Is he the sort who could kill? Even if it was just to get his fiancée off his back?'

'To be honest I've always assumed he likes the nagging. I can barely put up with her myself, but I don't have so much of a choice – one is rather lumbered with family, like it or not. But he could walk away at any time, so I thought he must enjoy it.'

Skins laughed. 'Probably not the murdering type, then. But other than those two, the coast's clear?'

'There's no one else about.'

'Let's do it, then,' said Ellie. 'I'm dying to see what's down there.'

Skins showed them how the latch worked and pushed the bookcase inwards.

'After you, then, Ells-Bells,' he said. 'Light switch is next to you, there.'

Ellie turned on the light and trod carefully down the stone stairs with Skins close behind. Once he'd made his own way inside, Dunn turned round and, with a wink, started to push the bookcase back into place.

'We'll knock like this' – he tapped 'Shave and a Haircut' on the wood – 'when we're ready to come out. If it's all clear, tap the same rhythm back – not the two knocks anyone else would do. That way we'll know it's you and that it's all right to come out. We can open the door from in here.'

'Got it. Good luck. Bring me back a present.'

Dunn laughed and clicked the bookcase closed.

At the bottom of the steps was a room that seemed identical to the one beneath the study. This one, though, was free of furniture and postcards. The other glaring difference was an iron-bound oak door on the outside wall.

'That's old,' said Ellie. 'Much older than the house.'

'Elizabethan?' asked Skins.

'Could be,' she said. 'Could be.'

'Ah, I get it,' said Dunn. 'So this could be left over from the original house. Which might mean it leads to—'

'The chapel,' said Skins and Ellie together.

'Well, don't just stand there, you idiots. Open it.'

Ellie grasped the ring handle and turned it to lift the latch. The door swung towards them on oiled hinges to reveal an arched, brick-lined tunnel.

To their surprise, the tunnel was lit.

'Those bulbs aren't an original feature,' said Dunn.

Skins pointed to the cables that ran from a hole in the wall above their heads to the right, went through a hole drilled in the old doorframe and then off down the tunnel. 'They've got all the modern amenities here, mate. Someone's wired it all up.'

Ellie led them off down the tunnel. It was tall enough for her to stand upright and she progressed quickly. Skins was fine as long as he remembered to duck for the lightbulbs hung at intervals from the roof. Dunn, though, was forced to crouch uncomfortably.

'People were a lot shorter in the olden days,' he said as he banged his head on the brick roof for the umpteenth time.

'Maybe it's just Catholic priests who were short,' said Skins.

'Or maybe Barty's freakishly tall,' suggested Ellie. 'We're having no trouble at all.'

'Or maybe he's normal, and I'm descended from a long line of priests.'

'Pause a while and see if you can work out why that's impossible,' said Dunn. 'You idiot.'

Skins chuckled. 'You make a good point, Barty boy. Now all we need to do is work out why this tunnel is so twisty-turny. You'd think it would be easier just to cut it in a straight line from the chapel to the house.'

Dunn thought for a moment. 'How about this? Suppose you were a priest. Suppose you were saying mass in the chapel and the queen's agents burst in. You manage to leg it down the escape tunnel, but they follow you. If the tunnel is straight, they can see you, no matter how far you've run. One of them has a crossbow. Or a gun. Did they have guns? Anyway, if the tunnel's straight they've got a clear shot and you're a dead priest with no one to give you the last rites. But if it's a little bit twisty like this one, you don't have to be far ahead for them not to be able to even see you, let alone take pot shots at you.'

'You're much cleverer than you look, Barty Dunn,' said Ellie.

'He'd have to be,' said Skins, ducking the slap aimed at the back of his head. 'How far do you reckon we've come?'

'I've no idea any more,' said Ellie. 'I started counting steps but then you started wittering on about short priests and crossbows and I lost count.'

'However far it is,' said Dunn, 'we're there. Look.'

A short way ahead of them was another oaken door. Ellie approached and confidently turned the ring handle. The door was locked.

'Oh,' said Dunn. 'That's disappointing.'

'Not wholly unexpected, though,' said Ellie. 'To be honest I was surprised the first one opened.'

'What do you reckon, then? Back to the library for a rethink?'

Skins nodded. 'Lead the way, Lofty. And mind your head.'

Back in the library, Veronica poured them all a cup of tea while they told her what they'd found.

'How very thrilling,' she said. 'Do you think you got as far as the chapel?'

'I tried counting my steps on the way there and the way back,' said Ellie, 'but these two idiots kept joking about and I lost count both times. We must have been most of the way there, though.'

'It might come up outside,' said Dunn. 'A lot of those secret tunnels do.'

'How do you know?' asked Skins.

'I live alone. I read.'

'How do they emerge, though?' said Veronica. 'Trapdoors?'

'Some have trapdoors,' said Dunn. 'Some are hidden in follies or grottoes. I read of one that came out at the back of a natural cave.'

'We've nothing like that in the grounds. We might have missed the secret doors, but we'd know all about follies, grottoes and caves.'

'Oh. Well in that case, if it opens anywhere at all it's probably in the chapel itself. Can you think of a likely spot?'

'There's a cupboard just inside the main door.'

'Gordon could easily have slipped into a cupboard while no one was looking,' said Skins.

Dunn was less convinced. 'Is it big, this cupboard? Big enough for someone to get in, close the door, then open a secret trapdoor?'

'Probably not,' said Veronica.

'You'd not want a tunnel entrance right by the main door,' said Skins. 'That's where the bad guys would be. "Excuse me, would you mind awfully stepping aside, only you're blocking my secret escape route." You'd want it in the body of the chapel somewhere.'

'Not the body,' said Ellie. 'In one of the side rooms. You'd need to be able to run, hide, lock yourself in and then disappear. If it comes out anywhere it'll be in the bathroom or the control room.'

'It'll be the bathroom, then,' said Skins. 'You said before that everyone was back and forth to the loo. Gordon could have snuck off to powder his nose any time after John left. Who would have noticed how long it took him to get back?'

'We need to find the key,' said Dunn.

'Well, quite,' said Veronica. 'But that's easier said than done, wouldn't you say? I mean, I've lived here since I was two and I've only just learned that there are two secret rooms and a tunnel in the house. And think how big a secret room is compared with a key.'

'It's got to be easy to get hold of,' said Dunn. 'If you were planning to make use of the tunnel, you'd not want to be ferreting about for the key. You'd want it close at hand.'

'Or in your pocket,' said Skins. 'We might never find it if the killer has it.'

'I wouldn't keep it with me,' said Ellie. 'It's incriminating evidence, for one thing – I wouldn't want to be caught with the key that might help to prove I murdered John Bilverton.'

'Good point,' said Dunn. 'And if more than one person knows about the tunnel, it's a bit of a giveaway if the key goes missing.'

'All right, then,' said Skins. 'But where would you keep it? If you keep it in the house, you can't get out of the chapel. If you keep it in the chapel you can't get through the tunnel from here.'

'Two keys?' suggested Ellie. 'One at either end?'

'I suppose that would do it. But it's a big old house and a big old chapel. Where do we start? The study? Or the butler's pantry? There were dozens of keys on that board in there.'

'It's hardly a secret tunnel if the butler has a key,' said Dunn. 'But it would be near the secret door itself. That's obvious, isn't it? If it exists at all, it's got to be in here.'

Skins swept his arm around the room. 'Somewhere in here, then. Among these hundreds of books—'

'Thousands,' interrupted Veronica.

'Among these *thousands* of books and dozens of knick-knacks. Where do we even start?'

'We think like a sneaky person,' said Ellie. 'If you were trying to keep the key available, it would be near the secret door, just as Barty says. But you wouldn't want it too close. If someone stumbles upon how to open the door, like we did—'

'I didn't stumble,' said Skins. 'I reasoned it out with the power of my towering intellect.'

'If someone figures out there's a secret door here by the sheer, breathtaking brilliance of their mighty brain—'

'That's more like it.'

'—then you wouldn't want them just to stumble on the key as well, no matter how powerful their brain might be. So I suggest we can rule out the whole of this side of the bookcase.' She indicated the section to the right of the fireplace. 'But you'd still want it to be handy, so I think we can rule out the other end of the room down towards the salon door as well.' She moved over to the left of the fireplace and pointed to the bookcase there. 'Which leaves this side.' She turned to her left. 'These shelves as far as the window.' She turned right round. 'And that section over there as far as the door. Barty? You and Ivor take those, Veronica can search up to the window and I'll take these shelves by the fireplace.'

'What are we looking for?' asked Veronica. 'What was the lock like? Big? Little?'

'It was a big, old-fashioned lock,' said Dunn. 'So the key is going to be chunky. Probably ornate, too – they went in for fancy keys in the olden days.' He held up his hands to indicate a key about four inches long. 'Something like that.'

'Right you are,' she said. 'Are we considering hollowed-out books?'

'I've always wanted to find something in a hollowed-out book,' said Skins.

'I guess we'll have to consider them in the end,' said Ellie, 'but I'd start with looking in trinkets first. Anything that might open, even if it's not an actual box. Then we can look behind the books. And then, Ivor my darling, we can start opening them up and seeing if someone has cut a compartment in the pages to conceal a key.'

'That's all I ask,' he said.

They began their search.

Veronica took down a porcelain figurine of a geisha wearing a blue kimono, and shook it. It belatedly occurred to her that if there were a heavy iron key inside it might smash the delicate china, but it appeared to be empty anyway. She peered into the hole in the base in case the key might be wrapped in something to prevent it rattling, but there was definitely nothing there.

She moved on to a Japanese puzzle box. She'd played with it as a girl and had long since worked out the secret of opening it. Inside, exactly as she remembered, were three coins and a jade bracelet. But no key. She closed the box and put it back on the shelf.

Skins and Dunn were also examining figurines with a similar lack of success, though theirs were European in origin.

Skins held up a figure of a woman in a floral dress wearing a long green jacket. She was sitting on a chair and holding a book while she stared into the middle distance with a vacant look on her face. 'No offence, Veronica, but this is hideous.'

'None taken,' she said. 'There are some absolutely ghastly things in this house. I used to long to break some of them – that one in particular.'

'You must come and visit us in London,' said Ellie. 'We have a porcelain ballerina that's badly in need of smashing, but the children never seem to manage it.'

'I should love to visit, porcelain ballerina or not. And when I do, just point it out to me and I'll do my best to bump into it for you.'

'Come for dinner when all this is over.'

Dunn held up a dark blue Fabergé-style egg. 'Does this open? Or will I break it if I try?'

'Twist the crown thing on the top and it'll pop open.'

The egg did, indeed, pop open to reveal a posy of enamelled violets. But no key.

The trinkets on Ellie's section of bookcase were all too small to hold the sort of key they thought they were looking for, so she had started removing the books one by one to see what was behind them.

The top shelf had yielded nothing, as had the second. She was working her way along the third when a title caught her eye.

'Would you guys hide the key to a priest's secret escape tunnel in a book called *The Mysteries of the Elizabethan House*?'

Skins stopped what he was doing at once and excitedly crossed the room. 'Open it and find out.'

Ellie pulled the book from the shelf. It was bound in dark red leather with the title debossed and picked out in gold leaf. It was hefty and, to their shared joy, made a clonking sound when she shook it. She lifted the cover, expecting to be able to leaf through the book, but almost all the pages had been glued together. Just two remained unglued so that the cover and the first few pages formed the lid of a heavy paper box, inside which was a chunky iron key.

'Well, that's not disappointing at all,' said Dunn. 'Shall we see if it works?'

# Chapter Fifteen

With Veronica on watch in the library, Ellie led the way along the tunnel, muttering under her breath.

'You counting, Ells-Bells?' said Skins.

'She might be,' said Dunn. 'Although I can think of twenty-six, maybe thirty-five reasons why she might not.'

'Oh, I'd have put it lower than that. I can only think of six or seven. Twelve at the most.'

'You're a couple of stinkers, you know that,' said Ellie. 'I've a good mind to take us back to the entrance and start again.'

'It doesn't matter now,' said Dunn. 'If the key opens the door, we'll find out where it goes without having to count anything.'

'You're still a stinker. And you're a double stinker, Ivor Maloney.'

'What have I done? He started it.'

'You joined in. You should defend me.'

'You're big and scary enough to defend yourself, my angel. We're here now, anyway.'

Ellie fitted the key into the lock and turned it. With a well-oiled clonk, the bolt withdrew. She turned the ring handle. The latch lifted, and the door swung open.

Ahead was another stretch of tunnel, exactly like the section they had already come through.

'See, now, if you stinkers had let me count, we'd have known we were only part way there.'

'There can't be much further to go,' said Dunn. 'Just round this next bend, I reckon.'

Skins shook his head. 'I say two more bends.'

'Half a crown?'

'You're on.'

Two more bends later they reached a third oak door and Dunn fished in his pocket for two shillings and sixpence to settle the bet.

Ellie tried the door and was relieved to find it unlocked. It opened into a small empty room, lit with an electric lightbulb hung from the same cables that ran the length of the tunnel. There was a flight of stone stairs in the corner of the room, disappearing up into the ceiling.

'You guys want to place a bet on where that leads?' she asked.

'Bathroom,' they said together.

She laughed. 'I agree, actually. Come on, let's find out.'

She led the way up the steps and found herself in front of a blank wall. It was darker at the top of the stairs, but it was obviously a dead end.

She started running her hands over the smooth plaster. 'We'd all have lost our money – it doesn't go anywhere.'

'It must do,' said Skins. 'Is it another trick door like at the other end?'

'Already looking, honey. Give me a second.'

Her fingertips brushed over a crack in the plaster. She traced it upwards. The crack was straight and vertical.

'Feels like there's a door here,' she said. 'I'm looking for the latch.'

With a click, the crack widened and a section of the wall moved slightly away.

'Found it.'

She pushed firmly but steadily, and the hidden door opened.

'We'd definitely have lost our money,' she said as the other two joined her. 'Look where we are.'

'Well, I'll be buggered,' said Skins.

Dunn looked around the recording control room. 'This changes everything.'

The wooden racks that held the recording discs were attached to the door and had swung into the room with it. Dunn looked around for signs of the latch, and soon found a small hook on the wall, hidden on the other side of the rack. There was a large iron key, just like the one in Ellie's pocket, hanging from it. He pulled on the hook and it moved outwards against the resistance of a spring. He couldn't see any sign of a mechanism, but he was willing to bet this was how the door was opened. He tested his hypothesis by pushing against the rack to close the door. It clicked shut and he briefly admired the way it was completely hidden before pulling on the hook to unlatch it again.

'It explains that weird thing Malcolm said when he was showing us round,' said Skins.

'What thing?' asked Ellie.

'He said it never got hot in here. Sometimes got too cold, he said. I should reckon having a draughty tunnel opening up behind the record rack would chill the place nicely.'

'It certainly would,' agreed Ellie. 'But I'm having trouble believing it's Malcolm.'

'It's the only reasonable explanation, though, isn't it?' said Dunn. 'We all assumed he was in here the whole time, checking the recordings. We could hear them till he shut the door, but then nothing. He could have been back and forth to the house as often as he wanted and none of us would have known anything about it.'

'But why?' asked Skins. 'And how?'

Dunn frowned. 'How? He went down the tunnel, shot his brother and came back up the tunnel again. It's not complicated.'

'There's still gaps in that – the gunshot Ellie heard, for one. But even so, there's no clear "Why?" is there?'

'That's the stumper, isn't it?' said Ellie. 'We know his recording business was sound, and well financed. We know from the unsigned new will that the two got on – John was going to make provision for the business to carry on here whatever happened. Actually, that might even be in the original will – we don't know for sure it was a new provision. He doesn't seem to have any real reason to want to get rid of him.'

'Now we know it's him—' began Skins.

Dunn interrupted. '*Think* it's him.'

'Think it would be difficult for it to be anyone other than him, then. But anyway. Now we know that, maybe we should take another look at the new will. I only skimmed it, after all. And if we can find the current will, that might help, too.'

'I agree,' said Ellie. 'Shall we do that now? There's not much point in trying to work out the "How?" if we've got the wrong "Who?", and the "Why?" should help us confirm it.'

'I . . . er . . . yes,' said Skins. 'So does that mean we're going back to the house?'

'It does. We shouldn't be hanging about here, anyway – if it really is Malcolm and he comes back and finds us snooping about in his control room it could all get a bit ugly. He's not above shooting people, after all.'

'And we need to lock the tunnel door and let Veronica know what we've found,' agreed Dunn. 'We can come back here later.'

'Right you are,' said Skins. 'I just want to check something before we set off, though.'

He rummaged around among the cables and mysterious electronics for a few moments, occasionally emitting what could have been murmurs of satisfaction and approval, but could just as easily have been indigestion. Finally, he stood up.

'Happy now?' asked Dunn. 'Can we go?'

'Lay on, McDunn.'

Ellie pulled on the hook to unlock the door and they all trooped in. Once again Dunn was left to close the door behind them and they made their way quickly back along the tunnel, each lost in their own thoughts. They paused briefly to allow Ellie to relock the door, then continued to the room beneath the library.

Dunn and Ellie mounted the stairs, but Skins was looking about.

'You coming up?' asked Dunn. 'Or should we just get Mickey to send some food down for you?'

'On my way, mate. Hold your horses. Just checking something.'

'You're not going to tell us what, are you?'

'Where would be the fun in that?'

Dunn tutted and gave the secret knock. A few seconds later, he heard it repeated back, so he opened the door and the three friends emerged into the library. Ellie turned off the lights and helped Skins pull the bookcase back into position.

'Well?' demanded Veronica excitedly. 'Where does it lead? The chapel bathroom? I bet it's the bathroom. No, wait. The cupboard in the vestibule. Or . . . or a manhole cover outside. Or—'

'It comes out in the studio control room,' said Ellie. 'I'm guessing it would have been the sacristy when it was an actual chapel? Or maybe the priest's private room. The priest could hide in there, then sneak back to the house. If anyone came looking for him, they'd just find an empty room.'

'How exciting,' said Veronica with a grin. 'Oh. But . . . but that means . . .'

'It's looking very likely, yes,' said Dunn.

'Oh no, he's one of my favourites. And why would Uncle Malcolm—'

'That's what we've come back to find out,' said Ellie. 'We're going to start by having another look at the new will, if you want to come.'

'The new will?' exclaimed Veronica. 'You found it? What do I get?'

'Sadly, we don't know,' said Skins. 'It's not signed, so the old one's still in force.'

'I'd love to see it, though, nonetheless. Are you going now?'

Ellie was already moving towards the door. 'Now, yes. We don't have much time. As soon as the motor coach gets here, we'll be ushered out and it'll all be too late.'

'Then let's go.'

◆ ◆ ◆

In the study, Skins was once again hunting about behind the gramophone.

Dunn had gone straight to the desk with Ellie and Veronica. 'Would you stop faffing about over there and come and show us the secret drawer,' he said.

'Just checking something,' said Skins as he pushed himself upright and joined the others. He motioned for them to move aside, then reached under the surface of the desk and ran his fingers along the smooth wood, as he had done before.

'There's a little catch like the ones on the shelves . . . right . . . here.'

With a click, the hidden drawer popped open, and Skins stepped back to let the others have a look.

Dunn took out the will and started to read. Meanwhile, Ellie and Veronica rummaged through the other files and papers.

'Did you look at this other stuff, honey?' asked Ellie.

'No, I was so excited to find the will I ignored all that other tat.'

Ellie and Veronica split the papers between them while Skins returned to his examination of the gramophone.

Five minutes passed with only occasional whistles and at least one 'Well, I'll be' from Ellie.

Skins had completed his own investigations and waited as patiently as he could.

Eventually, his curiosity got the better of him. 'Well?'

Ellie smiled enigmatically. 'I think I'm beginning to get an idea what might have made Malcolm do what we think he did.'

'And you're not going to tell me, are you?'

'No, honey, not yet. I need to figure some other things out first. Are you going to tell us why you keep rummaging about with all those wires?'

'No, love, not yet. I need to work some other things out first.'

'Touché.'

'If it makes you feel any better,' said Veronica, waving the file she'd been reading, 'I've only found some confidential ideas for a new line of biscuits, so I've no idea what either of you is talking about.'

Dunn held up the will. 'And this is exactly as laughing boy there described it the other day. There's nothing in here that would make anyone want to kill him. Not that I can see, anyway.'

'No,' said Ellie, 'it's got nothing to do with the will. Nothing at all. Trouble is, I still can't prove anything.'

Dunn replaced the will. 'Would it help if we could figure out once and for all how he did it?'

'It couldn't hurt. Maybe there's something uniquely Malcolmish about the method that would absolutely rule everyone else out.'

'I think I might be able to help there,' said Skins. 'Anyone fancy another trip to the chapel?'

'Rather,' said Veronica. 'And Malcolm's still in his room as far as I know, so we should be safe. I say, can we go through the tunnel? I'd love to see it.'

'I don't see why not,' said Dunn. 'Now we know where it comes out, we don't need a lookout in the library any more – we can just walk back through the grounds.'

'It would also suit my own plans very well,' said Skins.

'Would it?' said Dunn. 'Would it really?'

Skins tapped the side of his nose.

Despite having recently been given the news that her uncle may have murdered her father, Veronica was close to being giddy as Ellie and Skins led her down the steps from the library. Dunn closed the secret door and joined them in the cellar room, where he found Veronica closely examining the oak door.

'It's like an adventure novel,' she said. 'I can't believe we had something so utterly fabulous under our noses the whole time. Look at this door. Can't you just imagine some terrified priest scuttling through it? I wonder if it was ever used in anger. Oh, would he stay here? No, of course not. He'd run up into the house and then hide in the priest hole. If he'd been followed, he wouldn't want to be caught hanging around in a room at the end of the tunnel. Oh, I say, isn't it just too thrilling?'

Ellie smiled and opened the door.

'A tunnel. Oh my goodness, these bricks.' She brushed her hands against the red bricks that lined the tunnel. 'Laid by Elizabethan artisans. This is marvellous.'

She kept up her excited narration all the way to the locked door, then resumed as Ellie relocked it behind them. She finally relented as Dunn carefully opened the door at the top of the stairs at the other end. He checked that the coast was clear before leading them all into the control room.

Veronica looked back at the rack of discs attached to the moving section of wall. 'Oh, I say. Who would ever have thought it?'

'Not us, certainly,' said Ellie. 'Now, then, Mr Maloney, what are you up to?'

'Flick the tunnel lights off and push the door shut,' said Skins.

'It's unlike you to be so tidy. Why aren't you more like this at home?'

'Because we don't have a big rack of gramophone records at home that needs searching.'

Ellie looked at the dozens of discs neatly stacked on the wooden rack. 'You want to go through that lot?'

'I want you and Veronica to go through them, yes, please.'

Veronica looked a good deal more excited about the task than Ellie. 'What are we looking for?'

'First off, another copy of "Rhapsody in Blue", if you can see one. Then anything that doesn't look right. A peculiar title written on the disc. Or no title at all, maybe. A disc where only a tiny portion has been recorded and the rest is blank would be especially interesting.'

'And what important task will you and Barty be undertaking while we're doing secretarial work?'

'While you, my darling Ells-Bells, are looking for the disc upon which the sound of a gunshot was recorded, Barty and I will be checking that it was possible to play it from one of the machines in here so that it could be heard in the study while you were standing outside.'

'That explains all the ferreting about in dusty corners and the obsession with cables,' said Dunn. 'You're much cleverer than you look, as well.'

'Thanks, mate. There's two pairs of wires running along the tunnel. One's for the lights, obviously, but I needed to double-check that the other one connected the equipment in the study to the equipment in here. That's what I was looking for in the room under the library. One pair runs up to the light switch, but another one disappears into the wall of the postcard room. Well, I assume that's where it goes, anyway. From there it goes up into the study where it's connected to the terminals on the loudspeaker alongside the ones coming from the gramophone in there.'

'It's all a bit of a mystery to me,' said Veronica. 'You're saying that Papa's gramophone could play records in here?'

'Not exactly. In theory, the gramophones in here can play out through loudspeakers anywhere else, as long as there are wires connecting them. That's the beauty of these new electric ones – the sound travels along wires instead of through tubes. And there's a pair of wires going through the tunnel to the house, so you can put a disc on in here and hear it in the study.'

'Like a telephone.'

'More or less. But much better sound quality. So if Malcolm had a recording of, say, a gunshot, he could play it here and the sound could come out of the loudspeaker in the study.'

'But the gramophone in the study was already playing "Rhapsody in Blue",' said Ellie. 'I heard it.'

'You heard the tune, yes, and you saw the record spinning on the gramophone when you broke in, but that doesn't mean you heard that particular record.'

'I don't follow any of this,' said Veronica, 'but my own job seems clear: find a peculiar gramophone record.'

'That's it,' said Skins. 'We'll catch the bugger yet.'

Veronica and Ellie began the painstaking task of removing each disc in turn from the rack, taking it from its cardboard sleeve and examining it for peculiarities.

Meanwhile Skins showed Dunn where a pair of wires entered the room through a tiny hole drilled in the wall. Together they confirmed that the wires were connected to one of the boxes of electronics.

'So it could definitely be done, then,' said Dunn. 'You're a clever old stick, aren't you?'

'It's still only . . . What do they call it in the detective stories? Circumstantial evidence? That's it. It'll never stand up in court.'

'I couldn't tell you anything about that, but there must be other evidence. The clever ones never think they'll get caught so they always leave something. You take those drawers in that table, I'll check the cupboard.'

It took Dunn a few moments to force the lock on the cupboard door, but once he was in, it wasn't long before he let out a triumphant 'Oi, oi! Look what we have here.'

He held up an ornately engraved brass box.

'That's Uncle Malcolm's pandan box,' said Veronica. 'He brought it back from India. They keep *paan* in it – betel leaves, areca nut and spices, all mixed into some sort of paste. I think I remember slaked lime being mentioned, but I might be wrong. Then they chew it. It's a stimulant. Good for the digestion or something, I believe.'

'Oh, it's a stimulant, all right,' said Dunn. He opened the box to show them the fine white powder inside. 'But he skipped the betel leaves and went straight on to cocaine.'

'Good Lord,' said Veronica. 'Are you certain?'

'I don't use it myself, but I've met a lot of people who do – I'd know it anywhere.'

'It fits in with what I found in the study,' said Ellie.

'All I've got is a journal,' said Skins, holding up a leather-bound notebook. 'Oh, but I do have a door lock and some leftover lock parts. I'm going to bet it's the original one from John's study and the bits our murderer took out of the doctored one.' He showed them. 'How about you, Ells-Bells? Got anything?'

'I've found a couple of likely candidates,' she said. 'Shall we try them?' She held up two record sleeves, then looked at the gramophone. 'If I can figure out how to get this thing working.'

Skins was about to do it for her, but Veronica beat him to it.

'Oh, that much I do know,' she said. 'If it's anything like the one in the drawing room, you flick this switch here, turn that knob and retire to a safe distance while it hums to itself for a bit and makes you feel as though it could explode at any moment. This lever here will set it spinning, and the needle is like the old wind-up ones – just pop it on the record.'

They watched as she brought the machine to life and put on the first disc.

The familiar pops and crackles of the record sounded sharper through the loudspeaker. Then another set of pops and crackles, as though another disc had been put on. The familiar clarinet notes of "Rhapsody in Blue" filled the room. The piece continued entirely as normal until they heard a faint click. Then, with a suddenness that shocked even those of them who had been expecting it, there was a loud bang: the pistol shot that Ellie had heard on Saturday afternoon.

They let the disc run through to the end before Veronica lifted the needle.

'So how did he do that?' asked Veronica.

'Sounded to me like he played the original record into a microphone and recorded it on to a fresh disc, then fired the gun at the appropriate moment,' said Dunn. 'That click would have been the sound of him cocking the pistol.'

'That's it, then,' said Skins. 'He was the only one who would have known how to put all that together. I reckon all we need is the gun he used to record the shot and then we've got him bang to rights.'

'Do you mean this gun?' said a voice from the doorway.

They turned to see Malcolm Bilverton, his walking stick in one hand and a Webley service revolver in the other. The pistol was pointed at Skins.

'I should have liked to have used John's own gun,' said Malcolm languidly, 'but he'd have missed it if I pinched it – he liked to keep it cleaned and oiled, d'you see? Even if I got it back to his desk in short order, its absence might still have been noticed. Still, I reasoned that no one but me would be able to tell the difference in the sound, so I used my own.'

'There's four of us, mate,' said Dunn. 'You'll never—'

'Never get away with it? Oh, I think my pals in the local constabulary will happily accept my story of how the drug-addled musicians my nephew hired for the party broke in to my control room, intent on stealing my expensive kit to pay for their habit. Plucky Veronica tried to stop them, of course, but the bounders shot her. I came upon the scene, wrestled the gun from their devilish hands, and in the ensuing struggle, all three succumbed to fatal bullet wounds.'

'What about Hetty?' asked Ellie.

'Dear, ambitious Hetty? Tragic accidental overdose of a sleeping draught. Happens all the time.'

'What on earth did she do to deserve to be murdered?'

'She was poking about in here while I was trying to work. The silly girl stumbled upon the latch that opens the escape tunnel. She didn't realize its significance. Not then, at least. But it was only a matter of time. Bright girl. Had to go.'

'And Marianne?'

'Another bright girl. She was suspicious. John must have confided in her, or let something slip, so when he copped it she knew something was up. Confronted me. Had to suffer an accident.'

Dunn scowled. 'You're m—'

'Mad? Do you know, I used to worry that I might be. Had some terrible doubts about myself in my army days. But I've come to realize that actually everyone else is mad and I'm the only sane one. Wars, greed, crime – insanity. The only important thing is beauty. Music, art, Mother Nature. Everything else is insanity and wickedness. The old cocaine sharpens the mind, d'you see? Puts all the senses on alert. Helps me see things much more clearly. Put that box down carefully, lad, by the way. Precious stuff, that. Cost me an arm and a leg, what?' He gave a little chuckle as he tapped his false leg with his cane.

'Where did you record it all? Where did you fire the shot?' asked Skins.

Malcolm turned slightly and waved his pistol back towards the chapel. 'Had to do it in here – I told you, the loudspeaker is screwed down. Fired the shot out through the door. Bullet's lodged in one of the ceiling beams. I wondered about getting a ladder and digging it out, but I'm not much good on ladders and I thought it would be a nice reminder of one of my better-laid plans.'

He turned smugly back just as Dunn threw the contents of the pandan box in his face. Skins rushed towards the temporarily blinded former soldier and tried to wrestle the gun from his hands.

In the ensuing struggle the gun went off. Ellie screamed as Veronica fell.

Between them, Skins and Dunn managed to subdue Malcolm. They used Dunn's tie to secure his hands behind his back, and Skins unbuckled and removed the older man's false leg.

'You know, just in case you were thinking of hopping it,' he said as he put the leg out of reach in the corner of the control room.

Ellie was tending to Veronica.

'How bad?' asked Skins.

'Got her in the shoulder. I can staunch the bleeding for now, but she'll need the hospital.'

Veronica moaned as Ellie applied pressure to the wound, using the torn-off sleeve of her own blouse.

'She could do with morphine, too. Go and see if Doctor Whosit is still here. And let me have a look at that journal while you're gone.'

Skins handed her the journal and then, having checked that Dunn had Malcolm under control, set off at a run through the chapel and back to the house.

◆ ◆ ◆

He found Gordon, Howard and Dr Hurlston in the drawing room.

'I'm afraid there'll have to be an inquest,' the doctor was saying. 'The coroner has to rule in cases of suicide.'

'I understand,' said Gordon. 'That will delay the reading of the will, won't it?'

'I'm sorry, but yes. There'll be no death certificate until after the coroner's hearing.'

'Is that all you're worried about—' began Howard, but Skins interrupted him.

'We need the doctor in the chapel,' he panted. 'Veronica's been hurt.'

'Hurt?' said Howard. 'How?'

'Malcolm shot her. Call an ambulance – we'll need to get her to a hospital. And call the police. Doctor? Come with me please. And bring your bag.'

'Uncle Malcolm?' said Gordon in astonishment. 'Surely there must be some mistake.'

'No mistake, Gordon. We'll explain later. Just make the calls, please. Now. Doctor?'

Dr Hurlston seemed slightly flustered. 'I'll . . . I'll need to get my bag from my car. The chapel, you say?'

'The chapel. Quick as you can, please.'

The doctor went to the door with Skins following him.

'I can manage, thank you, Mr . . . ?'

'Maloney. I'll meet you there.'

Shaking his head at the old doctor's lack of urgency, Skins left through the other door, going back the way he had come through the dining room and salon.

Howard followed. 'I'm coming with you.'

'All right, but don't throw a fit on me, all right? Have you ever seen someone shot?'

'Where would I have seen—'

'No, of course not. Sorry. There's a lot of blood, but she's all right. Ellie used to be a nurse and she's taking care of her. Just don't . . . you know . . .'

'Don't throw a fit. No. Got it.'

They jogged to the chapel and Skins led the way to the control room.

'How's she doing?' he asked.

'I'm still with it, you know,' said Veronica. 'You can ask me.'

'Sorry, mate. How are you?'

'In a lot of bloody pain, if you must know. I don't know how soldiers bear it.'

'Never got shot, me,' said Skins. 'Got bonked on the head by a signpost, but never got shot.'

'I'd have bloody shot you,' growled Malcolm, still lying on the floor. 'Insolent whelp. I bet you thought you were the life and soul of the regiment. There'd have been a tragic accident in your trench, let me tell you. Accidental discharge of a weapon. Man responsible's on a fizzer for carelessness, but it was just one of those things. Pity about poor Maloney, but these things happen.'

'Malcolm?' said Skins.

'Colonel bloody Bilverton to you, boy.'

'Malcolm,' repeated Skins. 'Shut your face. I *was* the life and soul of the regiment, as it happens, but my mate there had a bit of a reputation for putting the boot in. It wouldn't do to upset him or you'll spend your first night in the police cells with a broken nose.'

Dunn, who had never kicked anyone in his life, tapped Malcolm idly in the ribs with the toe of his boot.

'Is the doctor on his way?' asked Ellie.

'As fast as his fat little legs will carry him,' said Skins. 'Gordon's calling an ambulance, too.' He looked over at Malcolm. 'And the rozzers, Malcy.'

'You'll be smirking on the other side of your face when I've finished with you, boy. I know the Duke of Sutherland. And the chief constable.'

'And I know Duke Ellington. Well, not to speak to, but I've heard his records. But that wouldn't help me if I'd murdered my brother and shot my niece in the shoulder.'

'Murdered his brother?' said Howard.

'What's that useless drip doing in here?' spluttered Malcolm.

'We'll explain everything later,' said Ellie. 'For now, will someone please hurry that doctor up.'

'No need, no need,' said Dr Hurlston. 'Here I am. Now then, young Veronica, it looks like you've been in the wars.'

# Chapter Sixteen

The ambulance arrived some while before the police, but Veronica had insisted – very much against the advice of Dr Hurlston – that they delay her trip to hospital until she'd heard Ellie's promised explanation of the events of the weekend.

With Howard's assistance, Ellie had managed to persuade all the Bilvertons, as well as the entire band, to gather in the library. They were joined by Dr Hurlston, Inspector Upton of the Oxfordshire Constabulary and a uniformed police sergeant whose name had not been given.

The room was easily big enough to accommodate the eighteen people, and a good few of them had found somewhere to sit. Malcolm – now free of his improvised restraints and with his artificial leg returned and refitted – sat in an armchair, fiercely guarded by Howard.

The inspector called for silence and then turned to Ellie. 'I have to tell you, Miss—'

'Mrs,' she said. 'Mrs Maloney.'

'Ah, Irish, eh?'

'American, but the name is my husband's. He's English. From London.'

'Is that a fact? Well, well, well. But as I was saying, I have to tell you that I'm wondering why you've called us all here. As I understand it from Dr Hurlston, there was a tragic incident here at the house on Saturday. Mr John Bilverton took his own life. There are other things for us to look into' – he glanced at Malcolm – 'but I'm not at all sure that the rest is a police matter.'

'If it were suicide, Inspector, I'm sure you'd be right. But we – that is, my husband Ivor, our friend Barty Dunn and I – strongly believe that John Bilverton did not take his own life. We believe he was murdered. Hetty Hollis's overdose was not accidental, either. Nor was Marianne Bilverton's fall. And we're convinced we know who was responsible for everything.'

She had anticipated the ensuing uproar and protestations from the family and waited patiently while the inspector regained control of the room.

'This is a grave accusation, madam, and one that I am obliged to take seriously. I hope you realize that wasting police time is also a serious matter, and that you could well be opening yourself to civil proceedings for slander if you're not able to back up your claims.'

'All I ask is that you all hear me out and decide for yourselves. I imagine everyone here remembers the events of Saturday afternoon, but I think it will make more sense to the inspector if we start at the beginning. So, on Saturday afternoon, everyone – all the members of the family and the entire band—'

The inspector was making notes as she spoke. 'Band, madam?'

'The Dizzy Heights. We were hired to play at the family's Midsummer Ball on Friday – or rather they were. I'm married to the drummer – I just came along to enjoy the party. But on Saturday we were waiting for the motor coach to come and pick us all up to take us back to London. The band had been recording in the chapel with Malcolm Bilverton, and towards the end of the recording session the family had come along to listen.'

'The entire family?'

'Everyone. It was raining heavily so there was little for them to do outdoors. Malcolm had suggested earlier that they might enjoy listening to the band, and at about one o'clock John Bilverton brought them all to the chapel.'

'Through the pouring rain.'

'I think they felt that it was worth enduring a drenching. The Dizzy Heights are more than worth getting wet for, and they're not the sort of family to let even a deluge like that stand in the way of their fun.'

'I see. It was quite the deluge, though, as you say. We've not seen flooding like it for years. Not since I was a lad.'

Ellie smiled. 'So everyone who was still here was in the chapel. A little before three o'clock, John excused himself and returned to the house to complete some work. There were a few complaints from his children, but he reminded them that he'd already told them of his intention to work that afternoon. He set off in the rain.'

'Alone?'

'Alone, yes. As it approached four, we all decided we were hungry. The cook had left a picnic tea, so Elizabeth, Veronica and I went to the house to fetch it. John had left strict instructions that he wasn't to be disturbed until after four, so I was standing outside the study, waiting for the clock to chime four before telling him that afternoon tea was served. As I waited, a gramophone record started playing inside the room – Gershwin's "Rhapsody in Blue"—'

'I'm not familiar with that. Modern, is it?'

'About a year old.'

'Ah. I prefer the old music hall songs, myself.'

'Many do. The music played, then the clock began to chime. As it finished, I heard a loud gunshot from inside the room.'

'The shot that killed John Bilverton.'

'Or so we were expected to believe. But I'll come to that in due course. Elizabeth and Veronica arrived while I was banging on the door. We tried it, but it was locked from the inside – Veronica went to the butler's pantry to get the spare key, and Elizabeth waited in the hall while I went outside to try and peer in through the window. I eventually managed it, in part thanks to a wheelbarrow, and saw a figure slumped in the chair. I went back in hoping we'd be able to enter using the spare key, but there was something blocking the keyhole. When we looked we saw there was a key already in the lock on the other side. Between us we managed to break open the door and I slipped in a tiny puddle of water as we tumbled in. I thought nothing of it at the time – the weather was atrocious, after all. And that was when we found John Bilverton, dead in his chair with a pistol on the floor beside him.'

'He'd shot himself, then.'

'So it was meant to appear, yes. Shot himself inside his locked study.'

'There was no sign of anyone else being there?'

'None. He had been drinking Scotch – there was a decanter and a single glass on the desk. There was a cushion from the library on the windowsill, but nothing else was out of place.'

'Did he leave a note?'

'No. We checked.'

'That's most unusual in cases of suicide.'

'It is, isn't it? Now, I served in the First Aid Nursing Yeomanry so I felt competent to examine the body.'

'The FANYs, madam? But I thought you said you were American.'

'It's a long story, Inspector. I was in love with a drummer. I wanted to be near him. I came to England. I volunteered. They were short-handed. They took me on despite my nationality.'

'I see, madam. Sorry to interrupt.'

'That's quite all right. There was a single bullet wound in the left temple. Mr Bilverton was left-handed. I've seen many bullet wounds, but few fatal and even fewer self-inflicted, so I wasn't completely sure what I was looking at. But when I described it to my husband and his friends – all old soldiers, of course – they said that the marks weren't what you'd expect from a self-inflicted wound.'

'What do you think, Dr Hurlston? Do you agree with the old soldiers?'

'Well,' said the doctor, thoughtfully. 'Actually, now you come to mention it, I suppose they might be right. I had no reason to doubt what I'd been told so I merely confirmed that life was extinct and noted the presence of a gunshot wound to the left temple. The . . . You'll have to excuse me, ladies, but I need to be blunt here. Despite being stored in the ice house, the body was in the early stages of decomposition. Even so, I was able to examine the wound, and now Mrs Maloney mentions it there was an absence of the sort of markings one might expect from a self-inflicted shot at close range. I was unfortunate enough to see one or two suicides in the trenches myself and, yes, I should have expected stippling around the wound – gunpowder and the like embedded in the skin. If the muzzle of the gun is in contact with the skin one gets a stellate – umm, star-shaped – pattern as the hot gases tear the skin. There was none of that, so, yes, it's certainly possible that the fatal round was fired from more than a couple of feet away.'

'I see. Continue, please, Mrs Maloney.'

Ellie nodded her thanks. 'We shared our concerns with Veronica and she agreed to help us try to find out what really happened that afternoon. This morning we finally pieced everything together.'

'So what did really happen?'

'When he retired from the army, Malcolm Bilverton set up Bilver-Tone Records, which he runs from the chapel. His army pension is generous, but it didn't come anywhere near to providing the capital he needed when he decided to re-equip the studio with a modern electrical recording system from America. For some reason – whether pride on his own part or reluctance on his brother's part, we may never know – he didn't go to John for the money, and turned instead to local businessman Valentine Baisley.'

'Mr Baisley is well known to us. "Businessman" is a generously euphemistic description of that particular gentleman.'

'So we understand. But the result is that Malcolm Bilverton is financially indebted to Baisley. He's tied to him in other ways, too. At some point Malcolm became addicted to cocaine. I honestly would have expected it to be morphine after losing his leg in battle – a lot of boys got hooked on the stuff after spending time in the field hospitals – but Malcolm's vice is cocaine. Perhaps he found it elevated his mood. We should have known something was up – he went off a couple of times and reappeared a short time later fizzing with energy and enthusiasm. It wasn't until we found a box of the stuff in his desk in the chapel that we finally realized why.'

'Where is it now, this box?'

Dunn piped up from his spot by the window. 'The box is still in the control room, but most of the cocaine is on the chapel floor, I'm afraid. There'll be some on Malcolm's jacket if he hasn't already snorted it off. I had to improvise a weapon. Sorry.'

'No matter. We'll be able to tell from whatever traces remain.'

Ellie continued. 'So, Malcolm is very much in Baisley's debt. Which is bad news for him, but was very good news for Baisley when John began serious investigations into Baisley's many business dealings. He was compiling a dossier and had strong evidence on a number of the shadier aspects of the Baisley empire. Somehow Baisley got wind of it – probably from a powerful member of the Oxfordshire establishment he has in his pocket. Obviously he couldn't tolerate that sort of risk, even with plenty of bribed officials to dig him out, so he put pressure on Malcolm to "sort things out".'

'How can you be sure?'

'Malcolm spent his whole life in the army. They say an army marches on its stomach, but it actually marches on a cloud of paperwork. He kept meticulous records of his dealings with Baisley in a journal we found in his control room. He made a careful, detailed note when Baisley said that he wanted John stopped at any cost. It was made plain to him that his own life would be forfeit if he didn't comply. That, I think, is when Malcolm decided to kill his brother, and he planned it as he would any military operation. The key to his plan was establishing in everyone's mind that he was alone in the chapel control room listening to his recordings when John died. He began by inviting the band to the chapel on Saturday to make a recording. He suggested that the whole family came down to watch so that they knew what was going on and wouldn't question his absence later in the afternoon – obviously he would still be in his studio checking that everything had worked. The storm forced him to adapt his plans, but if anything, that worked to his advantage. Now he had the whole family as well as the band in the chapel when John went off to work in the study at three, leaving the house empty but for the servants. We were all out of the way, and we were all able to provide him with an alibi without him having to remind anyone where he was. He let us hear him in the control room with his recordings, then he closed the soundproof door and we all assumed he was in there working on the discs. Once he was sure John was hard at work and we were all enjoying the band, he opened the secret door to the tunnel that leads to the house—'

'Secret door? Tunnel?'

'Yes. The house that originally stood here was built by a Catholic family in Elizabethan times. There's an escape tunnel that runs from the chapel to this room so that the family priest could flee if the authorities came calling.'

'In here?' said Howard.

Ellie pointed to the bookcase. 'Show them, Ivor.'

There were oohs, aahs, and one 'Well, I'll be blowed' as Skins opened the bookcase door.

'Once in here, he picked up a cushion from one of those chairs and took it with him. I'm not sure exactly how he proceeded next, but I'm going to assume he went down to the kitchen to fetch a piece of ice from the ice box in the larder. Lily the kitchen maid said she saw someone go into the larder that afternoon but doesn't know who it was.'

'Ice?' said the inspector.

'Yes, sorry, I'm getting ahead of myself. He'd worked out a way to rig one of the door locks so that it would lock on its own. We can show you the lock later. It involved modifying it with a spring mechanism held back by ice. So, with his trick lock and his cushion he went in to see John. This was the only part of the scheme that was a bit of a gamble, I think. He'd taken the chance that John would help himself to a glass of Scotch while he was working, so he'd dosed the decanter with Veronal. By the time he got to the study, John was out cold.'

'What makes you think he did that?'

'One of our boys helped himself to the whisky decanter from the study and put the whole band to sleep later that night. We have the decanter among our effects so you can check it for yourselves. With his brother out for the count, Malcolm took John's pistol from his desk and shot him with it, setting the scene to make it look like suicide. We assume he took the cushion to muffle the shot, but with the storm thundering away outside there was no need. With John unconscious, he was able to time the shot with a clap of thunder and no one would be any the wiser. He must have decided it would be too risky to be walking about with a cushion, so he put it on the windowsill and hoped no one would notice.'

'Where is the gun now?'

'Still in the study. It's a Smith and Wesson Ladysmith. A .22.'

'You know your guns.'

'A girl has to have a hobby. We believe he quickly searched among some files on the bookshelves, looking for any evidence John might have had on Baisley, but didn't find what he was looking for.'

'How do you know he didn't find it?'

'Because we found it, and it wasn't in the files – it was in a secret drawer in the desk. After that, he switched on the electric gramophone and put George Gershwin's "Rhapsody in Blue" on the turntable. But instead of playing it, he left the needle at the end as though it had just finished. He replaced the door lock with his modified version, leaving the key in it, then set off back to the library. As the last of the ice melted, the door locked itself. The little bit of water I slipped in when we burst into the room came from the melted ice, do you see?

'A couple of minutes later he was back in the control room and putting the original lock in the drawer, where we found it a little while ago. Then comes the technical bit that the boys figured out.' She indicated Skins and Dunn. 'When he knew Elizabeth, Veronica and I had gone off to the house, he kept a close eye on the clock. It's another assumption on my part, but I'm betting that the butler is fastidious about clocks. Veronica told us how he regularly checks the staircases for creaks, so I imagine he's fastidious about everything else and the clocks are all set to exactly the right time. Anyway, at a couple of minutes to four, he started playing his own, doctored copy of the Gershwin on the gramophone in the control room, which he'd rigged up so that it would play out of the loudspeaker in the study. As the clock struck four, I was outside the study where I heard not a gunshot, but a recording of a gunshot played on a gramophone in the chapel.'

'Going on your performance so far, I presume you have evidence of this, too?'

'We have the gramophone record he used, yes. Then, when we raised the alarm, he was in the chapel as though he'd been there all the time. We considered the possibility that it could have been almost anyone else, but the weather was so bad that no matter how sneaky they were, they couldn't have got to the house and back without getting soaked to the skin. Everyone was dry – or at least as dry as they could be given how wet they'd gotten on their way to the chapel earlier – and the only dry way to get to the house was through the tunnel. And Malcolm was able to keep an eye on the entrance to the tunnel because it's in his control room.'

'This is all very thorough. Is there anything else?'

'No, Inspector, that's more or less it. John Bilverton didn't commit suicide, he was killed by his brother in a quite astonishingly sophisticated plan that really ought to have worked. It was just bad luck that it didn't.'

'You said something about the two ladies.'

'Oh, yes. Hetty Hollis was murdered because she discovered the secret door in the chapel. Your police surgeon will be able to check, but it was almost certainly a drug overdose. Barbiturates would be my guess. And Marianne Bilverton didn't fall down the stairs, she was pushed – Malcolm admitted as much. She knew he was a bad lot, and something Malcolm said in the chapel makes me think she knew about John's investigation. Barty Dunn overheard Charlotte telling her to be careful – that must have been before she confronted Malcolm. I think she knew Malcolm had killed her husband.'

The family sat in stunned silence. The band nodded appreciatively. Another victory for Skins, Ellie and Dunn.

Malcolm, who had remained unexpectedly silent throughout, suddenly exploded. 'Balderdash!' he exclaimed. 'Utter poppycock. You're the one on drugs, Mrs Maloney, if you think any of that is true.'

The inspector shook his head wearily. 'Please be quiet, Mr Bilverton—'

'*Colonel* Bilverton. I earned my rank, Upton.'

'*Inspector* Upton – I earned mine too. You'll have your chance to speak later, though I should warn you that since you are now under arrest, you do not have to say anything unless you wish to do so, but that anything you say will be taken down and may be given in evidence.'

'Preposterous. Upon what charge, sir? Upon what charge? The word of this American woman and her musician friends?'

'We shall be investigating the allegations of murder, of course, but in the meantime possession of an illegal drug and reckless discharge of a firearm will be enough to be getting on with.'

'What drug? There's no drug.'

'That white power on your jacket suggests otherwise. And you can't deny the wound in young Miss Bilverton's shoulder. Take him out to the car, please, Sergeant.'

The unnamed sergeant handcuffed Malcolm Bilverton, who was still loudly protesting his innocence as he was led out.

The room erupted with questions, which the three friends tried to answer. Meanwhile, the two ambulance men were finally able to take their charge to the hospital. Howard went with her.

◆ ◆ ◆

It took almost another hour for Inspector Upton to finish collecting everyone's details and taking a few key witness statements. Ellie stayed nearby, eavesdropping on what the family said, but no one seemed to offer anything to contradict her own version of events.

Eventually the inspector was satisfied that he had enough to be getting on with, and said his goodbyes to Gordon as the head of the household. He seemed about to leave when he called Ellie over.

'I'm obliged to keep an open mind – innocent until proven guilty and all that – but I'm impressed by the effort you and your husband put into this.'

'And Barty Dunn,' she said.

'Ah, yes, the cocaine flinger. Well, I'm impressed. Have you any experience of this line of work? Or do you just read a lot of detective novels?'

'We helped solve a case a few weeks ago in London with a detective from Scotland Yard. Superintendent Sunderland.'

'He caught the deserter at the Mayfair club, didn't he? I read about that. You were involved in the case?'

'We were indeed. And I have a friend in Gloucestershire who has some experience in the field, too. Lady Hardcastle?'

'Good Lord. She's almost legendary. Well, I never.'

'So we're just enthusiastic amateurs, but we have friends to advise us when we need them.'

'It seems you do, madam. Well, I have to be off now – poor Sergeant Adams has been sitting in the car with Bilverton for quite a while. You'll be called for the trial if we decide to prosecute, of course. And between you and me, I rather think we shall. And this file on Valentine Baisley' –he tapped the pile of papers under his arm – 'might put an end to that toerag's shenanigans, too. You've done us a great service.'

'You're more than welcome, Inspector. I just hope the family doesn't resent us too much. It was hard for them to accept that their father had killed himself, but I don't imagine it's much easier to accept that their favourite uncle murdered him.'

'It will take time, but they'll come to terms with it, I'm sure. It's always better to know the truth.'

'I suppose so. Well, goodbye, Inspector.'

She found Skins and Dunn talking to Marianne.

'. . . of the will, of course. Once we all know where we stand, perhaps we can make a proper decision. Ah, hello, Ellie.' With a smile, Marianne reached out to shake Ellie's hand.

'We're so glad to see you up and about,' said Ellie. 'You gave us quite a fright.'

'It gave me quite a fright, too. One minute I was standing at the top of the stairs, the next I was waking up in bed with Dr Hurlston standing over me.'

'Do you remember anything at all?'

'Charlotte and I had begun to suspect Malcolm. John had told me about his file on Baisley, and of course we knew how thick he was with Malcolm. We put it all together and I went to have it out with him. He told me it was utter rot, of course, and invited me to get out of his room. I was on my way back downstairs and . . . and then I woke up in bed. He must have followed me and given me a shove. Given what he was prepared to do to John and poor Hetty, I'm lucky he didn't get a chance to finish me off.'

'Well, yes.'

'Thank you so very much for everything you've done,' said Marianne.

'You're entirely welcome, of course. But the boys here have to take two-thirds of the credit.'

'And I've already given them two-thirds of the thanks. Between you, you've saved John's reputation from the stigma of suicide. That sort of thing hangs over a family, you know.'

'Although we replaced one stigma with another. There's a murderer in the family, after all.'

'That's easier for society to accept, though. Actually, I can imagine one or two thinking it rather glamorous and romantic that John lost his life in his crusade against a gangster.'

'Well, when you put it like that . . .' Ellie smiled, then looked around to make sure they couldn't be overheard. 'What will you and Charlotte do now?'

'I . . . Oh, of course you know. You seem to know everything. Well, I'm not sure, to be honest. I was just saying to these two scallywags that until the estate is settled, none of us has any real idea how to proceed for the best. I can't help thinking that there'd be even more stigma and scandal if we ran off together. But then again . . .'

'Perhaps it's better to endure a little scandal than deny yourselves a chance at happiness?' suggested Ellie.

'Something like that, yes. We shall see.'

'I hope whatever you decide, you find some contentment.'

'You're very kind. Now, if you'll all excuse me, I ought to check a few things. I'm still nominally the lady of the house, even if Gordon thinks otherwise.'

She headed off in the direction of the kitchen stairs.

'Well, that's that, then,' said Skins.

'It does seem to be,' said Ellie.

'We never did find out what John did to upset Peter so badly, though.'

'I don't suppose he cares much now he's got all the Bilverton's Biscuits business,' said Dunn. 'But it would be interesting to know.'

'Oh, I'm so sorry,' said Ellie, 'I thought I'd already told you – John left an account of it in his notes. He and his brother had a thing about writing everything down, didn't they? Anyway, Peter had been engaged to act for Valentine Baisley in a business matter that John knew to be shady, so he warned him off. He knew the police would have to act once they had his own evidence, and he didn't want anyone in the family connected with criminal activity. Of course, he couldn't let on that that was why he was against it, so Peter worked himself up into an indignant paddy about being a fully qualified solicitor and able to make up his own mind, thank you very much. But John stuck to his guns and Peter resentfully caved in.'

'So he didn't ruin a lucrative deal, he saved him from gaol,' said Dunn. 'Are you going to tell them?'

'I probably ought. It'll come out soon enough, but knowing might make it easier to come to terms with . . . well, you know, everything.' She was wondering whether to go off and find Elizabeth and Peter when they heard Gordon calling from the Grand Hall.

'The charabanc's here.'

The Dizzy Heights gave a cheer.

By the time Skins and Ellie had checked that everything from their room on the second floor had been packed and brought down, the rest of the Dizzies were assembled in the Grand Hall with all their gear. Mickey was sitting on Skins's bass drum case, chatting to Eustace.

'Thanks for bringing my kit up,' said Skins. 'I owe you one.'

'Not sure you do, mate,' said Mickey. 'We knew what you three was up to, of course, but none of us had any idea it was all so . . . you know . . . so involved. And you cracked it. You caught an actual murderer. Again. Proud to carry your drums.'

'Really? Job's yours if you want it. I always wanted me own porter.'

'Don't get carried away, son. I was happy to get your stuff up from the chapel 'cause you were busy, but I ain't making a career of it.'

'Fair dos. You all right, there, Benny?'

'Just fine, thank you. I'll be glad to get home, though.'

'You and me both, mate.'

Katy came in through the front door.

'Come on then, you lot,' she said. 'Let's get all this stuff loaded up. The footmen will give us a hand, but the driver's keen to get going as soon as poss, so don't dawdle.'

The Dizzies stirred to action and started carrying their bags and instruments out on to the drive. The two footmen were there, helping the driver to heft the baggage on to the roof, and Skins handed up his and Ellie's bags before they both turned back to collect the first of his drum cases. They caught up with Dunn and were just about to re-enter the front door when a taxi pulled up on the drive and Howard hopped out. He paid the driver and loped over to the three friends.

'How is she?' asked Ellie.

'They were just taking her into surgery when I left,' said Howard, 'so I've taken the opportunity to scoot back to get her some necessaries. She lost quite a bit more blood than we thought, and it was, or so said the quack, "a nasty big old bullet" so it's made quite a mess of her shoulder, but they're confident they can put her more or less back together.'

'That's not wonderful, but it could be worse. Do give her our love, won't you?'

'Of course. And thank you for . . . well . . . you know.'

'I hope we've not made things worse.'

'Far from it. I can't say I liked the old man much, and heaven knows the feeling was mutual, but I'm not sure he deserved to die. Especially not at Uncle Malcolm's hand. I had no idea he was in so deep with Baisley.'

'No one did. Are you all right, though? What are you going to do? Didn't I hear you had a job in the City?'

'D'you know, I've been thinking about that. One way or another I'm coming into money, so blow the boring job – I'm going to go to New York. Who knows what exciting opportunities might arise while I'm there.'

'Are you serious?'

'Never more so, Mrs M. Either the gaffer left me money or Ronnie and I sell those postcards. Either way I can't let a windfall like that go to waste. I only took the banking job to annoy Papa, if I'm honest, so now I want to see the bright lights, listen to the jazz. Meet glamorous and exciting people.'

Ellie laughed. 'Well, good luck to you, Mr B. Oh, hold on.' She pulled a calling card from her pocket and handed it to him. 'When you're ready to set off, drop me a line, give me a call. Hell, you can come unannounced for tea if you like. But do get in touch. I can give you introductions to a few lovely people there – friends of mine. They'll make you welcome.'

'I say, thank you. Thank you very much indeed.'

'It's no fun being a stranger in a new town. You might not like them all – God knows Patty Ballantine gets on my nerves, for one – but at least you'll have a few people to call on. And they know all the swell places to go.'

'You're very kind. What say I take you all to dinner once my plans are finalized? You can show me the "swell" places to go in London before I leave it for good.'

'Even better,' said Dunn. 'We can help you brush up on your jazz knowledge before you ship out. Make you look less like a rube.'

'It's a date,' said Howard, brandishing Ellie's card. 'All I need now is to figure out what on earth Veronica might want to have with her in hospital.'

Ellie laughed. 'Get Elizabeth to help you.'

Howard waved over his shoulder as he mounted the steps. 'Capital idea, Mrs M. Will do.'

'I think they're all going to be all right,' said Skins.

'Seems that way,' agreed Dunn.

Ellie linked arms with them both and led them back towards the house. 'Then let's get the rest of our gear on the coach and we can go home and see if the children even noticed we were gone.'

# Chapter Seventeen

The journey home was a long but largely jolly and uneventful one. The usual groups had formed, with Elk, Benny and Eustace still trying to play pontoon on the bench – with exactly the same lack of success – while Puddle read her book and Vera her magazine.

Skins and Dunn occupied the rear seats and were still bickering about Dunn's song lyric, leaving Mickey sitting alone once more by the door with his paper bag and a tinge of green about his handsome face.

Ellie sat with Katy and they looked out of the window at waterlogged Oxfordshire.

No homes had been flooded when the river burst its banks, so the visible effects of the inundation were, for the most part, muddy roads and a herd of displaced cattle sheltering forlornly beneath some trees on a small hillock.

'How was your first proper engagement with the band?' asked Ellie.

'I've a lot to learn, but it was rather thrilling.'

'A lot to learn?'

'Oh my word, yes. I thought I knew all about musicians – having one in the family made me imagine I had them worked out – but there's a lot more to it, isn't there? And they're all so . . .'

'Infuriating? Badly behaved? Dim-witted?'

Katy laughed. 'So damn good, I was going to say. Eight of them, all playing and singing together. It's like magic, isn't it?'

'I suppose it is when you put it like that. I think I take it a little for granted, but you're right – they really are uncommonly good.'

'I just have to get used to all their little ways. I felt such a fool asking for eight chairs, for instance. A decent manager would know they only need five.'

'It'll come. They're not a very complex bunch. And they like you – that definitely helps.'

'They do? Have they said anything?'

'Not a word – that's how I know they like you. None of them is terribly good at expressing their appreciation, but they're not at all shy about complaining when things don't go their way.'

'That's good to know. As long as all the touring engagements aren't like that, I'm sure I'll be fine.'

'Like what? The murder? Oh, we seldom have murders.'

'Aside from this weekend, and last month at Tipsy Harry's.'

'Aside from those two, no one's ever been murdered at a Dizzy Heights gig, as far as I know.'

Mickey, still looking very sorry for himself, turned round. 'We've murdered a few tunes in our time, mind you,' he said. 'We're not always as good as all that.'

'Even at your worst, I'm sure you're better than many of the bands I've seen over the years.'

'That's the kind of flattery we need in a manager.' What little colour remained in his face drained rapidly. He turned back to address the driver. 'Pull over here, would you, mate?'

While Mickey was still leaning groggily against the front of the motor coach, trying to get his stomach and spinning head back under control, Katy knelt up on her seat so that she was facing the rest of the band.

'I know everyone's keen to get home as soon as possible,' she said, 'but I also know one or two of you live alone and won't have any food in. If our driver knows of a suitable one, I propose we stop at a pub before we get to London and have a bite to eat. Any objections?'

There were none, and the driver did, indeed, know of a suitable inn just outside Beaconsfield.

By the time they arrived, even Mickey was hungry.

They invaded the pub with the coach driver in the lead. He knew the landlord and, Ellie suspected, was probably offered a small cash incentive to take his passengers there.

The bill of fare was chalked on a blackboard. The choice was beef pie with boiled potatoes and carrots. Or nothing. They all opted for the beef pie.

◆ ◆ ◆

Skins and Ellie were dropped back at their home in Bloomsbury at about eight o'clock that evening. They had offered Dunn a bed for the night and he had gratefully accepted, so the three of them lugged their instruments and bags up the front steps together.

Skins was fumbling in his pocket for his door key.

'Just ring the damn bell,' said Ellie from behind him. 'Mrs Dalrymple can open it.'

'I don't like ringing my own doorbell. It ain't right. It makes me feel like it's not really my house. Oh, hello, Mrs D.'

The door had already opened, and the Maloneys' smiling housekeeper ushered them in.

'I heard the motor coach pull up outside and I thought it might be you,' she said. 'Then I heard Mr Maloney refusing to ring the doorbell and I *knew* it was you. Let me help you with that bag, Mrs

Maloney. I told Cook to put the kettle on and Nanny let the weans stay up past their bedtime, just as you asked.'

'Thank you, Mrs Dalrymple,' said Ellie.

'Will you be wanting any supper?'

'No, thank you – we ate on the journey.'

'Right you are, then. You just settle yourselves and I'll tell Nanny you're here.'

She offered to help them to bring the rest of their gear in, but they insisted they could manage.

Ellie pointed at a spot next to the coat stand. 'Just leave your bass there, Barty, it'll be fine.'

Skins began to stack his drums in the hallway, too.

'Are you just going to dump those there, honey?'

'We're going to have to take it all to the Preening Parrot tomorrow night. They'll only be here a few hours.'

'But people will trip over them.'

'If you'd let me have the "morning room" as a music room, they could go in there. But, as it is . . .'

'But I like having a morning room.'

'You never go in there.'

'No, but I like being able to say I have a morning room. It sounds so grand.'

'What actually is a morning room?' asked Dunn.

'It's an extra sitting room,' she said. 'For use in the morning.'

'What happens if you go in there in the afternoon?'

'Then you're drummed out of polite society and have to leave London at once.'

'Probably better let the lad have it as a music room, then. Sounds like a liability. You could put the piano in there.'

'Actually, Barty, that's not a bad idea. Then I could get a lovely baby grand for the drawing room.'

Skins brought in the last of his cases. 'You're a very expensive house guest, Barty boy. All I wanted was somewhere to practise, now you're getting her to spend who knows how much on a new piano.'

'Nothing to do with me, mate – that was all her idea.'

'We should probably think about it,' said Ellie. 'When the children are a little older I'd like them to have music lessons. It would be somewhere for them to practise, too.'

'That's more like it. We could get a family band going.'

Lottie the housemaid came up the stairs from the kitchen with a tea tray.

'Where do you want this, ma'am?' she said.

'Oh, Lottie, thank you,' said Ellie. 'In the drawing room, I think.'

They were just making themselves comfortable with their tea when they heard a thundering on the stairs. With a crash, the drawing room door burst open as Edward and Catherine Maloney burst in. They were, apparently, pleased their parents were home.

By the time Nanny Nora had rounded them up again and taken them off to bed, the tea had gone cold and Skins decided it was probably time for something a little stronger anyway.

With drinks in hand, they began discussing the events of the weekend.

By half past nine they were all fast asleep in their armchairs.

# Chapter Eighteen

***Saturday, 4 July 1925***

Four days later, on Saturday, the fourth of July, Ellie woke early and tiptoed from the bedroom. The Dizzy Heights had played their regular date at the Aristippus Club in Mayfair the night before, so she imagined Skins wouldn't have been home until at least three. She left him sleeping and made her way stealthily downstairs.

When Skins had been working she usually had a cup of coffee alone in the drawing room before calling Edward and Catherine down for breakfast. She was looking forward to some rambunctious silliness over the breakfast table, and to telling her half-American children what a special day it was.

Still slightly sleepy, she opened the drawing room door, plodded in and pressed the bell to alert the housemaid, Lottie, to her need for coffee. She turned to sit in her favourite chair but stopped suddenly.

The room, normally decorated in a tastefully discreet modern style, had been transformed. Miniature Stars and Stripes flags lined up on the mantelpiece. The mirror was bedecked with red, white and blue ribbons and matching paper fans. More broad ribbons were draped on the furniture and piano. Still more still hung from the ceiling, together with a banner that read "Happy 4th of July".

She was still beaming when Lottie arrived with the tray.

'Oh, my sainted aunt,' said Lottie, apparently not sure whether to be thrilled or horrified.

'I was about to thank you for being so thoughtful,' said Ellie. 'This isn't your doing, then?'

'No, ma'am. I checked all the rooms was in order before bed last night. It didn't look like this in here.'

'Mrs Dalrymple?'

'She went to bed before me with one of her headaches.'

'Then it must be Ivor. What an absolute sweetheart.'

'I wish I could find a bloke who'd do something like this for me,' said Lottie. 'Not for the fourth of July, obviously, that's your day. But . . . you know . . . maybe a birthday. None of the lads I've walked out with would ever think of this.'

'He's one in a million, all right.'

'Will there be anything else, ma'am?'

'No, thank you, honey. I'll get the children down in a little while and we can sing patriotic songs until breakfast is ready.'

Lottie left her to her private celebrations and heard Ellie strike up a familiar tune on the piano. She didn't know it was Sousa's 'The Liberty Bell', but she knew the mistress liked to play it from time to time to amuse her English friends.

Skins surfaced close to lunchtime and was amused to find his family still in the drawing room, with the children making even more flags while Ellie told them the history of the American Revolution.

'Daddy!' yelled Edward as Skins came in. 'Can we have a tea party?'

'I've not even had my breakfast yet.'

'Like they did in Busting. We can dump all the tea in the Turpentine.'

'I'm pretty sure it's "Boston", mate,' said Skins. 'And you probably mean the Serpentine.'

'That's what I said.'

'Yes. Yes, you did. Maybe Mrs Ponton can give us a little packet of tea and we can take your boat to the park. What do you reckon, Mummy? A little outing to celebrate your independence?'

'Sounds perfect to me,' said Ellie. 'Why don't you two run upstairs and get your shoes on? And find your boat, Teddy.'

The children thundered off.

Skins had brought something in with him from the table in the hall.

'Whatcha got there, Limey?'

'Just the post. The postman seems to be getting later and later.' He put down a handful of envelopes and examined the package that had also been delivered. It was a box sealed with gummed paper, postmarked Oxford. 'Looks like the Bilvertons have sent us something.'

He tore off the gummed paper and opened it up. Inside were a number of shellac discs in cardboard sleeves, and a note. He read it.

'It's from Veronica,' he said. 'It's the discs we recorded at Bilver-Tone. How fantastic . . . She says she's feeling much better, and thanks you for taking good care of her. The doctor said you might have saved her life.'

'I don't know about that,' said Ellie.

'No, she said he was very impressed. Apparently she'd lost a lot of blood, and if you hadn't been there, she might not have made it . . . Malcolm has been charged with two murders and an attempted murder, and will appear before the magistrates next week – they expect him to be indicted for trial at the next assizes . . . Baisley has been arrested on a number of charges thanks to John Bilverton's investigations . . .

Howard and Veronica are going to sell the French postcards to a mate of Howard's from university and he's already decided to go to America on the third of the month. Oh, but that was yesterday. Oh, yes, she says he said to tell us he was sorry he couldn't call in, but everything happened rather quickly. Umm . . . Marianne and Charlotte are going to buy a flat in London . . . and Veronica wants Barty's address.'

'He's thirteen years older than her. It'll never work.'

'I'm not sure it's our place to decide that. Umm . . . She wishes us well, and hopes to see us the next time she's in London.'

'Well, that's very sweet of her. I'll write to her later. What else have we got?'

He picked up the envelopes again. 'Nothing much – it's just bills, and some letters for you. One from Flo, one from the solicitors and something from New York.'

'The Old Country, eh? Hand it over. You can take a look at the solicitors' letter.'

Skins opened the envelope and scanned it quickly. 'Meeting of the 1st *inst* . . . satisfied that your arrangements still meet the requirements of the will . . . yours, etc.'

'Well, that's that over for another year.'

She opened the American letter and read it eagerly. She would savour the letter from her friend Florence Armstrong in Gloucestershire later, but news from the homeland couldn't wait.

'It's from my cousin Clara. She's married to some Wall Street high-flyer, remember?'

Skins didn't remember, but thought it best not to say.

'Blah, blah . . . Hopes we're well . . . Family news . . . Oh, here we are. Her husband is investing in a nightclub . . . He wants advice on the music . . . He wants more international acts, not just the usual New York crowd . . . Heard you were the best in London . . . Oh, and they want us to go over there and stay with them for a few weeks to help get things set up. She's sent us tickets for a liner leaving Southampton in two weeks' time.'

'Us? You, me and the kids? I don't know about that. They're a bit young for the crossing, I reckon.'

'No, she's only sent three tickets – you, me and "that tall, good-looking guy". She doesn't mention the children at all. I think she's probably forgotten we have any.'

Skins laughed. 'Well, that answers that, then. Why not? We could invite my mum to stay here with them. She'd like a break, I bet. And we haven't been away on our own for years.'

'We went away to Oxfordshire without the children last week.'

'Yeah, but I want to go away on our own without someone getting murdered.'

'That would be nice. Oh, but we won't be on our own – Barty's invited, too, don't forget.'

'We won't have to worry about him – he'll be in his element. London musician in New York? The girls'll be all over him. I bet we don't see him much.'

'You're probably right. Well, I'd love to go. I'll send her a telegram and let her know we're coming, shall I? You can tell Barty.'

'I'll tell him tonight at the Blue Pussycat.'

# Author's Note

Bilverton's Biscuits and Bilver-Tone Records are, as usual, entirely fictitious, as is Bilverton House. I can no longer remember how I came to make up the name.

The layout of the house is an amalgamation of ideas from a number of stately homes from around England. I drew a sketch plan of the house, and all the bits of it work together exactly as depicted, but the house as described would be architecturally impossible. There just aren't enough interior supporting walls, and the staircases, though useful for the story, seem similarly improbable from an engineering point of view.

I listened to a lot of Bix Beiderbecke while writing both this book and *The Deadly Mystery of the Missing Diamonds*, so if you want a feel for the jazz of the period, that's a good place to start.

The Sazarac Ellie drinks at the party is a cocktail invented in New Orleans in the nineteenth century. It features whiskey or cognac (it was originally cognac, but changed to whiskey in 1870 thanks to a cognac shortage in New Orleans), absinthe (or Pernod), simple syrup and a dash of bitters (Peychaud's for authenticity, Angostura for a little more depth). Absinthe was unjustly blamed for many of society's ills and production was banned in France in 1915, but Pernod Fils resumed production in Catalonia after the First World War. The Bilvertons would have had to go to some trouble to obtain a supply, but they would have considered it worth it for the cachet of having a 'forbidden' drink.

Electrical recording equipment was very new in 1925 and was pioneered by Western Electric. It's a stretch for Malcolm Bilverton to have 'all the latest gear from America', but it's just about possible. Enthusiasts find a way.

The first English stately home to open its doors to the public was Stoneleigh Abbey in Warwickshire in 1946, so Veronica's tour of Bilverton House and its grounds wouldn't have been a familiar idea. The role of tour guide, though, was well established, and the guides who accompanied young men on the 'Grand Tour' of Europe in the seventeenth and eighteenth centuries were known as 'bear-leaders' (from the old Oxford University slang that referred to students as bears, and the similarly obsolete term for one who trains actual bears).

Veronica mentions giving the house to the National Trust. The National Trust for Places of Historic Interest or Natural Beauty was founded in 1895 as a heritage conservation charity. It first purchased (or was gifted) land, and smaller threatened buildings. In 1907 it acquired its first large country house, Barrington Court in Somerset (which proved much more expensive to renovate and maintain than they had anticipated). In 1936 the Trust set up The Country House Scheme, and a couple of Acts of Parliament later was able to take ownership of country houses where the owners could no longer afford to maintain them. It enabled the owners to escape estate duty on the house but allowed them to keep living there as long as they allowed some public access. If the Bilvertons did get into financial difficulties, they only needed to try to hang on for another eleven years and they could stay in the house in exchange for allowing a few visitors. Veronica's tour guide experience might come in handy.

A brief note for American (and some Canadian) readers. In Britain (and, indeed, most places outside the USA), the word 'cider' refers exclusively to the alcoholic drink made from fermented apple juice, known to Americans as 'hard cider'. We do use the term 'sweet cider', but even that isn't the same as in the USA and is simply alcoholic cider that happens to be sweet rather than the unfiltered apple juice you might be expecting.

Although the book was written during the pandemic lockdown in 2020, the fact that the characters are stuck in Bilverton House is completely coincidental. The story was planned in 2019 and it was always my intention to trap them in the house somehow, but it wasn't until a trip to Stratford-upon-Avon in November 2019 that the idea of the flood occurred to me. We were staying at a country house hotel not far from the town and were prevented from visiting Anne Hathaway's cottage because the road outside it was flooded. It seemed like the perfect way to prevent my characters from leaving Bilverton House and of stopping anyone else from getting to them, even though flooding in late June is much less commonplace in England.

The right to silence has been part of English common law since the seventeenth century. The police caution ('You do not have to say anything,' etc.) is a little harder to pin down. It has taken many forms over the years and I haven't been able to establish whether it was given in the 1920s, nor precisely what form it took. I have taken the liberty of including it anyway.

# Acknowledgments

There's always a danger when writing acknowledgements that someone will be overlooked. A *lot* of people help make a book and I try to be sure to thank them personally, but perhaps setting it down in print would be good, too. So huge thanks go to Jack Butler, Nicole Wagner and everyone else at Thomas & Mercer who have looked after me – and the books – so well.

And . . .

I have been working with Jane Snelgrove since she acquired the first Lady Hardcastle books in 2015. She has guided and encouraged me, and has played a major part in the success of the Lady Hardcastle books and now this new series, The Dizzy Heights. Her editorial advice has been perceptive, clearly thought through and always, *always* right. Her friendship has been unstinting and uplifting. Without her, the books and I would have been merely OK. With her we have, to use one of her own favourite words, 'sparkled'.

Thank you, Jane.

# About the Author

*Photo © 2018 Clifton Photographic Company*

T E Kinsey grew up in London and read history at Bristol University. He worked for a number of years as a magazine features writer before falling into the glamorous world of the Internet, where he edited content for a very famous entertainment website for quite a few years more. After helping to raise three children, learning to scuba dive and to play the drums and mandolin (though never, disappointingly, all at the same time), he decided the time was right to get back to writing. A Baffling Murder at the Midsummer Ball is the second story in the Dizzy Heights series. His website is at www.tekinsey.uk and you can follow him on Twitter @tekinsey as well as on Facebook: www.facebook.com/tekinsey.

Did you enjoy this book and would like to get informed when T E Kinsey publishes his next work? Just follow the author on Amazon!

1) Search for the book you were just reading on Amazon or in the Amazon App.

2) Go to the Author Page by clicking on the Author's name.

3) Click the "Follow" button.

If you enjoyed this book on a Kindle eReader or in the Kindle App, you will be automatically offered to follow the author when arriving at the last page.